WHEN PL

Denthurion spoke [...] it over with."

All around Ordnung the black sky lit up. A hundred thousand Guard ships floated in orbit, optical carrier nets feeding power to collimated particle beam weapons.

Something like ultra-high-energy cosmic rays punched into the upper atmosphere, aurorae flaring and climbing, blue-white-green, into space. Showers of collisional particles sprayed into the troposphere, dividing, flooding the biosphere with ionizing radiation, through and through that little family.

"Daddy, I feel sick."

Empty houses, rotting meat. And in deep shelters the government of Ordnung would wait, sweating, for the Televox to come.

And judge them.

"A richly detailed, fascinating view of the far future."
    —John Stith, author of Redshift Rendezvous

"Truly a quiet gem, thought-provoking and colorful. The canvas is vast, covering distances and timescales that push to the edge of my sense of wonder. . . . I was truly impressed."
    —Kevin J. Anderson

"Compelling, fascinating and disturbing. Science Fiction has always asked the question 'what does it mean to be human?' This book suggests some unnerving, thought-provoking answers."
    —Roger McBride Allen

Previous Books by
William Barton

Hunting on Kunderer (1973)
A Plague of All Cowards (1976)

with Michael Capobianco

Iris (1990)
Fellow Traveler (1991)

Dark Sky Legion

an ahrimanic novel
by

William Barton

BANTAM BOOKS
NEW YORK · TORONTO · LONDON · SYDNEY · AUCKLAND

Dark Sky Legion

A Bantam Spectra Book / August 1992

ISBN 0-553-29616-7

Published simultaneously in the United States and Canada

Bantam Books are published by Bantam Books, a division of Bantam Doubleday Dell Publishing Group, Inc. Its trademark, consisting of the words "Bantam Books" and the portrayal of a rooster, is Registered in U.S. Patent and Trademark Office and in other countries. Marca Registrada. Bantam Books, 666 Fifth Avenue, New York, New York 10103.

PRINTED IN THE UNITED STATES OF AMERICA

RAD   0   9   8   7   6   5   4   3   2   1

Dedicated to
the Galactic Empires
of

Poul Anderson
and
Frank Herbert

Sense and Sensibility

"A dimension is opened up ... which lies between the thing and man, which reaches out beyond things and back behind man."
—Martin Heidegger

PROLOGUE: Fiat Lux

For the better part of fifty thousand years Metastatic Vectorship *Naglfar* had followed the gently curving line of an outward spiral, voyaging away from the Earth, following the receding frontier, falling ever farther behind. The starship drifted through a sea of diamond-dust stars, unmanned, carrying a cargo of information, transporting souls, visiting all the planets on its course, staying at each one a little while, moving on.

Naglfar was an extension of an early Red Millennium design, an irregular sphere of fuel tanks and machinery, its quantum dissociative engines pulsing violet light every now and again. It had a small crew cabin and life-support system, adhering to a regulation ages forgotten, but the bulk of the ship's resources went to supporting her neurotaxic computer system and optical resonance storage devices.

The ship's computer looked out through its sensors on a familiar scene. The main braking phase was finished, the inertial-relativistic rainbow faded into a haze of repetitive memories, the universe inflated back into a sphere. The target star, Shemesh, was a bright spark ahead, only light-hours away, a brightish G7 sun with the usual entourage of debris.

There were six planets here, distributed among the usual gravitational troughs, divided evenly between silicate-iron bodies and gas giants. The innermost world was a stripped planetary core, rich in metals and stirred mineral pools. Next came an Earth-sized world, the colony planet Olam, with its hazy blue skies and twin hundred-kilometer moons. Beyond that was a small, cool world, marginally habitable to mankind, then an unusually dense asteroid belt, thick with stony-iron material, poor in chondritic bodies. The gas giants were a varied lot; two small bluish worlds with a few nondescript moonlets, then Adomm, huge, sullen, red substellar object, with its vast, silvery ring system and complex, planetlike satellites. Beyond that an outer asteroid belt, mostly blackened ices, trailing off into the usual cometary cloud.

The ship scanned the system for anything that might pose a navigational hazard, reaching out with constantly evolving instrumentation down into the submicron range, until it was satisfied. *Naglfar* turned about its center of gravity, pulsed the engines once, then spun again, stopping twice for lesser bursts. A second scan showed a trajectory that would intersect Olam's orbit just as the planet happened by. Neurotaxa flowed toward each other and the world began.

The land around Asgard curves up and away in all directions, retreating from the thirteen halls of the great gods in an endless wash of green and gold. In Valhalla, benign Odin smiles over the feasts of heroes, gone to their reward. And the heroes dream.

As the one most recently delivered from the Valkyries' charms, the sixty-sixth incarnation of Maaron Denthurion, branch Thirty-three, sat at the head of a long feasting table, looking down the double row of his band of brothers toward the first incarnation. They were, he thought, not quite all alike. In fact, for doppelgangers, they showed a startling diversity. There sat the first brother, fresh and new, brought to life so long ago at Odin's unfathomable whim, father to a new line of men, representing of the Metastable Order. And along that line you could see the faces change, gathering wisdom and experience until the end of the table was reached.

Denthurion settled back in his chair, sighing, feeling the solid, sleep-inducing lump under his breastbone, digestive juices wringing new life from old. How long did I live? Five years on Kem? It didn't sound like much . . . but the lives of his brothers were within him. Five years? No. Three hundred years and more since the branching began.

The hall opened up around him, row on row of long tables, filled with animated men, a whispering sea of brethren. And all of them inside him as well; from times past, from overlays, from a common childhood in the remote and hazy past . . . a childhood that was, somehow, as fresh as those few bright years spent wandering the canal-crossed deserts of Kem.

A distant, fading memory of Tiy, sweet Tiy, flickered past, brushing him with feather wings of dark beauty. One long pulse of happiness touched him, like the recollection of a forgotten song.

How many years? It was hard to calculate . . . but Odin knew: Ten thousand years since the lines began. All the overlays converged. All the branchings became one, focusing on the original nexus of the many lives. Somewhere, in the cloudy far reaches of the great hall, the first incarnation of the first branching sat at Odin's side; and from him a thread reached out into the past and future. Their lives, as instrumentalities, added up. They were, in consequence, the aggregate lords of creation.

And where are we going? Onward, outward . . . Ten thousand years? No. All the incarnations of all the branchings were cumulative. We have eternity. And in that eternity I have lived forty thousand years. But . . . only five. Only those five bright years on Kem, walking the deserts, bathing in the silvery canals . . .

He saw himself under a brilliant night sky, standing naked beneath a sea of stars, small moon a sliver against the heavens, warm winds stroking his skin, cooling away sweat. Tiy reached up from her bed of feathery grass to stroke his leg, whispering to him, begging him to stay, but . . .

Lost. Lost to me.

Then, Odin whispered to him: Time to live. And Maaron Denthurion dissolved into the mists of memory.

shade his face — disappears in turn, hopping like a frog.

First Canto

Aurea prima sata est aetas, quae vindice nullo,
Sponte sua, sine lege fidem rectumque colebat.

The folk of that first Golden Age, completely
without punishment,
On their own and without laws, lived faithful and
upright lives.

—Ovid, *Metamorphoses*

Chapter 1

Kinnock Maclaren, Second Consul and cultural attaché for the Metastable Order on Olam, stood alone in the musty stillness of the Archive Center, waiting, in the seldom-used main transceiver chamber, for the Televox to appear. He was a tall, thin man, with curly, close-cropped red-bronze hair and a narrow, ruddy face, clad in the white tunic of a Servant of the Metastability.

The transceiver chamber, like the MAC building itself, was ancient, having been built more than twenty thousand years earlier during the first days of Olam's colonization. Its gray stone walls and floor had been worn smooth by the endless touch of hands and feet. A shallow gully was visible across the middle of the floor, a path leading from the door to the transceiver niche.

Get hold of yourself, he thought. Five hundred years ought to breed something like self-confidence. But in eight long incarnations, decades each on varied worlds, he'd never met a Televox before, nor any instrumentality more powerful than a Planetary Governor. Televoxes were the ultimate authority, their decisions irrevocable, beyond appeal.

No, not quite right. There was the Metastatic Senate, and the Congress of Planetary Deputies . . . on Earth, fifteen hundred parsecs away, better than five thousand years of linear travel . . . No, this Televox would come and his will would be done, not to be reversed until some other power happened to pass this way, centuries, perhaps millennia, later. Kinnock smoothed the front of his tunic, glanced at his flat, silvery Olamite wristwatch, and swallowed dryness. The ship had been in orbit for more than an hour, engine glow cooling away, silent since an initial terse message: Prepare.

Prepare for what? They knew there was a Televox in *Naglfar*'s registry, little more. And the last Televox had come to Olam more than twenty-five hundred years ago. What will he see this time? Kinnock felt a lump form in his chest, an expanding vein of nervousness. Nothing. Perhaps nothing. It was a formality. A Televox wandered the universe as he would, stopping at every inhabited world in his path, and any uninhabited one that struck his fancy. Perhaps this Televox would come, take a quick look around, then depart on his endless course. But the ship came from Kem. He'll be used to . . . quiet.

The dead stillness of the chamber was interrupted by a faint ticking sound from behind the stone walls, where age-old electronics lay embedded, then the transceiver niche took on a misty look as its teledyne nodes tuned up. Kinnock straightened his clothes further, throwing back his shoulders, waiting.

The mist cleared suddenly, the stone behind it taking on a crisp look, then the Televox spilled into existence, building up out of nothing, from inside to out, in a fraction of a second, an amorphous red mass, growing, growing . . . there. Kinnock took an involuntary step backward, stopped. Modern transceivers were decently enclosed.

Thick black hair, shaggy and irregular, cropped to a few inches length, long-nosed, square chin faintly cleft, greenish-brown eyes rolling to follow the motion of unseen clouds . . . Tall, evenly muscled, pale clear skin, smallish manicured hands . . .

The meaningless details disappeared abruptly and Kinnock Maclaren found himself looking at the Televox, attention sharply focused. Look at him, then. Handsome, young, alert as a hunting hawk, stooping from one of the tall towers of Hansa, intent on his prey. Young, yes. Very young? Is he twenty, then? Younger than that? Calm, attention on me, focused, taking in the room behind me, yet undistracted . . . Could be twenty, yes, but . . . I could believe him to be a thousand years old . . .

And the little voice in his head noted that this Televox, his aggregate self, at least, could be a good deal older than that.

The black-clad man in the niche looked down at him with interest for a moment, then he stepped down, offering his hand. He was a little taller than Kinnock, thin and muscular, in severely allopathic fashion. Kinnock stepped forward and took the proffered hand, then, in Ursprache, said, "Good afternoon, Mr. Televox. Welcome to Olam. I'm your servant, Kinnock Maclaren."

"Maaron Denthurion." The man looked him up and down and smiled. "Please speak the local language, Kinnock," he said in fluid Olamite.

God. A faux pas already! "Of course, sir." He motioned toward the door. "Would you like to freshen up?"

The Televox laughed. "I'm as fresh as I'll ever be, my friend. Let's go outside. I want to see the world."

Kinnock followed his Televox down the narrow stone corridor and up into the building, cursing a tongue-tied inanity. Nerves, he tried to tell himself.

Leaning on a smooth granite balustrade, Denthurion looked out over the valley of the Almana River, building a first impression of Olam. Not bad. Very Earth-like, but . . . different. Just a hint of the exotic. The Archive Center, a massive pile of gray stone, weathered until it had a soft, organic look, stood on a low hill at the western rim of the valley. Now, near sunset, Shemesh stood at his back, near the horizon, throwing the building's long shadow down the hill. There was a balmy wind blowing and the long, sword-shaped, bluish leaves of nearby trees were rustling against one another, waving in little repetitive undulations, singing.

Denthurion rubbed a hand over his face and brushed back his hair, brought forward by the wind. Something sweet in the air. I wonder what. Vegetation? Animals? Something man-made? You never knew with a new world, and *Naglfar* could only supply so much. Language, some history, customs, and literature. Just a little bit. No overlay from a recent Televox was available regarding Olam—just the news from Kem.

Below him, the valley was broad and shallow, receding into the distance, a sparse land of trees and bald, rolling hills. Kilometers away you could see the winding silver of the river and the shadowy blueness of the Sky Mountains. To the north the city of Perax was a rubble of white walls and low buildings, boxes in disarray, obscured by the hazy air.

He squinted upward. A typical sky, blue-green, a few isolated cumulus clouds just beginning to be tinted orange by sunset . . . Shemesh was an average star, a little cooler than Sol, a little closer, light a little yellower, less ultraviolet . . . He looked sharply then at the bluish vegetation. Well. There was no accounting for the vagaries of biochemistry. Still, the leaves should be greener, maybe spring green . . .

Denthurion shook off a sharp stab of déjà vu and moved on.

Olam was a large world, a little bigger than Earth. It had a somewhat heavier core and a surface gravity about ten percent greater. It didn't feel any different, but his legs seemed a little thicker than usual, especially after the slimness he'd worn on Kem. The computers took care of things like that during transmission. You had to be *right* for a world.

The haze was a little odd, too, for a world with a sharp atmospheric gradient. On planets where the air was compacted by gravity into a shallower layer, the strata of dust were correspondingly thinner. On the other hand, Olam's surface was more than fifty percent land, the interiors of the great "continents" full of gritty, uninhabitable desert. He looked back into the valley, watching shadows grow and spread, merging into pools of evening blue. If you looked sharply, there were little roads here and there—dirt roads—winding among the wispy trees. Not surprising. The colony worlds of the Metastable Order tended to be a bit pastoral, holo- and homeopathic norms widespread. Allopathic worlds could be jarring after that, all iron and ceramic and jostling hurry. Here, those things were hidden, off world, underground, heavy industry banished to the far reaches of the star system, where stinks and harshnesses could be themselves.

A scraping noise brought him to ground level. Kinnock Maclaren was coming out on the balcony, followed by a couple of bulky, green-uniformed men, bearing folding chairs and a tray laden with refreshments. As they began setting up, Denthurion said, "You're not locals."

The larger of the two, hashmarks on his sleeve, straightened up from his task. "Uh. No, sir. Guardsmen." He saluted. "Sergeant Olathe Harid, sir."

Denthurion stared at them curiously for a moment. "I see. Rather unusual work for soldiers, don't you think?"

Harid shot a nervous look at Maclaren. "Uh. Yes, sir." He saluted again, then he and the other man disappeared through the door.

Taking one of the chairs, Denthurion motioned Kinnock into the other. "On most worlds the habit is to hire locals for that kind of service. Metastatic Guardsmen, trained and transported from the stars . . ."

"Yes, well . . . I've been here for about fifty years, local time. The custom is to keep locals out of metagovernmental installations."

"Custom." Denthurion nodded slowly to himself. You had to be careful with a thing like custom. The major task of a Televox as he traveled the galaxy was to reinforce the status quo; but custom, like language, like everything else, could drift. People were very defensive, very proprietary about their customs. "Who started this custom, Governor, ah"—he searched his memory of recent history, uploaded since leaving Kem—"Governor Kartavilis?"

Kinnock shrugged. "I couldn't say. He's been in office for about eight hundred years, so . . ." He shrugged again. "Try some of this wine. It's called *davash*. It's very good."

Denthurion picked up one of the silver goblets and sipped the wine, feeling it burn sharply, evaporating off his tongue, filling his nose with a heady aroma compounded of roses and honey. "Very good." He put the goblet back on the tray. "Speaking of Governor Kartavilis, when will I meet him?"

Kinnock Maclaren stared into his cup, watching an interplay of light oils on the surface of the wine, still swirling from currents generated by the tipping of the fluid. "Tomorrow, sir. We've arranged a banquet. The Governor, some of his officers, Great Komer Ashaan of the Amud temple, and the principals of the planetary civil government."

"Business leaders?"

"There's no difference here."

"Ah." Denthurion picked up a leathery brown bit of sandwich from the tray and nibbled at it. Some kind of garlicky fish pâté. Denthurion put his feet up on the balustrade, picked up his goblet, and took another sip of the *davash*, savoring its sudden warmth. "I'll be interested to meet him." Interested? How many Planetary Governors have I met. A thousand? Ten thousand? *Naglfar* would know.

Maaron Denthurion, mark Zero, ten years old, sat in the living room on his mother's couch, bent over, pressing down the fastenings of his pneumotharsis athletic shoes, trying to organize thoughts still chaotic with sleep. They'd have a good pickup game today, probably beat the Featherstone kids . . . Maybe he and Cary could go hiking afterward and finish the day properly.

He stood up, basking for a moment in the crisp yellow sunshine streaming through the big bay window, staring at the transceiver in the corner. There was a temptation to pop over to Cary's house, by the edge of the playing field . . . It was an expensive allopathic unit, full of analytical algorithms, and would drop him off in perfect condition. He flexed his long, smooth arm muscles tentatively. No twinges. Well. He was in perfect condition already and the walk would be pleasant.

He palmed the linker platform and watched the miasma build up, then swirl into a comeye. The little homunculus waited patiently for his command, but . . . nah. He palmed the thing off and watched the comeye swirl away into nothingness.

"Denny?" The voice was high and soft.

"Coming, Mother." He walked down the shadowy hallway and into her bedroom. She was sitting on a blue-padded bench in front of her vanity mirror, pale brown hair piled high on her head, body wrapped in transparent azure chiffon. Through the material, her back was smooth, the double line of her spinal column bracketed by a sinuous musculature that blended smoothly into the sleek tendons at the sides of her neck. He knew his mother was considered unusually pretty, even for an allopath.

She twisted around to look up at him, hugging her arms across her chest so that her small breasts were squeezed together. "How will you be spending the day?"

"We have a game against Featherstone today. I was planning on lunch at Cary's afterward, then maybe a hike out to Italkor."

"What about school?"

"This is a catharsis week."

She nodded slowly. "It's hard to keep track . . ."

He bent to peck his lips on the soft, dry skin of her forehead, then went into his room and rummaged his Spanya gear out of a corner, looping the lanyards of the gray and black response-gloves over the long, thin wand, tucking the dull silver crack-helmet under his arm.

Outside, the morning air was cool on his legs, spring

not quite gone yet. In another month it would be blazing in Marumsko and the humidity would be beginning to rise. This was the best part of the year for outdoor activity. He put the Spanya gear down in a webwork chair and leaned on the sundeck's railing, looking uphill. The family's rambling house stood on a little rise in the middle of his father's kraal, a one-acre property of lawns, flowering bushes, and small fruit trees that was little different from the ones all around it. The village had a reputation for a certain subtle uniformity. Up the hill lay the Szomody's two-story house and, beyond that, the Ellis estate. They were naturopaths and had five children. It was difficult to imagine what life must be like for those ugly, naked little girls. All you could tell was that they were quite noisy.

Beyond the Ellis kraal was the big hedgerow that marked the end of the village ... He tilted his head back, looking up at the Landmark. The abandoned police cruiser, a vast, tilted disk more than a thousand meters in diameter, was balanced improbably on its blunt lower end. It had been there since the Salamander War, more than twenty thousand years ago, left there by its crew after an emergency landing.

The Salamander War had been a terrible thing, one of the major focal points they studied in history classes. When the humans had come, bearing the weight of an irresistible technology, the Salamander fleet had fled into interstellar space. The panic had been astonishing when, twelve centuries later, that same fleet had come crashing into the solar system, bent on vengeance. In the war's aftermath, filled with shame over the extinction of the Salamanders, the ruling allopathic regime had been overthrown, giving way to millennia of holopathic rule ... And never again would the Great Metastability of Humankind leave unexplored pockets of stars in its interior.

Picking up his gear, he turned and walked down the steps, then out across the lawn, heading down Stag's Hill.

The view that way was out across the valley of the village, a view of one-acre estates and parklands, the bushy ravine of the little Marumsko River, and the hedgerows of the far boundary. Beyond that, misty on the horizon, lay the pastel-hued, fairy-castle towers of Helium, capital city of the known universe, a volume of almost four trillion cubic light-years.

The next morning the sky over Almana Valley was a clear, cloudless turquoise, one of Olam's tiny moons a pale crescent rising little more than an hour before the sun. This one was called Baal. The other moon, Yshaa, was far away, a fat spark seldom visible in the daytime. Denthurion stood at the edge of the Archive Center's ornithopter landing stage, waiting for the machine to be unfolded and warmed up, looking out over the valley. The air was clearer today, a composite of morning clarity and calming weather patterns.

Good. I'll get a nice view. A little flyaround. The vegetation seemed even bluer today, striking yet another false note. I'll have to review the histories again. Something about this place . . .

Kinnock walked up to him from where he had supervised the unpacking of the flyer. Guard technicians were taking care of it now, checking all the connections, plugging it into the house electrical grid, running com lines into its nervous system. "Good morning, sir." Well. How do I say this? "Uh. Sir, are you *certain* you want to use this thing? I mean, Olam's transceiver grid may not be much, but it's . . . adequate. We can step through to the Governor's Palace. Or the Metastatic Guard Headquarters if you prefer . . ."

Denthurion's level gaze shut him up. "What are you so nervous about, Kinnock? I want to *see* this planet while I'm here, not jump from one room to another, like I was in one of those Hanseatic urban monads!"

"Nervous? I . . ." Kinnock had a sudden vision of the

great buildings of Hansa, kilometers high on a low-gravity world, cloud decks forming all around them. Strange. I never thought of the grid that way before. . .

"Well, sir, we don't use these things much. I don't know how old this machine is. It might . . ."

"Might what?" Behind them the engines on the ornithopter began to whine softly, a high, plaintive sound. They turned to look at it. The thing's red and black wings, drooping on the stone of the landing stage, were shivering, feather lattices seeming to stand away from their underlying infrastructure. One of the technicians suddenly shouted up to the pilot, "Release the aerolock, you idiot!" There was a loud clank and the wings lurched off the ground, folding up and tucking into the hull.

Denthurion laughed. "What's the worst that can happen? The wings fall off?"

"It's not out of the question."

"And what if they do? The impact won't hurt."

Kinnock blanched, shocked at the man's impropriety. "Sir. I'm not branched . . ."

"No?" He nodded slowly. "In a sense, neither am I. Everything since yesterday would be lost." Denthurion slapped Kinnock on the shoulder. "Come on, let's get on with it."

When they were ready, securely strapped into seats in the ornithopter's ventral cabin, the technicians uncoupled the machine from its moorings, then one of them, stepping back, gave the signal, whirling one arm over his head. The engines whined and the wings opened into a half-unfurled position, then the pilot applied vectored thrust and they lifted off, vertically, away from the MAC. As he watched the ground recede, dust clouds rising, Denthurion felt the thing throbbing through the frame of his chair and wondered just how long it *had* been. Dissociative reactor vessels weren't *quite* immortal.

The ground was sloping away swiftly now, the ornithopter banking as the pilot gained altitude and applied forward thrust. By the time they leveled off, a few kilometers up, the wings had opened to their full seventy-five-meter span. "Where to?" the pilot, in a green MetaGuard uniform, called over his shoulder.

"Just . . . around. Fly me around."

The pilot shrugged and made a long looping turn toward the west, out over the plains. The craft seemed steadier now that the strain had been taken off its engines. It was, after all, an excellent sort of glider.

Denthurion looked out the window with interest, watching the landscape unroll beneath them. The land was flat and sketchily forested, the occasional narrow lane passing below, along with widely separated buildings. Every now and then they passed over what looked like a patch of farmland, dark green terrestrial vegetation contrasting sharply with the bluer native stuff.

"What are you looking for, sir?" asked Kinnock when they'd cruised on in silence for several minutes. "If you'd let us know, we might take you directly to it . . ."

Denthurion waved him away, craning his neck forward. The land below was drying out, the patches of blue-green forest giving way to scrubland and occasional rocky outcrops. They were moving inland, toward the desert. Suddenly, fingers of bright green grass began to appear among the trees, then an occasional tall, pale stalk, something with a white trunk terminating in a puff of round, yellowish leaves. It was hard, though, to see any detail from this high up. "What are those tall things called?"

Kinnock squinted at the ground. "The pale trees? I don't know. I do know the pale vegetation is evergreen and the dark is deciduous. We had something like it on Albansburgh."

"Earth, too." He had a sudden memory, isolated, of flying over the area south of Helium in a parawing, looking down on a region where lanes of pine were snaking long invasion tendrils into an oak forest. Must have been winter, he mused. The oaks were bare. "Odd. I wonder why? Olam doesn't have much of an axial tilt."

Kinnock shrugged. "I couldn't tell you." He was begin-

ning to feel nervous again. This Televox was a distinctly
odd character. Why the Hell did he want to know about
the forest?

They were well away from the settled area now and
the true character of Olam was revealed. Settled areas
were surrounded by farming districts, quickly giving way
to wilderness, and all of it no more than green islands in
a sea of desert and scrubland. Watching the ground unreel, the ratio of light green flora gradually increasing,
Denthurion smiled with satisfaction, telling himself, *I
thought so. Strange that his predecessor, in preparing the
overlay file, hadn't thought to make a point of it. Still, it
hasn't always been illegal to alter biota like this. On the
other hand . . .* He tapped the pilot on the shoulder.
"Take me to Perax, now. See if you can set this thing
down in the big public square. What's it called?"

"Shaar Shamayim," said Kinnock.

"Okay." The pilot threw them into a steep climb, banking back toward the east, wind whistling through the
ship's pinion feathers with an eerie, multitoned voice.

When they stepped out of the ornithopter into Shamayim
Square, the bare, flagstone pavement was beginning to
shimmer a little in the midmorning heat. Denthurion felt
the warmth pushing through the thin soles of his light-
weight dress boots as he stood looking around. Apparently the square, something like a half kilometer on a
side, had been cleared of its occupants by local militia,
for there was a thin rime of people, giving off a soft rustle of whispered conversation, lining the south, east, and
west borders. Odd. The policemen, stationed a few meters apart before the crowd, carried slim rifles of some
sort.

The north side of Shaar Shamayim was dominated by
a vast, white concrete building. It was severely squared
off, walls sloping inward, perhaps two hundred meters
tall, topped by small crenellations. The middle of the

wall was dominated by a peaked set of bronze double doors, dark with verdigris. They stood open, and inside you could see another, smaller building, draped with hangings, covered with some kind of ornate scrollwork.

At his shoulder, Kinnock said, "The Great Amud. One of the few buildings on Olam older than the Archive Center."

Denthurion nodded to himself. First Landing on Olam had come something like twenty-five thousand years ago, and like many Frontier colonies, it had taken a score of centuries for the Metastability to catch up and put in an appearance. That single fact of life accounted for much of the destabilizing force against which the Televoxes labored. The Great Amud, now ... *Amud* meant "pillar" in Olamite. This place was supposed to be a loose theocratic oligarchy run under the aegis of a Metastatic governorship; not strict-constructionist, but with strong holo- and homeopathic tendencies. It makes my job harder, but these open worlds are so much *pleasanter* than ones run by the rule book.

A lane had been opened in the crowd lining the south side of the square and now a procession of bubble-topped hovercars slid in from the broad avenue, Dimyon Rexov, that bisected Perax. The Governor's Palace stood at the southern terminus of the avenue and these cars were blazoned with the webbed galaxy device of the Metastatic Guard. Looking at the cars, Denthurion said, "These are pretty up-to-date vehicles."

Kinnock nodded. "Based on a Hanseatic design. There's an underground factory complex in the Sky Mountains." At Denthurion's curious look, he continued, "The transceiver net was never extended, you know. Intercity, major sectors of the big cities ... and the extensive Guard/Government nets, of course." He *must* know all this ...

"How long do people live here?"

Kinnock shrugged. "A few centuries, I guess. Until something happens to them. The net is mostly holopathic, but"—he spread his hands helplessly—"we take care of things."

Once they were in the car, Denthurion settled back for the short ride down the avenue, looking out the window at passing architecture, peering down side streets at masses of people. They've cleared this one, too. The police must be fast and efficient. The buildings lining the avenue were squared off, whitewashed, facades mostly stone, with very little glass in evidence. There were small businesses everywhere, with little black and white signs lettered in ornate, serif-dominated Olamite characters.

They passed by one street in which the crowd had spilled back onto the main avenue, despite the best efforts of the police, and Denthurion looked at them with interest. There. Dotted among the crowd were any number of meter-tall, gray-furred bipeds, rather human-like, collared and leashed, many of them carrying packages. He turned to Kinnock and gestured at the crowd. "Hodai."

"Yes. They're more or less—ubiquitous." He squirmed unaccountably. "It . . . made me uncomfortable when I first arrived."

Watching them recede, Denthurion thought, there are too many people on the streets . . . I don't know. Something indefinably wrong. Well. Maybe nothing more than the fact that my most recent incarnation was on orderly Kem. We'll see.

By the fall of 42,063, the season of their thirteenth birthdays, Denthurion and his best friend, Melis Carthoradis, were getting their full growth, time terribly short now for both of them.

Today the woods were cool, breezes penetrating past fading foliage, curling around the backs of their necks. The sun was filtering down through the leaves, taking on color and losing warmth, illustrating what they learned in school, of how the world was emerging from a recent bubble of glaciation, ten thousand years of cold that had given the region around Helium a subarctic climate.

Denny walked ahead steadily, remembering the summer just past, trying to focus on the special things of childhood that seemed to be slipping away between his fingers, but Cary's voice, thickening with advanced puberty, broke in. "What are you going to do?"

"I don't know. Yule is still ten weeks away."

"That's not much time."

Denny shrugged, wishing he could avoid the topic for another little while, knowing he could not. "Time enough to think a little more. How about you?"

"My parents are fighting again. My father wants me to stay home with him and help with the family's epic poem. It pisses my mother off. She wants me to go to the Remedy School in Steinershafen."

Denny grinned to himself, glad Cary couldn't see through his head. "Like a proper homeopath, huh?"

"Fuck you. I don't imagine your dad's giving you much choice."

"Nope. The Institute for Metastatic Interpathy, nothing less, nothing more. Your family writes epic poems about the evolution of the universe, mine breeds Guard Commanders and Planetary Deputies."

"That piss you off?"

"Nah. I like Helium. Besides, IMI boys can get laid whenever they want."

"That seems like a pretty shortsighted attitude."

Denny stopped and turned to face the other boy. "What difference does it make? With IMI training I can do whatever I want, be an explorer or a poet; *anything*. I don't *have* to go to the Branchings College afterward. Not unless I want to."

They resumed walking as Cary said, "Explorer, huh? The Frontier is twenty thousand light-years away."

"So what? I'd catch up eventually . . . and the Frontier sure as Hell isn't going to disappear!"

"Could you dad get me into IMI?"

"You're a homeopath. What would you study?"

"Holopathic pussy." His voice took on an edge of frustration. "Shit, I don't know. Anything so long as it isn't nonsensical epic poetry or . . . *remedies*."

"Well . . . what are you interested in?"

"You know. Cosmology."

Denny nodded slowly. Of course he knew. The Last Mystery. Since the Red Millennium, forty thousand years gone, science had boiled down to just one question: *Why.* "I guess you'd have trouble studying the real issues anywhere else . . ." The various single-viewpoint schools merely presented their special mythologies. IMI, the government's training center, looked at all the angles. "Well. I'll ask."

After a while, they burst out of the woods, finding themselves on the edge of Dorvo Valley, and stopped, looking down. Denny remembered that first day, when they discovered it accidentally, stumbling out of the tangled summer undergrowth and halting with amazement. He could still recall Cary's muttered exclamation.

The valley was just as it had been, a broad, shallow, seemingly uninhabited bowl, fully of tawny grass, dotted here and there by gnarled and isolated trees. Just off center was a big crater maybe ten meters across, full of raw dirt that turned red when it rained. They'd spent many a day here, fencing with their Spanya wands or defending themselves from attack by the small berry bushes that grew in profusion. Denny smiled, then frowned. Oh, happy memory! But childhood is . . . over.

Denthurion stood at the head of a flight of broad, blue-carpeted stone steps, looking down into a vast, softly lit room. The tiered floor of the Grand Concourse in the Governor's Palace of Olam spread out across nearly two hectares beneath a vaulted crystalline dome of fine, optically reactive glass and spidery, metallic struts. On the floor was a colorful sea of Olamites, surging about each other in a slow, complex milling of interconnected cliques, above them, the bright, clotted stars of Olam's sky, static against a black background resonance.

Turning to the man at his side, Denthurion said, "Very nice, Governor."

Ardennes Kartavilis nodded slightly, the sharp essence of a bow. "I've always thought so, Mr. Televox." The Governor, eighth branching of a well-trained, experienced instrumentality, was a short, thick-waisted, and overdeveloped man, with a broad face, high cheekbones under curly black hair, his eyes dark brown and set in deep, shadowy wells, bracketing a short, blunt nose. Now, he was on edge, sifting every word for nuance.

Denthurion looked around, eyes darting here and there quickly, seldom lingering long on any feature in his field of view. The room was full of little ... touches ... bits of ornamentation, always understated, from the detailed attentions of human craftsmen. "How much do you suppose a ballroom like this would cost?"

The Governor was taken aback. Cost? What did that have to do with anything? He shrugged. "In today's economy? Billions of *gavishim*, maybe. I couldn't tell you what the interstellar exchange medium would do with it." He tried to look into the Televox's face, but found nothing. "Well. I can claim no credit for it, one way or another, since this place was built thousands of years ago. Back then ... I understand the work was done by human craftsmen and then-plentiful Hodai labor."

Back then ... Denthurion nodded slowly to himself. The sense of accumulating historical change was definitely present. Planets do that. Sometimes for better, requiring encouragement; sometimes for worse, calling for reform. We'll see. He smiled slowly and gestured toward the floor of the ballroom. "Shall we?" He started down the long stairs, not waiting for the others.

Governor Kartavilis turned to stare at Kinnock Maclaren. Finally, the other man said, "It seems to be the way he works. Digging a bit here and there, I mean. We'll have to get used to it, Governor."

Kartavilis looked after Denthurion's retreating back. "More than that, Mr. Maclaren. How we handle him may be"—he shrugged—"crucial." He started down the stairs himself, followed by his little entourage.

Despite a studied nonchalance, they were watchful on the floor. Above all, who was this little interloper, to interfere in the workings of their world? But . . . demigods have to be careful when real deities stop by, however benign their motives. Ashaan, Great Komer of Amud, chairman of the Council of Twelve, stood with his friends and watched the Televox move slowly through the crowd, closing in on them with steady deliberation. He was a small man, plump, moon-faced, bald under his pale green head-cloak, an unprepossessing supreme civil authority, with a stillness of manner that could be unnerving. "He's taller than the other one," he whispered to the man next to him, "friendlier."

Meltsar straightened up, smoothing the front of his favorite red tunic, running a hand down his dark beard with its two narrow stripes of white hair on either side of his mouth. You had to remember that the salient thing about this old fart was that he was . . . *old*. Ashaan had been here, a very minor priest-functionary, twenty-five hundred years ago, when the last Televox stopped by. "Well," he muttered. "The last one did nothing. We have nothing to be alarmed about. This is a well-settled world."

"I'm not alarmed. But things are different now."

Different. Meltsar felt a faint stirring of unease. "I don't see how. The world has changed very little since I was a boy."

"*You're* less than three hundred years old, Meltsar. A baby."

The Governor, Televox Denthurion, and that bland little Metastatic bureaucrat, what was his name, Maclaren, stopped in front of them. Ashaan drew himself up and bowed low before Denthurion. "Good evening, Your Grace. Welcome to Olam." He straightened up and nodded to Kartavilis. "Governor."

Standing a little to one side, not quite between them, Kartavilis said, "Your Grace, allow me to present Great Komer Ashaan."

"Your Honor." Smiling, Denthurion held out his hand.

Ashaan stared at it for a moment, then was glad the Governor had taken the trouble to brief him on Earth customs earlier in the day. He grasped the man's wrist and bowed low over the connection between them, while Kartavilis made a brief, formal statement about his position as head of the civil government.

"Charmed." Denthurion looked down on the little man and read the signs with interest. That fixed stare was probably perceptual, of course, but the smooth movements and stillness in repose bespoke long life. Interesting. People didn't usually last too long out on the holopathic worlds. Still, there were other influences in this part of the galaxy, contributing a liberalizing effect. He looked past Ashaan at a tall, heavily built man whose pale brown eyes were oddly highlighted by reflections off his red head-cloak. "And this is?"

Kartavilis started slightly. "A cultural institution, Your Grace. Mr. Meltsar is one of our finest authors," he said, repressing his anger at finding the man here.

Denthurion nodded. "Novelist?"

Gripping his wrist, Meltsar bowed. "At times, Your Grace."

"I loved them as a child. Perhaps I'll find time to read one of yours while I'm here."

"I'd be honored, Your Grace." Meltsar, smiling broadly through his beard, bowed low before him. "I'll have my favorite works sent to you."

The Governor stared at him in aggravation for a moment, then he gestured toward another man, some distance away. "Over here, Your Grace, is our Resource Minister, Mr. Shatiyax . . ."

As they moved away, Ashaan whispered to Meltsar, "If he reads *Hikanesh!*, our Governor won't be very happy."

"No. I suppose not."

Chapter 2

Kinnock and Denthurion sat in the back of a Guard transport that was part of a three-hovercar procession that slid swiftly through the streets of Perax under a hazy, blue-white sky. Hayah Boulevard, a main diagonal artery that led from the Governor's Palace in the South District to Universitaa Square in the West, had not been explicitly cleared of people, though there were black-uniformed Olamite security police in evidence, enough to thin the crowds.

Maclaren was trying to look out through the bubble glass, at the city, but he kept stealing glances at Denthurion. The Televox was leaning far back in his seat, legs extended before him, crossed at the ankles, eyes narrowed to slits through which a moist glitter was barely perceptible. The man had been silent all morning, puttering about the Archive Center, lounging on the balcony, then, after lunch, making them drive a circuitous route into Perax, wandering the back lanes of the countryside for hours.

He pulled his eyes away, not wanting to trigger any kind of a response. Eventually this nerve-wrackingly mysterious behavior would stop. The Televox would do his job and Olam would be a little bit different . . . or he would do nothing but bedevil them for a little while, then leave.

His interest in the vegetation, now, was an example of bedevilment. And I checked up on it. Kemitish flora was introduced into the region around Perax fifteen hundred years ago, and it's spread all around the southern shore of the Shennhavv Sea. Unlicensed bicontamination's been illegal since before Olam was colonized . . . but what's he going to do about it now? At worst, Ashaan's ass is in the fire. And that idiot Shatiyax.

Denthurion stirred suddenly, and said, "This will have to stop."

Now what? "Your Grace?"

"I'm not interested in an extended inspection of the Peraxian police." He turned to face Kinnock, laying one arm up along the seat back. "Please convey my respects to the Great Komer. Ask him to reassign the security forces to their regular duties."

No police? Kinnock frowned. "Uh. I'm not sure Ashaan's the one, Your Grace. Public Safety Commissioner Kevess . . ."

"Whomever. Kinnock?"

"Your Grace?"

"You and I are going to be working together quite closely for the next four or five years."

Four or five years? It would seem like an interminable agony . . . but, historically, a Televox would spend five years inspecting even a relatively tranquil planet. If he stayed longer, things must already be down the shitter. "Yes, Your Grace."

"My name is Denthurion."

He looked up into an open and friendly face, stared at shifting, expressionless eyes. "Yes, uh." Denthurion. And I am Kinnock. Not Denthurion and Maclaren. Certainly not Maaron and Kinnock. Does that mean something? Possibly. But no one called Olam's other Earthman Ardennes. It was always Governor Kartavilis. Or Governor, informally. Ashaan just called him Kartavilis. He shrugged. No way I can work this out. He smiled. "Denthurion, then."

The little convoy slid into the great square before the Universitaa, whispering softly over the pavement, and the Televox said, "Well. I spoke precipitously. Obviously Perax has a most impressive police force . . ." He grinned. "Unless Commissioner Kevess has called in men from all over Olam to protect the city from my depredations."

Their path was marked by a double row of black-clad armed men, and once again the inhabitants of a public square had been pushed to its outskirts. The Universitaa, on the western border of the square, was a complex of white stone buildings, squared off like all Olamite architecture, structures stepped back as they grew taller, and the whole was surrounded by a low masonry wall, more symbolic than otherwise.

The car scraped to a stop, then the bubble slid back. The noise level increased dramatically. This crowd, unlike the one in Shamayim, was not subdued. There was a steady roar of conversation, occasionally resolving into a babble of individual words. Sometimes you could hear shouts, entire sentences, something about *ovvedim*, "laborers," and *hofeshsh*, "liberty," but they were too far away for the whole sense of it to be made out.

Kinnock stood up before his seat and stared about the square. Ashaan ought to be able to suppress something like this, even on short notice. "Your Grace, uh." He gestured toward the gates of the Universitaa.

Denthurion stood in his turn and looked through the gates into an empty campus, at a double row of armed guards, obviously keeping everyone out, then around at the snarling crowd. "These people seem mad at us, Kinnock. And if you don't stop calling me 'Your Grace,' *I'll* be mad at you."

"Yes ... yes." He gestured toward the building again. "Let's get inside." His heart was speeding up a little bit. There was no point in dawdling out here ... In the background the people seemed to be chanting something, but they kept getting mixed up, their words an out-of-sync gabble.

The Televox put his hands on his hips and was staring at the milling masses around the square, seeming to listen to their discordant cries. "This was a very bad idea, Kinnock. We'll be taking it up with Ashaan." He glanced at Maclaren. "Well. He didn't seem very bright at dinner, did he?"

"No. No, sir." Look at them! Hands were waving in the air, head-cloaks, dominated by the green and white stripes of Universitaa undergraduates, flapping like flags.

"I'm not here to stir up trouble, nor to let foolish local authorities stir it up for me." He listened to the crowd again, watching as the people pressed closer to the police line, moving in little tentative surges. "What does *leshamenn* mean?"

"'Lubricate.' It's a euphemism that the students use. It means, uh . . . 'fuck you.'" But he made the infinitive correctly. Why ask? "I think we should go inside now, Your . . ."

A distinct chant began again, the human mass making individual policemen step back: *Bah-YEET, bah-YEET* . . . and more clearly between the shouted waves of sound, *bayiit shelanu, "our* home."

Something flickered over the heads of the police, sunlight glinting on clear glass and a small, fluttering blossom of yellow fire. The bottle tumbled toward them and smashed on the pavement a dozen yards away, burning fluid spreading into a fat, fiery puddle in moments, spilling under the feet of nearby policemen, making them dance out of the way, stamping fire from their boots. Kinnock grabbed the Televox and forced him back down at his seat, screaming to the driver, "Dome! Dome! Get the Televox out of here!"

As the hovercar's dome slid up, police truncheons were out everywhere, rising and falling, and the crowd snarl was changing into screams as the people tried to surge away from the point of trouble. The sound cut off as the dome snapped shut and they were already moving. Denthurion turned in his seat, looking back toward the square as they slid off down Hayah Boulevard. "Those men are using their rifles on the crowd." He looked forward, then back. "We've lost one of our Guard cars." He stared fixedly at Kinnock, then. "Are the Metastatic troops armed with dissipators?"

Maclaren felt himself trying to shrink out of sight. "Yes, Your Grace."

"Driver."

"Sir."

"Take me back to the Archive Center."

"Yes, sir."

As the hovercar slid up a side street, circling out through the western sectors of the city, passing south of the Universitaa via a narrow belt of low, unremarkable suburban dwellings, flat-roofed houses of white stucco and small windows, Denthurion lay back in the seat again, arms folded, eyes slitted. At several points Maclaren tried to get his attention, start a halting conversation, but he was ignored.

Well. We will find out the roots of this problem, and what it may be related to . . . Stupid administration, certainly. That business of throwing the students out of their own university . . . What do they think I am?

But . . . these things simply *happened*, as well. He let his head fall back onto the soft, leatherlike padding of the car seat and stared out through the shifting tints of the bubble glass, watching the haze deepen with the first hint of sunset. Not many clouds. Just haze. He shut his eyes, remembering the student riots on Great Porphyry, some incarnations back. Whole cities burned to the ground, a fury of angry, directionless young people, aglitter with arcane war paint, tearing through the countryside, leading to devastation, to famine, and, finally, to outright generational war.

I had to change everything, the educational system, local customs of parenting, ideas about birth control, marriage, and interpersonal relationships. It was twenty years before I could get away. A very long incarnation . . .

And yet, Great Porphyry had been a strict-constructionist allopath world, with a difficult, complex, and dehumanizing society, the sort of place that made you say, "These things happen." Here, now . . . We shall see.

In the summer of 42,068, Maaron Denthurion was still seventeen years old. He was taller and rangier now, kept close to some hypothetical ideal by periodic passage through an allopathically tuned transceiver, his face handsome and unlined, long nose and high cheekbones artistically framed by a halo of glossy, wavy black hair, green-brown eyes bright with health and intelligence.

Standing by his side in the darkness, Melis Carthoradis was a study in subtle contrasts. He was stockier, a little shorter, his midsection lightly padded with fat, long, dark hair straight and lit with red highlights. Homeopathic transceivers had given him a variation on the original holopathic ideal, studying his genes for some clue to the intent of his Platonic source code. Where Denny was an individual based on the generalized theme of Man, Cary was an individual based on the precepts of the Carthoradis family line.

All around them, soft winds were blowing through the night, cool summer breezes rippling the tufted, spongy grasses of Edmundshaven Park, stirring the branches of leafy deciduous trees until they gave off a sweet chlorophyll perfume and filled the night with their sandpaper sound. The dim circle of a new moon, faint and coppery, stood low in the western sky, an hour or so from setting. The blackened heavens were thick with stars, the wan glow of the Milky Way filtering through thin clouds, narrow black shapes, visible only in outline, as they drifted slowly toward the southwest.

They walked slowly through the darkness, booted feet whispering over the grass, sneaking up on a pool of light and sound, and Denny felt touches of excitement building within. It had taken them weeks to nerve themselves up for this, amid much demurring and recalcitrance. Should we or shouldn't we? The ethically correct answer was "shouldn't," of course, but interest had won out over prudence. Now they crawled into a strand of bushes, pushing through an undergrowth of feathery grass, and looked out into a lighted clearing.

The Crimson Dancers were a legitimate holopathic sect, but they were uncommon, nonetheless, regarded as verging at all times on heresy. You heard about their activities, of course, but seldom had a chance to actually *see* them. They had a local chapter in Helium, all legal groups did, but this was the first Red Cradle to be held on the IMI campus in about ten years. In all probability, the bushes were just full of prying eyes, but you couldn't see them and the Dancers seemed unconcerned.

The clearing was lit by a circle of open-flame hydrogen sponge torches, flickering, throwing an unpredictable blue-yellow light everywhere, brightening the backs of a dozen naked girls, throwing long shadows before them, like spokes, commingling on the grassy ground at the circle's hub, making a patch of greater darkness where the umbrae overlapped.

"Shit," whispered Cary. "What do you suppose they're up to?"

Denny shrugged. You heard rumors, but these girls were a pretty closemouthed lot. "I guess we'll find out shortly."

Outside the circle of torches, perhaps another three dozen naked girls squatted, clustered into nine groups of four, drums clutched tightly between their knees. The twelve girls in the middle stood silently, staring up into the night sky, arms relaxed at their sides. Suddenly the girl at the south end of the circle lifted her hand overhead, pointing at the western sky, and shouted, "She waxes!" Immediately, the four girls sitting to the north, the only ones in the outer circle on a cardinal compass point, banged their little drums in unison. The flat, high sound echoed off the buildings surrounding the park.

The girls in the circle reached between their legs and fumbled there, plucking something out and discarding it in the grass, then they began to dance, and the drums began to sound. The drummers struck in a complex patterning, across the circle, but precessing through their odd number, each set of drums tuned to a slightly different timbre. Every fourth cluster struck its note more loudly than the others, giving the drumming an aboriginal four-part rhythm.

The girls danced, bending, seeming to stagger, and Denny could see that dark rivulets were beginning to spread down the inner thighs of some of them, looking black in the blue hydrogen light, snaking apart into forked rivers, like little bolts of lightning. Cary muttered something in the background, echoing his own thought: This is grotesque.

The girls began to spin as they danced, whirling out, then in again, voiceless, their faces frozen, eyes dark pits in pale faces, long hair flying out in midnight arcs. After long minutes of circling, the heels of their feet stamping into the ground, the girl who'd stood at the south node, the one who'd started things with her shout, changed the pattern, spinning into the center of the circle, standing on the dark confluence of spasming shadows. Now she spun solitary, the other girls dancing around her, the circle closing in. "She flows! She pulls me free!"

To Denny's amazement, the girl thrust both hands into her crotch and brought them up to her face, smeared with blood. Two quick strokes and there were four red lines on each cheek, like war paint. The other girls shouted, a high, ululating cry, and the drums banged once, in unison, then resumed their four-part pattern.

The circle flew apart again, twelve girls in twelve places whirling about beneath the flickering torches. Now they all reached downward and began painting themselves, smearing blood over their faces and around their bouncing breasts. Cary whispered softly, "I feel like I'm looking back in time."

Denny nodded. It was like something from that other alien half of human history, the ages of mankind that existed before the coming of the Red Millennium. Something in him rebelled at this ... barbarism. Forty thousand years had gone by since the Red Millennium, forty thousand years of selective modification, of civilization and expansion into the cosmos. You'd think this sort of thing would be gone forever, or at least banished to primitive Frontier worlds ...

But it plucked at some unpleasant chord within him, stirring him on a hormonal level. There was a faint wish building up, a desire to burst from the bushes and throw himself on these girls ...

The drums banged again, suddenly, in unison, and the dancers halted, arms upraised, filling the circle with a crosshatching of shadows that continued the dance on some other plane. The drummers stood silently, and then began to stream out of the clearing, taking their drums with them, vanishing into the night. When the last one was gone, the twelve girls stepped out of the circle, each extinguishing a torch as she passed by, then they too left the clearing, walking away, back toward the spoke containing the various holopathic dormitories.

One of the girls walked close by the bush under which Denny and Cary lay concealed, bringing with her as she passed a strong, musty odor of menstrual blood. Denny squinted out into the darkness after her and was shocked to recognize one of the girls from his seminar on Metastatic Imagery, a leading intellectual of the class.

He turned to look at Cary, whose face was almost obscured by shadow. "Two weeks ... We should come back here again for the Full Moon. I understand the White Cradle is something else again ..."

Denthurion sat under the vaulted blue ceiling of the Archive Center's small dining room and contemplated his third dinner on Olam. *Neshikaa*, this stuff was called: ground *kivsaa*, which seemed to be the meat of a small mountain reptile renowned for its plaintive call, artfully arranged with a whipped blend of Inca potatoes and some small, round, yellow pods he'd never seen before, all smothered in a thick, grayish sauce that smelled of the omnipresent *shuum*. He tasted it. Not bad, but definitely inferior to the tomato-dominated Kemitish fare of his previous incarnation. Maybe that's what's wrong with these people. Too much garlic. That sparked a trickle of amusement. ·

The soldier who was serving him poured a tall goblet of tawny *davash* wine, set the carafe down beside it, and departed, leaving him alone with a fidgeting Kinnock Maclaren. No time like the present. "All right, Kinnock. It's time we began talking seriously about my job here."

"Your Grace."

"We will begin better if you resolve to stop calling me that."

That brought a slightly pained look. "Mr. ... Denthurion, the niceties of Metastatic etiquette were firmly drilled into us on Hansa. It'll take some time for me to break that conditioning."

"I know." He smiled. "And as a nonbranched entity, you may pass the broken conditioning on to a future incarnation who will get in trouble."

"Pass it on to *me*, I think." Kinnock frowned, staring down at his steaming dinner. "*I* believe the incarnations have continuity, don't you? It's such an *old* question ..."

Denthurion laughed, genuinely amused, but thought, Old and unanswerable, for the branched few. After forty thousand years of accumulated composite memories, my feelings are still mixed. The memory of those early days still strikes cold. He picked up his goblet and sipped stinging, flowery sweetness. "How does the soul know where you went? We'll leave that one to naturopathic worriers."

Kinnock nodded slowly. "I've read any number of books from the late Red Millennium, around the time teleportation was being developed. They worried about it a great deal."

"Well. So does anyone who uses anything more sophisticated than a planetary transport net. You start thinking about crystal time." He smothered the tack of the conversation with another, longer drink from his goblet, then refilled it from the carafe. "Kinnock, what do you think a Televox does?"

"Ah . . . well." Signs of faint dismay surfaced. A philosophical discussion about the nuances of matter transmission clearly would have been more to his taste. "You travel the universe, making sure the Metastable Order is properly enforced."

"You regard me as a sort of wandering Inspector General, making sure the Metastatic Guard forces don't fuck up too badly?"

He shrugged. "Well, sure. That's the general idea."

Denthurion pushed his plate aside, largely untouched, deciding to concentrate on the wine, which was beginning to make him feel a little light-headed. "The Planetary Governor and his Guardsmen sit on the one node, in isolation, seeing that it keeps within certain local bounds. My job is to make sure that node doesn't drift away from the totality of the Metastable Order. I am the voice of humanity, flung out to the stars."

"That's not so different from my supposition."

Good enough. Conditioning and "niceties" or no, he's not really afraid of me. "Irregardless, what I do is little more than a stochastic process. Kinnock, what's wrong with Olam?"

Maclaren picked up his goblet and took a drink in turn, looking a little to one side of Denthurion. "I don't know that anything's wrong here."

"To late for *that*, Kinnock. You have to talk to me now." He stared at the man for a few seconds, watching his eyes drift around the room. "Well. Let me put it another way: If they'd thrown a firebomb at *you* . . ." He shrugged. "Petty terrorism's not that uncommon, just illegal. When they throw one at *me*, well, it may be the end of everything for Olam."

That got his attention, pulled the wandering eyes onto Denthurion's face. "What do you mean?"

"Kinnock, the notion of an expendable Televox is only partly true." He considered, gauging the necessary effect, then said, "The loss of Maaron Denthurion, mark Thirty-three, incarnation sixty-seven, would be a small one for the Metastable Order. Just a few days experience; one more regrettable *lacuna*. Incarnation sixty-eight would be down here tomorrow, straightening things out, wishing he knew what the devil I'd been through. The loss to *me*, of course . . ." He spread his hands and smiled. "The point is this: Without faster-than-light communication, much less travel, humanity is held together by nothing more than the likes of me . . ."

"What about the Metastatic Guard? What about Governor Kartavilis?"

Another shrug. "Without the stabilizing continuity of the Televoxes, they're nothing more than imposed military dictatorships, isolated, drifting apart. As far as this world is concerned, I *am* the Metastable Order. A blow against me is a blow against everything that has value in our lives."

Maclaren frowned. "That's what they say . . . and I do understand what you're saying." He sat back in his chair, draining his cup, then reached out to refill it from the carafe. "I'm curious: What if they killed you? What if they managed to shoot *Naglfar* out of the sky? What then?"

"Surely you know the answer to that one, Kinnock. In a century, or maybe two, a fleet of Guard contingents from the surrounding worlds would come, under the command of a Televox. And when they were through this world would have a different name and different people." Memories of other worlds, other lives, welled up to trouble him. I say it so blandly, but the reality is there. The image of cities in flame is . . . unhappy. "I'll ask you again, Kinnock: What's wrong with Olam?"

Maclaren sighed, then looked him in the eye, obviously seeking belief. "I honestly don't know. Maybe nothing much; nothing like what you're talking about. Economic unrest, philosophical ferment, the students . . ." He shrugged. "They bandy about ideas not taught in the schools. I couldn't tell you where it's coming from."

"And the firebomb?"

He shrugged. "The students demonstrate . . . it's not so unusual on a world like Olam. They even have an organized movement they call *Shearah*, a pitiful thing, really . . . I'm sure it was just the act of an unthinking individual. There's been nothing like that before. No assassination attempts or . . . anything like that."

Shearah. "Storm." Interesting. "Still, *I* haven't been here before," he said, "or anyone like me. Ashaan would make a pathetic target, after all."

"He's cautious, in any case. What about the Governor?"

Shows that you're thinking, at least. Denthurion smiled. "Kartavilis has been here longer than most Olamites live. He's as much a fixture as the Great Komer. Tell me, Kinnock, have things changed much in the time you've been here?"

"Regarding the unrest?"

"Of course."

Maclaren rubbed his chin reflectively. "I—suppose they have. Not the economic component, though, and the business with the students seems to go back before my time. The mythosocietal business of, uh, *Koxavonia* . . ."

" 'Starship'?"

Maclaren nodded. "It's a minor sect, I guess. Charismatic philosophy has always been part of the Olamite culture; something of a sociopathic metastasis that I understand is widespread in this sector."

"This region is a fusion between two colonization streams, one allopathic, the other holopathic. Your neighbor Kem is considered a perfect fusion of opposing liberal and conservative elements, a precise balance between homeopathic and sociopathic lines." Don't get distracted now. Follow this taxonomy. "What about this *Koxavonia* sect? If it's so minor, why did you bring it up?"

"Well . . . I don't know. I guess it's just . . . that . . . it's growing, in ways the other philosophies don't. It seems to have sprung up about twenty years ago, out of nowhere."

"And what are its major precepts?"

"It's a mythology about the supposed Starship of God. How we are all his crewmen, stuff like that." He looked troubled. "I really don't know that much about it. I'm sorry."

"Don't be." He refilled his goblet one last time, marveling at how fuzzy-headed he'd become after draining more than half the carafe, which held something like two liters. "It sounds like a standard readaptive mythology, mostly borrowed from the larger reality of the Metastable Order. Well. We'll look into it tomorrow. Right now my sensibilities are . . . drowned in liquor."

Kinnock Maclaren looked relieved.

Denthurion sat wedged in the broad, open window of his bedchamber in the Metastable Archive Center, one slippered foot pressed against the frame, the other curled under, knee to one side. His back was against the cool stone and the sweet smell of alien vegetation was wafting in on a slow, warm breeze. Overhead, the stars glittered, faint color visible in the brighter ones, pastel oranges and barely hinted blues, and the back side of the Crab Nebula was a thumb-sized smudge of dim haze, hard to make out unless you knew it was there.

Interesting. The stars seemed thicker the other night; now it's more like on Earth; a spattering of stars, thickening where the Milky Way arced low over the northern horizon. He remembered lying on his back in an open field somewhere near Marumsko, staring up at the stars, chatting for hours with Cary, wondering about the endless sea of men overhead, and about the vast, humanless universe beyond. Melis Carthoradis. Ten thousand years on his way, outward bound. In all that time I've lived forty thousand subjective years and come fifteen hundred parsecs from home. And he's gone more than twice as far and lived . . . not at all. Right now he sleeps in the crystal, the same Melis Carthoradis I said good-bye to all those long ages ago. When he awakens, in another ten thousand years, out on the Frontier, I wonder where and what I'll be?

He smiled to himself in the whispering darkness. It was useless to speculate about such things. He'd met men before who'd had eighty and ninety thousand years of composited subjective experience. Sometimes they were very odd indeed, but usually they were just men.

For we are the essence of the Metastable Order. And we discourage change in civilization by discouraging change in the individual man. Below him, down in the river valley, individual lights could be seen, marking the occasional rural dwelling place. On the northern horizon, Perax was a low glitter.

So. The task begins. Where am I now?

Item: At some time in the past few thousand years this planet was seeded with sweet-smelling Kemitish vegetation. Why? Does the native vegetation smell bad? Is it ugly? After all this time, you'd think they'd be used to it. Was this an accident, or deliberate? Did they think they could get away with a gross quarantine violation?

Item: Despite the fact that this is a holopathic world, the ruling elite uses allopathic life-prolongation techniques. If nothing else, that is a recipe for civil unrest. Are they stupid? The ones I've met don't seem overly sophisticated, despite millennia of subjective experience.

Item: Despite eight hundred years on the job, despite the accumulated experience of eight previous branchings, Governor Kartavilis has let things get out of hand. Is *he* stupid? Is the Metastable Order manufacturing incompetent Planetary Governors now?

That brought a momentary jolt of memory. Ardennes

Kartavilis dates from the same time period as my father. And my father . . . Well. I wonder if the originals know each other? Almost certainly.

So, again.

Item: The politics of Olam seem excessively complex. There *is* civil unrest, classical ferment in the cities, quarrelsome students, odd philosophical cults . . .

Since the last Televox came to Olam, all during the lifetime of Great Komer Ashaan and his colleagues, change has come . . . and, in the last twenty years, accelerated.

Revision? He nodded slowly to himself. We'll see . . .

One. Talk to the responsible parties. Get an unbiased view of what they think is going on.

Two. Review the Archives, find out what the Servants of the Metastable Order observed, in aggregate, over the centuries.

Three. Get out into the culture and discover the truth.

Well. A hard task, that last; easy to say, hard to do . . . And yet I've done it, again and again . . .

He turned into the dark room, easing off the windowsill, and sprawled facedown on the cool, stiff sheets of his bed, feeling the wind curl on the exposed skin of his back. *Tsemmer-gefen* this material is called, he thought muzzily, yet I knew it on Kem as *qoutn*, come all the way from Earth . . . and fell asleep.

An allopathic laboratory is a place of white enamel and bitter smells. It reflects the philosophical tenets of its technicians, as they reflect the precepts that led them to their tasks. The sights and smells are mere stage dressing, of course, for an advanced and subtle technology gives no sign of its existence.

Maaron Denthurion, mark Zero, sat in a little side chamber deep within the bowels of the Branchings College, robed in white, clustered with his fellow initiates, waiting his turn. Waiting for the Doubling Ceremony to begin. I'm . . . unnerved, he realized. It wasn't surprising; not really. He'd been thinking about this moment, on and off, for the last four years, ever since graduation day at IMI and his sudden decision to enroll in the Branchings College after all.

Calm down. It's no different than stepping through a transceiver. A little flicker of cultivated simultaneity and it'll be all over. You'll still be standing there . . . unchanged. He noticed that the initiate next to him was shivering, eyes squeezed shut.

For it was different, after all. He was all that he remembered himself to be. He was the Maaron Denthurion whose body vanished into the maw of a transmitter, whose soul transmitted itself through space to appear in the receiver, in a new and reperfected body. Now . . . who would this other Denthurion be? Me? No, I'll still be me. But this other Denthurion will be all that I remember myself to be. And that is all that I am. Memory is continuity. The flesh is . . . ephemeral.

All the philosophical studying in the universe, all the thoughts of all the thinkers who had come out of the Red Millennium, whose ideas had led to the Metastable Civilization, were not enough when you came down to this cold moment. But . . . me. *I'll* still be me . . .

"Denthurion."

He flinched, bumping against the initiate beside him, feeling, momentarily, the continued shiver. He smiled as he rose, thinking, Bye, Sammy. You're next, but I'm . . . first.

He turned and followed the white-clad technician out of the waiting room and into the branching lab proper. As the man stood aside, letting him enter the room, the door melting shut behind them, he smiled. "Nervous?"

Denthurion nodded.

The technician smiled. "Everyone is, but you needn't be. Nothing's going to happen to *you*."

Taking a deep breath, Denthurion thought, I'm *prepared* for this. I'm *ready*. And he supposed he was. Years of classes, of studying on his own, prowling through the deep databases that had come out of the Red Millennium, marveling at the sophistication of an age more than forty thousand years gone, sundered from him by a hundred trillion man-millennia of directed thought. They'd come up with all the answers in those days. And what had gone unknown during those years of concentrated discovery was unknown to this day. There were still questions . . . probably forever beyond human ken.

The laboratory was a study in simplicity. It was just an open room, hemicylindrical, the bowed wall composed of tall, green-tinted windows, facing out into Einstein Park. Against the flat wall, between two doormarks, an entrance and an exit, stood a big, unshielded transceiver and a small control node at which sat three Metastatic engineers.

The transceiver itself was odd-looking. Instead of the usual enclosed box, it was two disks, one set in the floor, the other in the ceiling. On the lower disk were two little gray daises, one against the wall, the other away from it.

One of the engineers, a tall, handsome man with pale skin, blue eyes, and coal-black hair, rose, watching him cross the room. "Maaron mark Zero incarnation zero Denthurion, by accepting this branching, by participating in the Ceremony of Doubling, you will have agreed to serve the interests of the Metastability of Mankind for all eternity."

Denthurion tried not to stutter as he spoke his line: "I have agreed to all this. Humanity is my life, now and forever."

"Then the ceremony proceeds. When you speak again, it will be as two beings: one to remain here on Earth, grounded at the center of all life, a guiding hand for the Metastatic Race; the other to wander the heavens, doubling and redoubling again and again, the far voice of the Metastability, preserving its unity across all time and space."

Well. When you put it that way . . . It seemed silly just

then, and terrifying as well. Denthurion fought an urge to run out of the room, as he knew so many others did, instead turning to face the transceiver, stepping up on the rearmost dais, facing out into the room.

As the engineer resumed his seat before the control node, Denthurion found himself staring out through the windows, out into the bright and sunny park. The sky looked a little odd, bilious, the clouds green-tinted, but it was a beautiful day. I . . . feel like I'm about to die. I wish I were outside, with the wind in my hair, feeling the soft turf bounce under my bare feet. I . . .

The room jumped suddenly, and he found himself staring into his own face. Odd. I never thought I'd look like that. I . . . His heart began thudding suddenly. It's happened! The other Denthurion stepped away from the wall, holding out a hand to him, smiling gently. "Welcome . . ."

He spun around, looking wildly around the room, turning to stare out the window once more. The day was unchanged, still bright and sunny, the trees of the park bending slightly in the breeze. "My friend . . ." said that other Denthurion.

He whirled again, facing the other man, who stood with his back to a white wall. "Son of a bitch," he whispered. "I'm the *duplicate*."

Maaron Denthurion, mark Zero, put a hand on his shoulder, squeezing gently. "Of course you are." He smiled again. "You know, I never thought of it this way, before. I just *assumed* I'd be the original and the duplicate would somehow *know* . . ."

Maaron Denthurion, mark One, stepped back, fighting down an almost overpowering panic. "My God," he said, tears welling up into his eyes, gathering on his lower lashes to blur his vision, "my God, I'm the *duplicate* . . ."

Denthurion stood in the middle of Ardennes Kartavilis's office in the Governor's Palace of Olam, feeling a certain grimness settle in. Walnut paneling, walnut furniture with inlaid teak patterns, brilliantly polished oak floor showing around the edges of a certificate quality Persian carpet ... Well. This fits in, doesn't it? Kartavilis was sitting behind his desk in a high-backed black leather chair, staring at him expressionlessly, waiting. Behind him, broad, latticed glass doors stood open, giving access to a balustraded balcony and the brilliant sunshine of a clear Olamite morning.

"Welcome to my study, Your Grace. Please be seated." He gestured to a smaller chair, set slightly to one side of the room, facing the desk.

Denthurion sank into the chair, smelling the fresh scent of a lemon-based leather cleaner, and crossed his legs, allowing himself to smile slightly. Work into it gradually, but get there. "Very nice. You do well by yourself, Governor."

Kartavilis frowned. "Thank you, Your Grace."

"Do you think this kind of ostentation is a wise idea?"

The Governor leaned back in his chair, fixing his gaze on the Televox's face, intending to stare him down, but was disturbed to notice the man's eyes were wandering again, flitting across bookcases, evidently reading titles. He shrugged. "The room itself predates me, Your Grace. The furniture ... they've been raising walnut and teak commercially on Olam for twenty thousand years. It isn't really very expensive."

"And the rug?"

Kartavilis's face hardened slightly. "Personal property, brought from Earth at my expense when I took office."

"Come now, Governor. You're nothing more than a doppelganger of Planetary Deputy Ardennes Kartavilis. You never existed anywhere but on Olam."

Bastard! How dare you say something like that to me ... Kartavilis's eyes flashed, but he held himself in check and spoke calmly. "It's a tradition with us, Mr. Televox. Kartavilis, mark Zero, sends a rug out with each of his representatives."

"A copy of the one on the floor of his office in Helium, perhaps?"

"No, sir. A certified original, relayed without backup into the transport crystal."

"Rather an expensive tradition, don't you think?"

"As you say. Your original is a Metastatic Senator and"—Kartavilis's eyes gleamed momentarily—"my original knows your father. You are aware, I'm certain, of the privileges that attach to Planetary Deputation."

Denthurion's smile broadened. Got me there. "A display of wealth on Earth is meaningless, Governor. Earth is the center of the universe. Olam, on the other hand, is not. I may understand these things. What the Olamites think is rather more important."

Kartavilis stared at him motionlessly, waiting.

To business, then. "Governor, who authorized the importation of Kemitish flora onto Olam? Was there an import license?"

Kartavilis's eyes began to flicker and shift then, mimicking Denthurion's natural pattern. "No, Your Grace. It happened before I came to office, long before Ashaan assumed the Great Komership. We don't know who was responsible. It may even have been a transport accident involving no more than a single shipment."

"It seems unlikely that they would accidentally download a biocanister. Has this infestation caused any problems?"

"A few. A limited number of Kemitish predators were included in the shipment, if that's what it was. While they didn't bother the native animals much, they seemed to have a considerable appetite for Terragenic livestock."

"I just came from Kem, Governor. It's a well-known problem."

Kartavilis nodded slowly. "They had to be hunted down over a period of time. Whoever did it seems not to have thought things out."

"Obviously." Denthurion couldn't keep the dryness out

of his voice. "I take it you don't know the whole story then?"

"No, sir. It seemed like a done thing. Not worth investigating."

So. Not worth investigating. How would he come to a conclusion like that? "I'm not pleased by the things I've seen here, Governor. I notice your civil unrest has progressed to the bomb-throwing stage."

"Your Grace, I . . ." He paused and took a breath, then said, "It's true that there's been a good deal of . . . *trouble* lately. The developing ferment centered on the Universitaa has caused increasing dissatisfaction, but . . . I think these are minor disturbances, easily handled by the local authorities."

Garbled. Uncertain. This isn't the sort of thing one expects from a Planetary Governor . . . Denthurion suppressed his puzzlement and said, "The local authorities don't seem competent to handle anything of consequence. If your Great Komer had said that, I wouldn't be surprised. You, sir . . ." He let it trail off into an accusing look.

Kartavilis sat forward in his chair, cheeks whitening with suppressed anger. "Mr. Televox, I tell you this: It was sheer mischance that placed you in the middle of that demonstration! There haven't been any assassination attempts or . . ."

"Perhaps, Governor. Yet they threw that incendiary device at *me*."

"Did they? We don't know *that*. I suspect few of them were even aware of your identity."

"No? And whose bright idea was that?"

"Ashaan thought . . ."

"Ashaan?" Denthurion crossed his arms over his chest and smiled ironically. "You're here to manage the affairs of this planet, Governor, not look to poor little Ashaan for excuses."

"Dammit! I . . ."

"Don't be damning me, Kartavilis. There are important things at stake here."

The Governor grew pale and still, his rapid pulse a faint but visible flexing at the base of his throat. "I'm sorry, Your Grace. I grew excited."

"So I noticed. It's not an appropriate trait for a man in your position."

"No, sir."

Denthurion let him stew for a while, watching the amplitude of his eye movements slow, gradually returning to a more usual fixedness, seeming to focus mostly on the surface of his desk, occasionally glancing up into the rest of the room. All right. Point three. "Governor, I notice the Peraxian police are usually armed with automatic rifles. Do you think this is a good idea?"

Kartavilis was slow to answer. "Well . . . Police Commissioner Kevess . . ."

"Kevess will answer to me in good time. I'm asking *you*."

"No, sir. I did not."

"But you did nothing to intervene?"

"No. It didn't seem appropriate." He saw the growing disapproval on the other man's face. "I've used certain methods in managing Olam's affairs. In that time I've met with nothing but success."

"So, in the context of eight hundred years experience, you felt it wise to let locals make your decisions for you."

He shrugged. "I saw no reason to reverse their decisions."

"I see." Right out of the manuals, but . . . staggering incompetence. "Governor, why did elements of your Metastatic Guard force participate in the suppression of that . . . riot?"

Careful. Careful . . . "Despite their armament the local police have been unable to deal with some civil disturbances expeditiously."

"So you felt it appropriate to let the local populace

feel the instrumentalities of the Mestastable Order were their enemies."

"I never viewed it that way, Your Grace."

"And you felt it appropriate to let them conduct these activities using dissipators."

"That has been their standard arm since the beginning of my term in office."

Denthurion got up out of the chair and came to stand before the broad walnut desk, looking down at Kartavilis. "You've made some bad decisions, Governor. You'd better pay close attention to your duties from this point on, for I assure you, nothing is beneath the notice of the Metastable Order."

Kartavilis opened his mouth to speak and immediately closed it again, visibly working through some inner strife. Finally, he said, "I'll try to abide by this advice, Your Grace."

"It's . . . more than just advice, Governor."

Chapter 3

Mexonaa Prospect leads due south from the Governor's Palace to the outskirts of Perax and then onward, becoming a country thoroughfare in Almana Valley, following the winding course of the river for many kilometers before crossing the mountains to the provincial city of Givaa-Tapuwax. Now an unmarked hovercar slid sedately down the road, staying toward the middle, well away from the pedestrian and bicycle traffic that spilled off the sidewalks, dodging to one side occasionally to avoid an oncoming vehicle.

Maclaren sat beside the Televox, staring at the driver's green-uniformed back, and thought, First no transceiver net, then no police guards, now no escort! He shook his head slowly. This nonsense was dangerous and unnecessary. *Shearah* wasn't a *real* terrorist conspiracy, but . . . no telling what these young assholes might do. If they were stupid enough to throw a homemade firebomb at *anyone* . . . He turned to look at Denthurion, who seemed to be gazing placidly out the window, watching the street scene with passive interest. "What will you do next."

The man glanced at him and smiled slightly. "Next?" He shrugged. "My original plan was to interview the civil authorities, Ashaan and his people, before doing a full-scale literature search. After talking with Kartavilis . . . I'd better take a closer look."

That didn't sound too promising. "Meaning what?" he asked.

"I'll review the Archives, download an appropriate overlay set, and get started on an in-depth investigation."

"And what do you intend to do?"

Denthurion's eyes steadied on his face suddenly. "Set matters straight. We'll know how when we understand what the problems are."

Oh, great. What was coming might be anything from mere procedural changes in the way Olam was run to the arrest and deportation of the entire civil government. He sat back in his seat, staring at the driver's back again, visualizing a number of potential scenarios, none of them particularly plausible.

Watching the crowds, afoot in colorful garb, rolling along on their plastic-framed bicycles, robes flapping behind, Denthurion began to marvel at the concatenation of variety and sameness. There's a variation here, but stylistic unity; more than there ought to be.

Behind the people, the little shops were a steady succession of identical white storefronts, differentiated only in the black lettering of their signs and small advertisements. There seemed to be an unusually large number of men congregated in front of one building and Denthurion read off its sign. "Does *pizhaama* mean the same thing in Olamite as it does in Ursprache?"

Of all the ... "Sort of. The usual context is 'nightshirt.'"

"And on the front of a shop? What do they sell, lingerie and sleepwear?"

"Well ... no. Um, as you may know, Olamitic custom encourages a certain amount of prostitution. In this context a *pizhaama* is a whorehouse." Why do I feel this resentment boiling up? It isn't *my* planet.

"How about *glulaayim*? 'Pills'? Is that a drugstore?"

"Yes."

"Legal or illegal?"

"Both." The resentment built a little further. I've been here long enough that I feel a certain proprietorship and local pride. Perhaps it's time I applied for a new assignment. "Glulaa stores supply liquor, amphetamines, and other recreational drugs, such as particulate carcinogens, which are illegal here, though popular. Medical drugs come from the *Apotheka*."

"Interesting that they use the Ursprache word. What do you buy at a *merkahhat*?"

"Homeopathic remedies." I wonder where I'd like to go next? Someplace less absorbing and amorphous—a high-tech world, perhaps, or some newer society, closer to the Frontier. It had a certain allure: someplace different, close to the blaze of the galactic core, or out under the dark nights of the rim worlds. There might even be extragalactic colonies by now, though the news wouldn't have had time to diffuse inward yet.

As they continued onward, passing through a shopping district that included a variety of meat, bread, and vegetable stalls, Denthurion tapped the driver on the shoulder. "Slow up a little bit." The hovercar decelerated gently, sliding through a particularly crowded section of the street. Outside, on the nearby sidewalk, a white-robed, veiled fat woman was holding her gray-furred Hoda on a short leash, jerking the chain, shouting at the little biped, pointing angrily to a crushed melon by their feet. She slapped it across the head, jerked it upright, and then slapped it again.

Denthurion turned as they went past, watching closely, but remaining silent as the scene disappeared into the crowd behind them. Well. Call it human nature. Just human nature . . . if petty meanness is natural. Think of the way people treat their children. But it didn't seem natural at the moment. Suddenly the profusion of Hodai filling the interstices of the crowd seemed to jump out at him. Leashes, everywhere you looked, and Hodai under burdens, Hodai with fanciful grooming, obviously female Hodai led around by jowly, thick-waisted men . . .

He reached forward and tapped the driver again. "Get me back to the Archive Center. I've seen enough for now." The hovercar began to accelerate again, filling Maclaren with a certain relief.

By the fall of 42,071 they were entering into their last days on Earth. Melis Carthoradis, Journeyman Explorer, walked along a broad, grassy avenue between the tall towers of Helium with a Maaron Denthurion on either side, head down, hands in the pockets of his pale blue tunic. As they strolled toward the center of the city the dim midmorning light picked out pastel highlights in the translucent-seeming walls of the buildings. Long ago the structural materials of this architecture, from the dawn of the Metastable Order, had been imported from other star systems, from the mines of other, now vanished, civilizations.

To Cary's left, Denthurion mark Zero walked carelessly, eyes straight ahead, ignoring his surroundings, intent on their conversation; to his right, Denthurion mark One looked everywhere, eyes darting ceaselessly, head turning occasionally to shift his field of view. The world fascinated this doppelganger, the hazily clouded sky and fuzzy-leaved trees, decorating the little parks that marked every intersection, caught his attention, snatching it from the delicate beauty of the tall, slim buildings. There was wildlife in the city, too, gray squirrels and starlings, little wrens and robins and the occasional darting chipmunk. When winter fell Helium would fill with grosbeaks, dashing their brains out on the sides of buildings.

All gone, thought mark One, going away from me before I've had half a chance to appreciate it. Mark Zero paid his surroundings no attention at all. He would be here on Earth almost forever. There was no sense in exhausting the details of his only real world. Sometimes he thought about the televoxic lives that would fill him up, but it seemed somehow . . . unreal.

"I never thought this day would come," said mark Zero. "I picture myself here in Helium, wandering the woods about Marumsko without you . . . I can't believe it."

Cary nodded. "A part of me wishes I could divide, be here and travel the cosmos, but . . . the rules."

"Sometimes I wish I'd chosen differently. We could be going out there together."

Listening to them, mark One felt a certain pleased bitterness. Let these innocent Originals babble on. Only he and his branched brethren understood the truth . . . He pulled his thoughts back from that one, knowing he still had a lot to work out with the Branching Team counselors.

"I wish you had," said Cary. But the words were falling flat. Do I wish that? No, maybe not. His training period, traveling about the solar system, exploring the complex debris of a forty-thousand-year-old civilization, had been a liberating experience, enough to make him realize that his relationship with Denny had long ago come to its natural conclusion. No, we're just raking over the burned-out coals of childhood one last time. We're through with each other.

"Who knows," said mark One, "maybe sometime, a hundred thousand years down the road, we'll run into each other out there. There are Televoxes on the Frontier."

Cary regarded him levelly, then smiled. "Maybe we will. Likely one of a thousand duplicates you'll have by then. Will it be the Maaron Denthurion I know?"

"Does it matter? What I have in common with you . . . we *all* will."

"Marumsko . . . and here. A little more than twenty years out of a hundred millennia. Will that be enough?"

Walking past a little copse of thick-waisted oak trees, all yellow-brown leaves now, they emerged into Helium's Inner Plaza, the heart of the city. Mark Zero looked around uneasily, then said, "If it isn't enough . . . well. In some sense those linked childhoods are what bind the Metastable Order together."

"But for how much longer?" mused Cary. It was a good question, asked more often with each passing century. Despite everything, Earth's hegemony was getting too big for centralized rule. The Frontier was endless thousands of years away at sublight travel . . . and nothing else was possible. Sooner or later, unless the technology changed, as it was unlikely to do, satellite empires would split off, daughter metastases, and the Metastable Order would come to an end.

Before them, in a broad disk of parkland, towered the circular ziggurat of the city's Transceiver Matrix. In some sense, in this latter day, foci like this were uncalled-for. Helium, like the rest of Earth, was as networked as it could be, each door a door to elsewhere, to anywhere on Earth, if need be, to places beyond the sky. But it had been here since the end of the Red Millennium, since terrible Cpaht built his city on slightly older ruins and made it the capital of a budding human universe. Back then, this had been a necessary link to the exostation in the southern countryside. Now it was merely tradition.

Cary stood silently, hands on hips, looking up at the tiered and glassy structure. "So," he murmured, "one last passage through the fire and I am away." He turned to face the two images of his friend, reaching out to grasp their hands. "I knew this good-bye would be hard, but . . ." He shrugged. "Long lifetimes await us all."

Long lifetimes . . . thought mark One. He wanted to say something, just a phrase, a happy wish that would call closure on a shared childhood, but the gleaming crystalline beauty of the Transceiver Matrix kept catching his eye, making him look up over Cary's head, into his own tomorrow. A thousand long lifetimes, incarnations and branchings until this moment is lost in a sea of yesterdays . . .

Mark Zero reached out to hug Cary gently. He shook his hand, grinning, and said, "Good-bye, then. We'll . . . hear from you."

Melis Carthoradis looked from one Denthurion to the other, nodded slowly, turned away, stepped through a beckoning arch, and was gone.

The two of them stood there for a while, looking at the building amid the soft rustle of thin crowds, little clusters of men and women walking past, coming and going, then they turned away, walking back down the avenue from whence they'd come, toward the southwestern part of the city and IMI campus.

"Almost noon," said mark Zero. "Hungry?"

Mark One felt a slight pang, more or less simultaneous with the other's words. "I guess," he said, and thought, We haven't diverged enough yet. The mirror of our thoughts is undistorted . . .

And in both their minds, couched in nearly identical phrasing, was the stark realization that they were unalterably changed, that they'd crossed some kind of major boundary, sundering them from a much simpler past.

Denthurion sat alone in his room, bare feet up on the windowsill, staring out into the white light of midday. The breeze coming in through the open window seemed hotter than usual and the sky had taken on a pale cast, now that yellow Shemesh was so high. He tried to relax, gathering his thoughts, and ran one finger down the length of his tunic, releasing the front seam and letting the black material fall open. His chest felt cooler immediately and he ran his thumbs under the stretchy waistband of his underpants, smearing a bit of trapped sweat, making it evaporate. It was too hot now, but the dry climate around Perax seemed invigorating.

Well. No time like the present, then. "House Archive," he said into the empty room.

A flat, expressionless face formed in the swirled material of the white plaster wall, a little to one side of the window. The comeye seemed to turn slowly toward him, re-forming in different aspects to give the illusion of dimensionality. It opened red-highlit beige eyes and looked at him wearily, then, "Televox," it rustled. "I've been waiting for you."

Denthurion regarded the tired disk face with interest, watching the lips move in an imitation of speech that didn't go beyond forming a dark, flexing oval of a mouth. This then was a very ancient sort of AI device, something from the dawn of civilization. "Good afternoon. Were you installed with the construction of this building or are you an add on?"

"My circuits are part of the original structure."

Old, then. Very old. "Was your neurotaxis completed at that time?" The functionality of something this old might be problematic. How much of the odd, stylized face was obsolete technology and how much was cultural preference?

The comeye's lidless orbs remained fixed on him, motionless during an unnervingly long pause. "No, sir. I was brought in as physical cargo from Earth, where I'd become obsolescent."

That was rare, but it did happen. Even premodern computers were too complex for electromagnetic transmission, which was why they were usually grown in situ. "Earth, huh? How long ago?" It could have been very long ago indeed. Precursors to the OTANNs, the optically trainable artificial neural networks on which neurotaxic devices were based, had seen their original development in the middle centuries of the Red Millennium. They were the supreme legacy of that age, on which stood the whole foundation of the Metastable Order and its civilization.

The comeye said, "I was constructed to supervise the reterraforming of Venus, beginning in the thirteenth century of the Metastable Order."

Fifty thousand years! Denthurion was taken aback. "You must have stressed the computational design facilities of that time."

"I was unsurpassed as a neurotaxic device for more than five thousand years."

It was hard to imagine how the universe must seem to

a thing like this ... "Would you like to be decommissioned?"

This time the response was immediate, with a faint trace of tonality added to the comeye's stage whisper. "No, sir. Life becomes more precious with each passing moment."

"I understand." My own multiple lives ... those shared forty thousand years ... The machine and I can go on for quite a long time. But the machine would spend its millennia right here, inside the walls of this crumbling edifice. "I have questions."

"Proceed."

"I'm interested in the origins of Olam and its people."

"A topic of no small depth. Do you prefer linear, hypermatrix, or volitional?"

Denthurion considered the choices. Linear was out, of course, since it would ignore the complex nuances of historical reality. Hypermatrix ... he could wander at will through the databases and, without luck, get lost with ease. "Volitional." Let the comeye figure out what he wanted to know. This thing was troublingly ancient ... but it had been designed as a planetary engineering system and must be inconceivably more sophisticated than an individual human being.

The face stared at him through yet another long pause. "Why are you asking about the origins of Olam?"

"I want to understand the social problems I am encountering, so that I may prepare a proper solution, in the context of the Metastable Order."

The aspects shifted as the face imitated a slight nod. "I have been aware of these things ..." Another pause. "But the data are difficult to synthesize for one in my position. I'm glad you've come. It was ... necessary."

That disturbed him. When a comeye talked like that you knew it was operating on the periphery of its rule-sieve parameters. Perhaps it was just old age. "Tell me what I need to know."

The walls of the room faded away in three dimensions,

leaving him in a dark night that, with deliberate slowness, filled with light. A black, starry sky appeared and he was looking down on the northern hemisphere of a cloudless Earth, feeling a detached ache at the sight of a tiny sliver of eastern North America. Helium of the ectypes; and the Marumsko of my frozen dreams ... The globe rotated and the background stars whirled by as the point of view shifted, come to rest again above a bit of land that was embedded in a complex of small seas and peninsulas. It was really an isthmus, though that was hard to perceive because of the general layout of the land.

"The problem," whispered the comeye, "began in an area that premodern historians called 'the Levant.' It is the meeting point for the major components of the World Island and is the region where the first human civilization evolved, in the period spanning some eighty to one hundred centuries before the Red Millennium." Areas of the map were spinning off ghosted details, visions of villages growing into printed, mud-brick cities, columns of toiling Sumerians and their political gods. "It was here too that the major pathologies of the Red Millennium evolved, which, in concert with the Western Renaissance, gave rise to the social and technological seeds of the Metastable Order.

"During the Red Millennium itself, the Levant filled to overflowing with aggressive proponents of post-Classical mythologies, primarily endlessly interrelated variants of what came to be called the Yehudi, Muslami, and Ixtiani cults. Following the terminus of the Red Millennium, during the violently transitional Century of Cpaht, the entire population of the region was deported to the then newly discovered colony world of Zantac, fifty-four parsecs from Earth."

A ghost image formed, spanning the globe, of a severely emaciated man, dark eyes blazing out of a pale, angular face, thin mustache rimming his upper lip, dropping outriggers down onto the sides of his chin, the whole framed in long, lustrous black hair. "During his brief time of absolute power, the self-styled Second Universal Emperor Cpaht succeeded in exporting approximately forty billion human beings, roughly eighty percent of the extant population, to the stars." Ghosts of small, globular dataships, quantum dissociative engines flaring violet, fleeing into the void. "The bulk of the remaining population was composed of his own Alpino-Mediterranean ethnic complex, accounting for the present persistent racial characteristics of Earthmen."

A cluster of serious-looking men appeared, arrayed before a long table, holding a chained Cpaht in their midst. "The Council of Reform, laying the framework of the Metastable Order, determined that it would be both impossible and unwise to recall Cpaht's Exodus Fleet. Since the concept of the Human Metastasis was already accepted, it was determined to expand the Exile into a wider, more useful format. The Council decided that each of the twenty-five hundred ships would settle a different habitable world, so the human race set out on the trail of the first explorers, dropping down in the wake of the evolving Frontier." The room filled with an expanding globe of stars, set against the vast backdrop of an entire galaxy.

"Eventually, the dataship *Diaspar* was directed to deposit its cargo on the vacant colony world of Khazar, some two hundred twenty parsecs from Earth, right at what was then the edge of human exploration. The people of the Levant were dropped there, complete with everything they had owned on Earth, and took up where they left off, a mixed population at war with itself." The globe of Khazar formed out of black apace, a Prussian blue jewel of vast shallow seas and many small island continents, throwing off ghosts of unhappy, rioting men and women.

Another giant formed astride this new globe, a pale, black-haired man, like a healthy Cpaht. "When the first Televox came to Khazar, in the sixteenth century of the Metastable Order, he made a first pass at restoring order by suppressing the Levantine Cult Complex. What remained to differentiate the people then were the seven major languages of the Levant. The Ivrit, Arabiyah, Turki, Gruzinski, Armani, Kurdiyah, and Azeri speakers settled into separate enclaves, the nuclei of nation-states tolerated by a succession of careful Planetary Governors."

Denthurion, himself a muscular allopathic reflection of mad, skeletal Cpaht, considered the data. So far, an ordinary beginning for an ordinary world. A whole people gathered up willy-nilly from a sector of old Earth and cast away into the great Metastatic Surge.

Displaying a passive, fragmented world, the comeye continued: "How Khazar and the Khazarians would have evolved is no more than a matter for conjecture. There are many models to work from, many undisturbed Source Colonies, and, presumably, Khazar would merely have been one of more; it was, however, not to be, for, in the fortieth century of the Metastable Order, that sector of the then slowly expanding Frontier impinged on space dominated by the Hhurull."

So! The complexities, the vast, looping catenaries of interrelated causality chains, began to unfold. The Hhurull War had been the first and worst of humanity's battles against other star-faring races, and the only one decided by mankind's reliance on matter transmitter technology. "Up to this point, how do you rate the impact of their terrestrial and Khazarian origins on the Olamites?"

The comeye appeared to consider, staring blank-eyed out of an interstellar space previously untenanted. "Without the context of later events, rather small. By the time the Hhurull came on the scene, they had been reduced to a common early holopathic society. Later reinoculations with Red Millennium and even Classical pathologies were more significant."

Not surprising, given that by then they were further from the end of the Red Millennium than it was from their era of origin. "And the Hhurull impact?"

"Large. Without that great discontinuity they would

not have been susceptible to reinfection." The universe closed in again, portraying the Hhurull dispersal into a whole quadrant of human space, then their coming to Khazar, deep within the Metastatic interior. "It would be difficult to overestimate the consequences of the Hhurull radiotelepathic entities on the small human populations that survived the invasion and ensuing wars of occupation and liberation. On Khazar, for example, something like ninety-eight percent of the human population was killed outright." New ghosts evolved into sight, tiny, primitive bands of nomadic human beings, short-lived, suffering and dying across two hundred unending generations; hiding amid the incomprehensible glory of the mute Hhurull civilization.

The comeye stared at him fixedly, its pseudoface shifting back and forth slightly in some kind of indefinable rhythm. "Televox, I don't know how much you know about the Hhurull, or what your feelings are ... They were a danger to humanity, yet they seemed in many ways kin to artificial intelligence."

And what does this old artificial mind think about them? Denthurion smiled in the soft darkness of the enveloping display, which now presented ghosts of still-faced individual Hhurull, communing with each other, and their machines, in absolute, holistic harmony. "In any case, the Hhurull were destroyed." And no one was left to explain their enmity, why they had made no attempt at communication.

There was another long silence, then the comeye spoke with a hint of wistfulness: "To be sure. Utterly destroyed." Brilliant flashes of white light enveloped the blue globe, searing red scars into its face. "By the time the Frontier had been pushed back to Khazar, in the ninety-third century, the Hhurull were putting up a strong resistance. Thermonuclear demolition units were required to dig them out of continental-root bunkers, rendering the planet uninhabitable in the process. Approximately fifty-eight thousand human survivors were rescued at that time, including roughly seven thousand Ivrit-speaking tribesmen." Scenes of bug-eyed, skin-clad men, women, and children, shaking with horror, surrounded by armored warriors, being shoveled into the waiting maws of transceiver units; flash, flash, flash, off into space.

Denthurion didn't need the prompting of the ghost display to imagine the feelings of those pathetic beings. Five thousand years hiding in the shadow of incomprehensible monsters had rendered the memory of the earlier civilization mere mythology; now the world was burned down around them, now they were gathered up whole, plucked from their hiding places and incinerated by demons.

The comeye continued: "Khazar, of course, was cleaned up and resettled a few centuries later by Russian-speaking colonists who were pouring into the sector in the wake of the Hhurull defeat. By the hundred tenth century the whole region had been renormalized." Images of great, spired cities, gleaming with technology, for the Russian strains of humanity tended to be allopathic.

"In the wake of the cleanup, the various Khazarian ethnic groups found themselves scattered about this sector, embedded in the Russianized population, one of many tiny subgroups that represented a pre-Hhurull stratum. It was a pretty little problem for the local authorities, crying out for the intervention of Televoxes." Images of angry-looking men and women, haranguing each other, of riots and clashes with the ruling majorities. "Over the next few millennia, numerous attempts were made by the ethnics to return to Khazar, sometimes resulting in large-scale suppression by Metastable authorities. By the hundred seventieth century, Khazarian groups had grown so numerous that a return to Khazar would have crushed the planet's resources."

The comeye seemed to consider judiciously. "In and of itself, this would have caused no real difficulty; unfortunately the Khazarians were scattered over hundreds of planets now, creating a scale effect that was hard to overcome. At this point, events drove the disaster to completion. The Ivrit produced a scholar-historian named Jehohannon, who determined to re-create the pre-Classical pathology among his people." The ghost of a tall, swarthy, bearded man, with mad, dark eyes, stood before them, howling out the Truth. "It took a thousand years, but the worlds of this sector began boiling with Jehohannonists." Again, riots were marching before his eyes.

"When violence broke out across the sector, Metastatic authorities began their slow reaction. By this time, of course, the Metastable Order was complete, one great effect of the Hhurull War's organizational drive. Televoxes and Metastatic Guard slid into place, ethnic Khazarians were gathered up and placed into storage crystals, and the Russian worlds were put to rights." Glittering cities under tranquil skies, humming with allopathic productivity.

"It took seven thousand years to complete the ingathering and associated labor, but, in the end, the Khazarians, subject to in-transit redefinition, were transported to different worlds, out near the new Frontier, then lying between fifteen hundred and two thousand parsecs from Earth. The Ivrit, left with little more than their language and the bare outlines of a holopathic culture, were brought to Olam."

This new world was no jewel, rather it was a muddy, red-brown disk, disfigured here and there with the splotches of lakes and isolated seas, mostly desert and mountain between shrunken icecaps. The scene closed in on landing sites, where mass transceivers were set up and activated, columns of bewildered Ivrit marching out into a new, yet uncannily familiar world. Olamites? Us? Yet they went forth.

Finally, the comeye said, "The relationship of the new Olamites with the mesolithic Hodai was peaceable, but the natives dwindled under the impact of a burgeoning human civilization." Scenes of little abode villages, some with two- and three-story temples, of Hodai trading with the humans, losing their ancient skills, cities crumbling into mud. Scenes of Hodai in the wilderness, dwindling into smaller and smaller bands, clothing turned to animal skins, then to nothing. "In twenty-five thousand years, the civilized Hodai have become household pets, and the wild Hodai have all but vanished."

The scene froze on a lone Hoda, walking away into the yellow-green forest, looking back over his shoulder, then dissolved back to the imperturbable face of the Archive comeye. Denthurion relaxed into his chair, propping his feet back on the windowsill. Outside, the light of midday was as it had been. "Well," he said, "an uncommonly complex origin. What is the likelihood that some pre-Classical pathology remains after all this time?"

"As a minor situational contaminant? Low, I would imagine."

Denthurion nodded. "Incalculably low." He stood up and walked slowly away from the staring wall, out of his room and down the cool, whispering, air-conditioned hallway, focusing his thoughts on the process of understanding, working to digest this fresh knowledge.

The kitchens of the MAC center were, at best, semiautomatic. The house AI had some input here, could reach into the backs of mechanisms with teledyne arms, operate, make transfers, do things . . . but not so much, after all. Denthurion stood in the doorway, surveying a kitchen that was mostly old-style refrigerators and cabinets and manual stoves. Somehow, not totally unexpected . . .

He walked over to the nearest refrigerator and opened the door. The thing was full of shrink-wrapped parcels, unlabeled, their contents plainly visible. He picked one up. Fresh food, Olamitic ingredients, preprepared and rendered instant. He shut the door and looked around.

Yes, there *were* microwave ovens here; and the lack of labeling on the packages said something about Olam's cooking style.

He went to the next refrigerator and opened it. Mostly small bottles of what looked like chocolate milk, with tiny Ursprache labels full of chemical names, reflecting an imitation of a popular allopathic ersatz beverage ...

"We do have some real stuff, Your Grace ..."

Denthurion looked up, turning back into the room, recognizing the Guard sergeant who'd brought him breakfast on that first morning. "Real?" Name. Name ... Olathe Harid, pronounced full and broad, accent on the second syllables, matching the Olamite linguistic environment.

The sergeant grinned, beckoning him over to yet another refrigerator. "As real as we can make it."

Denthurion pawed through a collection of brand-name-adorned packages, selecting a mix of things he'd encountered on different worlds, carrying them to an oven and heating them, along with Harid's snack.

When they were seated, eating their hot miscellany, drinking cold pseudochocolate, Denthurion said, "How long have you been on Olam, Sergeant?"

"Oh, twenty years, I guess ..."

"About due for a rotation?"

"Mm ... Won't be *too* long, now. My contract is for twenty-five-year rotations."

"You like it here?"

Harid shrugged. "It's all right. I'm ready for a change, though. Twenty-five years is enough ..."

"I think I know what you mean. How many incarnations is this?" It could have been an impertinently personal question, but this was a Metastatic Guardsman, after all, and a properly deputed legate of the Metastable Order ...

"Uh ..." Harid's eyes tipped back, accessing a visual memory of worlds across time, then tipped right, accessing left-hemisphere math with which to count them.

"Uh, forty, I think . . . no, only thirty-nine. Unless you want to count my birth world . . ."

Denthurion smiled. "Why not? So you're, what? Eleven, twelve centuries old?"

"No . . . not quite. Only a little more than a thousand years. Ulnaqq is a Sosh world. I got off as soon as I could."

Sociopathic. Right. Advanced, modern, and all that, but . . . controlled. Life spans curtailed. Access to services somewhat limited. "You've been around, though."

"I guess. Thirty-nine planets is a fair number . . ."

But nothing like the thousand incarnations an experienced Televox can muster. You can see his wheels turning. "A fair number. What do you think about the situation on Olam?" There. Watch his eyes flicker.

"Um. Your Grace. I'm just a Guard sergeant. I . . ."

"Come on, Harid. Give me your honest opinion. I won't tell on you."

"Well, sir." The man looked around uneasily. "It's not the best I've ever seen . . ."

"Why?"

The squirming grew more pronounced. "Your Grace. Governor Kartavilis is my superior officer. I just don't feel I can talk out of turn . . ."

"No, I suppose not. I think you've told me enough in any case." He stood, clapping Harid on the shoulder. "Cheer up, Sergeant. Your next posting's bound to be better. See if you can't set down on a naturopathic world . . ."

That brought out the shadow of a grin.

Back in his room, late in the evening, relaxing after a walk in the wood around the Archive Center, Denthurion stared levelly at the flat-visaged comeye on his wall. The detail of Olam's recent history, the long lifetimes since the last Televox had been by to check up on things, was inchoate, formed largely from the bits and pieces of the comeye's guesswork. Over the last ten thousand years, since the final reduction of the Hodai civilization to a race of household pets, the world had taken on the timeless sameness required by the Métastable Order. Televox Dorian Lakadaemon had come on the scene, taken a quick look around, staying a mere eighteen months, then gone on his way. Situation: Normal.

But normal, how? A dozen Televoxes had seen this world since its founding, and not one of them had found fault with the business of the Hodai. No reason? Perhaps not. The Interpathic Spectrum was a smooth continuity, with room for many pathologies in its compass. There were other enslaved species of course, the poor Salamanders, for the little while they lasted, the several dozen sentient races liberated from trans-Frontier Hhurull colonies. So long as it didn't lead to a drift away from the circumscribed path-set allowed to humanity, there was no reason for intervention.

Why then is this society drifting away from its pathological tensor? Why now, after all this time? This nonsense about the *Shearah* student movement . . . He turned away from the comeye and put his feet back up in the windowsill.

And there was the fact of the trees. The comeye had been unable to pinpoint the actual introduction of Kemitish flora onto Olam. Some time between fifteen hundred and two thousand years ago it had simply started spreading down onto the coast from a source point in the interior. An accident? No. Seeds brought in attached to some traveler's clothing would make no more than tiny incursions. Even a vegetation more virulent than Kem's could do no more than sweep the world with a monospecific, easily combated tidal wave. This was a balanced ecology, the obvious contents of a Transfer Casque. There should be records, but there aren't.

Well. There isn't a lot wrong here, but enough. Olam must be assessed . . . and Ordered. Even the fact of decision was satisfying.

"Set up a comlink to *Naglfar*."

The still-faced comeye gave him a clearly wistful look, and said, "As you wish." It disappeared abruptly and the wall space where it had been became three-dimensional once more, the ragged, open door to a shadowy, cavelike chamber.

Odin, the comeye manifestation of *Naglfar's* synchronoptic operating system, stared out at Denthurion, stroking his gray beard, while the eyes of Hugin and Munin, ablaze with sentience, darted about the room. "Good day to you, Televox." His voice was a smooth and even baritone, echoing just a little in the stone-lined chamber.

Denthurion folded his hands across his abdomen, and said, "The situation here is somewhat different than was indicated by the Archives on Kem. I'd like to uplink my experience stream of the past two days and download my central overlay file into the house neurotaxy." Get it done. Get some sense of organization imposed.

"I take it we'll be staying here for an extended visit."

Denthurion nodded. "Once I'm sure I have the tools I need for my investigation I'll send you out to take a look at the various technogenic installations around the Shemesh system."

Odin seemed to smile, his lone eye brightening. "Done and done. Olam's naturalistic economy is supported by an extensive network of resource drivers."

"I'm not surprised. Shall we begin?"

"Uplink sequence commenced."

Denthurion's scalp prickled slightly as the room's teledynes, operated from the orbiting spacecraft, sorted through his head, comparing data sequences with those stored in the ship's hydrogen-crystal mass storage devices, plucking new event streams forth and spooling them into compressed archival files.

"I've established a downlink net interconnect with the house comeye. The Archive Center mass storage systems are antiquated optical palimpsests. Rather than use them,

I have preempted a little-used neural trunk, placing its contents in temporary storage."

How, Denthurion wondered, would the MAC comeye feel about that?

"The trunk space is inadequate to implant a complete overlay system . . . I'll set up a rotisserie modulus here, giving you quick uplink access."

"Thank you." The dry statement covered an information interchange that exceeded the typical annual data-processing needs of a holopathic planet.

"Will that be all?"

Denthurion nodded.

"I'll await your call." The blue-shadowed cave rolled into a misty ball and disappeared, replaced by a shocked and pale comeye. "Are you all right?"

The flat face nodded, in comparison with Odin, even more an imitation of life, its eyes faded to salmon pink.

"What was in the trunk I preempted?"

"I . . . don't have the faintest idea."

Did that mean it had never known, or that the pre-empting had taken that knowledge with it? The comeye wouldn't know that either. "Please activate my overlay drivers."

"As you wish, Televox." Along with the comeye, the room and the world beyond it snapped out of existence and he was surrounded in a familiar blue and gray sea of square, shadowed buttons, each little placard a window into some other time and identity.

Let's see now. Assessment and ordering. Problems arrayed in decreasing substantive order.

1. The question of enslaved autochthonous populations; their effect on humans as masters; the penetration of nonhuman cultural detail into the Metastable Order.

2. The question of illegal interstellar biocontamination; positive effects done without license;

negative effects of successful illegality on the local
pathology.
3. The question of holistic societies under incompetent leadership; as an import effect on pathological
drift; as an export effect on the regional Metastable
Order.
4. The isolated question of the competence of Ardennes mark Eight Kartavilis; extending to the
competence of the Ardennes Kartavilis line; extending to the training of Planetary Governors on
Earth.

That last troubled him. If it went to that third level, its
echoic effects might extend throughout the Metastability.
If it went that far . . . this could be the branch-point for
the Order itself. Unlikely. Deranged Governors had developed before. And even distorted lines. These things
happen.

As he thought about the evolving problems of Olam,
poorly understood now, but delineated after a fashion,
the buttons swarmed around his head, reorganizing
themselves as the AI driver interpreted his musings.
Four placards arrayed themselves in front of his face,
larger than all the others, reddening as they grew in im-
portance. One at a time then.

The first incarnation blossomed:

Maaron Denthurion in an awful place called The
Mauve Star's Planet, barely suitable for humankind, red
sun swollen in the sky, big dense planet orbiting near the
star's outer envelope, euentropic shields altering the climate . . . Squat, crablike beings in the mines, slaving
under the seas, a thin leavening humanity, the crew of
one of Cpaht's exiled colony ships, lost, come to an inap-
propriate world . . .

And again:

A courtroom scene, Maaron Denthurion, the Televox,
in judgment of his fellow man. Even before the coming

of humanity, Zold had been a paradise planet, brilliant dappled green beneath a fine yellow sun, an unending splendor of field and forest, glaciers like diamonds in the mountains, glittering blue seas filled with life. And yet, it hadn't been enough. Now the overlords of this world, pale-skinned, white-haired, blue-eyed men, stood sorrowing before their master, heads bowed down . . .

And again:

Haldane's Fastness was an incomprehensible world. Maaron Denthurion, freighted with experience, marveled, never having seen its like. In a mere three thousand years the Committee of the Five had taken a prosperous going concern and reduced it to desert and famine and death. Why? Apparently for no more reason than simple greed . . .

And again:

Kalkis Tharmunin stood before a seated Maaron Denthurion, trying to explain himself, but it was no use. There were no excuses that fit the magnitude of his failure. He said his apologies, made his obeisance, and found himself relieved of his governorship, sent home to Earth in disgrace . . .

To work, then. Squat Germanic demons, Odin's trolls marching off into the sunset, pickaxes over their shoulders, strong ropes looped around upper arms, brass carbide lamps on iron helmets, ready to light the darkness. *Heid-ho, heid-ho . . .*

Later, finished with his preliminary research, Denthurion sat in his chair by the open window, staring out into the night-shrouded landscape. Lights on the horizon. Lights in the sky. Starlight to guide my path, out in the dark between the worlds. A whole world out there, for me to mold or destroy. I feel . . . rather alone.

It always began this way, of course. You came to a world, saw what was happening there, changed it or let it be or even wiped it away, as if it had never been. It called for a cold steel soul, modeled again and again on an original cast from some harder alloy. Look back at your childhood, as all the Denthurions must be looking back on that same childhood, those who live now, those frozen away in cold black ice . . .

My coming is always the same. Always, everywhere I go. He could remember stepping out of the transceiver on Kem, beneath that world's Metastable Archive Center, just as he had stepped forth onto Olam, just as he would step out of the transceiver on Adenen-yo, next world in this region's long line, a few years hence. On Kem, there had been a stable local functionary waiting for him, just as on Olam, white-robed, reaching out to greet him: "Welcome to Kem, Mr. Televox. My name is Arwen Talmoun, Your Grace. I am here to serve your needs."

All well and good of course. And always the same. Kem had been the same, as one world after another . . . No. Kem was not the same. Only my passage through the ice makes it seem that way. Kem was different. Quiet. Perfect. I stayed on Kem the full five years, though I was not needed there.

Kem was different. Kem had Tiy.

He could see her now, dark and slim, silhouetted against a bright, starry sky, waiting for him, as she always waited, knowing he would one day leave forever.

No forever for them, of course. Only a brief lifetime, then gone into a darkness I'll never know . . .

Happy five years, at peace with myself and all the people around me, in a world at peace with itself. It was . . . almost as if I belonged there . . .

But you belong here now, Maaron Denthurion. Here, where you are most certainly needed, where there is work for you to do. Forget peaceful Kem. Forget Tiy and happy moments in the darkness, stolen from a universe of endless time. Olam is your universe now.

Still, the pain in his chest refused to go away.

Chapter 4

The Great Hall of the Civil Administration Building in eastern Perax vaulted overhead, a smoked-glass mosaic dome surrounded by concentric rings of mezzaninelike hallways. Small clots of people moved about, trailing the colored head-cloaks of semiformal Olamite daywear, shadowy groups on the hall balconies, larger clusters crisscrossing the blue-carpeted floor of the Hall at odd angles to each other. At the cardinal points of the compass, broad flights of gray stone stairs lead upward to the first tier of offices.

Denthurion stood with Maclaren at his side and a little cadre of green-clad Guardsmen at his back, hands on hips, surveying the scene, and found himself marveling at the slow pace of what was, after all, a planetary government. Even on the most backward, nondevelopmental worlds, you expected a certain amount of . . . bustle.

Before him, a small, thin, astonished-looking man stood, shifting from one foot to the other, backed by a little knot of wide-eyed, crimson-uniformed government workers. "Why," he said, "this is such an *honor.*"

Could they really not have known I was coming? Denthurion turned to glance at Maclaren, who said, "This is Tenth Komer Evshaar, Principal Functionary for the Civil Secretariat of Olam."

The man bowed low. "Your Grace." He straightened up and said, "If we'd known, we would've . . ."

Denthurion listened to him babble for a moment, then interrupted with, "That's all very well, Mr. Evshaar, but I'm here to interview certain members of the Council."

"Why, ah . . . yes." He licked dry lips, swallowed, and said, "I'm a member of, ah . . . the Council."

Denthurion smiled. "I'll get to you, Mr. Evshaar." Why is he turning so pale? This fellow is positively green . . . Very odd. There's not enough wrong here for these people to fear any special consequences. And this Evshaar acts like a schoolboy caught cheating on exams. "Meanwhile, I've put Mr. Kevess first on my list."

"I'll . . . I'll *summon* him right away! If you'd care to use my office . . ."

"No, Mr. Evshaar, we'll go to him. If you'd care to lead the way?" He gestured toward the nearest flight of stairs.

Evshaar seemed to struggle with himself, trying to walk and bow at the same time. "Yes. Of course. This way, Your Grace." He turned and barged through the middle of his group of followers, scattering them. Denthurion and Maclaren followed, the latter motioning for the Metastatic Guardsmen to hold their position.

The Commissioner of Public Safety, Second Komer Kevess, was already out of his desk, standing beside a wide-open window looking out over the rooftops of Perax at a bright, cloudless blue sky. "Mr. Televox. Come in. I'd heard you were in the building."

Kevess's office was the opposite of all the others he'd seen so far. Its walls were covered with white paint, done up in a decor of framed pictures and certificates, the desk a complex thing of metal and glass. On a pad near one corner of the desktop shimmered the homunculus of a modern comeye, waiting patiently, looking at the chair, rather than about at the room or the men. "Good morning, Commissioner. I'm sorry we didn't get a chance to chat the other day, at Kartavilis's little get-together."

Kevess was a tall, slender man, trim and smoothly muscled, dark-eyed and dark-haired, clean-shaven and altogether allopathic-looking. As Denthurion joined him at the window, he said, "Perhaps we can remedy that now, Your Grace. What can I do for you?"

Reading out a cultivated sense of confidence, Denthurion smiled. "Just tell me a few things about Olam, Mr. Kevess. Nothing official; I can read the records when I want that. Just give me your impressions."

Spreading his palms blandly, Kevess smiled and said, "Anything I can do to help out, Your Grace. I and my people are yours to command."

Make me dig then. So be it. "I'll keep it simple, then. Tell me something about *Shearah*."

He leaned his elbow on the windowsill, turning to face Denthurion, eyes blackened by shadow. "I'm sure you already know the basics. It's a . . . free speech movement that's spread among the university students in recent decades. Free speech. Academic democracy. De-emphasis of the Amud core curriculum. They like to sit up all night talking, when they should be studying. Mostly, they get bad grades. Not the leaders, though. There're demonstrations, exam strikes, marches . . ."

"Throwing bombs at visiting Televoxes."

Kevess turned to stare out the window again. "These people are children, for the most part. Sometimes they get carried away, believing in their own nonsense. I'm sorry you had to be involved."

"Have you caught the one responsible?"

"Positive ID? No. We rounded up the entire part of the crowd from which the bomb was thrown, filtered out six or seven known *Shearah* members, and assigned them collective responsibility. They'll be punished."

"How?"

Kevess looked at him and shrugged. "Expulsion from school. A few years on a collective irrigation project in the highlands. That ought to be enough."

"I suppose so. Have you thought of rounding them all up? Putting an end to things?"

Another shrug. "What for? It'd just spring up again.

These things have to burn themselves out. You know the theory."

"How far has it spread?"

"Not too far. It's in all the upper-level general educational institutes ... but the professional students—doctors, engineers, and the like—are too busy for bullshit. It's just starting to trickle down into the preprofessional schools, the really big student populations. As you may know, that's usually the end of these things. When the elitist feeling becomes diffused, the cycle swings the other way, breeding a generation of tight-assed conservatives."

"So they say." He glanced at the other two men, standing over by the closed door. Maclaren was still, following the exchange expressionlessly; Evshaar was relaxed and smiling. "How do you gauge the effect on the general populace?"

"Not much. Ferment in the intellectual families, not totally outside their tradition. Hard-won education in worker families ... well, it leads to no small bitterness between fathers and sons. They'll survive—and these notions *will* die out. They always do."

"I'm sure. Don't you think this *Shearah* business is a little extreme?"

"Maybe so. But this is a holopath-dominant society, with a focus on holistic education. There's a natural pendulum that swings through events in a society like ours. This time we've taken a particularly big swing; I'm sure the backstroke will be just as bad. This oscillation will die out, in time." He laughed. "And 'Time Is the Metastability's Principal Ally.' "

"I'm sure you know your catechism better than I do, Commissioner." He stuck out his hand. "I'm glad we had this little talk."

Kevess, smiling broadly, had a firm, dry grip. "Anytime I can be of service, Your Grace."

Denthurion turned to the other two again. "Well. It's time we paid our visit to Mr. Ashaan. Shall we?"

As the door closed behind them, Kevess turned to face his comeye. "Tell Ashaan they're coming," he said, "and then see if you can find Meltsar for me. We need to talk."

The little homunculus snapped off a crisp salute, "Aye-aye, sir," and vanished in a curl of smoke.

Well, now, thought Kevess, sinking into his chair. Just how transparent *am* I? I've gotten very smart over the last five hundred years. Just how smart would I get if I had a hundred times as long to hone my skills? Careful, Kevess, just . . . careful.

Great Komer Ashaan, Prime Minister of the Olamite civil government and high priest of the Amud theocracy, sat in his office and waited for the door to open. He waved a dismissing hand at the comeye and watched as it and its dioramic displays wisped away. Bah. Your Grace, this; Your Grace, that. Bastard chewing our assholes off without just cause. And Kartavilis! It was hard to believe the reaming out handed to the Planetary Governor, of all people! Ashaan had served as Great Komer through the terms of three Metastable officers now, had gotten used to their ways. Supreme authority; brook no bullshit; make no trouble. Now, *this*.

What am I supposed to *think*? That meeting with Meltsar, though. Got to be careful about shit like that . . .

The ornate door opened and Denthurion strode in, followed closely by Evshaar and that useless Kinnock Maclaren. Nothing more than a secretary. Look at him: face frozen, pretending to be stern, the Arm of Authority. Probably doesn't know what's going on either, just happy to see us terrorized. He rose to his feet, smiling: "Your Grace! I'm so pleased to see you again. We all had such a delightful time at Governor Kartavilis's soiree . . ."

Denthurion seated himself in a high-backed occasional chair near one wall. "Good to see you again, too, Ashaan. I'm looking forward to your planetary ball."

"Ah, yes! We've begun planning already! No more than ten days away!" This was a safe topic ... not that I know anything worth relating about *Shearah* or that damned plant business.

"It should be interesting." He paused, steepling his hands before his face, then said, "Ashaan, I'm interested in 'starships,'" he used the Ursprache word. "What do you call them in Olamite? *Koxavoniayim*, isn't it?"

The Great Komer sat down slowly in his chair. *Starships*. Well, so much for safe discussions. He dithered internally, taking his time, shifting into a position of maximum comfort. Well. No sense in pretending ignorance ... but there's a lot I *can* say. "*Koxavonia*. I assume you're referring to the, ah, *philosophical* cult?"

Denthurion smiled. "Indeed."

The first incarnation of Maaron Denthurion, mark One, stood in the parklike surround of Helium's Transceiver Matrix beside his source code, essentially saying goodbye. Mark Zero was quietly cheerful, steadily growing ever more bland, as he had been, day by day, with this moment's approach. Well, let him be that way. Blandness may be what is called for, over time ... And it stretched before him now, an ugly totality, somehow unending.

Mark Zero gripped him by the upper arms, smiling into his face, mottled, green-brown eyes chips of mossy stone, face unweathered, unlined, eternal young adulthood in flower. "Time to move on, at last." He shook his head slowly. "I can't believe it. Since Cary left ... You've become less a part of me and more a friend. Now you're going, too."

The will to listen to this forced nonsense was flooding away fast. Have done with it ... "Part of each other. Our shared memories won't end. We'll have that, just as we do with Cary, wherever he goes." Platitudes. Bullshit. Do I really mean them? No way of knowing.

Mark Zero grinned and shook his hand. "Televox and Senator. I'll wait to hear from you."

As his hand was released, mark One suddenly felt dazed. Wait to hear from me? The overlays would come back at intervals, one at a time, his life without him, flitting ghostlike about the cosmos. Something else to wonder about. They could reconstruct me from the overlays. Something like a soul ... but soulless. Something like that. He rubbed his hands together and smiled wanly. "Time to go."

Zero clapped him on the shoulder one last time. "Good-bye, then. I'll be seeing you."

Indefinable feelings welled up, threatening to break out, but mark One turned away, stepped into a transceiver booth, and let the door slide shut before he turned around. No more views of the past. Make it a clean break. Clean as fire. The inside of the box was pale pastel green, featureless, its inner surface slick, with something of the feel of wet plastic.

Time to go. He lifted a hand, but hesitated. And what about me? Where am I going? Old fears, atavistic fears, reared out of the darkness. The flame devouring you, sending you away into eternity. This body vaporized, fed into the power storage grid, soul recorded on hydrogen ice. Maaron Denthurion, mark One, incarnation One. Maaron mk01i01 Denthurion. Name and Number goodbye. He shivered. What the hell. Going nowhere.

As he gestured to the functional uplink node, the first incarnation of Maaron Denthurion, mark One, muttered, "So. *Pars aeterna.*" Then the teledynes wafted him away.

Relays. Transceiver Matrix to main exostation in the countryside south of the city—temporary storage, a few thousand wait states ticking over—then *Harvest Sky* drifted overhead. A bolt into the blue, transiting the link mechanism receiver, into a storage ring circuit for another few thousand clicks, then written into the cold, dark crystals, black ice forever and an address on the file table . . .

The ship circled in its orbit for a few more days, bedding down its manifests, contemplating the darkness, dissociative reactors bubbling over quietly. The comeye looked down on the blue-white-brown of Earth, bright sky shield like so many other worlds, cool and dispassionate, waiting leave to go. It came.

The engines flared soft violet at last, bending *Harvest Sky*'s ground track into a polar orbit a few thousand kilometers up. Easy now; gently, no hard radiation to sink through ozone and air, cooking delicate evolutionary mechanisms. Spiral away, taking hundreds of hours, out beyond the yellow-white Moon, beyond the million-kilometer mark, engine flares gradually waxing.

Look around now, wary sensors checking for other space traffic—this was an insufferably busy star system. All clear, and go. The ship's engines spawned their full power, winding up over a few sharp seconds, acceleration building to ten thousand gravities and more. Go. *Harvest Sky* was visible for a few minutes as a bright violet spark in Earth's daytime sky, fading, diminishing, gone.

In the dark between the stars, *Harvest Sky* drifted, the comeye alone, content in its natural element. This was a quick run, six brief years to another landfall, then down into orbit again, around another bright shield world, blue and white and brown, two brilliant suns in the sky, manifests compared, down- and up-loading tasks begun. But, meanwhile, the clocks ticked slowly over a world of black ice . . .

Step between the stars, he thought. Into the transceiver in Helium and out again in Oldenburg, capital of Urheim, oldest human stellar colony, circling close by Alpha Centauri's lesser sun. Over in subjective Planck time, no more than stepping from Helium to Marumsko, two score kilometers away . . .

Where? He floated in a sea of mist, staring blindly into dim light. There were frosty white mountains in the distance, remote crags, Alp-like, but enormous, far away, trans-Himalayan in their magnitude, backed by drifting clouds of white fog. Where? Urheim? No. Urheim was a world of warm, orange sunlight, K-star swollen in a blue-green sky. This . . .

His perspective was motionless, like some kind of ersatz, generated point of view, like talking directly with the comeye. The mist about him was independent, no swirling about body, no cold wind, no condensed plume of breath jetting out from somewhere beneath his eyes. No eyes, in fact. No where. No when.

Suddenly he was looking upward into a nighttime sky, watching the clouds blow across the bright, featureless disk of the Moon, waxing and waning, black ghosts becoming backlit, brightening, glowing across the face of the Goddess, silhouette shapes running before the storm, going away, turning dark again, vanishing into the night. The essence of a shiver swept him. Frozen demons closing in, waiting, waiting . . .

Cry out to the Gods! Save me! Save me, All-Father!

The Goddess looked down coldly, laughing at him.

I am all that is real. Myself and green nature. The Sky Gods, the Warriors . . . No more than imagination. And fear.

Wishful thinking.

Where am I, then?

Forget reality. Forget the dream. Forget the Goddess . . . and all the Gods of imagination and fear.

Downlink time already. There is world enough, now and again, but never time. Live again, Maaron Denthurion, for just a little while.

Mark One stepped through the flash-night of Helium's Transceiver Matrix and out into the midday light of Oldenburg's Central Receiving, startled by dimming daylight and slightly shrunken weight, his incarnation counter clicking over, unnoticed, from one to two. Over in an instant, he thought wonderingly, stepping between the stars . . .

The city around him was low, rambling, and ancient, gray stone buildings never more than two or three stories tall under a cloudless, windless sky tainted with a faint hint of green. Alpha Centauri-B was a fat, blinding ball in the sky. Not a hole into Hell, like Earth's sun, but too bright to look at nonetheless. It stood high overhead, at maybe seventy degrees in the . . . south? No. Oldenburg lay far down in Urheim's southern hemisphere, deep in the antarctic temperate zone. The northern sky then. And it was . . . Afternoon? No way of knowing. The clues were too subtle to absorb easily.

A tall, handsome, dark-haired couple stood before him, man and woman, faces remarkably similar, smiling at him out of identical black eyes. They were dressed in silvery, gray-green clothing, loose trousers tucked into low, mottled brown boots, baggy shirts of some shiny, silklike material, silver necklaces with embedded blue-green stones looped about thin, stately necks, long hair swirling around their shoulders in tandem waves.

The man stepped forward, holding out his right hand, showing teeth in a thin, pleased-looking smile. "Welcome to Urheim, Mr. Televox. My name is Klaes and this is my sister Zoe. We'll be your hosts during this final phase of your training regimen."

Maaron Denthurion took the proffered hand, smiling, nodding, and thought, Klaes and Zoe, in Oldenburg, on Urheim, out among the fixed stars. And the final phase . . .

The unmarked government hovercar slid endlessly along a broad main avenue of Perax, southwestward from the civil administration center, heading toward the Governor's Palace. Denthurion slumped in the backseat beside

Maclaren, brooding, trying to shut out the bright sky beyond the tinted bubble.

All right. Was that a crucial sequence or not? These encounters are difficult to ordinate in the long context of local history. Men who know they're incompetent. Men who don't know they're incompetent. That Mr. Kevess, now . . . The worst kind of incompetence. Thinks a situation can be allowed to fall into any kind of disarray, confident he has the magic touch to set things right, at leisure. Denthurion smiled slightly to himself. If only the bastard *knew* what trouble was, he'd think differently.

He had a sudden vision of his life as a composite, wandering the galaxy at will, endless crisis and confrontation. Hell. These assholes can't handle a few unruly children. What would they do in the face of an unruly world . . . Or a little pocket empire growing like a cancer in the heart of the Metastability? Well. My job, not theirs. Turn back to the problem at hand.

The Amud itself. Something to be said for a planet run by a theocratic bureaucracy. Not much, though. Have to look into it. I wonder if they realize how close to their roots they still are? After all the millennia, all the terrible changes, the people of the Levant are still soaked in something like religion. It was interesting, of course, and the natural, blended result of holopathy in the static context of the Metastable Order.

Governor Ardennes Kartavilis, mark Eight, now . . . By damn. A *trained* administrator. One of our own. No excuse for these mistakes. Time to set *him* straight, at least . . .

In front of them the driver cocked his head to one side, listening intently to an inner voice. "Have to make a detour," he called over his shoulder. "There's some kind of trouble ahead."

Denthurion clapped him lightly on the shoulder. "Just drive right by it."

"But, Your Grace . . ." said Maclaren, looking alarmed.

"We're not in any danger, Kinnock."

"But the bomb . . ."

Denthurion laughed. "Commissioner Kevess is an extremely clever man."

"Kevess?" The look of alarm waxed rapidly. "Are you saying you think *he* was responsible for the attack?"

"Don't get carried away, Kinnock. He just doesn't want me to see these little altercations anymore. Trouble is, I *have* to see them."

The road ahead of them was partly closed off by a small, milling crowd, surrounded by several squads of armed and armored local militia. As the car slowed up, edging around the mass of people, Denthurion pushed over to the edge of the seat, leaning close to the glass, looking out. The demonstrators were mostly stripe-clad students, boiling around the front of a tall, ornately facaded building, hammering on its bright green bronze doors, shouting incoherently. Several of them carried pole-mounted placards, all bearing the single phrase *Kessev Kafuu*. Frozen Money.

The police were placid now, standing around the edges of the crowd in little knots, faceplates tipped up, chatting with each other and tapping their thick black wands on the ground, against their boots, holding them across their chests, all of it innocuous but suggestive.

Some of the students turned to watch the passing hovercar slide by with idle interest, then one boy pointed at them, shouting something, his mouth working inaudibly. There was a sudden flurry of movement, spreading all through the crowd, then one demonstrator brought down his sign, cracking its pole over the head of the nearest policeman. Two other officers closed in immediately, one of them stroking his wand across the offending demonstrator's head, bringing him down, face splashed with bright blood.

"What's the name of this building?"

The driver glanced quickly over his shoulder and said, "The Student Loan Bank."

They drove on, Denthurion turning in his seat so he

could watch the receding mass break into a melee, police and students beating each other with sticks. No gunfire today. Not worth the effort. Or . . . maybe orders to the contrary. Despite appearances, this is a modern world. Kevess could have put the word out in the time since I left his office. He settled back in the seat, slouching down again as the car picked up speed. Clever man, Kevess. But local. He just doesn't know.

"Kinnock, what do you think?"

"About the demonstration?"

"No. What's your general impression of the Amud Council members? You've been here awhile."

"Well . . ." Maclaren struggled with reticence. Do your job. Do your job. "As a whole they're . . . ineffective. Harmless, though. They seem to mean well. As individuals? Hard to say. Kevess, I think . . ."

The driver said, "There's another problem ahead. This one blocks the entire road. We'll have to go around."

Interesting. "Pull into a side street near the whatever it is and stop."

"Sir?"

"Do as I say, please."

Listening to his voice, the driver pulled down a long, narrow alleyway, the sides of the car scraping periodically against brick and stone, and out onto another broad road that paralleled the one they'd left. Tsarfaati Street. As they continued their southwestward travel, the front of one shop caught Denthurion's eye, its signs and windows larger and more colorful than most that he'd seen before. *Arcane Lore.* Wonder what that's all about? They pulled up in front of a big building and ground to a stop, ignored by the street's passersby. Denthurion motioned for the driver to raise the bubble and stepped out into hot midday air.

The building they'd stopped in front of was a little taller than the others, four or five stories, at least, made of the ubiquitous pale, sandstonelike dimension stone of Olam, with fairly big glass windows through which peo-

ple could be seen working away at what appeared to be
comeye terminals. That meant the building had either an
embedded AI or was netted to one somewhere else. He
looked up at the big sign over the broad glass doors.
Northwestern Olam Central Bank. The AI was probably
on-premises.

"Are you sure you know what you're doing?"

Denthurion smiled. "You're not supposed to ask me
that, Kinnock."

"*I* don't know what you're doing, then."

"Just my job. Come on. If I'm not mistaken, this hallway will go all the way through."

The corridor was about five meters wide, the walls
mirrored, the floor done up in elaborate tilework. The
hall sloped gently upward past entry doors to the bank's
various departments, then opened out into a kind of indoor plaza containing a number of little shops. These
stores were frontless, their interior rooms opening directly into the corridor, their goods on prominent display.

Walking toward another set of glass doors on the far
end, Denthurion looked into each storefront as he passed
by. An interesting lot. Craftwork, restaurants, souvenir
minerals. Crap essentially. The stores seemed well pa-
tronized, though, colorfully cloaked Olamites pawing
over material that could serve little function in their ev-
eryday lives. The mineral store seemed to attract a particularly large clientele, men and women holding various
colored crystals up to the light, comparing them, murmuring softly to each other. The sign over the shop said,
Mehhetmol, "Since Yesterday."

Denthurion walked on toward the glass doors, then
stopped suddenly and went back to the mineral shop and
looked in, staring at the customers, then at the merchandise. Each little bin of stones had a small sign over it,
dark Olamite lettering. *Yesh li shiyul.* "I have a headache." *Hitstanaanti.* "I have chills." *Haitaa li teunaa.* "I
have had an accident."

An accident? What does that mean? Pissed your tunic?

How very odd. He shrugged and turned away, walking up
the corridor and out through the glass doors. The corridor continued outside along a balcony, more shops on
the inner edge, the outer edge some eight meters above
street level. They went around a corner, onto a plaza
filled with stone benches. The corridor continued on into
open space, becoming a bridge over the main avenue,
disappearing into a windowless structure only a little
smaller than the bank. There were a fair number of people here, crowded against the railing, looking down into
the street.

Denthurion and Kinnock walked out onto the pedestrian walkway, forcing their way between people until
they were leaning on the rail as well. The street below
was filled with ring after ring of people, surrounding a
little platform that had been set up on the sidewalk.
There were police among them, clustered into a little
bunch near the platform, standing together, facing each
other, talking. They'd probably been sent to keep order
by a supervisor who'd badly misjudged the attraction of
whatever was going on here. There seemed to be at least
two thousand people collected in the broad avenue, the
crowd growing now of its own accord, an attractor in its
own right. The people on the outskirts probably had no
idea what was going on.

Two bearded men mounted the platform, clad in lavender tunics bearing a bright gold sunburst on the upper
left breast. One of them cradled a cubic plastic sculpture
in which a slanted spiral of silvery metallic glitter had
been embedded. Denthurion shaded his eyes, trying
to focus on the thing. Difficult to see at this distance,
but ... Uh-oh. The spiral was surrounded by a thready
black net. A net that appeared to be torn to pieces. He
felt his attention sharpen as the unencumbered man began to speak, face earnest, eyes bright with ... something.

"Welcome," he said, "to the New World. I speak for
the Starship, and its Captain." The voice was deep,

rolling out over the crowd without amplification, catching their attention, quieting them easily. "They call me the Recruiter."

"An honest man," Denthurion whispered to Maclaren. "What a surprise."

"You think you know the world around you, but you do not. What you know is fifty thousand years of lies. Fifty thousand years. You know the story of Olam and the Olamites, of the sad, horrible path that led us to this world, out among the fixed stars. You know the story of the fall of the Levant, of Cpaht's terrible exodus, the story of the Hhurull and of the Reawakening. These are lies. What you know is a fairy tale, told to keep you satisfied with what you know as history. Told to keep you from seeking out the Truth.

"It would be enough," cried the man, "to keep us quiet for all eternity, had not the Truth accidentally gotten out. The Pilot, you see, the *Pilot*, knows the Truth. Now I am telling it to you."

"Tell us!" said somebody in the front of the crowd, followed immediately by a different voice, almost echoic, shouting, "The Pilot!"

Very interesting. Laymen who know the cant or a planted clacque? Denthurion suddenly felt a sense of exhaustion stealing over him. Again and again. Ages beyond numbering spent rooting out this nonsense. Like . . . Like . . . He had sudden memory of an open field he and Cary had found south of Marumsko, a field buried under a thick growth of Kudzu. Like that. You pluck it out, burn it down, 'dyne it into an alternate reality, and the following summer it's back again, as if you'd done nothing.

"We," said the Recruiter, "are crewmen on the Starship of God. The Great Commander, Captain of our Fate, lays down the Course in his Omnipotent Wisdom . . ."

Well. Different. I wonder who thought *this* one up? Whoever it is must be getting a solid return on his investment of cleverness.

"The Navigation is complete. The Pilot knows the course. Now I come to you, citizens of lost Olam, to tell you the Truth. Come with me. Learn the Ways of the Starship. In due course, we'll *all* board the Great Starship of God, join the crew in Eternal Salvation . . ."

The murmur of the crowd was dying down, faces turning to watch the Recruiter and follow his words. This, now. Odd. Nothing special in these words, just a clever mythology. Why the careful attention?

"You *know*," said the Recruiter, "that many of us have already gone aboard the eternal Starship. You have the Pilot's word. The Pilot, who has gone to heavenly bliss and come back of his own accord, come back into mud and misery, just to tell us the Truth . . ."

A dangerous gambit for a charlatan. Sooner or later you get caught, even if the authorities miss dealing with you. Denthurion turned to glance at Maclaren. "I think we'd better go see the Governor now, Kinnock."

The other man nodded. "As you say."

They turned and melted back into the crowd, the Recruiter's voice ringing out behind them over the heads of a silent audience.

Under a forty-thousand-year-old geodesic dome, originally the coronal courtyard of mighty Cpaht, the Metastatic Senate of Humanity sat in full session. The room was a vast Greek amphitheater, ring after ring of gray stone tiers descending to a central dais, a little more than five hundred meters across, the whole shielded from wind and rain and sun by a flattened dome of photoreactive glass triangles.

Mark Zero sat on a bench at the foot of the dais, embedded in a row of six new Senators, clad in flowing, silver-trimmed black robes, modeled on the academic ceremonial costumery of the Red Millennium. The room was filled now with black-clad men and women, the cool, conditioned air whispering with a rustle of voices and soft cloth. The dome was filled with light, filtering down, diffuse, through the gray glass overhead.

If you looked closely, you could see the countryside without, rolling hills, sparsely clad in trees, broken by an occasional angular rock outcrop. The Great Ice of a few thousand years back had scraped away the land, changing its aspect considerably.

Mark Zero took a deep breath, wishing the vast room had *some* kind of odor, even if only the smell of massed humanity. There were six thousand Senators here, the visible manifestation of two hundred thousand and more Televoxes who wandered a quarter of the galaxy, dispensing justice . . . No, more precisely, *order*.

A metal-clad gavel rapped from the dais, clanging on a steel plate, echoes ringing briefly through the chamber. The Senators came to order, facing forward, listening for a voice that would be conveyed technologically to the outermost row.

Metron Ariston, Vox Humana for the past few millennia, rose to stand behind his ancient teak podium, gripping the smoothly worn black wood with large, bony hands. He was unfashionably tall and thin, angular, largely without a visible musculature, representing the allopathic style of a long-gone age, evidence that, despite everything, change continued its sluggish crawl. "Call to Order. The forty-two thousand and seventy-ninth annual session of the Metastatic Senate of Humanity now begins."

There was a polite rustle of pro forma applause. "Standard routine business today: investiture, State of Humanity report, annual agenda setting, standing committee reassignments as necessary. We'll conduct the old business review tomorrow. Those of you with special items that require active processing this year will be permitted to submit them to the Agenda and Assignments Committee on Wednesday. All right. New people. Mrs. Panayotis?"

A short, roly-poly woman rose from her seat near the

podium, carrying a fistful of silver-chained medallions. As chair of the small Homeopathic Caucus, Andraakiya Panayotis had a permanent seat on the dais; as secondmost senior member of the Senate, she acted as Chief of Protocol. She and Metron Ariston lived in neighboring compounds out at the Reston Exurban Center. There were some standard jokes ... Now she and the Vox Humana stepped off the dais, down to the floor before the six new Senators, motioning them to rise.

"Ladies and gentlemen," said Metron Ariston, "welcome to the Metastatic Senate of Humanity. Your training is complete, your first Televox is on the way outward, your first overlays will not be long in coming. Now the business of humanity is before you." The two moved to one end of the line and began strolling down it, the Vox Humana shaking hands and smiling, fat little Panayotis flipping necklaces over bent-down necks. "That's it, then. Go the back benches, then. I'll talk to you again in a few thousand years." There was additional soft applause as the two turned away, resuming their places on the dais.

As he walked up the long central flight of stone stairs, headed for the outer periphery of the chamber, Denthurion mark Zero lifted the silver medallion off his chest. Black etching on a shiny mirror finish, the galaxy's spiral embedded in a spider's web, another spiral and radial lines. Around the edge of the emblem, a motto: *Tempora mutantur, nos et mutamur in illis.* "Times change and we are changed within them." Strange. I knew it all along, yet ... It seems different now.

He took a vacant seat, almost up by the giant pylons that supported the edge of the dome, mind whirling. Times change? No. Our job here is to see that they do not. A warning then. If we change, the times change with us.

Denthurion and Kartavilis stared at each other across the teak inlaid surface of the latter's walnut desk. The Governor was leaning forward, elbows on the hard surface, broad, blunt hands folded, fingers interlaced, dark eyes bland in an expressionless, craggy face. "All right, Mr. Televox. You've spent a couple of days wandering around the capital city of my world. Now you've come back to me with something on your mind. I'd like you to tell me what it is straight off."

Arrogant bastard. Denthurion leaned back in the soft leather of his chair, folding his arms loosely across the lower part of his chest. Too long in one place, I suppose. On the other hand, that's what Planetary Governors do. Stay. Stabilize. Send overlays back to their originals in the Congress of Planetary Deputies. He smiled faintly, glancing at Kartavilis, let his eyes rove around the room behind the desk, flitting from feature to feature. "Straight out? All right, Governor. First of all, it *isn't* your world."

A look of suppressed irritation crossed Kartavilis's features. "Just a manner of speaking, Your Grace."

"A figure of speech? No, Governor. Olam *should* be your world, but it isn't." He picked up a piece of pink crystal off one corner of the desk, turning it over in his hands. Rose quartz, not too common on the colony worlds. On the other hand, Olam was quite . . . minerally. "The Metastability sent you here to make this world your own. Whether you did that successfully in the past, I can't say as yet. Just now, you've let it get away from you."

The knuckles of Kartavilis's hands whitened briefly, then he unclasped them and sat back in his chair, dropping his hands onto the armrests. "I think not, Mr. Televox." The words were measured, as close to uninflected as the Olamite tongue could manage. "You've been here for four days. That's hardly enough time . . ."

"On the contrary. I've been elsewhere for forty thousand subjective years, I and my going-doubles. I know when a benchmark has been exceeded."

They stared at each other silently for a few seconds,

then Kartavilis said, "So. Tell me where you think I've failed."

"Failed? I hadn't thought to use that word." He replaced the quartz crystal on the desk. "All right. *Shearah.* You say it's just disgruntled children, demonstrating about tight student loans, about being inconvenienced by overzealous bureaucrats. I've seen this sort of thing before, Governor. 'Storm.' They *will* live up to their name."

"Really, Your Grace." Kartavilis picked up the crystal and held it close to his chest, rubbing his fingers slowly over the smooth, angled surfaces. "The firebomb incident . . ."

"Hardly a proper litmus test. I know how these things are argued." He waved a hand between them, cutting off an attempted interruption. "Let me go on. *Koxavonia.* Governor, the Starship of God cult is *illegal.* Why hasn't it been suppressed?"

"I . . ." Kartavilis rubbed his other hand across his chin. He sighed. "I hadn't thought of it as a religion, Mr. Televox. Not in the context of the Amud theocracy. It seems more like a moral philosophy, quite in keeping with the history and traditions of Olam."

"Go listen to one of their Recruiters, if you will. Go listen to them call the Metastable Order a lie."

"I think you're misinterpreting their words. I really do. I've been to rallies. I've never heard anything . . ."

"Then tell me this." He leveled a finger at Kartavilis's chest. "Who let the Red Millennium Crystal Mythology get a foothold on this planet?"

The Governor looked down in surprise, opening his hand, staring at the bit of rose quartz. "Crystal Mythology? Of all the idiotic . . ." His cheeks took on a hint of color, darkening slightly, throwing a glint of anger into his eyes. "Your Grace, this is an *art* form! How could you be so stupid as to think . . ."

Denthurion held out his left hand, palm up. "Give me the crystal, Governor."

Kartavilis looked at the thing doubtfully, then shrugged

and dropped it into Denthurion's palm. Denthurion smiled, then flicked his wrist, tossing the crystal out an open window. Kartavilis turned to watch it go, flinched as it went *crack* out on the balcony.

"Why so upset, Governor? Just a nonrepresentational work of art."

Pale, Kartavilis turned to look at him again. "Mr. Televox. That thing was worth money. My money."

"Worth *money*? To a planetary ruler?" Denthurion grinned. "Tell me more. I love to be entertained."

Kartavilis stood up, pushing his chair back, cheeks reddening with anger. "*Mister* Denthurion . . ." He grated.

"Sit your ass down, Ardennes mark Eight Kartavilis. I'm here to give you your instructions."

The Governor's knees appeared to buckle as he dropped back into his chair, mouth open in an "O" of astonishment. "But . . ."

"Point one: You will see to it that the *Shearah* student movement is infiltrated. I want the organization subverted from within and rendered harmless.

"Point two: You will see to it that the Starship of God religious cult is disbanded. I want its leadership rounded up and identified . . ."

Kartavilis gripped the arms of his chair briefly, fingers sinking into the leather. When he spoke, it was with a calm and level tone. "Listen to me, if you can. This is a mistake. You don't understand the people of Olam. Look around you and you'll see that suppression from the outside can only make things worse. These problems have to find their own solutions . . ."

Denthurion stood up. "Maybe so, Governor Kartavilis, but I fail to see it. You have three days to prepare a detailed plan. After your presentation, I'll decide how or whether to proceed."

"But . . . But . . ."

"Three days, Governor." He turned and strode from the room.

Kartavilis sat back in his chair, white-faced, staring at

the closed door. Bastard! Bastard! What now? Do I just *proceed*? Impossible! What if I refuse? Recalled. Back to Earth. At least I'd get a fair hearing, that way, get this madness overturned.

Sharp regret. But then Olam is lost, to me at least, maybe to everyone. Earth is a fifteen-hundred-parsec voyage, the round trip a one-way passage ten thousand years and more into the future . . .

He waved his comeye awake and said, "Get me . . ." Who? Ashaan? Asshole. Kevess. No. Useless. "Get me Mr. Meltsar, please."

Do something, damn you. Anything.

Chapter 5

The mist whispered in a sunless well. Great Mimir see for us ... Odin's other eye shines bright, a pale star in the impenetrable dark ... The winds of change rustled through the branches of the Great Tree, shaking its foundations from Nithogg to Weatherdraggled. Chattering Nibbletooth fled, shrieking ... Lies! All lies. Gods and Goddesses one with nature and humanity at last, embedded forever in the cold, black ice ...

Frail Denthurion, composite, shattered, floated forever in a dark and crystalline sea. Lost. Lost. No where. No when. Step between the stars, Great Televox. Become one with the Aesir ... and their nothingness. Black ice. Lost. Part of eternity ...

A light grew in the mist, swelling from a suddenly noticed pinpoint to an oval of foggy seeing, the long table laid out on a floor of swirling cloud stuff. The incarnations sat together at their feast, silently eating, soundless spoons to soundless mouths, endlessly relaying imaginary food to imagined alimentation.

Time again, the ragged Chorus whispered. Live again! One more little venture into simple mortality ... the *koax*-frogs sang in the background, not their traditional piping cries, no, but:

Heid-ho, heid-ho ... The denizens of Darkalfheim stooping to their eternal labor ...

Maaron Denthurion awoke. All darkness. What a strange dream ... He stirred, rolling over on the bed, sliding his face to a fresh spot on the stiff linen sheet, feeling a night breeze come in through the open window and stir across his back. The air was sweet with the smell of Kemitish vegetation . . .

The sleep haze continued, letting him coast aimlessly from place to place, bits and pieces of consciousness surfacing, bobbing about for a little while, sinking again into the still black pool of the past. Fifteen million awakenings and more, me, all me . . . No more.

He drifted again, skirting the edge of sleep, dipping into its gentle surf now and again, and found himself on his back once more, staring out the window into a pool of stars. They made pretty patterns, these almost colorless jewels . . . What a strange dream.

Black ice. Cold. You've dreamed this dream before. Not just in other incarnations, in other branchings as well. Other branchings. Hard to accept, despite everything; them, not me, but . . . me, nonetheless, those other beings whose lives flow into my own. Overlays. Call them overlays.

And where does the black ice come from? What overlay is that? The sky outside the window began to lighten, pink tints edging upward, but he fell into the black pit of nothingness for another little while.

When he awoke again the sky was bright blue and featureless. He sat up on the edge of the bed, rubbing a slightly oily face on his palms, then stood and stretched. There was already a hint of warmth in the air, but the day was still fresh, yesterday's dust suppressed by the relatively cool night. Waving the comeye alert, he said, "I'll have breakfast on the deck."

The papery face opened on the wall, timeshared to featurelessness, and whispered, "Very well. What would you like?"

"Um, fresh fruit. Coffee."

Out on the stone balcony he sat waiting, staring out over the now-familiar landscape. All right, you've given them instructions and a time frame. Now what will *you* do with that same period? What indeed? A tall, thin naturopathic-style Guardsman brought out a big, steaming mug of coffee, and a shallow bowl full of varicolored melon balls, pink, orange, blue, and bright green, stuck through and through by little spears of straw-colored wood.

He pawed through the fruit, finding fibrous yellow cubes among the spheres, and tasted one. Some species of pineapple, light and sharp-tasting. The little bits of melon were heavy and sweet, probably grown with the usual forced-agriculture techniques.

Storm and Starship. Idiotic developments, but . . . curious. The student thing was familiar and would be easy to subvert. The religious thing, on the other hand . . . The doctrines of *Koxavonia*, what little he'd heard of them, had a curious appeal. Yet, that *was* the reason why these things persisted. An appeal to the irrational, to the shared fears of mankind. Immortality. Never disappear into the yawning gap between reality and dream.

Everyone *knew*, had known for all the thousands of years, that the immortality conferred by the matter transmitters wasn't *real*. The talk about souls, flitting instantly from one place to another, dividing between bodies and branchings, had died down long ago. Copies were copies and what was physical was real. And that was an end to the matter. You just died. One way or another. And the pretense was life.

Well. They've made a powerful appeal, come up with some really novel idea, to gather adherents in any number, even here in a holopathic sea. Climb aboard the Starship of God? Ashaan's statements hadn't made any sense. Gobbledygook about the Boolean logic of a Life-and-Death Gate . . . It would be hogwash, of course, but *convincing* hogwash. People weren't completely silly, just primed by tiny fears.

He snapped his fingers overhead and the house

comeye blinked on in the exterior stucco, rendered irregularly three-dimensional by the gritty stone surface.

"Bring me some Olamite clothing, please."

The featureless eyes stared at him for a moment, then it said, "As you wish." It irised away to a bright spot, light going down the drain, and winked out.

Denthurion stepped from a public transceiver box into the brilliant late morning sunshine of Gaan Tashluum, at the center of Perax. A light wind whipped his dull tan head-cloak, lifting it away from the back of his neck, cooling the skin a little bit. The transition from the Archive Center's dimness to full daylight made him squint, a twinge from his eyes signaling an adjustment rate too rapid for normal compensation. This was a primitive, generalized transceiver that made no attempt to modify its cargo: just make the copy and leave it at that.

The square kilometer of Payment Park, a low collection of grassy knolls, was covered with a variety of wooden stalls and multicolored tents, people milling between them, buying, selling, haggling, generally filling the air above them with a continuous squawk and rumble. He rubbed a sandaled foot over the spongy, green-brown grass. One of the terrestrial *gramineae*, specially engineered for the "paving" of heavily used public parkland.

He walked slowly away from the booth, sliding into the loose crowd, ambling between two rows of stalls, pausing now and again to look into them and examine their wares. The Gaan Tashluum marketplace was, of course, entirely focused on "nonmanufactured" goods. Olam's partial industrial economy, under the aegis of the Amud, produced hard goods with a simple efficiency no private enterprise could hope to overwhelm. If you wanted a car or a Public Net comeye terminal ... there were robot-dominated asteroidal and cometary mines and orbiting factories that would, without careful management, flood the world with impossibly cheap goods. What these petty entrepreneurs sold was "personal quality."

He came to an open area near the center of the park in which benches had been scattered, facing each other at more or less irregular angles and intervals. The benches were occupied by a variety of idlers, well dressed and ill, and Denthurion joined them. No better way to begin an investigation like this than to sit and listen.

Opposite him, a couple of meters away, two pudgy men sat, chatting idly. Denthurion relaxed, slitting his eyes against the sunshine, watching them unobtrusively. Unremarkable, fat men in gray and olive-drab talking about some sporting event they'd seen the previous night. Live? No. A Public Net presentation.

One of them held a small female Hoda on his lap, a small biped with a puglike face and a small, shiny black nose. Its hair was a curious brown-blond shade, almost iridescent in the sunlight, and the man was stroking its fur gently, running broad hands over its sides and back in an absentminded fashion. The creature butted its head against his chest, making a little sound halfway between a purr and a whine. The man ran his hand up one of its thighs and stroked between its legs for a while. Odd. Like scratching a cat's belly?

No. These are sentient beings. They were slaves before they became pets . . . And before we arrived? The lords of creation. The man dug his fingers under the fur, making delicate adjustments, while the Hoda whined softly and rubbed its face against his tunic. The other man took no notice, chattering on gaily about the declining quality of this year's All Olam Makel Kaduur League.

Makel Kaduur. Denthurion translated the words to himself. Well. Spanya. That might be worth looking into. It brought back flickering memories of a thousand well-spent afternoons . . . He got up and walked away from the unpleasant little tableau, strolling down an avenue full of people and lined with merchants' stalls.

The merchandise here seemed to echo the things he'd seen in the little indoor mall the previous day. Amid stalls selling homemade food and clothing were merchants selling rock crystals and what looked like small art objects. One stall, manned by a sullen-looking fat woman, contained a fair number of exquisitely well-made statuettes of Olamite wildlife, carved from some kind of clear, colored, soapy-feeling material. The animals were, presumably, well rendered, though except for a few delicate little Hodai, he recognized none of them.

Komer shel-Maazal. "Luck-priest"? Odd. Denthurion went over to the booth, which bore a seal indicating official Amud sanction. A black-bearded, red-clad man sat behind it, paper and stylus on the wooden bench before him, beside a bowl full of little black cubes. "What are these for?"

The priest looked at him in amazement. "Are you simpleminded?"

Denthurion grinned. "No, just a foreigner."

"What do you mean, 'foreigner'?" He waved one hand around, seeming to indicate the crowded pathways of the park. "There are no . . ." He sat back in the chair, eyes widening. "From . . . off-planet?"

Denthurion nodded.

"Well." The priest rubbed a hand in his curly beard. "Kem?"

"Most recently. I arrived aboard the *Naglfar* a few days ago."

The man nodded. "I'd heard there was an interstellar vessel in orbit." He looked at Denthurion speculatively. "I've always wanted to travel. What's it like on Kem?"

Interesting. "Interstellar vessel," not "starship." "Not terribly different from Olam. Bigger oceans, island continents, lots of irrigated land under cultivation. Deserts . . . maybe not so dry, but widespread nonetheless."

The priest sighed. "I know that from books. I suppose there's no way to convey the *feel* of another world . . ."

"No. Human-inhabited planets tend to be similar in

any case. And discounting superficial things like language and costume, so do human cultures. Olam is lucky to have native inhabitants. It gives your world a little flavor all its own."

"Native inhabitants?" He seemed puzzled for a moment. "Oh. You mean the Hodai. We're . . . too used to them, I guess."

Denthurion nodded. "That feeling's not so uncommon." He waved a hand at the little black boxes. "You still haven't told me about these."

The priest stared at his wares, obviously not much interested in discussing mundanities. "*Tvilaa.* 'Prayer shells.' " Not seeing comprehension on Denthurion's face, he continued, "You tell me what you wish for. I write it on the paper and say a blessing. It goes in the little box and you shove the box up under the front of your head-cloak and keep it there all day. Maybe your wish comes true after that."

"I see." Another piece in a puzzle of superstition.

Not far from the priest's booth was a little stall from which emanated a faint pall of smoke and a variety of strange smells. There were a half-dozen small tables on the grass in front of the booth, people seated at them, eating and talking. Denthurion wound his way through them to the front of the stall and looked over the counter. Inside, a handsome, dark-featured woman stood before a smoking, flat-metal grill surrounded by piles of bready-looking disks, an assortment of cooking utensils, and some steaming, covered pots.

She looked up at him, smiling. "What'll you have?"

"Uh." There was a paper menu taped to the counter. "A, uh, bullring"—whatever that was—"and, let's see"—he looked over at the column of drinks—"a bottle of Two Horses beer."

"Sit. I'll bring it out to you." She handed him a dark brown bottle, popping it open so that a wisp of vapor spilled from the neck.

He sat down at the nearest unoccupied table, while

sizzling noises, followed by a very strange odor, came from the tiny kitchen. He sipped the beer. Thick and bittersweet, sharp with alcohol. Odd. The label was done up primarily in Ursprache—one of the few Olamite legends on the bottle said, "Two Horses, from an Old Terrestrial Recipe." Unaccountably, there were no horses in the label's fancy scrollwork, just an assortment of cabalistic-looking mathematical symbols. More magic and mystery here, but . . . the Ursprache word for "horse" was spelled wrong and . . . He put the bottle down, feeling a mild pang of exasperation. Someone had confused "horse" with a popular slang term for the algebraic *rebus* symbol: *hekwis* instead of *hekkis*. He sipped it again. Not bad.

The woman brought out a plate and set it before him. "Ten and six." He handed her the money and watched as she walked away, white tunic sleek over solid, meaty buttocks.

The thing in front of him was one of the bready disks, rolled into a tube around some sort of filling, fried, and covered with a spoonful of white fluff. He picked up his knife and fork, then tasted the moist gobbet. Sour cream. He cut the thing open and looked inside. Good God. Horrid, recognizable ingredients: sauerkraut, black olives, mashed, fried beans, chunks of some kind of hard, dark sausage. Well. He popped a forkful into his mouth. The meat was strong and smoky, the overall mixture of flavors harmonious, particularly when followed by a mouthful of the strong beer.

As he ate, savoring the concatenation of pungent-musty-sour flavors, he began to focus in on his surroundings, distinguishing types in the flow of people down the aisle between the shops, listening to snippets of conversation between people walking by and at the neighboring tables. Despite the fact that Perax seemed to enjoy a monotonously stable climate, the weather was a major topic, "Dry today . . . dusty . . . high haze seems to be keeping things cool . . ." Variations on a theme. A pair of teen-aged girls passed by, flapping head-cloaks made mostly of white lace, one of them leading a bedraggled Hoda on a leather leash. They were chattering merrily back and forth, boys this and boys that. Sipping his beer, Denthurion smiled. For the most part, life here seemed as pointless as life anywhere else.

A pair of women sat at the next table and were soon digging into huge salads wrapped in some kind of crunchy yellow blanket, topped with a gooey gray dressing. One of them, round and soft-looking, spoke around a muffling mouthful, "I'll miss Baarvazaa, but it's all for the best."

The other, a taut, stringy, nervous-looking woman, picking diffidently at her food, said, "I don't see why you have to let her go . . ."

"It's what she *wants*, Shliiha!"

Shliiha seemed dubious. "I don't know, Melaxuutit. Children have to grow up, but this *Koxavonia* thing . . . it seems such a *waste*, going out to a wilderness camp, living like a wild Hoda! And what happens when she's done? 'Boarding the Starship of God,' my asshole!"

Melaxuutit seemed nonplussed. "I don't know. I just don't know. How could I stop her?"

"There's college . . ."

"College? She'd get involved with *Shearah*. I'd rather have her out in the desert with these 'Starship' people. At least *they* have some sense of moral identity . . ."

As he listened, Denthurion found himself marveling at the layers of primitive reasoning. Life has to have a purpose, a sense of identity and belonging, some reason to *be* . . . Go ahead and laugh at their pitiful attempts, Mr. Televox. *Your* life has a purpose . . . Of course it does. Travel and travel and travel, see the worlds, become the force of, what . . . sameness? Of course you have a purpose.

He drained the last of an increasingly bitter beer, got up, and wandered off, thinking . . .

• • •

In the time of Cpaht, decisions were made. Members of the Konservaat, committee designers of the forced interstellar migration, made their plans in accord with government policy—and the soldiers of Cpaht carried them out. All over the world, transceivers were set up. In Zaire, as elsewhere, the idle peasants were snatched from their entertainment nets and fed through the maw of the Machine, fearful and uncomprehending, into the hydrogen ice matrices of Starship *Thelathini*, outward bound for a newly discovered world. And shortly before the quantum dissociative engines began to spill their violet fury, the citizens of Kiev were marched at gunpoint to reprogrammed public transport booths and sent to join them.

Maaron Denthurion, ninth of his line, sat amid the pillars on the front portico of Gospodin Renko's manor house, sipping *chai* so cold it hurt his teeth, watching purple sunset crawl up into the pale indigo of sky of Nyegrai. The air was cool, the wind growing brisk as the fat orange sun, banded with stripes of black cloud, sank below the horizon. The wind rustled the thin leaves of olive-drab trees, rippling the surface of a soft, brown lawn. In the middle distance, down by the lakeshore, a small band of *rabi*, white tunics brilliant against ebony skin, were hauling sailboats out of the water for the night, detaching keels, laying the hulls up on blocks, lowering the masts to horizontal, folding up varicolored pastel sails, stowing them away. The sky was darkening gradually and the sharp smell of wood smoke and grill-cooked food tainted the air.

Metal chair legs scraped on stone and Civil Rightholder Yaroslav Renko sat down beside him, frosty bottle of *kvass* in one broad, blunt-fingered hand. Denthurion nodded to him, smiling distractedly. The Kievan Rus, as they called themselves in memory of a long-gone time, were a handsome folk, tall and muscular, ruddy skins well set off by red, blond, or light brown hair, and small, bright mulberry eyes. Renko himself was typical of his kind, a strong-looking, weather-beaten sociopath, of a strongly conservative bent. "Natural man" was a phrase you often heard here explaining the lack of tuning effects in the transceiver net.

"Enjoying your stay, then, Gospodin Denthurion?" The language was a blend of east Slavic dialects, mostly Russian, but with no little Ukrainian flavoring the mix.

"Your hospitality has been quite flawless . . ."

"I thank you." Renko took a long pull on his bitter, watery drink. "We don't see many Televoxes out here in the Pustynya. It's been a little unaccustomed excitement for us all."

Denthurion smiled. Not many Televoxes, at all . . . Only twelve parsecs from Earth, Nyegrai saw a steady stream of government agents, one every few years, usually raw from the training mill, on their way out into the darkness. The flow through this world was unnecessarily large, one visit a century probably more than enough, but you made a point of seeing the archetypal old colonies, in adumbration of much to come. A year here was an important educational credit. "I've enjoyed myself. The climate here is . . . as good as anything I've seen."

Renko beamed at the compliment. "Well. I've lived on this estate for close to fifteen hundred years. We have some rough weather, especially in winter, but, by and large . . ." He waved a hand at the fading purple sky.

Looking down across the lawn to the lakefront, Denthurion saw that the *rabi* had finished their task and were walking away into the darkness. If it hadn't been for their white clothing, they would have been invisible. "How old are you, Gospodin? If it's not an intrusion."

"No, not at all." He mulled the question for a moment, then said, "A little under two thousand, I think. You?"

A little under two thousand . . . Well, a "natural man" you may be, but the medical teledyne services are doing their part. "Hard to say. I am the ninth incarnation of this particular branching, so in that sense I may only be forty years old. Or six weeks old, if you want to look at it that way! On the other hand ..." He shrugged. "It's complicated."

Renko nodded sagely.

Odd how reticent I feel before this bland old monster. Why *shouldn't* he know this is my first branching, that mark Zero and I, between us, have only had a century or so of conscious experience? From the other side of the building came a harsh clanging, the sound of an iron bar being whirled in an iron triangle.

"Ah! The dinner bell!" Renko put down the *kvass* bottle and rose, rubbing his hands together. "The steaks'll be crispy tonight!"

Crispy, thought Denthurion, without a doubt ...

The next morning they went out to ride under a brilliant silver-blue sky puffed with a scattering of tiny white clouds. The Nyegraian *loshadi* were not exactly horses, but obviously something bred from equine base stock over the last several millennia, big, broad-bodied, maneless, covered with coats of long, fine hair. Denthurion's *loshad* was mostly brown, with patches of white here and there, and it looked to him like some kind of enormous, fat dog.

Renko kept pace beside him on a fluffy, yellow-white *loshad* as they rode off into the woods surrounding the manor house, following a wide, rutted track between the trees. "It's a fine day for a ride, Gospodin. I trust you passed a restful night?"

Denthurion nodded, thinking of the *devka*'s black skin, glistening with beaded sweat, and her dense, crisp, woolly hair. "Restful, as you say, citizen. Where are we going today?"

"Out and about. I thought I'd show you some of the plantation's main features. I like to keep track of these things myself."

The path they followed wound upward through the

woodlands, heading toward ever higher ground, where the vegetation grew increasingly sparse. The patches of blue sky grew larger overhead, trees blocking less and less, until they burst entirely out of the forest onto a broad strip of barren land at the sharp edge of a cliff.

Denthurion edged his mount over to the precipice and looked out into space. A caldera-like bowl had been cut into the side of this low mountain, the trees torn away, soil stripped off, bright white stone cut out in terrace after terrace, concentric steps leading down into the earth. At his side, Renko said, "Nyegrai marble—finest in the known universe."

They rode along the rim of the man-made canyon, then down an inclined trail cut diagonally across the terraced stone. From close-up Denthurion could see that the individual "steps" of the excavation tended to be between ten and twenty meters high. Gangs of sweating black men labored against the face of the stone, drilling, hammering, slicing away at the marble with things that looked like enormous chain saws amid a high-pitched power-tool roar. The air was filled with a fine mist of rock dust and the sweet, sharp tang of burned ethanol.

Down at the lowermost level of the pit, where marble slabs were being pulled vertically out of the ground by a small crane, they found a little encampment of sorts, a tent with a paramedic and emergency supplies, a little cookstove gang that proposed to feed the thousand and more workers of the quarry. Sitting astride a big, gray and white striped *loshad*, shouting what sounded like abusive orders to the crane operator, was a tall, thickset black man, dressed in the omnipresent *rabi* white. This one, though . . . an indefinable air of authority, the master of the house in his own domicile.

Denthurion listened carefully to the speech. Bantu. Probably the descendant of some Swahili-based trade language. Odd that it would get here . . . but the Zairean sweep had been a big one. Still, people plucked from the trans-Mitumba . . .

The man whirled his *loshad* as he heard them ride up, hooves cracking on stone louder than the putting, creaking groan of the crane, his look of concern swiftly changing to a beaming, obsequious smile. "Gospodin! An honor!" He bowed low in his saddle.

Renko gestured to the man. "Gospodin Denthurion, this is my *kulak*, Grigor Ndarya, chief of *Gulag Kalemi*, manager of the Renko Mines and Quarries Industrial Enterprise."

The man bowed again. "Pleased to make your acquaintance, Gospodin." There was a sudden snapping crash from the center of the pit and the *kulak* spun in his saddle, a look of fury taking over his features. The crane, transporting a big marble slab, had swung wide on its course, striking the side of the pit, breaking an entire corner off the valuable stone. Ndarya bowed sharply to Renko with a muttered "Excuse me," then turned his back on his master, shouting, "You there, Nyareri! *Down* from that crane!" He rode off to deal with the incident, switching to the native dialect, words booming and thumping from his chest.

As they watched him thrash the hapless crane operator with his riding crop, splashing droplets of blood on the man's white clothing, Denthurion said, "Nothing like him in the cities."

Renko smiled. "No. It wouldn't do, you see. The city folk are . . . effete. *Kulaki* belong in the countryside, with us."

"Do these other *rabi* speak Russki?"

Another smile. "Seldom. Household servants. Managers and native chieftains, yes. The rest have neither the need to know nor the opportunity to learn."

"How long do these people live?"

Renko shrugged. "How long do human beings live? My *rabi* have access to standard medical services. Maybe twelve or fifteen decades. I hadn't given it much thought." The bright blue eyes seemed untroubled by the question.

"And this Nydarya fellow. A hundred and fifty years for him as well?"

"Well, no. The *kulaki* are paid salaries for their special work. I give them passes on a regular basis. They can go to the regional medical centers for special treatment . . ."

"So?"

"Well, I promoted Grigor to his present position more than three centuries ago."

"So a *kulak* might live as long as a Kievan Rus?"

Renko laughed. "In principle. Yes, I suppose so. Grigor's predecessor might still be on the job had he not gotten under a piece of falling marble."

"An accident?"

The smiling eyes were shadowed. "I understand what you're getting at, Mr. Televox. No, not an accident. The *rabi* harbor grudges and resentments, just like other human beings. The *kulaki* make satisfactory targets."

"Do Rus ever have such accidents?"

"Of course not."

"Never?"

"We've had forty thousand years to teach the *rabi* what a mistake that is." He sat up straight in his saddle, suntanned and proud. "What would *you* do in our place?"

"I'm . . . familiar with the process of history, Gospodin Renko."

Midafternoon Olam was a darker, hotter version of the midmorning world. The sun was still high in the sky, but descending to the west, promising night in nothing but direction. Denthurion stood embedded in a small crowd, watching and listening. Wandering around at random, he found a little square to the north of Gaan Tashluum, dominated by a wooden dais, by the voices of men and women talking together.

Up on the platform, a slim, handsome young auctioneer described his wares: ". . . and now, gentlefolk, a fine lot of young Hodai, straight from the breeding grounds of Itaalki Farms in Pniym Province." A dozen of the little bipeds were led out in a coffle to stand side by side on the stage, bewildered, dark eyes glazed and uncomprehending. "The Itaalki factor, Mr. Shovaats, asks that the bidding be started at five hundred *gavishim* a head or five thousand for the lot."

Someone in the crowd whistled angrily and a woman near Denthurion muttered, "Must be good little poodles for all that!"

"Prospective purchasers come forward and make their inspections now," said the auctioneer.

Denthurion watched as men and women stepped out of the crowd and up onto the dais, descending on the hapless and frightened Hodai. There was a flurry of pawing, hands stroking fur, forcing mouths open to inspect little yellow teeth, poking at eyes and ears. One man went along the entire line of Hodai, making them bend over, inspecting their anuses, poking an index finger into their cloacalike genitals, admiring the fluid thus extracted, wiping it away on his handkerchief before going on to the next animal . . .

No, not *animal*, Denthurion reminded himself. It was hard to think of the Hodai as thinking beings when you saw them like this. Little remained of Olam before Man, the golden cities long ago ground away to dust, great highways no more than a few pieces of paving stone lost in the wilderness, seagoing cargo ships erased as if they had never been, nothing left but a few ancient digital images, nothing left, essentially, but the physical evidence of the Hodai themselves, up on the stage, bodies invaded, souls shrunken away to nothingness. Denthurion felt a faint burst of inner surprise. I'm starting to sound like some kind of naturopathic simpleton . . .

The bidding, once begun, was brisk, and soon the Itaalki factor was happily counting his seven thousand *gavishim*, the coffle being led away by their new owner, the cloaca-fingerer. A Hodai breeder, himself, perhaps. Or, something else.

He watched as the next lot was led out and the process more or less repeated. This batch were worker Hodai, big and muscular, and increasingly hard to sell. They went for less than two hundred *gavishim* a head, to their seller's disappointment. The woman near Denthurion said, "What does he think? Who uses Hodai for *servants* anymore?"

The next batch were glossy-coated household pets and the talking woman bought two herself, young females barely out of kittenhood, frightened, staring about wide-eyed. The woman took them away in her arms, cooing in their ears, nuzzling her face between their astonished heads.

All right, you're seeing this and somehow not taking in any meaning. Yet you keep *seeing* these Hodai. Think. Denthurion watched the auction proceed through lot after lot, yet found himself unable to make any logical connection. Have you seen something like this before? Of course you have. Human slaves. Animal slaves. Even other enslaved alien intelligences. Why does this seem different? Odd.

All right. Make the connection then. When did you first see sentient nonhuman beings under the yoke of humanity ... Hmm. So many worlds. Too much time. I may need to consult *Naglfar* ... No. Wait. Of course ...

Vinylhaven ... of the Gnaw-Xhan ...

So *long* ago. Almost lost in the mists of childhood ...

The eleventh incarnation of Maaron Denthurion, mark One, stood alone in a dark and enormous wood, creeping among the roots of vast and ancient trees, lost in a gloomy twilight world. Soon enough. Soon enough. He could hear a snuffling sound in the distance, slowly growing closer.

I suppose I had to come here, he thought, remembering his mother's furniture. Odd, how the petty things of childhood clung to you for all eternity. Maybe not, though. My eternity is just begun, my first century hardly expended. Who knows how I'll feel in a thousand years, or fifty thousand. I don't know who I'll be, or even how many . . .

The great trees of Vinylhaven, bases a hundred meters and more in diameter, towered into the darkness overhead, trunks disappearing toward a remote and cloudy canopy that, by itself, determined the climate of this entire world. The snuffling grew louder and Denthurion pulled his weapon from his shoulder, checking its gauges. It was just an old-fashioned lasgun, based on the military weapons Cpaht's men had used, able to project a five-megawatt beam of coherent X rays in millisecond bursts. He thumbed the charge button and listened to the condenser's fifteen-kilohertz whine. In less than a second a violet light, invisible to Vinylhaven's denizens, winked on. Ready.

What the Hell are you *doing* here, Televox? Well. Paid your licensing fee. Picked up your legal weapon, and walked off alone into the jungle. So. Here you are. Now what?

There was a sharp scrape from far overhead and a little debris, mostly bark and leaf fragments, began to rain down. Denthurion aimed the lasgun straight up into the darkness and lined his right eye up with the ambient light grid. A gray-green shadow world appeared before him, bounded in a tiny square.

"Good God . . ." he whispered. You saw pictures of them, even PsychImp tapes, but it was meaningless.

The Gnaw-Xhan clung to the side of the tree, a thousand meters overhead, a fat slug of shiny brown leather more than a hundred fifty meters long. Its jaws were scraping against the bark, *crunch, crunch, crunch* . . . Something screamed, briefly, as it was sucked out of its hole and down the immense gullet. The thing turned and began rippling slowly down the trunk on its powerful belly-foot, stalk-mounted ears sliding over the bark as it listened for its prey, stalk-mounted eyes gazing out into the darkness, searching the environment, soaking up infrared radiation.

All right. Make your decision *now*, before it sees you ... Too late. A score of Gnaw-Xhan eyes swiveled in his direction. The beast stopped, staring down at him, probably estimating its chances. No way to avoid the lasgun beam, no cover big enough to slide behind, not in time, anyway ...

Aroooooo ...

Long, eerie cry. Death challenge. I am lost. Go with me into Hell, demon!

The Gnaw-Xhan slid forward, accelerating down the tree trunk, belly-foot keeping a tenuous hold. Aroooo ... Good God. It was like a starship falling on him out of the night.

He took careful aim and triggered the lasgun. The forest around him lit up with brilliant violet light, *snap*, a flashbulb going off, almost-invisible beam, no more than excited, fluorescing air, arrowing into the creature's side, then gone, darkness once more, no afterimages.

OWWWWW ... The Gnaw-Xhan's anguished bellow filled his head. It grabbed the tree, almost coming to a stop, writhing momentarily, then it started down again, close to releasing its grip, closing the gap with maximum speed, leaving spots of dark blood wherever it touched. The condenser whined and he fired again. Another lancing flashbulb.

OWWWWW ... It let go of the trunk and fell, screaming, snarling alien words. OWWWWW ... Denthurion shrank between two big roots, cowering down into the thick leaf mold, hoping it wouldn't fall on him. The ground surged, bouncing him into the air as the thing hit no more than fifty meters away.

When he regained his feet, thankful for not losing the lasgun, the ruined hulk towered over him, twitching, rolling slightly from side to side, tail tip thrashing in the distance. He walked around to the head and looked. Some of the eyes were gone, torn away by the impact, but many remained, lit by an inner fire, looking up at him with an unquenchable fury. "Owwwww ..." it whispered to him. "Owwwww ..."

Denthurion lifted his rifle, the condenser's whine loud in his ear, and fired again, right into the bright nest of eyes. The thing spasmed and screamed, then lay still on the forest floor.

"God damn you, human," it burbled at him, and died.

Denthurion stood for a long time looking down at the Gnaw-Xhan, considering the matter, but there was nothing more to conclude. Finally, he marked the carcass's location on his inertial compass for later retrieval, and walked off into the steady, dim light of a twilit world. Exit incarnation eleven, he thought. Time to move on.

Toward evening, the sky of Olam was burnished brass overhead, the sun a bloated red ball bisected by the edge of the world. Denthurion, pleasantly tired, walked down a side street in the western sector of Perax, musing, letting the day's wandering replay inside his head. A world was a complex place, layer on layer of detail, hard to understand, even for one trained to the task. Ten thousand real-time years since I left old Earth, two score subjective millennia of experience ... And yet this one city tended to defy definition. Maybe the task of Metastability is hopeless. Are there a million habitable worlds in our quarter of the galaxy? We don't even know anymore.

A hunger pang scratched for his attention, manifesting as a slight, itching ache under the ribs of his left side. All right. Dinnertime? Home? No. Keep on going ... He pictured Kartavilis and the others, frantic with worry, calling out the Guard and combing the city. What, they must wonder, would happen to officials who managed to lose a Televox? The ironic answer was, of course, nothing. It's happened before, even to me. The memory of *la-*

cunae pulled at him softly. Memory? No. Just an empty place where memory ought to be.

He strolled down a narrow alleyway and stopped before a good-smelling storefront bearing a little red and black sign: *Davaar Adomm*. Not too auspicious, but then, what is? He pushed open a slatted wooden door and went in.

The tavern was full of men and women, sitting at little tables, sitting at the bar. The air over their heads was foggy, a mixture of illegal smokes and the tangible smells of cooking steam. There was laughter here and a low growl of conversation. Well. No harm in this.

There were no waitresses here, but a serving line formed to the left of the bar. He stood behind the last customer, waiting his turn, staring up at a grease-spotted menu posted on the wall. Eventually: "Let's see. I'll have a *maak-gdolaa*, *tapuwax adamaa tsorfaati*, and, mmm . . . a Blackstyle beer." The fat woman behind the counter shoveled steaming food onto a plate and took his money.

Well. The stuff certainly had a *smell* to it. He backed away from the counter, clutching plate and bottle, and wandered around the edges of the room until he found a table with an unoccupied chair. He stood behind it, looking down at a pair of beefy, red-faced men, eyes hazy with food, drink, and smoke. "Do you mind?"

One of the men waved him into the chair. He sat, unwrapping the food, focusing at first on his plate. Bread, meat, bits of minced vegetable. There was a shine of grease on the bread crust and some kind of thick red sauce oozed from the sides of the sandwich. He took a bite and almost choked on the heavy flavor. Garlic and onion stench assailed his nostrils, cutting right through the greasy meat smell. He washed the mouthful down with a sip of beer, grateful for the clean, bitter taste of the alcohol.

One of the men was looking at him oddly. "Not quite to your taste?"

Denthurion shook his head. "Too big a bite. I was hungry."

"Got to watch that, friend. Folks have died that way." He held out a big, moist-looking hand. "Name's Bohaanan; this is my old *zuug* Tanar."

Denthurion shook the hand, which was as sweaty as it looked. "Ah, Mahalets, here."

The man grinned thinly. " 'Corkscrew'? That a nickname?"

Denthurion nodded.

"People used to cal me Shohr—'ox'—but I got old and flabby and it died out. How'd you get a name like Corkscrew?" He looked over Denthurion's muscular frame. "You a fighter?"

Denthurion nodded, relieved. His imposed physical conditioning was a little out of place here . . . but illegal combat sports were widespread in the galaxy, enough to explain away much of the difference.

"Never saw you around here before. You from Perax?"

"No. Just visiting."

"Looking for a match?" Bohaanan and Tanar looked at each other, filled with dawning surmise.

Denthurion shrugged. "Maybe."

"Well. I might be able to do something for you. I've got some friends . . ." He looked at the mess in Denthurion's plate. "No wonder you gagged. You shouldn't be eating that crap."

"I'm sort of on vacation."

"Where you from?"

So. You keep backing yourself into these little corners, Mr. Televox. Where *are* you from, Mr. Fighting Man? "Up north."

You could see the wheels turning in little provincial minds. Sort of on vacation . . . a fighter from the outback, on the run from, what? The law? Hooligan promoters? An injured adversary's kindred? Didn't matter. This could be a money-making opportunity. "Stick around, Corkscrew. We'll find something for you."

He dug into his meal, eating the fried *tapuwax* strips slowly, sipping his beer, listening to the two men talk about the details of the local prize- and club-fighting scenes. It was interesting, but . . . not exactly what he'd come for. He drained the dregs from his bottle, and said, "We're hearing a lot about Starship up north."

Bohaanan looked at him oddly again. "*Koxavonia*? That's a silly thing for a fighter to be interested in."

"I'm interested."

The man's lips twisted bitterly. "Yeah, so's my fucking wife. More interested in the Starship than my dick, sad to say."

"Wish those cocksuckers'd get the Hell out of here," interjected Tanar. "Messing with people's heads, that's what."

"People up north think it's a pretty good thing."

Bohaanan waved to the woman behind the bar, some kind of complex hand signal, and three bottles of beer came tumbling through the air to be caught, one after another, and plunked down on the table. "Assholes around here think the same way. Not me, though."

"No?"

"You listen to me, chum. It's all bullshit. Crewing on the Starship of God, for pity's sake!" He shook his head angrily. "Leave that outer space stuff to Governors and their Guardsmen. Far as I'm concerned, Olam *is* the universe."

"Never been curious about the other worlds? Not even a nearby one like Kem?"

"I can't *go* there. Why should I care about places I'll never see?"

"Well . . ."

"All this *Koxavonia* shit does is fuck with people. My wife. People's kids wandering off . . . They can keep it."

Denthurion popped the cap off his beer and took a long swallow. It was some other, sweeter brand, not as Earth-like as either Blackstyle or Two Horses. "You're the first person I've heard with anything bad to say."

"Yeah ... Hell." Bohaanan fell silent for a minute, then said, "Where you staying tonight?"

Denthurion shrugged noncommittally. "I'll find someplace."

"Come home with me. You'll learn more'n you want to know about that Starship crap. Levanaa can't keep her fucking mouth shut for two consecutive minutes."

Go home with a real Olamite? That's about the best I can hope for. On the other hand ... by morning there'll be panic in the streets ... "All right."

Bohaanan clapped him on the shoulder. "Good-oh!" They went on talking a while longer, drinking down the sweet beer, then finally rose to go. "You coming, Tanar?"

"Sure. I got no wife to go home to."

"Heh. You're not missing much. Come on." They made their way through a sea of men and tables and on out into the night.

Across the alleyway from the tavern door stood a bulky man, clutching a thick rod in one hand, rawhide thong wrapped around his knuckles, clapping it against the palm of the other. "Well," he said. "Mr. Televox, I presume."

Bohaanan and Tanar shrank back suddenly. "This guy after you, Corkscrew?" Their fear was almost palpable in the darkness, faced by an obviously dangerous hooligan.

The big man laughed softly. "Corkscrew? How inventive."

"Just hit him, Gili," said a voice out of the darkness. "Get it over with."

"As you say." The man took a step forward, lifting the rod over his head. "Bend your head down and I won't have to hit so hard." The rod started to descend.

So. Denthurion reached up and caught the stick with his palm, stopping it. Gili grunted with surprise, then started to scream as the rod was twisted, breaking its rawhide thong and dislocating the bones of his big hand. Denthurion pulled the thing away, noticing abstractedly that it was a big, smooth wooden stick, then he rapped the handle into Gili's mouth, extracting shattered teeth, feeling it grate against the bones of his hard palate. Gili's head banged against the stone wall and he fell to the pavement, breath a soft, bubbling wheeze.

"God," said another voice from the darkness. "Good God!"

"Shut up," said the first voice. "He can't take us all."

Tossing the club aside, Denthurion sank into a slight crouch, knees bent, hands cupped before his abdomen, about level with the bottom of his rib cage. Dark forms were gathering about him in the night, ten, maybe twelve bodies outlined against the lesser dark of the walls. So. Not impossible odds. He listened as his heart rate came up to a steady 120 beats, the prelaunch stage for fight-or-flight biochemistry, sharpening his senses, recalling synaptic training.

"Your little friends are gone, Mr. Televox."

It was true. Bohaanan and Tanar had disappeared back behind the closed door of the Davaar Adomm bar and grill. Didn't count on *them*, of course, but they don't know that . . .

"We can take you, sir. Easy or hard. Your choice."

Very polite. They know who and what I am. "Don't count on it, friends."

"I see. Gili didn't even make you breathe hard, did he?"

"No. You won't either." But his breath was deepening nonetheless, oxygenating his tissues for the coming battle.

"Well. We figured you were pretty smart, Mr. Televox, but . . . have it your way. Pick up some rocks, boys." The dark figures bent down, picking up loose cobbles and bits of debris. "See? Don't have to live forever to be smart. Just have to *be* smart, that's all."

Denthurion ducked the first stone that came his way, but two more flew by, the second one striking him in the middle of the forehead, obliterating the world in a flash of white light.

Second Canto

Entia non sunt multiplicanda sine necessitate.

Entities should not be multiplied
without necessity.

—William of Ockham, his razor

Chapter 6

A heavy smell in his nose came first. No light, no dark . . .
Gray? Impossible to determine. Sightlessness had the
quality of velvet. What *was* that smell? Copper? Improbable. Seaweed? Ridiculous. No seaweed on Olam . . .

"Watch it! You're bumping his fucking head on the
stairs!"

"Who gives a fuck? Gili's *dead*! I'd like to put this bastard over the railing. Headfirst." The voices sank to a distant rumble, echoes from the bottom of a deep mine.

Thump. Thump. Thump. Hollow sounds. A block of
soft wood bouncing off stone. The smell got stronger. The voices rustled, pattering like rain as they came
back.

"Careful, for God's sake! You've opened up his cut."

"I don't *give* a shit! Gili's dead . . ."

Thump. Stillness, the smell waxing into a distinct itch.

"Listen to me, asshole. We can't make this a personal
thing. I'm sorry your brother's dead, but . . ."

Denthurion tried to focus on the velvet voices, but a
sharp whining began to buzz in his ears, two-toned, simultaneously rising and falling, crossing frequencies with
a brief heterodyne. A sound now to go with the peculiar
smell. And what is this sound? An electric drill . . . Into
my head . . . They're drilling into my head! Momentary
panic made his heart race, the sound and smell waxing
together. No. Impossible. What about the pain? A splinter started up somewhere above his eyes . . . Eyes? No.
No eyes. But the drill . . . The pain sharpened, pulsing
back into his head, echoing off the bones of his skull.

The voices came back with a roar, batting the pain

around, angry voices, arguing, then the world appeared abruptly, rising out of a black mist, focus swiftly sharpening.

"Shit! He's awake!"

Denthurion surged off the splintery wooden steps, feet pressed together, arms twisted behind his back, and fell over on one side. Wrong way. Back. Fall *through* the railing, down into the darkness.

Strong hands grabbed the front of his shirt and slammed him back down, head making its hollow-wood sound on a sharp-edged riser. The pain echoed once, driving through his brain, rebounding from the occiput and back out through his eyes, decorating the night with bright flashes.

A pale and shadowy face swam before him, eyes pools of night, mouth a flickering oval. "We've got you, *Mister* Televox. Securely tied. Trussed up like a mad Hoda on its way to the furnace. Got you, and we intend to keep you."

Mad Hoda on its way to the furnace ... The imagery clicked into place. Something sharp trickled into his left eye, blinding him. Denthurion shook his head, trying to clear it, then groaned and lay still. The pain from his forehead was dying down swiftly, trained nerves doing their job of reintegration ...

The shadow face before him laughed softly. "Hurts, eh?" The oval flattened and became toothy. "Good. It took Gili fifteen minutes to die, while we carried you both. I bet he hurt a lot worse."

Denthurion blinked his eyes hard, triggering tears to wash the blood away. He tipped his head slightly to one side, letting the blood flow over his cheek and funnel down his neck.

The face above him, crisp now, leered. "Look at the sorry bastard cry!"

Denthurion's voice was a thick and gluey rasp. "Blood's making my eyes water ..."

A sudden slap drove his head to one side, spraying black droplets. "*Cry*, damn you! Gili cried ..."

"For God's *sake*, Nahhag! It's not a personal thing . . ."

"My ass."

Denthurion waited for the pain echoes to damp down. It was happening faster with each passing second, and he could feel a scab starting to re-form on his forehead. "Making a mistake."

Nahhag looked down at him sharply. "What did you say?"

"You're making a serious mistake, boys. This is no little demonstration you're pulling off. They'll kill you for this . . ."

A babble of other voices, at least the ten—nine? eleven?—that he knew about, out of which there was a clear, "He *knows*! How the fuck does he know who we are?"

Nahhag scowled. "Fuck. He *doesn't* know. Just fishing."

Denthurion essayed a crooked smile. "Execution, boys. Think about it. What a sorry end for *Shearah* . . ."

Nahhag slapped him hard across the face, starting a new stream of blood, spilling more light into the darkness, little receding flickers that danced awhile and were gone. "Shut *up*!"

"Come on. Let's get him inside."

Denthurion tensed his body, feeling muscle tissue snake across his back and up over his shoulders.

"What the *fuck* . . ."

There was a loud report as the bonds around his wrists snapped and his arms came free, whipping around his sides, numb but functional. His legs stuck together, caught at an awkward angle, still tightly bound.

"Hey . . ."

He brought his fist up and struck hard into the shadowy oval still hanging over him, felt nose bones crush under his hand, blood spraying out over the man's ears. Nahhag went over backward, boneless, and fell, carrying someone else down the stairs with him in a shouting tangle of limbs. Denthurion rolled right, through the railing, down into the darkness.

Facedown. Facedown. Arms outspread, legs together, no choice about that. Long fall? No. He hit the ground, trying to take the shock on his arms, failing, his forehead banging on the pavement. Pain echoed like the ringing of a bell.

"Gods ... He's *loose!*" Voices were echoing from all around.

Denthurion thrust himself upright, struggling to break the bonds around his legs. No use. No time. He turned and began hopping away into the darkness, just around one corner, anything ...

Something hit him on the back of the head, gonging the pain back into preeminence. He turned, head ringing, unable to think, and faced his attacker. Shadows and pale ovals, swimming at him out of a red-tinted night ... The whatever it was hit him over the head again and he went down. A sharp wedge of pain drove into his side, spreading ribs briefly. One last coherent thought: The bastards are kicking me ...

The whatever it was thumped against his shoulder, followed by a second kick in the ribs. "Hit him again! Hit him again!"

A rain of blows fell, one after another, a succession of triphammer jolts, pushing him back down into a soft velvet world in which pain did not exist. The voices became an incomprehensible roar, then a mutter, rain pattering on dry grass, a whisper, then nothing. All that remained was that sharp, coppery smell, then, in a little while, not even that.

The ice was crisp, yet slick as oil, clear, looking out into the darkness beyond. A world out there ... No. Nothing. His point of view rotated, expanding, until he was at the center of a 360-degree field of view, spinning ... No. End over end ... No. Three-axis rotation, chaotic elements creeping in, his field of view becoming three-dimensional . . .

Lost. No. Just back in the ice . . . No. Back in the dream. Warm. Comfortable. Secure in my bed. Just dreaming . . . that same cool nightmare of a hundred thousand sleeps . . .

Call out to God . . . Clouds passing swiftly over a brilliant crescent Moon . . . Freezing . . . freezing. Demons closing in on me . . . Odin! Save me! No. Whom? Ah. OTANN . . .

Fall, then. Where? Downward. Downward. Into the past . . .

The darkness accelerated past him, viewpoint descending, wind whistling through ectoplasm. The light below grew, enveloping, ruddy with the light of a billion cool flames. Warmth, comfort, safety . . .

Heart banging like a distant kettledrum, Denthurion regained consciousness all at once, pain ripping his forehead like a broken saw blade, alternately sharp and dull, cutting his head into two unequal parts. He kept his eyes shut for a moment, struggling to gather shards of thought from different obscure mental corners, light a red-gray haze on the other side of papery eyelids. He moved slightly.

Arms behind my back, stretched around the back of a chair, wrists tight together. Legs down and apart, tied separately to the legs of the chair. Very uncomfortable.

The chair was wood, perhaps, the seat hard and flat against his buttocks, slightly sculpted, suggestive but not vulgar . . .

There was a rustling sound from the middle distance, then sharp footsteps, leather boot heels on an uncarpeted floor, echoing from the walls of a small room. A broad hand fell on the crown of his head, thumb on forehead, lifting his face up, more toward the light, making him flinch involuntarily where it skirted the edge of his pain.

"Awake, then." The voice was a light, pleasant baritone, unaccented Olamite, edged with a soft burr, a hint of natural roughness.

Denthurion opened his eyes, the lids separating with only the slightest touch of gumminess, rolling up across an expanse of cornea and disappearing from his awareness. The light from the room's electroluminescent panels sharpened his headache briefly, then faded.

"Welcome back, Mr. . . . Televox."

The face hanging over him was round and smooth, chin lined by a short, somewhat-patchy beard, brown eyes bright, yet heavy-lidded. Head-cloak absent, he wore his hair long, drawn sharply back into a ponytail, short, white scar interrupting the hairline, slightly off center. The man was smiling slightly, eyes shifting back and forth, the overall effect one of secret amusement.

"Nothing to say? Well." He released Denthurion's head and straightened up, folding his arms across a barrel chest. "They call me Naamer, Mr. Televox. I am what passes for a leader in the *Shearah* Rebellion."

Naamer . . . He searched his implanted memory briefly, pleased to find it still intact. Some kind of Olamitic carnivore, big and ugly, preying on the large herbivores that lived in the string of tropical swamps south of the Ashpaa Sea. As he watched, Naamer brushed a hand over his hair. The movement set a small earring, worn in his left ear, to swinging rapidly. Denthurion focused on it briefly, some kind of small yellow crystal, topaz perhaps, embedded in a copper disk. Finally, he said, "Sorry I beat up your friends."

That brought a slight frown, brief, quickly replaced by blandness. "I was impressed. I sent twelve men to capture you, Mr. Televox. Now two of them are dead and another has broken ribs and a concussion. I never imagined you'd be this tough."

Denthurion stretched in his bonds and smiled, willing a stab of pain into the background. "No? Your imagination seems to have very strict limits then, Mr. Naamer.

I'd be interested in hearing what you hope to achieve by this madness. Other than your own destruction, of course . . ."

Naamer stroked his patchy beard for a moment, staring at his captive, then said, "Bold. Surprising. I imagine you think you've got some secret power over us. You don't, though."

"That imagination is betraying you . . ."

Naamer turned away, stepping across the room and opening the door. "He's awake."

There was a rustle from the other room, compounded of voices, stirring bodies, hard shoes on another bare floor. Denthurion stretched again in his bonds, which felt like some kind of insulated wire, and took in his circumstances.

The room was small, perhaps five meters long, no more than two and a half wide, rough plaster on three walls, the fourth a long one of pale, crumbly-looking brick. His chair was in one corner, between the long brick wall and the short plaster one that had the room's lone tan-curtained window. He tried to listen beyond the sounds of the people crowding into the room, for street sounds, a hint of noise from other apartments. There was nothing.

Focus. Focus on these people.

Naamer was back before him, the others clustered around, looking over his shoulders, over each other. There was no inconsiderable amount of fright here. One face, bruised, bandaged above a tightly strapped chest, glared at him from puffy, blackened, pain-filled eyes. Denthurion smiled at him. "Good day to you, sir. Do I look worse or better?"

Naamer's lips twisted briefly to one side. "Much better, Televox." He glanced at his circle of friends, then said, "There's no point in bravado, or further verbal game playing. We have you and we mean to follow our plan."

"Or kill you . . ." muttered the bandaged man.

Naamer said, "Enough, Kerren."

Denthurion shifted to a more vertical position, as stiff and upright as his bonds would allow. Seeing him helpless, fear was fading from the faces that surrounded him, signs of boldness and determination welling up from obviously young personalities. He scanned their faces, memorizing, then looked down into the shadows between them. Three, no four Hodai ... No collars, but what appeared to be belts and straps of some plant-derived material.

Naamer said, "Don't you have any curiosity about ..."

"I can hazard a guess at what you want, Naamer." He smiled at the man again. "You have political aims of some kind; now you'll hold me hostage to achieve them, or threaten to turn me over to Kerren, and your friend Gili's kindred."

"And Nahhag ..." muttered Kerren.

"No curiosity about what those aims are?"

Denthurion shrugged. "Human curiosity enough, but ... it really doesn't matter. Release me and you'll be caught and sent to prison. Kill me and *Naglfar* will send down another incarnation of the Televox Denthurion in the morning. You'll have gained nothing but death for yourselves and a global restructuring for the people of Olam." He chuckled, a single, short sound. "Something which may happen in any case."

Naamer reached behind his back and unsheathed a long, slim knife, whipping it around, light glittering on a blue-tinted blade, moving it in a short arc that ended at Denthurion's throat, sharp edge just breaking the skin, blood an itchy trickle on his neck.

"Well, Televox." He smiled gently. "I can *see* your fear ... making a lie out of that pretty speech."

Denthurion leaned forward slightly, digging the knife blade in a little deeper. "The fact that I've died before and will die again doesn't make me view the prospect with equanimity, child. Whether you kill me or not is immaterial. The consequences will come from elsewhere, now."

Eyes shifting uneasily, Naamer pulled the knife away from Denthurion's throat, wiping it on his shirt and resheathing the clean blade. "I don't believe you, Televox."

"Then do what you will." Denthurion felt his heart thudding in his chest and willed it to slow down. No point in this. No point. Either compel him to end it now or go on, think if you can escape with a cargo of information . . . Decide.

Naamer stood up straight, hands on hips, eyes troubled. "You're not what I expected, Televox."

"Sorry. Tell me what you expected and I'll try to oblige."

"Sarcasm won't help."

"What will?"

The man looked at his friends, at their mingled expressions of anger and confusion, then back at his captive. "That's an odd thing for you to say, Televox. What . . ."

Denthurion broadened his smile, willing it to fill with sincerity. "*Your* fate is sealed, Naamer. The best you and your little friends can hope for is long prison terms. But . . . you have me here now, a captive audience. Regardless of the punishment you earn for yourselves, if your aims are just, they may yet win out . . ."

"What the fuck are you saying?" Naamer's eyes had become narrow and suspicious, his former air of superior, detached amusement vanished.

"Well. Think what I am. The Televox comes, bearing the authority of the whole Metastable Order. He sees that there is some serious cultural deficit on Olam. His right *and* duty is to set things straight. Suppose you tell me what's wrong here. Tell me what made you throw your lives away."

"He's *lying* to us!" hissed Kerren.

"Think again." He stared into Naamer's eyes. "You *seem* like an educated man . . . Remember what the

Saints of Disorder used to say? 'God will forgive me,' they used to say, 'It's his job.' " And there are the signs I was looking for ... Snap. Naamer and the whole of *Shearah* lock into their place in this vast Olamitic puzzle. He felt a faint twinge of disappointment. What was I hoping for? Something more ... interesting? Saints of Disorder, then ... Boys dreaming of a different age, when things could be different, somehow. Huss and Wycliff and King and the whole array of men and women martyred by Cpaht: *Ours is the pain and the travail, the wind and rain in the fields* ... "I'm like that God, Naamer. Regardless of what happens, or how I feel, it's my job to listen. Your evidence is no less valid than anything those fine, self-satisfied men in the Amud could say. Or my own vaguely incompetent Governor Kartavilis."

Snap. Sold. Naamer rubbed his beard again, eyes doubtful, entropy eating his determination. "You're just not what I expected ..." He looked at his comrades, searching their faces, then turned back to the Televox. "You know that the Amud must fall?"

Denthurion nodded.

"Why are you opposed to us, then?"

"That's my job, too."

"I don't understand you, Televox. If you realize the whole system on Olam is rotten, why don't you just go out and pull it down, give us the freedom we need?"

Freedom. What will he say when I begin to laugh? "I will pull it down, Naamer. Or someone will, in the not-too-distant future. And when that happens, the whole idea of freedom will vanish. What was your dream, then?"

Naamer's voice was slightly subdued. "There was a world once, before Cpaht, before the Metastability, when men were free to dream. Here on Olam we'd like to"—he waved a hand helplessly between them—"start dreaming again."

Pathetic. Red Millennium trash. "So. You thought

you'd kidnap me, someone visibly more important than the entire authority structure of Olam, and, what, force the resignation of the present Amud Council?"

"It seemed like a good place to start." Naamer's voice was hardening with renewed defiance.

"Then?"

"Freedom, Mr. Televox. Men ruled by their own laws."

Don't laugh. He still has that knife . . . "What about the Metastatic Guard? What about your Planetary Governor?"

"Why should they interfere, so long as Olam is calm and competently run?"

"Surely you can't be *that* naive. Our Governor is a rather staunch supporter of the Amud regime . . ."

The man's anger was palpable. "But . . . what about the *rules*, Mr. Televox? Why should he support incompetence and greed when . . . when . . ."

Denthurion smiled again. "I am the rules, Naamer. Without me, Governor Kartavilis has only his own flawed conscience." He shrugged in his bonds. "And you forget the scale of the human Metastable Order. Let us assume you overthrow the Amud, and the Guard. Let's even suppose you somehow defeat the forces available to *Naglfar.* We will come again. And again. And again. Until *things* on Olam are however we wish. The universe is against you now, Naamer. You can't . . ."

There was a sudden clatter from the floor and then one of the Hodai, male from its upright, tufted ears, was standing on the chair between his legs, clawed toes against the cloth that surrounded his testicles. The little being grabbed the front of his tunic, leaning close, sour breath washing over his face and filling his nostrils. "Humans call me Shgiah, Televox. My name is Sessiri-wohnith." Its voice was thin and harsh, a little deeper than he'd anticipated.

So. A new element. Surprised? Maybe not. "Interesting. Why *mistake*?" The Hoda's eyes were ringed brown on brown, in subtly differing hues, its stubby teeth tinted blue.

"You seem pretty smart. I made the name up myself. You figure it out."

"I think I can do that." The hair on the back of his neck suddenly prickled atavistically. "What's your interest in this affair?"

The Hoda hissed through its teeth, spitting gummy saliva onto his cheek. "You're not stupid, Televox. I don't have your history, nor your buttons to push. Human culture is meaningless to me."

Denthurion grinned at it. "I think not, Mr. -wohnith. Is that the correct shortened form? Twenty-five thousand years. How much Hoda culture is left?"

It grated, "Enough."

"What will you do when the Amud has fallen? Overthrow humanity? Kick us off Olam? We beat the Hhurull. What chance will you have?"

The Hoda clasped his face between its hands. "We called our world *Suuwurith*, Televox. 'Happiness.' "

Naamer tugged the Hoda gently away from him and lifted it down to the floor. "The Hodai have a place in our plan, Mr. Televox. Maybe they helped cause it. You've seen how they are treated. But they're thinking beings, not dogs and cats. When we make our Rule of Law ... Hoda like -wohnith will help build the new world."

There was a rustle from the back of the room as someone came through the door. "Daylight coming. We'd better move on."

Naamer suddenly looked tired. "Right. Let's get everything together. Kerren, get your rifle." He looked down on Denthurion. "I'm going to untie your legs now, and pull you out of the chair. If you try anything, Kerren will shoot your nuts off."

"You'd better tell him to kill me."

Naamer looked at him dubiously. "Maybe so, Mr. Televox. It's become easier for me to believe that you'd pocket whatever was left of your testicles and kill us all bare-handed . . ."

On the late afternoon of his two hundredth birthday, Metastatic Senator Maaron Denthurion strolled slowly down one of the grassy streets of Helium, moccasin-shod feet whispering over spongy, drying grass. It was getting cool now, an early-evening breeze raising occasional patches of gooseflesh on his bare legs. Time, soon, to get out the leggings, jackets and trousers to follow. Winter still came early at this latitude, though the epoch was warming. They couldn't move the capital, because Helium was . . . Helium. With time, though, the climate would make its way here.

He looked up, toward the west, where the fat orange sun was falling down among the tall buildings, slanted rays splashing angular shadows on the street, then at his wristwatch. Time to stop this woolgathering and finish off the day's work. He walked to the corner, where a public transceiver booth stood, small picowave dish pointed at its cellsat. He stepped in, let the door slide shut, and said, "Home, please." An element of the city's nervous system looked into the cubicle, triggering its teledyne net, boiling him away to Marumsko, a few dozen kilometers to the south.

In recent years, tiring of the city, Denthurion had taken up an abandoned villa not far from the old school grounds. It was on the rim of the valley, directly opposite the crashed police cruiser, a few thousand meters uphill from the Carthoradis estate. From its deck, when he looked, he could see his parents' home on the far slope.

He stepped out of the antique latticework transceiver booth into a gloomy living room decorated in a brown and orange theme of smooth walnut and dyed cotton cloth, moccasins almost soundless on a tan carpet. The house had a fair amount of tinted glass along its southern side, ruddy light sloping in, young willow trees outside making a maze of chaotic shadows. They'd been in the ground less than twenty years, but their trunks were already thick, roots systems spreading. Time soon to 'dyne them out of the earth, send them away to an appropriate forest, and put in new saplings ...

He went into his study and sat down in the soft, high-backed chair, propping his feet on the desk, and said, "House."

A comeye unfurled from the desktop, becoming a slim, red-skinned homunculus a little less than a meter tall, clad in leather straps and feathered helmet. It waited patiently, watching him for cues.

"Status on *Waraqa*?"

The comeye bowed slightly, a bit of affectation, and folded its arms. "The ship is in its parking orbit, full engine-powerdown condition, manifests down-loaded to the planetary net, matrices downlinked."

"And for me?"

The little man smiled. "Sector Marshal Huduri's report on the Pleiadic Incident Set, as you expected, and a new overlay file from mark Three."

Three! Denthurion tensed slightly, taken by surprise. Another branching, only twenty years after the last. That was inordinately soon. Something ... interesting must have happened.

"There's also an update from mark Two," said the comeye.

"Mm. Link, then, and integrate ..."

"As you wish, Senator." The comeye faded out, then, after an appreciable pause, the room went with him, dropping away abruptly into a dark universe.

Denthurion listened for his heartbeat in the charcoal night, catching it, just briefly, before the sound and lights came up. A man scrolled into existence before him, smiling wryly, character lines radiating from the principal features of his face, Denthurion, but ... not.

"Mark Two here. As you might have guessed, there's been a spot of trouble." Behind him, an Earth-like planet spread itself across the black sky, blue ocean, bands of white cloud, here and there a green-gray-brown smudge of continental land. Mark Two gestured at the thing. "Torsdahn. One of the old colonies, about fifty parsecs out. Small, mixed population descended from Millennium-boundary colonists. Cpaht's fleet never made planetfall. Easy integration to the Order . . ."

Easy enough to know about. He'd never heard of Torsdahn, but then, there were thousands of old colony worlds within fifty parsecs of Earth.

Mark Two said, "No problems worth mentioning here, boring people leading ordinary lives. I'd been on Torsdahn for about six months, and was considering moving on, when . . ."

The manifestation of the overlay file wiped out of existence feetfirst, leaving the planet to hang by itself against a star-dusted backdrop, dominated by a slightly enlarged, more numerous Pleiades. Count heartbeats, two, three, four . . . Out of the corner of Denthurion's eye, a rat-bitten peanut drifted into view, tumbling slowly, dropping toward Torsdahn. The rock was silver-gray, a class M asteroid now more than a dozen kilometers down its long axis.

Too bad for Torsdahn . . . Earth, its comprehensive Red Millennium technology more or less intact, was protected from these encounters, as were the most important few hundred allopathic colonies. The rest . . . tough luck. A fully evolved terrestrial world, in a Tanner Stage Five solar system, could expect a major impact every ten to thirty million years. Given the size of the Metastability, that meant a colony world, somewhere, took one up the spout every generation. Still, interesting luck that brought *me* here to see it . . .

The rock grew tiny as it dropped toward Torsdahn's temperate north latitudes, almost disappearing, then . . . a small brilliant disk appeared against the face of the planet, red-hot embryo-bleme opening a little hole in the world. Not too bad. The rock was too little to crack into the planetary mantle ... a continental impact, besides, with reduced climatic effects ...

Count heartbeats, five, six, seven ... A pressure ring began to expand around the yellow-white plasma mass, propagating through the atmosphere at transsonic velocity, caught up with itself, trapped, sweeping the surface with a thousand-atmosphere overpressure, dropping, dropping ... At this stage, forests would be swept away, leaving bare rock behind. Only later would they merely lay down in the face of a terrible wind.

Back at the impact site, a hollow cone of debris was beginning to climb out of the atmosphere, inner jets heading for outer space, outer jets merely turning over, reversing stratigraphy in an instant, creating a fresh ejecta blanket for the surrounding, stripped terrain.

A fat little starship swept around the limb of the planet, engines flaring gaudy violet as it twisted frantically away from its deadly ground track, accelerating in the one-tenth megagravity range. Underneath, red-lit ground boiled away into lava and cities disappeared in puffs of oily steam.

Mark Two reappeared beside the planet, accelerating Torsdahn's time flow. The region around the impact darkened, forest fires breaking out all along the periphery of the zone of total destruction. A dark smudge spread outward from the crater, rock dust ground to flour and emulsified with the air, smoke sucked inward by the hot vacuum of the displaced atmosphere. In short order there was a black disk more than a hundred kilometers across covering the whole area.

"They couldn't have had worse luck. Taarus, Torsdahn's planetary capital, was only twenty kilometers from the impact. The government didn't even attempt to get away. Neither did our fine Planetary Governor ..."

Below, the smudge began to drift, taking on a teardrop shape, elongating, slowly at first, then faster, eddies breaking away, throwing the land below into night. In a matter of days, the cloud had gone completely around the world, filling an entire climatic zone, then spreading laterally, Hadley cells handing the dust over to each other. In a season it would cap the northern hemisphere and begin to spread south.

Mark Two said, "*Shan Hela*'s computer estimates the climatic adjustment time in excess of five years." The overlay smiled. "There are, of course, rules for dealing with this sort of thing." A second Denthurion scrolled into being beside him, motionless, eyes blank white fields. "Enter mark Three."

Denthurion nodded slowly to himself in the outer darkness. Rules, indeed. Mark Two wiped again and mark Three stood, waiting. Time, then, to uplink the overlay. The thought was the deed, and Denthurion felt himself fall forward through space, tipping abruptly down into a new and different life . . .

He stepped out of the transceiver and looked around. He was in some kind of large room, a terminal center perhaps, one wall lined with transceiver booths, the other a huge window, decorated by two long, irregular cracks. Outside . . . Dark, cold, blustery winds. The sky was totally overcast, black, the light levels about on a par with a moonless night on Earth, erratic wind scraping the bare branches of the trees against each other. Some kind of dust was blowing on the ground, black, like ash.

A green-clad, haggard-looking man stepped forward, offering his hand. "Welcome to Torsdahn, Your Grace. I am Captain Teyyahinn, commander of the surviving Guard contingents."

Mark Three greeted the man distractedly, still looking out into the windy night. In the distance, the lights of a large city could be seen above an invisible horizon, wan through a pall of smoke. Good. They still had power. Torsdahn maintained a fusion-based civilization akin to what had been on Earth in the boundary era. Good luck. Most colony worlds would have fallen into a nontechnological state in a matter of days. He clapped his soldier on the back, and said, "Let's go. Work to be done."

Captain Teyyahinn smiled weakly, glad to release his burden to a superior authority.

In the growing light of a dull dawn, they'd taken him to the outskirts of Perax, car sliding through a maze of back streets, avoiding major thoroughfares, getting out of the city and into the countryside with a minimum of contact. At one point, Denthurion had suggested stepping through a transceiver booth to some point nearer their destination, but . . .

"No. Our rather slim transmitter net is run by the Amud's computer system. If they're looking for you yet, they'll look there."

Finally, they were in the dooryard of a rather unkempt-looking farmhouse, the buildings weathered and overgrown with brush. While Kerren stood away from him, rifle pointed, he and Naamar watched the other men pull away loose, fading vegetation, liberating sweet smells into the morning air. Underneath was a black-painted machine, boxy cabin squatting on a tripod of wheels under a long, slim-bladed rotary wing.

Denthurion looked it over with interest. Old, old hovercar design. "Where did you get this thing?"

Naamer laughed, pleased at having elicited a response. "We've been ordering them from the autofactory, Televox. No one notices. It's called a *nahhash*, after the legless salamander of the Tuhhin River district . . ."

"I know what it is, Naamer. Your ingenuity in re-creating the Red Millennium's most effective aerial weapons platform is commendable."

Naamer laughed again.

When the brush was cleared away, they got into the machine, accompanied by three of the men. Naamer took the pilot's seat with Denthurion beside him, next to an open door, Kerren and two others in the back. "If you try anything, Kerren will push you out. Perhaps you'll survive the fall."

"I look forward to the experience with interest."

They were sitting in bucket seats before an elaborate instrument panel, radar and radionavigation equipment overhead, inertial guidance and engine monitors in front of their knees. Naamer had two controls at hand, a slim joystick sprouting between his legs, a larger one mounted at an angle to his left, itself burdened by additional controls and instruments.

"Is this thing armed?"

"There's a small particle beam weapon concealed in the nose." He looked over at Denthurion. "Just a welder/cutter with the governor disabled, hooked to the engine alternator system."

"That might work."

"It seems to."

Naamer reached out and punched a button in the center of the control panel. Various indicator lights and dials came on and the onboard computer screen displayed a sequence of terse sentences, status reports on the various systems. The design was more than primitive, dating back to a pre-OTANN technology.

Naamer said, "Power on." Various idiot lights winked to life.

"Engine start." There was the stuttering whine of a rotating electric motor, followed by a muted throbbing that died down quickly into a faint vibration in the hull.

After inspecting various cryptic dials and readouts, Naamer said, "All right. Engage rotor clutch." The big wing overhead began to turn, slowly at first, then faster, stirring the bushes around them, raising dust in the dooryard, climbing to a steady speed, accompanied by a sharp, pulsing slap of sound.

"Hmm. Collective pitch full low." Naamer thumbed the throttle with his left hand and the speed of the rotor began to build. "Three thousand engine, three hundred rotor. Good enough." He lifted the thick collective pitch control lever beside him with his left hand and the craft wobbled briefly, then lifted off the ground, climbing smoothly until it was hovering at about thirty meters, just above the tops of the surrounding trees.

Denthurion leaned out the door slightly, watching the remaining men run away from a malestrom of wind and dust, retreating to their car. Kerren's hand suddenly locked in his collar. He smiled over his shoulder. "Just looking. I won't jump."

"Let's go," said Naamer. He depressed the left rudder pedal and the *nahhash* turned about its axis, toward the northwest. When he pushed the cyclic control stick between his legs forward, the ship tipped obligingly, assuming a nose-down attitude, and began to accelerate, staying just above the treetops, vegetation whipping underneath at a quickening pace.

"Where are we going?"

Naamer grinned at him. "No place you'd know about, Mr. Televox. A long way."

Denthurion settled back in his seat, watching the trees slide by underneath, waiting for the Kemitish fauna to peter out and be replaced by the paler and yellower Olamitic stuff.

Interesting developments. More interesting than you could have hoped for. Is this a selfish attitude? Maybe not. These men must die in any case. You would have torn their world apart before you were done . . .

And in ten thousand years, or forty thousand, life becomes a flat and dreadful burden. If this incarnation survives . . . Well. Something for the memory fund.

Mountains began rising, blue on the horizon ahead. Naamer raised their altitude, allowing the world to spread out below with increasing detail. There was nothing but forest there. No roads, no houses. No fields. Just forest, cut through and through by narrow rivers. Beyond the mountains, he knew, lay the dry highlands of Olam, a land without cities, just a few mines and protosite factories, dotted here and there with the swiftly vanishing relics of the Hodai world that had died so long ago.

Interesting, that. What will I have to do? Change the human world of Olam, of course, but I knew that. What about the Hodai? Salvation? Dissolution? What do they deserve?

We'll see.

Below, the mountains spread out in cold and craggy relief.

Chapter 7

After they crossed the last exposed ridge of the Meirhhav Mountains the land flattened out again, opening up into a brown and dusty vista, barren wasteland sloping away from the foothills, complex patterns of eroded gullies becoming a hard-packed, stony desert, well away from water and rain. They swept down the decline, loosing altitude and speed, finally flaring out above a dry, bowl-shaped valley nearly a thousand kilometers from Perax.

Holding the *nahhash* in a steady hover, Naamer looked over at him. "Welcome to your new home, Mr. Televox."

As the ship began to descend, Denthurion leaned out the door, looking around and down. Not much to choose from. Backward, to the southeast, the looming gray line of the mountains, forward, farther inland, nothing but desert, dry and crusty dirt, then sand, increasingly hostile.

The valley itself, spreading out beneath them, dust beginning to rise in a vortex from the rotor's downward thrust, lay in a scrubby land that benefited from the last of the mountains' influence. There was a little central pool, evidence of a spring, and it was full of mixed vegetation, most of it the yellowish native flora. The *Shearah*, setting up housekeeping in tents and rude little cabins, had put in little gardens of terrestrial food plants, and scattered among them were patches of Kemitish flowering shrubbery.

Naamer pushed the collective down slowly and evenly, decreasing the lift from the rotor until the ship was sitting lightly on its undercarriage, blowing dirt in all directions, tent sides everywhere flapping vigorously, then he thumbed the throttle back and the blades slowed to neutral. Curious. The hum of the engine became a low groan, punctuated by a high-pitched sound as each rotor swept over the open door, almost like the chirp of some enormous bird. He disengaged the clutch and killed the engine, letting the rotor grind to a stop.

Looking out the door, Denthurion could see people emerging from their little shacks, walking over between rows of tents and buildings. The dust was settling quickly, back on footpaths and rooftops. He looked over at Naamer. "What do you call this place?"

The man seemed surprised. "We don't call it anything. Just . . . the Meirhhav camp."

-wohnith leaned forward between the sheets, head turned upward, eyes glittering dark. "It used to be called *Uukohwa*," he said. " 'Gateway.' "

After greeting their followers and settling him in a tent of his own, Naamer and -wohnith had stayed for the night, talking with him, trying to make sense of his position and win him over to their point of view, finally leaving instructions with the permanent residents of the camp, the conditions of his captivity. He was to remain in the camp, unbound but watched by the *Shearah* here, free to move about largely unrestrained.

"After all," said Naamer, preparing to board the *nahhash*, "what will you do? Run away into the desert? You're not a Hoda. Either we'd find you again, or you'd die. The nearest town is four hundred kilometers away, on the other side of the mountains; the nearest mantended industrial site is nearly that far in the other direction, on the other side of the Kikaar Erg . . ."

And there were no transceiver booths here, nor any other means of machine transport. Naamer and -wohnith climbed into the flyer, taking Kerren and the two others, waved to the people on the ground, and wafted away on their whirlwind into a pale blue sky, a sputtering dot that grew smaller and fainter, until it was gone.

Denthurion spent the balance of his first full day in the camp exploring the boundaries of this small world, climbing to the edge of the valley, and staring off across the desert, toward a parched and rubble-strewn horizon. To the northwest, the land grew ever flatter. No more than a few dozen kilometers away, he knew, lay the beginning of a very large dune field.

Southeast, back in the direction of Perax, the mountains towered blue and gloomy. The sun rose over them every morning under a reddish-yellow sky, leaving the camp in shadow for more than an hour each day. The Meirhhav were craggy and new, having risen sometime in the past few million years. The peaks were broken spires, Alpine in texture, on their way to Himalayan prominence.

Not too intolerable. The peaks were snowcapped, the bright glitter of glaciers visible here and there, but there would be many passes in a mountain range like that . . . So what do you do? You could walk back to Perax, through unknown terrain, in fifteen days; with luck find a town in three or four. Run? No. Follow this to its conclusion; at least follow it for a little while.

Down in the camp, they assigned him a moderately large tent for his personal use. His jailers seemed a little frightened by his presence, afraid to talk to him, or do anything but watch him uneasily. Perhaps they'd been told the circumstances of his capture by Kerren and the others. When he walked the rim of the valley, a couple of sturdy-looking young men followed him at a discreet distance. What will they do if I head out into the desert? They probably don't realize I can outrun them . . .

Toward evening, he'd seen everything available to him and was down at his tent, sitting in a folding chair before its entry flap. The sky overhead was turning a brilliant red, freighted with the day's cargo of desert dust. Lights were coming on here and there in the camp, each dwelling, like his own, equipped with a battery-driven electrical system, the whole camp wired together to a solar array on its southern rim.

This thing must really stand out from orbit. But Olam, despite its deep-space industries, was not given to orbital surveillance. Maybe *Naglfar* would notice it . . . But *Naglfar* was out at Adomm, inspecting the industrial matrix that powered Olam's civilization.

A slim young woman walked up, bearing a covered tray and a little folding table. She stopped before him, dark eyes wide and uncertain, waiting. Finally, Denthurion said, "Yes?"

"I . . ." She swallowed and started again. "I've brought dinner, Your Grace."

He smiled and shrugged. "Thank you."

She set up the folding table before him and set the tray on top of it, lifting off the cover, stepping back and waiting again. The food was in bowls, hot and steaming, the garlicky odor of *shuum* filling the budding night. He looked up at the girl. "What is your name?"

"I . . . Shvirah, Your Grace."

Shvirah. "Lace." It seemed, somehow, an appropriate name. The girl was tall and willowy, face bland and unformed-looking, chin narrow and smooth, eyes large and dark under a wavy sweep of red-highlit black hair. She was jittery and concerned-looking now, tending to come up on the balls of her feet, as if about to bolt into the gathering darkness. "Well, Shvirah. There's far too much of this delicious dinner here. Would you care to help me eat it?"

Her eyes widened and she took a step back. Traps? Danger? What do you *do* when the lion invites you to take a bite out of his antelope? Run? Run?

Denthurion smiled again. "Shvirah, no one's spoken to me since Naamer left. You people are treating me like a dangerous animal. I'm going to get mighty bored and lonely if I have to sit out here in the desert and talk to myself for however long I'm held captive. Come. sit."

There was another long pause, a hesitation, while she conceptualized, then her eyes filled with a faint hint of compassion. Push those buttons. Denthurion gestured to another folding chair, leaning against the wall of the tent. Shvirah smiled, said, "Of . . . of course, Your Grace," set up the chair, and sank down at his side.

He handed her a bowl and they ate in silence for a while, spooning up stewy gobbets of unidentifiable meat and vegetable. The food was highly spiced, its preparer taking refuge in the great secret of the incompetent cook. The girl was eating steadily, head down, staring into her bowl, keeping her consciousness locked away.

Maaron Denthurion, Great Terror of Olam . . . He smiled to himself. Maybe not totally unjustified. I wonder if these children realize how much trouble they're in? The evidence was against it. Naamer was clearly playing a game with himself, playing a role, Naamer the Terrorist, Hero of the People, Despair of Kings. Maybe -wohnith understood . . . But the Hodai had absolutely nothing to lose. Maybe their lives meant something to them. Maybe not.

He shifted slightly in his chair so he could look at the girl more directly, fixing his eyes on her, letting them wander over her form in an orderly manner. She was dressed in a light and silky white tunic that molded itself to her body, dropping across gentle curves, failing to mask them. And underneath it, she was thin, breasts small, standing away from a narrow rib cage, nipples definite bumps in the cloth, abdomen flat, hipbones a noticeable elevation, legs long, thin, and smoothly muscled . . .

He felt a sudden, long-drawn-out hormonal stirring flood through his body, familiar and welcome, yet simultaneously unpleasant, pulling him apart into two separate beings. Well. Welcome back, Mr. Denthurion, despoiler of innocent peasant women. I wondered when you'd return . . .

Dismiss the self-loathing, Televox, you are what you

are. And what they made you. Time changes nothing, nor all your petty concerns about life and its ephemeral inhabitants . . .

He glanced back up at her face and saw that she was looking at him out of the corner of her eye, clearly unnerved.

"Why don't the *Shearahim* wear head-cloaks?"

She looked up at him, seeming stunned. "Why . . ." She looked away, into the night, then back. "It's a symbol of Amud oppression."

Denthurion smiled. Right out of the Red Millennium texts. I wonder if Naamer knows about the Manchu pigtail edict? "Interesting. And why are you a member?"

This rapid focus on herself as an individual was shutting out the night and, with it, her sense of unease. "Because I believe in freedom, Your Grace. We all do."

That word again. "What would you do if you had perfect freedom, Shvirah? Besides live in a tent in the desert, that is."

She put down her bowl and sat forward, staring at him intently. "Oh, not for me, Your Grace. I have all the freedom one person can practically use. My family has money and . . . everything."

"Who, then?"

"The Hodai, Your Grace. I want freedom for the Hodai." Her voice was softening as she spoke, eyes retreating into some indefinite past.

"An animal lover, then?"

"Animal?" She seemed brought up short, come back to the present for a flickering instant. "No . . . no. I had a Hoda when I was a little girl. When Raakaa died . . ."

Denthurion watched the girl's eyes mist over with dismay. What an appallingly fragile personality . . .

And, suddenly, she looked up at his face, eyes clearing, and said, "Why are *you* here, Your Grace?"

Now what? He shrugged. "Stock answer? It's my job."

"They sent you to Olam, specifically?"

"No. I just came here, right after Kem . . ."

"And you wander all the worlds, riding frozen on the Starship, stopping here and there, at your whim . . ."

He heard the special emphasis she put on the word "Starship," and said, "Not my whim. The Starship decides where we'll go next, and when."

"The Starship decides . . ." Her dark eyes were unfathomable, almost invisible in their shadowy wells. "It fascinates me . . ."

"What, that the Starship decides what we'll do next?"

"I read all I could about the last Televox who came here; and about the ones who came before him. You know you're only the twelfth one to visit Olam?"

Denthurion nodded. "It's on record." Interesting that she's so deftly seized the conversational initiative. I wonder where this is going?

"Your lives fascinate me. Endless incarnations on world after world, branchings and overlays without number . . ." A light breeze sprang up, coming down cool off the mountains, making her shiver. "And where are you between incarnations? Where are you when you're no more than data, frozen into the hydrogen ice?"

Denthurion stared suddenly into a dark dream full of mist and demons. "Nowhere," he said.

"Nowhere . . ." She was staring at him intently. "I wonder. But that's not what they teach us . . ."

"Who teaches you?" But I know this answer.

"*Koxavonia*, of course."

Of course. Starship. "How long have you been a member?"

"Since . . . Raakaa died." She sank back into that interminable past for another little while. "My parents sent her to the oven. It seemed so . . . unfair. Raakaa was a *person* to me, but . . . just a little Hoda. I listened to the Recruiters . . . sometimes. And every week I spent my allowance on transceiver jumps. I kept hoping I'd . . . go to Heaven." She came back to the present, eyes burning. "Where I think you must spend your time between incarnations!"

Black ice. Dark mist. Long rows of tables, tiers of brothers strung out through eternity. Odin. Heaven? Hell? Just a *dream*. "If I spend time there ... I don't know it."

She nodded slowly to herself. "I've read everything I can about the Televoxes ... Maybe you're just asleep ... Maybe, someday, you'll awaken ..."

"Maybe ..." He stood up suddenly, pushing away a flood of dark dream images. Ten thousand years! And in all that time, what, three thousand incarnations? More than that. Some of his older branchings were approaching the thousand mark by themselves ... And between every incarnate pair, a few years of frozen night. And those dreams.

He walked into the dimly lit tent, aware of Shvirah's eyes following him, and stood still for a little while, facing away from the entrance. Well, Denthurion. Televox. Barbarian. Man ... Suddenly he reached up and pulled off his tunic, leaving himself in a pair of narrow silken shorts. He turned to face the girl.

She was staring at him, astonished, looking over a muscular allopath frame, frozen in a moment of youth and perfection. "You ... have a beautiful body, Your Grace."

"That is what was intended, Shvirah. Beautiful. Perfect. Preserving the fires of adolescence forever." And no need to mention what the millennia do to a man. The changes are ... gone for now.

Shvirah stood and came into the tent, pulling the drawstring loose, so the entry flap closed behind her, shutting out the world.

Sometime in the middle of the night, it was dark and shadowy in their tent, yet not pitch-black. They had the door flap open to admit a soft desert breeze, billowing the material of the tent in and out, gently, like the breathing of some vast animal, the gauzy insect screen closed, admitting moonlight from without, strained through the thin material, casting etched and tinted shadows all around.

Shvirah sat naked on the narrow bed beside Maaron Denthurion's sleeping form, listening to the soft whisper of his breathing, feeling the mattress move under him, a delicate back and forth roll. His breathing was very slow, almost frightening at times, deep, with pauses between finished exhalation and the next slow intake. When she touched his warm, slightly damp side, she could feel a distant heartbeat, also very slow, somewhere down below fifty beats per minute. Not like a dying man, though. The rhythm of a perfectly conditioned athlete . . .

Perfect. Was this perfection?

And why me? I'm not drawn to many men, and never so easily . . . He just pulled off his shirt and . . . *things* in me unreeled out of nowhere. She looked down at him, at the craggy shadows around his quiescent face. Handsome. Unreal. Alien. In his sleep he looks even younger. Younger than me . . .

Am I too young for this? No. Nineteen. This is the perfect time for me. Perfect. His perfection and mine and the perfection of our times. How did I come to be here? She wanted to wonder again at the forces that had impelled her, will-less, into his bed. Drawn to him physically, no doubt, and more strongly than to any of those few other men she'd shared herself with . . . Something else, though . . . I was afraid of him, but . . . not that, no. I would have run, not let him rape me, if that's what it would have been. The power here? This force that alters worlds? That affects women, but . . . not that, no.

Looking down at him, watching the slow rise and fall of a smooth, muscular chest, she could feel the same physical stirrings, calling her attention to residual sensations between her legs, dampness, a slowly devolving pushed-apart feeling . . .

Sex with him had been remarkable, yes, but nothing she could lay her hand on now. They say he is ten thousand years old, so he must truly know what he is doing ... Not remarkable, though. Not in so many ways. Considerate of me, yes, but almost incidentally, as if my pleasure were a vehicle for his own ...

Denthurion stirred in his sleep, sighing, rolling slightly to one side, pressing his face against her thigh, squirming, then going still again, resuming his regular breathing, breath now a feather touch on her skin.

Sudden, intense stab of memory. Shvirah was sitting up in her own bed, naked then as now, back home in one of Perax's better residential neighborhoods, reading by the light of a soft bedside lamp. What book? I can't even remember. Some silly romance or other, young women with secret sexual stirrings, their beauty bringing a flock of men, men whom they could command with a sigh ...

Raakaa lay sleeping in the bed beside her, curled up, breath a gentle stirring on the skin of her leg. She had reached down and touched the little Hoda, brushing down a place where her fur had become disheveled, the small being mewling in her sleep, squirming, snuggling against her leg.

I was only fourteen then, and had had Raakaa for three years. Got her from a pet store, lonely and forlorn, face pressed longingly against the glass when I looked in ... Mama so mad that I would spend the hundred *gavishim* I'd saved up on a pet Hoda ... Flea-bitten, miserable, mangy little mutt ...

Raakaa had been a very nice pet, her soft, lisping speech evolving as Shvirah talked to her. You could treat a dog as a confidant, or a cat. Raakaa could talk back, in due course had learned something about Shvirah's feelings and concerns, even learned to read a little bit, at Shvirah's urging ...

And one day, when Raakaa was seven and Shvirah sixteen, some facts of Hoda life intruded, for Hodai reached maturity a little bit faster than human beings. Shvirah had been appalled at first, finding Raakaa in the backyard, bent over in a corner, some strange male Hoda mounting her, growling softly in his throat while little Raakaa cried . . .

Other people deal with it. We could have done something . . . It happened again a week later, while her mother was watching, and the next day Raakaa was gone.

Shvirah came back to herself and the night with a start, feeling an itch on her inner thigh, where something wet had commenced to trickle. She looked down at Denthurion, stroking his dense black hair, looking at the angles and planes of his still, untroubled face, and thought, So pretty. I wonder what he dreams?

In the eighth century of the forty-third millennium a vacuole of trouble formed in the vast internal space of the Metastable Order.

The stars of the Hyades cluster, at an average distance of some forty-six parsecs from Earth, have been a fertile breeding ground for humanity. The stars themselves are young, none of them on the main sequence for more than a half-billion years, planetary systems only recently regularized, planetesimal bombardments fresh in geological memory, impact rates still high . . . But there are more than two hundred potentially habitable planets in the Hyades, concentrated in the space of a half-thousand cubic light-years.

The cluster was reached by human exploration teams at the end of the Red Millennium. Cpaht was gone before news of his coming reached the terraforming colonists, down on their primitive, near lifeless worlds. They looked up, briefly, at a still-empty sky, then went back to their labors, unconcerned. And the new order came, filled up their sky with its pathologies, smothered them under a wave of methodical stillness.

The ships that streamed into the Hyades during the first millennium of the Metastable Order were part of the early Great Experiment. Cpaht's metastasis was a random one: get humanity out to the stars, anywhere,

anywhere at all. The first Senators, seeking order, consulted the ships' manifests, and sent them to particular worlds, to particular places.

Cultures have origins and tensors of development. In the early conceptualization of the Metastability, they were assigned identities. So. Sociopathy: cultures strong in some form of group dynamic. Psychopathy: cultures with a strong sense of mentality. The ships were gathered from wherever they had gone and redirected. This one to that Hyadic world. That one to another. Psychopath, sociopath, in alternation, until all the worlds were filled.

The twenty-third incarnation of Maaron Denthurion, mark Four, floated above the deck of the command bridge aboard Starship *Manniska*, marveling at his surroundings. All this time, four great ships, and I've never been here before. The ship was in free-fall, leaving him to swim in the air, one hand clamped down on the leathery back of an ancient pilot's chair, looking out broad windows of radiation-proof glass at endless night.

Seen over a bank of mysterious instruments, outer space was a dusty sea of stars, the planet Otokonoshto and its large moon Hujin distant crescents, brightly lit by a fat orange sun. This deep in the cluster, the sky was dense with high-magnitude stars, provided you knew what to look for, other Hyadic systems, not too far away.

He drifted slowly over the chair, pulling himself down and strapping in, waiting patiently. The First Senators asked for this. What a wonder this problem took so long to brew. Somewhere out there Ordnunger starships were drifting into the system, one of many they would conquer. Psychosocial Jihad. Idiotic concept. The war had been evolving in the Hyades for almost a century—it took that long for Metastable forces to notice what was going on, even this close to Earth. Now, the Republic of Ordnung was in for its first terrible shock ...

The ship's comeye, Stelmaanen, tall, thin, head ablaze

with wild white hair, scrolled into being at his side, standing on the gravityless deck, leaning over the control panel. "Time. We're picking up sideband vector particles."

Denthurion nodded. The Ordnunger fleet had decelerated well outside the star system and spent months drifting in, sneaking up on their hapless victims. Victims, indeed. Coming in through the Hyades, he'd stopped off at a few subject planets, made some clandestine reconnaissance runs . . .

Well. Everything is in place now. This is the first blow. Guard units had been slipping into the cluster for a long time now, taking up positions outside dense and dusty new Oort clouds.

"There."

Violet lights began winking on, bright new stars making an unfamiliar constellation against a black and starry sky. Ordnunger ships, hundreds of them, were beginning their strike run. On Otokonoshto, sociopathic peasants, engaged in endless group endeavor, would be looking up from primitive fields, mouths open in wonder. "All right. Notify the wing commanders."

The comeye scrolled out of existence.

The violet lights were moving in swiftly now, the pattern of pretty stars becoming three-dimensional, gaining reality as it drew close. On the night side of the planet below, he could imagine people coming out of their houses for a quiet evening stroll, looking up at the sky in bewilderment. It can't be starships, they would be saying. Starships come one at a time, no more than four or five a year . . .

The space around Otokonoshto was lit up, brilliant blue-white, the little planet picked out in brief, universal daylight, then darkness returned, slowly, to a sky filled with small, fading globes of light, violet to white, white to yellow, yellow to red, fading, fading, gone.

Stelmaanen scrolled back into existence at his side. "Monitors show plasma clouds heading into the upper radiation belt. They'll have some terrific aurorae. Very little debris."

Denthurion nodded. Sideband vector particles. Nothing more. The Ordnunger ships were . . . good, by nonallopathic standards. But the Metastatic Guard fleet was invisible, invincible, silent. There was nothing to it, really. Long-range teledynes reached around leaky baffles into boiling dissonance reactors, pushed everything up into a smooth platform-release state . . . The explosions were, fortunately, insubstantial. Only the reactor's momentary flux mass converted to energy. The rest of the ship was merely blown to plasma.

Or to Hell and gone, if you wanted to look at it that way.

A hundred ships. Maybe a million psychopathic marines sent on their way out of reality, in no more than an instant.

A trifling thing, really.

Well. There was work to be done. Ordnung had taken over more than two score Hyadic worlds and the little Metastable task force was hardly adequate for the task . . .

The next day, after a long morning spent lazing in bed, Shvirah packed a light picnic lunch and led him off down the long axis of the valley, southward, away from the central encampment, where the sloping walls narrowed, becoming more ravinelike. Other *Shearahim* watched them go, eyes dark and mistrustful, but declined to follow.

As they walked along a narrow path, Denthurion fell in behind the girl, watching her slim, straight back, admiring the movement of her narrow hips under the thin cloth of her tunic. Rhythmic. Pelvic girdle tipping slightly from side to side with each stride. Evidence of evolutionary failure, of a time not so long ago in Earth's African Rift Valley, when human brains grew so large that women's ability to walk was compromised. He felt a smile tugging at his mouth. What are you thinking about? And why?

Still. I feel like I've been ... resurrected from the dead. Nothing so terribly untrue about that. Born in the transceiver flame, from careful notes taken down on an alien world ... But reborn now, all right. Bitter, self-directed humor. Reborn? Out of a little mammalian instinct-play? Don't be so pretentious, Mr. Televox. *Inter anem et urinam* ... Ah, yes. The Miracle of Life ...

And what about her? Complex motivations there, feelings somewhere, but locked away from me. Everything is hidden under this ... pseudocultural layer somehow made unreal. He thought, very briefly, about Tiy and Kem. I wonder ...

He pulled away from the shrinking circle of his thoughts, pulled his eyes from the twist-flex of Shvirah's buttocks, and looked around. The valley was quite narrow now, no more than twenty meters wide, the yellow-green vegetation diminished to a tangle of head-high brush. A little breeze ... Sniff. What? A faint, sour tang on the wind. Reminiscent of ... something. He rummaged in his memory. Not out of the overlays. A real memory, something laid down at random, in another incarnation, but in this branching, or earlier, out of childhood ...

He forced the matter and was suddenly rewarded by a brief flash of memory, a dinner table, outdoors, on a warm night, some kind of insect singing in the distance, or amphibians maybe, world and time unknown. Four dark men sitting around a table, reaching with two-tined forks into a central wooden bowl, spearing cold brussels sprouts and bits of marinated artichoke heart, dipping them into a hot sauce compounded largely of molten butter, oiliness cut by some dark, spicy vinegar ...

There. That smell. That *precise* smell ...

The valley narrowed farther, then the vegetation gave out and they were climbing a rise made up of broad, flat, sun-warmed stones. The valley came to an end here, in a little bowl of land, like a little room with walls less than a meter high. Shvirah put down the picnic basket and spread the blanket she was carrying, then turned and looked at Denthurion, face a little serious, but trying to smile. The wind of the desert floor was stronger here, and dryer, lifting her hair, separating it into thick clusters of strands, blowing them around, some across her face, others away from it. She motioned toward the blanket. "Shall we?"

He sat cross-legged on the blanket and watched as she squatted, unpacking the bits of food she'd brought along. A curious thing, her attachment to him, deliberate on his part, unfathomable on hers. Mostly, she seemed pretty and uncomplicated, but . . . Right. She was here, after all, which must count for something . . .

In the final analysis, people were equally complex. Whatever else they might seem to be was superficial, no more than concretized memory, erudition and experience, ending where the source of their mannerisms let go.

I'll understand her at some point. I always do. Tiy again, in faint memory profile.

The lunch was mostly fruit and cold cuts, some kind of thinly sliced reddish-brown meat, pieces of thin gray bread, with a sharp, bitter taste, little pots of mustard and bottles of some thin ale. Bringing supplies to this remote camp, presumably just one of several, must cause the *Shearah* a small logistics headache . . .

And it says a great deal that they've solved it. If this were a world alone in the universe, their plan might well succeed. Too bad for them that it isn't.

"Shvirah."

She looked at him, eyes blank and incurious.

Denthurion was slightly taken aback. *What did I want? Is there a person in there to answer my questions?* "What does *Koxavonia* tell you about Heaven? Where are you expecting to go?" *Odd. Not what I was thinking about at all . . .*

She frowned prettily, pushing hair away from her face, tucking it behind her ears, looking down, careful not to let him see her eyes. "Mostly they talk about the Starship, and about Tayash, the Pilot's experiences there." She shrugged, putting down her food, moving a little closer to him. "After Raakaa died, I wanted to go ... tried to. I heard them talk, but it was all vague. You know, just promises ..."

He nodded slowly. Not surprising.

"I think I just wanted to die. Get away from my thoughts. One of my friends, a boy from school, gave me a copy of *Hikanesh!*, Mr. Meltsar's book about *Koxavonia*. It was the first I knew that people were really going to Heaven; that they'd figured out the truth ..."

Hikanesh ... The word meant "enter," couched as an imperative. You saw it painted on glass doors on the front of large shops; enter and exit. Denthurion smiled slightly. Maybe manual doors, too. Might there be religions whose Bibles were called "push" and "pull"? So. There is a book about the Starship of God, a drawing card for the cult ... by Mr. Meltsar ... Something crystallized then, and an image of the man's smiling, black-bearded face came up. So, Mr. Meltsar. Interesting.

Shvirah was continuing to talk: "... I learned about the training camps and philosophical retreats they maintain; I went to a few of them, studied, saw people preparing for embarkation ..."

"*Koxavonia* maintains camps like this one?"

She nodded, eyes remote. "There's one in the mountains not too far from here, maybe ninety kilometers away ..."

Steer her away from that. If she thinks too hard about what she's just told me ... "Why didn't you stay with *Koxavonia*, Shvirah? Why are you here?"

She stared at him, eyes still unfathomable, lips thin, mouth compressed to a straight line. "Raakaa," she said. "They tell me the Hodai don't go to Heaven. At least, not to ours. Maybe they have their own Starship,

Tayash doesn't say and neither does Meltsar. I have to save them. I think I owe that to Raakaa, before I can go to Heaven myself . . ."

So. A purpose and a means, ready to hand. "Tell me about Raakaa."

That got another long stare, then, "No," she said, "I . . . just can't do that." Her face seemed drawn and unhappy.

Denthurion looked at her carefully. "Raakaa was that special to you?"

Shvirah nodded, still, apparently, unwilling to speak, rummaging in the picnic basket again, closing him out.

Well, he thought. Hard to imagine how deep this goes. We'll see . . . And it seemed, somehow, almost silly.

In the *Shearah* wilderness camp, in the middle of the night, Maaron Denthurion sat in the wan light of his tent, on the foot of his futon, staring at Shvirah's sleeping form. She lay flat on her back, head turned into the mass of her own hair, snoring softly, breasts flattened by gravity, nipples dark, wrinkled little islands on gently quaking seas. Her stomach was flat, rising and falling slowly, skin stretched between sharp hipbones. Her right leg was bent double, thrust up, resting against the material of the tent wall, left leg flat on the bed, knee slightly flexed, toes turned outward.

He let himself stare at her vulva for a while, hair still damp and flattened, dark fold of clitoris protruding slightly, little gluey smear of semen marking his exit.

So. Once again, in a new incarnation. At some time past, in some other branching, it had pleased him to think of each new incarnation as somehow virginal. A pleasant enough fiction, but eventually, like everything else, tiresome. God. You go on forever. And the machines keep you young and young and young.

Shvirah stretched in her sleep and then rolled over onto her right side, leaving him to face her slim, smooth buttocks and a dark, hourglass-shaped stain on the futon's sheet.

Look at her. The reality of youth. Only once. The light of the tent's electroluminescent lamp was glinting off sweaty patches on her back, making a little shadow in the valley of her spine, picking out a tiny haze of dark fuzz at its base. Smooth. Young. New, unlike my own ancient hide . . .

He looked down at himself. His skin was covered with a dense fur of short, fine, crisp black hair, but . . . Right. Young. Forever. How old am I then, really? Twenty? A week? Dream your uncomfortable dreams of eternity . . .

Wake . . . Sleep . . .

He slid off the futon and walked to the other side of the tent, dropping into one of his folding chairs. From this distance, Shvirah was an even smoother apparition, dark hair covering one end of a smoothly curved back, small hips globing up from the other. I suppose I could just go over there and wake her up . . . After all, I *am* young . . . we both are.

A small comdeck, flat and metallic, sat on a box beside his chair. He waved at it, bringing the thing to life, a primitive sort of homunculus popping up out of the deck. "Yes?" it whispered.

"Newsnet?"

The homunculus was replaced by a scrolling imagescan, flickering pictures of this and that, current events, current concerns. He raised his hand, stopping the scroll, bringing the homunculus back to life in the middle of a scene dominated by what looked like automated farm machinery.

"What's happening with the visiting Televox?"

The scene cut quickly to the orbital space above Olam, to an image of a giant starship drifting ominously above a supine world, and the sound came on. "Summoned from its investigation of the industrial complexes around the gas giant Adomm, Metastatic Vectorship *Naglfar* has resumed its position in the Olamite sky," whispered a thin and frightened-sounding voice. "Metastatic Guard contingents under the command of Planetary Governor Ardennes Kartavilis have been directed to search Perax for the missing Televox . . ."

The scene shifted to the ground, green-clad Guardsmen all through the city, entering buildings, seizing students, holding interrogations. It cut to an interior view of the Governor's Palace, a wild-eyed youth forced to his knees before the Governor, enraged, defiant. Well. Well. Mr. Naamer, I presume . . .

More scenes, Kevess and Ashaan giving interviews, both of them looking rather frightened, Shatiyax and the others in the background, looking ready to drop with dread. And a tall, bearded man, almost smiling . . . Denthurion peered into the little scene. Who? That writer . . . Mr. Meltsar . . . So.

". . . the ship's computer has stated that unless the Televox is found, it will place Olam under martial law and enact an economic interdict . . ."

Denthurion sat back in his chair, no longer listening to the program, staring into space. Predictable, but faster than I expected. Kartavilis must have called the ship back as soon as I disappeared. Well. What now? Let them tear the planet apart looking for me? Might be a good start to a program of rearrangement . . .

And if I don't turn up shortly, Odin will split off a new incarnation from my Kemitish self. If I live. A new branching. If I die, lacuna . . .

So what do I do now? Run away into the wilderness? That will take too long. Events will have begun to move. Hope *Naglfar* will notice this camp, direct the Guard to move in? No. Hope is worthless. What, then?

You can die. You can always die.

Suicide was a simple solution to a pressing personal problem. Kill yourself, be removed from the equation. *Shearah*, having lost its hostage/weapon, will give in immediately. Suicide will show them you spoke the truth. And a new Maaron Denthurion will come down, mourning this new *lacuna*, and set things straight once and for all . . .

He waved the comdeck to silence, stood up, and walked over to where Shvirah lay sleeping. What, then? Die now? Or . . . No. What difference would it make if the experience is lost? You're just an incarnation. Nothing more. You can live again . . .

A brief, formless longing pulsed through his body. Right. And if this incarnation's data is lost, that death is as real as any other.

And now, as a thousand times before, I find that I *do* love life . . .

He knelt on the futon beside Shvirah, pushing her over onto her back, watching her eyes open, foggy and bewildered. "What . . ." she began. And smiled.

Ordnung was a substantial marble in the Hyadic sky, growing steadily in *Manniska*'s viewport, defenses down and helpless. Denthurion sat in his bucket seat, feet propped on an inactive control panel, mind ticking over in a slow mode developed during a subjective decade of intermittent crisis management. All over now. Climax passed, no more than a vast plasma cloud and spinning debris mixing with this system's still-chaotic Oort cloud. Nothing left but the denouement.

The ship's comeye slid sideways out of the air behind him, and said, "All set. Elements of the fleet will be taking up englobement orbits with us. Time is minus one hour."

He nodded to himself. The Ordnungers were finished, their last fleet vapor, occupying forces handed over to the retributive populations of various worlds. Now the Metastatic Guard fleets would take up staggered, highly inclined synchronous orbits about the mother world . . .

And on my word . . .

He could look down there in imagination, see the proud folk of Ordnung waiting . . . The planet in the window was mostly blue and brown, its frosting of clouds thin and transparent. The sky above the Ordnungers' heads would be clear and bright, the light of its yellow-orange KO sun warm and sweet . . .

Do I really want to do this? Do I *have* to?

It was too easy to look down and see them as doppel-gangers of all the men and women he'd met through the subjective centuries, simple people by and large, swept up in a mass hysteria of conquest, taking on national pride in the face of their own humble roles; the deeds of the leaders as their own. Now they would will the responsibility of those deeds back into the collective hands of that leadership. It was, of course, too late.

The image that came back to him, this being a psycho-pathic world, was of an urban family, mother, father, boy, girl, living together in a classic high-rise apartment building, somewhere just away from the center of one of Ordnung's largest cities, Mittagsberg, perhaps, or Arnzeiss. Now they would be standing together, clutching each other, out on a warm and windy balcony, hundreds of meters above the street, staring anxiously into an inviting sky.

And, of course, the air-raid sirens would begin to blow . . .

He smiled at the image. Pure drama, fit only for the sensory nets of some technologically advanced world . . . A world much like Ordnung, in fact. Too much like Ordnung.

They blamed the trouble generated by psycho- and al-lopathic worlds on things like drama. Back in the beginning, in the opening millennia of the Metastable Age, there had been so many studies. Give people ideas, they act on them . . . Crime. Passion. Violence. Hatred.

But a thin leavening of allopathic worlds was all that made humanity continue its expansion into the cosmos, and psychopathic worlds were their inevitable consequence.

Order and progress, then.

And this the price.

The hour passed swiftly, Denthurion and the comeye silent beside each other, until the ships were in place. Commanders reported in, computer systems tipped through their virtual spaces, checking nodes, readying energy sources.

Denthurion glanced up at Stelmaanen's wild white hair, at his gaunt, curiously impassive face. "All right. Get it over with."

The comeye smiled, briefly, and vanished.

Left alone, Denthurion stared out at the bold blue world below. He was almost over the subsolar point, the face of the planet so nearly full that he couldn't tell it from a perfectly lit sphere.

I wonder why they do that? Early programming? Hard to say. The ships' OTANNs were close to independent entities, vastly more complex than a human being, or anything else the natural universe had to offer.

They can transport us, in endless numbers and combinations, but not each other. What could it be like, to be more complex than an entire world of human beings . . .

Maybe I'll know, one day. There are five of me now, counting the original, and, what, close to two hundred incarnations? Something like that.

And the manifestations of the neurotaxic computers took the trouble to mimic human mannerisms, false fronting their inner mechanism, far more than was necessary for ease of discourse . . .

All around Ordnung, the black sky lit up.

No subtle, advanced teledyne systems this time; a planet was just too large and a few volcanoes and earthquakes would do little to rectify matters . . .

A hundred thousand Guard ships floated in orbit around Ordnung, their quantum dissociative reactors boiling over with released energy, optical carrier nets feeding power to collimated particle beam weapons, the carefully tailored particles themselves the by-product of the reactors.

Something like ultra-high-energy cosmic rays punched into the upper atmosphere, aurorae flaring and climbing, blue-white-green, into space. Showers of collisional particles sprayed into the troposphere, dividing, dividing, flooding the biosphere with ionizing radiation, through and through that little imaginary family . . .

"Daddy, I feel sick . . ."

Empty houses, rotting meat. And in deep shelters the government of Ordnung would wait, sweating, for the Televox to come.

And judge them.

The sky was dark now, Ordnung fizzing below, the lights in its sky brightening, curtains of light shining, beautiful, in the heavens. Denthurion looked up in time to see the comeye slide into being, waiting.

"Let's get out of here," he said. "This incarnation is over. In a thousand years someone can come back and . . . put this house in order."

Below, the Ordnunger generals waited in vain.

Finished with sex again, Denthurion and Shvirah knelt on the futon facing each other in the damp stillness of the night, sweat evaporating slowly, light glinting off wet places, making glossy patches on their skin. The girl's hands, doubled into small fists, were clasped between her knees, her head down, partially hidden by a wavy veil of black hair.

Waiting for a response, Denthurion stared at her, knowing two days of talk and sex had had time to take effect. But what effect? Am I so skilled at manipulating primitive personalities that I can predict the outcome of my efforts? Best not to be so . . . what? Confident? No, merely egoistic. "You'll help me, then?" Better to force things to their conclusion, bring it out of her.

One hand came up and toyed briefly with some beads of moisture on her abdomen, then returned to its hiding place. "I can't think what's the right thing to do."

As if there were such a thing . . . "These decisions are hard to make. I'm sorry I have to put you in this position."

She straightened up, brushing her hair aside, looking at him. "But these people are my *friends*. I can't betray them for . . ." The hollows under her eyes were wet, merely an accumulation of sweat, but it made her look teary.

"Not for me, Shvirah. For everyone else in the world." Not a lie; not the truth.

"Why me?" She rubbed a hand across her face, smearing moisture. "Why do I have to come? You can just run away. I'll . . . say you left during the night."

Close enough, but . . . "We've talked about this already, Shvirah." He reached out and took her hand, holding it gently. "You convinced me this morning, out on our picnic. You know where the *Koxavonia* encampment is . . ."

"You could find it." Transient expressions were flickering across her face, mirroring the turmoil of indecision, sullen resentment at this difficulty thrust upon her, but desire, as well . . .

"I know that . . . I need you there with me. I could get out of here, even just into the wilderness, and find some way to signal *Naglfar*. What you've told me about Starship . . . I have to *know*, now. If there's a truth out there, I need to find it."

The desire to believe him began making war on her doubts, overwhelming them, the result evident in the relaxing tension of her face. "All right," she whispered. "When do we go?"

"Now." He stood up, looking down at her, smiling.

"Now? It's almost a hundred kilometers through the mountains!"

"I know. And preparations for a long trek would do no more than delay us, make sure we'd be caught. If we go now, we may succeed."

"But . . ." Her bewilderment was no more than a search for final excuses. "What will we eat?"

Picking up a soft towel, wiping away sweat, he pointed to a little bowl of fruit on the table. "It's only a two-day walk, Shvirah. We won't starve to death or even weaken in that little while."

The girl got up slowly, toweling her own moist places, reaching for bits of clothing, looking up occasionally to watch him dress. He smiled at her again. "Don't worry, Shvirah. It's not a *real* wilderness anymore. There's nothing out there that will eat us . . ."

No, not anymore. Not after twenty-five thousand years of human colonization. No jungle monsters to pursue us, no savage red aborigines to take us captive . . . On Olam, not even little bugs to bite us . . .

Outside, the camp was pitch-black, stars arcing overhead like diamond dust, in patches and lanes and queer constellations. Denthurion stood in the cool darkness, looking up at the sky, breathing in a semisweet night air compounded of many elements. Odd. I've been watching that sky form for the past dozen incarnations—the sky over Kem and Kirenayka before it . . . The moons were down, robbing it of its little Olamite individuality, but still, it was an alien sky, forbidding and unfamiliar.

He touched Shvirah's arm and walked off into the night, stepping between lanes of dark tents and little black-windowed cabins, out into the area of silent gardens, where the valley wall began to steepen.

The silence was so nearly absolute that the whisper of their feet on coarse sand and cloddy dirt was loud in the absence of competition. When they stopped moving, a soft, very slow wind could be heard hissing out in the desert, seeming far away. Curious. I know they have dogs and cats on Olam . . . Fewer. Ever fewer. The Hodai are taking their place. Hodai in laps, on leashes; dogs and cats able to talk and understand.

And insects. Buglike things. Even in this desert environment, not so different from Kem, we should hear them singing on the wind . . .

They walked up the slope of the valley wall, using their hands where it increased to a semblance of vertical, then they were up on the rim, standing on the desert floor. The light was brighter here, the light from a whole sky of stars shining down on them, save in the south where it was blocked by the mountains. They could feel the wind here, too, a soft, cooling breeze that barely stirred their clothes.

Denthurion turned, looking down into the valley, seeing nothing. The light from the sky had already altered his eyes so that the *Shearah* camp was no more than an inky well, a bottomless, depthless crater cut into the gray landscape.

Shvirah shivered at his side for a little while, seeming out of place in the warm night, then said, "We'd better get going. There's only four hours 'til dawn. We have to make the forest before that."

"It's twenty kilometers to the foothills. Think we'll make it that far in four hours?"

"No."

Denthurion smiled again in the darkness. "I think we have more time than that. They know I've been screwing you silly, Shvirah. They won't expect us to stir before midmorning. Seven hours, at least."

She looked at him, trying to see through the night into his dark and shadowy eyes. I *want* to believe this is the right thing to do, but . . . No. I'm not betraying them, nor they me. I joined them for Raakaa's sake, and that's why I'll do this . . .

But the doubts remained.

Denthurion took her limp, reluctant hand and they began to walk away toward the black shadow of the mountains, steady and silent.

Chapter 8

By dawn, walking steadily, they were far up in the foothills. Denthurion and Shvirah sat on a rocky outcrop, resting amid scrubby vegetation, mostly stunted trees, eating a breakfast of raw fruit whose taste was masked by the increasingly strong cabbages-and-vinegar smell of the woodlands around them.

Crunching one of the applelike things, Denthurion looked back the way they'd come, downhill, out into the desert. The sky overhead was dull indigo, slowly brightening, but clear and featureless. Does that mean something? Unknown. A poor sort of overlay ... Still, I've experienced millennia of meteorology, mostly on Earthlike worlds. I ought to be able to synthesize something. Still air. Low dust level. Good seeing for ground-based astronomers. What does that mean in the context of a planet with this much desert? A cloudless day? Unpleasant if we're caught in the open, without even head-cloaks for cover. Well. Dark hair will have to do.

He looked over at Shvirah. She was frowning, looking down at her food, extremely long-faced. Too bad. Broken your word. A lot of questions about yourself now ... "We'd better get going," he said, motioning uphill. She nodded, silently putting the fruit back in her bag, and they walked on.

The day brightened slowly, dawning clear, deep blue, the sky fully lit long before the sun rolled over the horizon, already small and yellow. The woods thickened, eventually growing tall enough to throw a patchwork of shadow on the ground, the sour smell waxing with each passing hour, becoming unpleasant in the rising heat of the day.

Walking uphill with a measured pace, sweat gathering in the hair of his brows, occasionally spilling with a sting into his eyes, Denthurion let the cloying stench fill his nostrils, wondering when his olfactory sensors would shut down, masking the odor. It never happened. So. This certainly explains the Kemitish incursion. It's a wonder they didn't simply apply for a permit to convert the planetary ecology . . . That got a wry smile. Maybe they did. Where do you apply for these things? To Earth? To a passing Televox, surely. Maybe an application was made, two or three visits ago, and rejected. An answer to their appeal wouldn't have had time to make a round-trip to Earth . . .

The shortcomings of the Metastable Order laid bare . . . With civilization this big, the appeals process couldn't work. Long ago, it had been time to institutionalize the work of the temporary Sector Marshal appointments . . . But, no, too much fear of spawning daughter empires . . . They want nothing above the Televox but his Senator . . . Who, they? We. I. Regularize the circuit? Make sure every world is visited by a Televox every few centuries? How? And what would that do? Localize authority, obviously. Again, that call for a permanent Sector Marshal.

But we've lasted this long. Local disturbances take so long to spread . . . The destabilization won't come until, what? Another Hhurull, of course, or worse . . . Another us . . .

They stopped for their noon break in a thick and shady copse of trees. Shvirah bedraggled and sweaty, her clothing clinging to her in patches, dark half-moons marking armpits and the underside of breasts, a wet stripe down the middle of her back. She threw herself down on a broad, flat, cool piece of stone, pushing locks of moist hair out of her face, staring up into the tree above, at its round, yellow leaves.

Denthurion remained on his feet, standing beside her,

sipping water from his flask, letting the light breeze wash his face, drying the small rivulets of sweat.

She looked up at him, eyes sullen. "You're not even tired."

"No." He reached out and smoothed the sweat on her forehead, spreading it out, making it evaporate faster. "Rest for a little while ... but we'll have to start walking again quickly. It's too early in the day to stiffen up."

She sighed, said "Right," and closed her eyes.

Hanging his flask back on its belt hook, Denthurion stretched, looking around the clearing, dappled here and there with small patches of bright yellow sunlight, then back at Shvirah's resting place. The stone was curiously flat, squared along one edge, the remaining surfaces sheared off and jagged. He bent close to the surface and rubbed his hand over the stone. Small, regular indentations. Odd.

He bent and, picking up a handful of dusty soil, scattered it on the surface of the rock, smoothed it carefully, filling in hollows, clearing off high places. Hmh. Basrelief carvings appeared, faint and hard to make out, almost worn away. Long rows of angular letters, almost like Norse runes, separated by straight lines, interrupted occasionally by tiny pictures, animals, what appeared to be buildings, humanoid figures ...

He worked his way along the stone, dusting and examining. Something that looked like a map. Or an amoeba. Square meters of text. More cities, mountainscapes. What looked like a comet in the sky over a great metropolis. The city below the comet was in fragments, carefully scribed fracture lines, zigzag bolts of lightning, breaking the buildings in two. Near the end of the stone, where irregular spalls were beginning to break into the text, was a scene of humanoids kneeling before a pair of enormous demons. One of the demons, the smaller of the two, was pushing a humanoid into its mouth, while the other menaced the crowd before it with a bolt of lightning.

Well. There was that. He tapped Shvirah gently. "Time we moved on."

She rose, stretching, silent and resentful, and followed him off into the midday forest, wishing for gloom and deep, cool shadows.

Not long after nightfall, when the sky was still deep purple, they made camp, laying out their thin blankets, sitting cross-legged on them in the gathering darkness, eating the last of their fruit. Denthurion pulled off his tunic and lay back naked on his blanket, savoring the cooling onset of night. Before dawn, he knew, it would get almost cool, making him wrap up in the blanket. For now . . .

Shvirah moved over to his side, sitting, looking down at him silently.

"Still sorry you came?"

She shrugged. "I don't know that I have been sorry . . . I'm tired . . . My friends . . ." She lay down, curled up against his side, head on his shoulder.

He stroked her hair, still damp with sweat, staring into the darkness above, watching the stars twinkle between moving leaves. "You haven't betrayed your friends. Nor they the world. This had to happen, one way or another . . ."

"You keep telling me that. How do I *know*?"

"How does anyone?" Platitudes. Forty thousand years and I give her platitudes . . .

Out of the darkness a soft voice whispered, "Woh! Yuman-ha! Yes? Smell you bitterstink!"

Denthurion sat up quickly, spilling Shvirah from his shoulder. They were surrounded by small, dark forms, none more than waist high, tufted ears projecting above their heads, all bearing sharpened sticks in the neighborhood of a meter long. He put his hand on Shvirah, pressing her gently down. Remain lying on the blanket. She seemed to be shivering, with good reason. "So. These must be the famous wild Hodai . . ."

One of them stepped forward, still masked by darkness, and put the point of its stick on his chest. "Wild-ha? You bet, kuwurru. Shearah Sessiri-wohnith say Yuman-ha no come Hoda-hill again. You Starship-ha forget?"

Denthurion put his hands up, palms forward, and smiled gently at the dark face. "Don't worry. We're . . . your friends . . ."

The Hoda hissed softly, took the stick away from his chest, and plunged it down into the ground, puncturing his blanket, thrusting into the soil below. "Friend?" There was something like outrage in its tone. "No! No friend Hoda-ha. No friend ever. Sky God evil ha-Chewiss . . ." That last, whatever it meant, trailed off in a long, sibilant hiss. The Hoda pulled its stick from the ground and stepped back. "Go back you camp, Starship-ha. No come Hoda-hill again. Keep *Shearah* promise."

Shearah promise. He remembered -wohnith standing between his legs, hissing with anger, spraying spit into his face. Well. This goes . . . further than I thought. *Shearah*. Hodai. *Koxavonia* camps in the mountains. Hard not to jump to conclusions. "Understood. We're headed for the Starship camp now. We just got lost in the woods."

"Lost-ha! Yes. Tomorrow gone!" It turned to its comrades and said, "Flee!" And they merged into the darkness, gone, silent.

He listened to the night for another little while, hand on Shvirah's shivering flank, hearing nothing but the soft sounds of Olamitic nature. Nothing. Little wind-wraiths. He lay down beside the girl, stroking her softly. "Over. Nothing to worry about."

"They could have killed us," she whispered.

"Could have, yes. But they didn't. They were afraid to."

"Afraid?"

He chuckled softly, then, imitating the Hoda's soft, high-pitched voice, said, "Sky God *evil ha-chewissss* . . ."

"My mother used to mock Raakaa like that."

Denthurion ran his hand over Shvirah's hip, pulling up the hem of her tunic, rubbing his fingers on her soft, bare skin. "*My* mother used to mock the mating call of our tomcat. Drove him crazy, in the end . . ."

Shvirah rolled back a little, so he could rub his hand over the taut skin of her abdomen, just above her pubic hairline. "What was his name?" she asked.

"The tomcat?" He thought for a minute. "You know, I don't remember. Funny. I can still see him, plain as you please, a big, fat tabby-tom, black and white, with just a few streaks of orange on his face, but . . . maybe he didn't have a name . . ."

The twenty-ninth incarnation of Maaron Denthurion, mark Four, crouched with his back to a gray stone wall, winter wind dusting the air with thin, icy snow, clutching a lasgun to his chest, freezing cold, tired to the point of paralysis. Come to this, then, he thought. Come to this.

A sharp voice, somewhere outside the pile of rubble he was using for shelter, called, "Come out, *aap-man*. We have you now!" There were faint after-echoes, bouncing around inside the ruins.

Kattekwaad could be a pleasant world, had been. Not now. Come to this. Very simple, or so it seemed. Take command, Mr. Televox. Lead your Guardsmen up into the mountains. Find the rebels. Kill them. Show that simpleminded Planetary Governor how the job was done. Clean the place up . . . And you, sir: Relieved when I'm finished. Back to Earth. Your whole line called into question. Your Planetary Deputy, perhaps, cast out in disgrace. What are you, third branching? You should know better than to let it go this far . . .

"We'll give you another minute, *aap-man*. You'll be sorry if we have to come in after you . . ." The broad, flat vowels of Kattekwaans had an ominous ring, backed by a sharp sussurus of echoes.

Voorwaarts Kattekwaad, the rebels called themselves, *vrij uit burgerschap*, their motto. "Free from citizenship." And worth a giggle, too. The words were similar enough to Ursprache that they sounded like something else . . .

"All right, *aap-man*. Time's up." There were the sounds of men moving about, footfalls, scuffling. They were slithering into the open nooks of his hideaway, stepping over the dead bodies of gunned-down Guardsmen, boot heels muddying torn green uniforms.

Come to this, then. And it had seemed so simple . . . The rustling of cloth, muttered comments of frightened men braving a dangerous situation, came steadily closer. Have to move. Decide what to do . . . And the worst thing is, they don't even know who I am, or what this means. Just one more government *politieagent* brought down by the clever rebel *kommando* . . . Move!

He scurried away from the voice, scrambling upward through the pile of rubble, moving toward the light.

"I hear him! This way! This way!" Thudding feet, a curse, someone falling down a hole, loose rock falling after him. "Owww, Heinzie, my arm's broke . . ."

"Shut up, you fool! He can hear us!"

Echo, echo, echo . . .

Denthurion burst out into gray light atop the ruins, lasgun clutched across his chest, snow thickening, blowing around his head, whipped by a freshening wind. The storm was building up. Another hour and visibility will be very low. If only . . . Yes. If only another hour. But there were men all around, already spying him up here, lasguns lifting, pointing, this way . . .

"There! There! Shoot!"

He spun, saw his target standing on a hilltop, not far away. He pulled the gun up fast, muscles driven by an allopathic fury, and fired, the snowstorm tinted briefly by a violet glare. The rebel leader Hans Jongewaard spasmed, stiffening, and fell over backward, disappearing in the snow amid a babble of shouting . . . Ah, what intense satisfaction . . .

Maaron Denthurion was transfixed by a dozen bright bolts, hot nails through vital organs, long wires of flame cooking his meat. He dropped his gun and fell, facedown, in the snow, sliding a bit, grinding to a stop.

God. God, he thought. Me. Over. Finished. Me. The world filled with haze, pulse faltering, limping to a halt. Over. New incarnation next, but . . . No. Not me. Gone. Lost . . . His thoughts came apart, simplifying, losing texture, then the world darkened and came to an end.

In the late afternoon of their second day in the mountains they crossed the sloping shoulder of a long ridge, coming out of the shadows onto the south side of the Meirhhav range, finding a broad outcropping of weathered, gray granite, where they stopped for a rest, sitting silently on the sun-warmed rock. The rays of Shemesh, an oblate orange ball low in the western sky, slanted between small, slow-moving clouds, spilling across an endless lowland sea of yellow-green forest.

Shading her eyes, Shvirah pointed into the middle distance, where the last rolling foothills flattened out and disappeared. "There. The camp."

Denthurion squinted into the sunshine, saw a pale curl of white smoke, below it an area cleared of trees and the faint outline of tiled rooftops. A little village, then. That round thing . . . Squint harder. Satellite dish. Not far enough from Perax for communication needs . . . Transceiver net? Odd . . . Associations closed in on each other, meshing. Tayash. The Pilot. Shvirah spending her allowance on transceiver trips, trying to get to Heaven. Questions. Where am I when I'm frozen out? He felt a cold prickle then, presentiment of an unpleasant possibility . . .

Near the horizon, there was something else, down in

the atmospheric haze, blocky blue shapes, almost invisible. He pointed. "What's that?"

She squinted where he indicated, shading her eyes with first one, then both hands. "I . . . can't make it out. What does it look like?"

"Some kind of big town."

"Uh . . . Yom Shishiy, maybe. A long way from here."

They got up finally and walked on, angling down the rock, back into the sour shadows of the forest, picking a trail between patches of native bramble. There weren't really paths in these woods, just areas not completely filled with brush. The paths on the north side of the mountains had to belong to the Hodai . . . who never came here, on mankind's side of the world.

Remember the woods around Marumsko? Odd woods, beautiful. Endless intersecting paths, running through clean, piney woods, over spongy dead needles, making hard-packed dirt roads through patches of oak-dominated inclusion. We always wondered who made the paths? Dogs? Us? Other children who we, somehow, never saw? We spent a decade wandering those paths, seldom met other human beings, then, more often than not, some eerie, frightening adult, lost in a bath of uncontrolled centuries . . .

Just a single decade, out of ten thousand years; so important to me. Cary's image came up suddenly. Frozen out, for so long. When he comes back to life, out on the horizon, that single decade will still be most of his life . . . Ten thousand years . . . The uppermost miasma of his dream came back to tantalize him briefly, cold mist and black ice. Melis Carthoradis had been in the hydrogen ice for every second of those ten thousand years . . .

He shivered, hurrying after Shvirah. Ten thousand years. I don't even want to think about the possibilities . . .

•   •   •

Against all odds, they made the *Koxavonia* camp not long after nightfall, when the clouds still had a purple tinge and the dimmer stars were still hidden under skyglow. They stood on a little rise between trees marking the end of the forest, looking down into the camp, which was fairly well lit up. The buildings were small, cabinlike, made from the wood of the surrounding forest. Even the roof tiles were shakes, thin slabs of skillfully hand-split wood. They were clustered in a rough circle about an open central square, which held a mass of machinery, most of it unidentifiable at this distance, dominated by a big satellite dish.

Funny that it points almost straight up . . .

Denthurion glanced at the sky, then back at the dish. Aimed nowhere near equatorial synchronous orbit. He looked at the sky again. Hard to tell without getting under it, getting a good alignment fix, but it seemed to be aimed solidly onto the ecliptic plane . . . He tipped his head back a third time. Right. Hard to miss that one. Adomm was a dull red spark in the sky, negative second magnitude, close to the negative three boundary . . . Hell. Maybe just symbolic. At close to two percent solar mass, Adomm was well into the brown dwarf category, *almost* a star, a symbolic star the followers of "Starship" could get close to without much difficulty.

Have to talk to Odin, when I get back. *Naglfar* would have had time to spend at least a little while out at the Adomm Industrial Complex . . .

Down in the camp, people were moving about, walking down well-lit paths, and you could see Olamitic bugs fluttering in the light of the electroluminescent panels, batting themselves against hard surfaces. Occasionally one would fly down to ground level, buzzing groups of people, never alighting or attacking. As sour to them as they are to us . . .

He looked down at Shvirah. "Well. We might as well go in."

She looked up at him unhappily. "What am I going to tell them?"

Should have thought of that by now ... He smiled. "Just the truth. Who you are, who I am, where we came from. We have to get back to Perax pretty soon. They have to know that ... and believe it."

They walked down into the unguarded camp, and then had trouble finding someone in charge. People ignored them, thinking they belonged here. Finally, they found themselves standing before some kind of camp commander, sitting at a desk, dressed in the pale lavender tunic of *Koxavonia*. He stared at them impatiently. "Make it quick, crewmen. I've had a long day."

The girl stepped forward. "My name is Shvirah, third-level engineering sorority, uh ..." She looked back at Denthurion, briefly, seeming at a loss.

The man smiled. "Good evening, sister. I'm Hashuuv, corresponding fraternity. What brings you to my office so late?"

"This is Maaron Denthurion. We've just walked overland from the *Shearah* camp on the other side of ..."

Hashuuv was staring hard at Denthurion, eyes bleak and suspicious. "Outsider?" He turned on Shvirah suddenly, interrupting her. "You brought an outsider *here*?"

"Brother, I ..."

He was staring at Denthurion again, cheeks slightly flushed. "You've made a serious mistake, young woman. I don't know what the consequences will be for you. And your friend ..."

Denthurion smiled.

Shvirah took another step forward, to the edge of the desk. "Hashuuv, listen to me. This is important. This man is ..."

Hashuuv interrupted her again, anger flaring. "You little fool! How *dare* you bring a ..."

"God damn it, Hashuuv! This is the missing Televox!"

Denthurion stepped into the long, motionless moment that followed, extending his hand. "Good day to you, Mr. Hashuuv. I wonder if I might borrow your transceiver node for a quick trip back to Perax . . ."

Hashuuv, pale now, eyes wide, whispered something to himself, a single syllable, then convulsively jerked open a desk drawer. His hand came up bearing some kind of pistol, a chemical-drive handgun of unknown design, which he pointed more or less in their general direction. His hand was shaking enough to make the barrel waver visibly.

"Careful with that . . ."

Hashuuv whispered, "Tallo . . ." then, *"TALLO!!"*

A skeletally thin man appeared in the doorway, stopped suddenly, aghast at the tableau. "Hashuuv, what . . ."

"Get some men. Lasguns, Tallo. Issue them lasguns."

"But . . ."

"Fuck you, *do* it!" Tallo stared for another fraction of a second, then backed out of the room, running and shouting instructions to someone unseen.

It only took about an hour for the frightened camp leaders to get them situated. Hashuuv stood in the open doorway of their prison bungalow. "Meltsar will be here in the morning. *He'll* decide what to do. Meanwhile, you can't escape; there're guards at every window and . . ."

Denthurion waved a quieting hand at the man. "Don't worry about us running off into the forest again, Hashuuv. How about something to eat, instead?"

Hashuuv stared at them silently for a moment. "This is *my* cottage, Mr. Televox. There's food in the refrigerator. Help yourselves. There's a tub, too. You both smell like the jungle . . ." He closed the door, latching it, and in a second his shadow was gone from the little curtained window.

Denthurion stood and stretched, smiling at Shvirah. "Well. Something to eat?"

"I'm not hungry." She pulled her tunic off over her head, breasts bouncing as the cloth released its grip. "I'll be in the tub. I'm tired of stinking." She turned away, dressed in sandals and her thin, silky underwear, walking across the dimly lit room, sweat on her back still glistening.

"All right. I'll fix us a snack and join you."

Denthurion padded out to the kitchen, opening the little refrigerator and inspecting its contents. Not good. The man has a perverted taste for Olamitic convenience foods . . . Still . . . He began pulling out ingredients, pouring drinks, fixing a few little sandwiches.

Meltsar, now. In the morning. I'm beginning to get an awful clear picture of what's going on here. *Hikanesh!* What else? Or what else does a "cultural institution" do with his time?

Question is, does this *mean* anything? The Red Millennium was full of prophets-for-profit, from Joseph Smith to L. Ron Hubbard . . . Even Cpaht, before he assumed temporal power, called himself the Great Seal of the Prophets . . . and made a very good living from the tithing of his followers.

What a Hell of a mess. Whatever else happens, Ardennes Kartavilis is recalled. Ashaan and the rest . . . we'll see. Have to talk to Naamer again . . . and Meltsar . . . Well. Tomorrow.

He picked up his tray of food and walked softly toward the bathroom, with its thunder of running water. From the doorway he could see Shvirah, nude now, bending over the tub, swirling her hand in the water.

This means more to you than you'd like to admit, doesn't it? Of course it does. And it's happened before . . . any number of times . . . What do they say? A girl in every port. Only you never come back again. Love happens, because it's easy to make it happen. Because it's so meaningless. Because life is such a shallow and temporary thing. And because these feelings evolved to hold together our little human bands, because they now persist into a great Metastable Universe . . .

And a passion for order gone mad.

Metastatic Senator Denthurion sat on the deck of his house on a late summer evening, looking out across Marumsko village. The August sunset had been brilliant, painting the sky in streaks of orange and dull red, following the lines of clouds, color reflecting off the smooth upper surface of the old police cruiser, throwing evening light down into the valley for a little while after the sun set behind its tree-covered ridge.

The sky was black now, all the stars come out, covering the sky with rivers of light, save where low clouds blotted them out, the Moon a narrow, bright crescent in the east. It was still hot, the air clotted with the unpleasant mugginess of an Atlantic coastal plain summer, sweat springing up under his tunic, rolling into every pocket and fold of skin, refusing to evaporate.

He put his feet up on the railing, opening the front of his tunic a little wider, rubbing the sweat around, brushing it up into the hair on his chest. *How old am I now?* He reached down and picked up a frosty glass of iced tea from the floor of the deck, the ice cubes tinkling against each other, clicking on the glass, and rolled the cool, wet tumbler across his forehead, then took a sweet sip. *Am I two thousand years old? Hell, I don't* know *anymore . . . They announce the date at every session of the Senate I go to . . . What is it? Fourteenth August, 44,786 . . . Meaningless.*

By God . . . In another six weeks I'll be . . . 2,736 years old . . . Meaningless. Meaningless, all right . . . And the incarnations . . . Eight branchings now. Close to a thousand incarnations . . . adding up. Something like nine thousand years of subjective experience accumulated . . . on top of my own days and nights.

Doesn't add up. Not to me. Overlays coming in every now and then, flowing into my life's experience. I feel like I'm drowning under the weight of it. Just a little while. And every day the same.

Life after life soaking in; world after world . . . What the Hell's the point of all this? Do they live forever in me? Or I in them? Directives going out to the stars, messages to the Televoxic many, from the Senatorial few . . .

Immortality. And *lacunae*.

Life and death.

Bullshit.

Dream.

And dream no more.

The ship's comeye, together with notes from the first incarnation of mark Six, made a reconstruction. We think it happened this way . . .

The forty-seventh incarnation of Maaron Denthurion, mark Five, was alone in a room with his adversary, staring her down. This was a reactor control room, the main power switching center for Elhaaria, capital of Nunsurru Province, on the northern hemisphere of the allopathic focal planet Faih-Andor. He stood in the doorway, gun in hand, slowly closing the hatch behind him.

Sector Marshal Saaraai Atem-Koridis grinned, dark eyes harsh, hand closing tightly on the red handle. "Put your gun down, Televox. I'll pull this thing . . ." She was tall and severely thin, downscaled feminine musculature visible on her exposed arms.

Denthurion walked over to another chair, a few meters from the woman, and sat. He put the gun on the control panel and folded his arms across his chest. "Why? What can you gain now?"

"You haven't beaten me yet."

"By being here in this room with you, I think I have."

"One of us may walk away, still living. That one is the winner."

Denthurion shrugged. "Senator Koridis is impeached. All her Televoxes are under a recall edict. You're the only one . . ."

"I was *always* the only one!" Koridis leaned forward, throwing further tension on the red handle, voice thick with passion.

"Well. You've certainly made plenty of trouble. We've never had a renegade Sector Marshal before."

"And God damn you all. I *solved* your little problems for you! I want what's mine."

"Nothing is yours, Koridis. You know what we are. And what we remain."

"You maybe, and all the other sniveling little bastards . . ."

"Give it up. The universe is against you."

"It's been that way since the day of my elevation. Precious little help I got from the rest of the Metastable Order . . . You think I can't beat the rest of you at this game? Watch me."

Denthurion smiled. "I'm *here*, Koridis. That means you lose."

"Bastard!"

Denthurion stood and walked slowly across the small gap between them, still smiling, his gun left behind on the console. "Come, now . . ."

"I'll *pull* this thing!"

Denthurion laid his hand on Koridis's clenched fist and grinned. "So will I, Sector Marshal Saaraai Atem-Koridis . . ." His arm muscles bunched as he tripped the switch, completing the circuit.

From orbit, it was a pretty sight. When the dissociative reactor's flux mass underwent simultaneous conversion, it triggered nuclear reactions in the surrounding material. A bright ball of plasma boiled up out of nowhere, ripping open the planet's crust, pushing a shock wave through Faih-Andor's troposphere, an expanding ring that spread out across the hemisphere, rolling over the limb of the planet, dropping beyond the horizon.

Cities a thousand miles away were blown to the ground, towers two and three kilometers high toppling, grinding millions of people away into dust and swiftly drying moisture. The starships surrounding the planet backed away, saving themselves, noting the scope of destruction.

It would take generations before Faih-Andor was a fully productive allopathic world once more. If, it seemed, the survivors still thought that was their appropriate pathology . . .

On the deck of his house, Senator Denthurion sipped his tea and stared into the nighttime sky. There was some kind of diamond sparkling on the night side of the Moon, waxing and waning in a hard-to-perceive irregular pattern. Wonder what's going on? Not much action left up there. The Moon had never been a top-notch industrial site, poor in minerals even in the days when that had been necessary to human civilization. Just handy, that's all, hanging up there in the sky . . .

Some of the stars were drifting overhead, dim bits of purple glitter, shedding their own faint light, starships in orbit around the Earth, gathering in their data cargoes, sending down the information produce of all the worlds.

I'd like to get on one. Just fly away. Nothing more to care about, just a tourist among the worlds of mankind . . . Or . . . is that what I *am*?

It just didn't matter anymore.

After a while, he fell asleep, a cool breeze beginning to blow, drying his sweat, making him dream formless little dreams, overlays dominant, experience a dim question mark outlining the void.

Meltsar stepped down out of the *nahhash*, passing beneath the slowing thump of its rotary wing, head-cloak flapping as he strode through a thin cloud of falling dust. "All right, Commander. What was so important you had to break comnet silence to get me here ahead of sched-ule?" Let them know who's in charge right away. No break in a rigid facade of authority.

Camp commander Hashuuv saluted, back straight, palm out, face frozen. *Don't* smile, it's more important than that, but, oh, the pleasure of seeing the next expres-sion on his face . . . "We, uh, have the Televox, sir."

Meltsar started to return the salute, let his hand drop back to his side, started to turn away, but stopped him-self. *The* Televox. He looked down on the camp com-mander, keeping his face still, reaching up and stroking his beard, smoothing it almost absentmindedly. I should have been afraid of this. The kidnapping. That *Shearah* camp on the other side of the mountains. Always stirring up the Hodai . . . Fucking little bastards.

"How did this happen?" His voice came out soft, pitched a little high.

"Uh. He turned up last night, sir." Hashuuv saw the quickly controlled flicker, felt mild disappointment. On the other hand, this man did rule *Koxavonia*, in the name of the Pilot.

"Just turned up, huh? Came wandering in out of the forest by himself?"

"Well, no." Now for the bad part. "He walked here from the *Shearah* camp with a, uh, girl . . ."

Interesting. "One of *them*?"

"Sort of. And, uh, one of our people, as well. She be-trayed us to him . . ."

Interesting choice of words. The overlap between Star-ship and Storm was small but significant; partly because it attracted similar sorts of people, partly because *Koxavonia* needed to have a hand in every affair. "Any idea why?"

"No, sir. We haven't questioned them."

Meltsar eyed the commander with increased respect. Probably smarter than you think you are. I'd've been an-gry if you had . . . "Time we got to that now. Find an ap-propriate place, then bring them, no, just him, to me."

Hashuuv nodded, glad he'd guessed correctly, made proper preparations. "Yes, sir." He saluted. "This way."

As they walked across camp, away from the *nahhash*, Meltsar found his thoughts turning over rapidly. God damned *Shearah*. This has to be Naamer's doing. Too much shit from them lately, now *this* . . . He tried in vain to suppress the turmoil. Got to get my thoughts in order. Bad things happening, but maybe I can extract *something* out of it. His instructions to Kartavilis . . . By God . . . Already making my bailout plans . . . Maybe not. Hell. Too much. Maybe I wasn't cut out for this game . . .

As they walked into the now-vacant community center, Meltsar straightened his shoulders, trying to banish fear. Too late for that sort of self-doubt now. You got yourself into this, serene in the knowledge no one would intervene. Now get yourself out of it in one piece. Got the germ of an idea. Go with it . . .

Denthurion and Shvirah sat cross-legged on their bed, facing each other, waiting. They'd been dressed for some hours now, talking on and off, falling into gulfs of silence. The staccato sound of the *nahhash* landing had brought them up short, leaving a mood of building anticipation.

"What do you think they'll do to us?" Shvirah was very much small-girlish now, queasy with unformed fear.

Denthurion smiled. "Nothing. We'll be back in Perax by nightfall, I think. That ship will have brought somebody important. Mr., ah, Meltsar, I would imagine . . ." Tell her that. But you don't know what these people have at stake. If *their* lives and short-term desires mean more to them than the eventual fate of their world . . . Death won't mean much to me, but Shvirah . . .

Right. Keep telling yourself that. One life is the universe to her, while you have an unending supply. Keep telling yourself you won't mind being snuffed out once again . . .

She shivered. "Meltsar . . ."

"What do you know about him?" Distract her. And yourself. Maybe this knowledge will be useful.

"I met him once." She shook her head. "Just once. He won't remember me. It was at a God's Mast ceremony ... Rewards and punishments handed out. He presided before Tayash himself gave me my sorority pin ..."

"You've met the Pilot?"

"Yes." She looked briefly troubled. "No. He was just ... there. Meltsar did all the talking and touching ..."

Talking and touching. Well. Someone has done his research well. The laying on of hands, accompanied by what amounted to hypnotic, sometimes hysterical, preaching; "witnessing the truth" was a historical standard with this sort of operation. I wonder how much information is actually available on a world like this? The worlds of the Metastable Order weren't completely self-contained, after all, though they sometimes came close to it. The flow of data from planet to planet was irregular, outside the normal channels of the Metastability. Something to be looked into, at any rate. There's more than enough Red Millennium nonsense here. This Meltsar had a deep well of mythology to draw on ...

Footsteps crunched on the gravel walk outside, shadows falling across the curtained windows, then the door latch grated and the door swung open, bright sunlight framing Hashuuv, leaving his face dim, body little more than a silhouette. "Good morning, Mr. Televox." The man stood straight, his voice betraying excitement more than fear.

Denthurion stood, smiling and nodding. "A fine day, I see. Is Mr. Meltsar ready for us now?"

"Uh, yes, sir."

"Well. Your military courtesy is commendable. The proper honorific is 'Your Grace,' however."

Hashuuv frowned for a second, then said, "Your Grace." He gestured out the door. "This way please."

Denthurion stretched out his hand to Shvirah, but Hashuuv said, "Just you, not the girl."

Not the girl. Of course not. He considered countermanding Hashuuv's order, forcing them to let her come along, but . . . "Don't worry. I'll be back for you in a little while." He smiled down at her.

"This way, Your Grace."

They walked out of the shadowy room into bright sunshine under a sky as blue as lapis lazuli.

When they were gone, Shvirah lay back on the bed, trying to relax, to regain some of the inner calm that had deserted her in recent days. She stretched, feeling twinges in her joints and a certain soreness in the tendons on the inner sides of her thighs. Long, long walk, through wild woods, sleeping outdoors, preceded by more sex in two days than she normally had in months.

She rubbed her hands on her face, trying to force some of the graininess from her eyes, reached down and rubbed the tops of her thighs, stilling the ache. I ought to get undressed again. I need a nap. He'd be back, and who knew what he'd want to do then . . .

Their sex acts were already beginning to merge into one another, taking on a fused unreality. Cold, at times. Then suffused by an almost-inhuman heat. One moment it's like love, the next it's like I'm being raped in my sleep. Like I'm a mannequin he uses, like some kind of masturbation tool . . .

The thought was almost, in some palpably sexual way, appealing. She knew some women used artificial devices to aid in masturbation, along with an assortment of *glulaa*-provided lubricants, that, for some reason, men rarely did. Nor do I. It always came easy to me; easy when I was young, easier now that I'm older . . .

She thought suddenly of her friend Shvetletha, who played teasing sexual games with her pet Hoda, Guraayd. Creepy. Not me, though. Raakaa too nice, too cute . . . She'd even been cute that day in the backyard, crying while that ratty old male humped away on her.

Talked to me about it later, a little bit. Confused, though ... Talking about wanting it, as if it were food, nothing to do with her, nothing to do with all the girly things we talked about ...

Raakaa not a human being. Subject, after all, to Hodai wants and needs. I was so wrong to make her read with me, about women in castles and strong, brave men who saw to their needs ...

She thought then about the Hodai in the forest, coming at them in the night, lisping out a barely comprehensible human speech. Hodai, yes, as they were, as they ought to be ... No. Not as they were, not proud, not strong, back in the lost days when they never heard the sound of human voices, but at least Hodai free to be themselves, wild and masterless ...

And after they were gone, vanished back into the darkness, he fucked me like an animal, like that male fucked Raakaa, holding her down, bent over the edge of my old sandbox, pumping his hips at her ... She could still feel Denthurion's quick orgasm, warm semen flooding her insides. She shivered and realized the memory was making her body undergo its little involuntary changes. If he came through the door right now, he'd find her ready ...

Like an animal ... More memories of Shvetletha, telling her secrets. Don't tell anybody. One night, thinking about masturbating, she let Guraayd get on top of her ... Don't tell anybody, but it was ... Shvirah shivered again. Crazy bitch couldn't keep it to herself. Shvetletha was doing time in a mental hospital, while poor little Guraayd went to the furnace ...

That was the way it worked, of course, always had worked on Olam.

Denthurion, now ... Maybe this was the way men were supposed to be, not so much like the begging, argument-worming little boys she knew, tricking her into their beds, lying, always lying ... Denthurion, like the Hoda male, lying on top of her, doing what he needed to, no pretense of "doing it for you," just doing it, and, somehow, making her happy as well . . .

Human beings were a long damn way from nature.

Him, now. Maaron Denthurion, Televox. Man. Sleeping out between the stars, maybe sleeping his years away, tucked in some happy corner of the Pilot's Heaven. Make him feel it when you love him, Shvirah. Hope for Starship. Hope for Storm. Change things here, forever.

Maybe the last best hope the poor Hodai would ever have . . .

Meltsar sat in the community center's meeting room, relaxing in a softly upholstered chair, legs crossed, waiting. All right. This is your one chance to set things straight again. Or as straight as they can ever be. Sell those little assholes down the river . . . A strong, nagging doubt flowed through his thoughts. Do I *have* to do that? Am I this opportunistic? Save my own precious hide by throwing my friends into the pit? I guess so. Only . . .

The Metastable Order just doesn't seem *real*. Does it really have the power to come here and upset our whole world? History says so . . . but is *history* real? The data flow comes from outside, after all . . . If they had the power, wouldn't there be enough Televoxes to make a slightly more frequent show of authority? Twenty-five hundred years!

Then again . . . Kartavilis. A half-million Metastatic Guardsmen always on-planet. *Real* starships in our sky . . . *Naglfar* alone enough to lay Olam waste . . . Even if we managed to marshal all the forces of Adomm and defeat the ship's comeye, *two* starships might come . . . Yes, if the Metastability owns two starships, we are lost . . .

The door opened, spilling sunlight onto the carpet. Denthurion and Hashuuv came in, closing the door behind them, cutting off a brief view of the armed escort that had accompanied them here.

Remaining seated, looking up at the men, Meltsar gestured to a pair of chairs drawn up opposite his position. "We meet again, Mr. Televox." He smiled. "Please be seated, won't you?"

Hashuuv quickly took a seat, but Denthurion remained standing, walking over to his chair, resting his arms on its back. "Hello, Meltsar. I'm sorry now I didn't take the time to read some of your books . . ."

Take it easy. You're still in command here. "I'll make certain you're given a copy of *Hikanesh!* before we go back to Perax . . ." There. That lets him know your intention. But the Televox wasn't smiling, just staring at him, little pools of light reflecting off the wet surface of his corneas. Unnerving.

"When do you plan to send me back?"

"Today, but . . . I'd like to talk to you first." Just get it right out in the open. You know what he said to Ashaan, Kevess, and the Governor.

Denthurion came around to the front of his chair and sat, a faint smile glimmering somewhere. "You have something to say. Might as well say it now."

Is that an attempt to throw me off balance? Why play games? "All right." *Play* it this way then. See what happens. "You've found out I'm more or less second in command of *Koxavonia* . . ."

"A little higher than that, perhaps."

Meltsar waved a hand in slight irritation. Stop trying to distract me . . . "Perhaps. And I know you told Ashaan and Kartavilis you wanted our group suppressed . . ."

Denthurion smiled, teeth flashing briefly. "The Planetary Governor isn't going to thank you for saying that."

Damn it. Stick to a linear path here. Stay out of trouble . . . "I just want to know why."

Denthurion stared at him again, eyes fixed on his face, then said, "I hadn't really decided what I would do. I just asked Kartavilis to come up with a plan. Maybe you're deciding *Koxavonia*'s fate right now."

Meltsar felt a little flush of anger begin to heat the surface of his face. Playing games with me. "Televox, we don't *have* to give you back."

A grin. "No, you don't, Mr. Meltsar. But you know what will happen then . . ."

"Will it happen anyway?"

"Maybe."

Meltsar sighed, taking his eyes off Denthurion's face, planting them firmly on the floor. Time. "Mr. Televox, I really believe in Tayash and his Starship. I want to save *Koxavonia* . . ."

"What can you do?"

I can lie, that's what I can do. He hesitated, striving for a look of bedeviled sincerity. "I can offer you a deal."

Denthurion's grin widened. "Go on."

Get that look of troubled earnestness up front, where it can do the most good. *Fool* him, damn you!" My agents have penetrated *Shearah* completely, Mr. Televox. Let us live and you can pull them down without trouble. Leave Olam as you found it, just a little smoothed over, the top layer of disturbance wiped away . . ."

Denthurion continued to stare at him, smiling, rubbing one hand across his chin, rasping along whisker stubble.

One last push. "Damn it, sir. We *help* people here! You just *can't* put us down like bad Hodai . . ."

Something seemed to crystallize, Denthurion's smile fading fast. "I'll tell you what. I'll stay here for a few days, get to know your 'Starship' a little better, read *Hikanesh!* Then I'll decide. Meanwhile, I'll put in a call to Kartavilis, get the search called off . . ."

Meltsar let out what seemed to be a held breath. A concession. A concession, at least. Give me a full day and I'll convince him . . . "You have a deal."

As they walked across the dusty compound to the camp's communications center, Denthurion looked down at his feet, watching the little puffs of yellow dust he was kicking up rise, expand, and blow away.

What am I doing here? Still exploring, without purpose? No, of course not. It's just easier this way. Why throw away the evidence and make more work for a successor incarnation? Just give them your word that they have a permanent reprieve, gather the rest of your evidence, go back to Perax and . . . do the deed.

Does it bother you, misleading them?

No, of course not.

He thought of Shvirah, of the troubled conflict on her face while he talked her into betraying a major part of her belief-set. Natural. Only natural. We each think ourselves central to the ongoing processes around us. Just instinct, in a being without real purpose . . .

Even I am just a memory, endlessly played out and re-recorded . . .

Why don't I believe that anymore?

Chapter 9

By noon the community center cafeteria of the *Koxavonia* camp was a minor chaos of people bustling about, spicy smells wafting in on a carrier wave of steam from the small, semiautomatic kitchen, people carrying trays to tables, talking, eating, the scrape of utensils and clank of ceramics punctuating a range of voices. The room was, by and large, a sea of lilac and lavender, Starship crewmen in various shades of similar color, variations on a theme, badges of rank in gold and silver glinting here and there. A few people were clad in more usual Olamitic garb, some including head-cloaks, possible instruments of the "Secret Missions" alluded to by certain building labels.

Denthurion sat at the end of one long table, Shvirah to his left, around the corner. The girl was dressed in lavender, wearing her metallic symbols of rank and sorority, spooning up a thick, clear soup, silent, seeming to have regained some sort of inner harmony.

As if they told her in my absence, It's all right. You did the right thing.

Important, that feeling. No one, not even the sheerest villain, wants to regard himself as "bad." She looked attractive in the sleek, clingy uniform, her badges, in silver, mostly abstract, worked from designs rooted in the Olamite alphabet. Her collar was closed by a small brooch in the shape of a kneeling female Hoda. Her "theme," thought Denthurion.

He looked down the table. People eating and talking, a steady transit of bodies, enjoy your lunch but don't tarry, there's work to be done. The sense of purpose here was almost unpleasant. These people think they're up to something . . . Nothing new. Most people think that. Only on worlds in decline . . .

Odd thought. If there were *nothing* like *Koxavonia* on Olam, if this were a world withered in spirit, I might have to introduce something . . . Unpleasant thought. You've been too many places; seen too many worlds in transition, one way or another . . . Did you really want to pull them down? Probably not. The *form* of it, though . . . There are so many ways they could have chosen to accomplish this end. Why *this* one? Accident? Talk to Meltsar.

What about Naamer and his *Shearah* in this context? What about Amud? Is it just these few little things . . . or has the whole culture gone sour? Remember their history. Olam may be ripe for dispersal . . . but it's been tried before.

A subconscious awareness of Shvirah caught his attention, a cessation of her movements in the corner of his eye. She'd finished her soup, was sitting quietly, staring at his profile. When he glanced at her, she said, "They told me what you promised."

So, Mr. Meltsar. How big a coin *is* my promise?

"It's important that you're giving us this chance. Starship may be . . . everything to Olam . . ."

Belief is its own reward . . . He shook his head, smiling. "I'm not going to judge you without . . . looking at all the evidence." He stood up, beckoning to her. "Let's go out and see what there is to find."

A little while later they sat on the carpeted floor of a big room, near the rear wall, behind the last echelon of a group of white-clad "cadets." In the front of the room stood a man in a uniform so dark its color verged on plum, gold braid decorating his collar, badges of rank and service clinging to his chest.

"Welcome," he said, "to the Great Meirhhav Embarkation Center. You have all, I know, followed the Starship for a long time, working among the laity, serving in the ranks of the support infrastructure. Now you come here, having earned graduation to the officer corps, wearing your cadet tunics, bearing great hopes ..."

He paused, looking them over, smiling at the upturned faces. "You hope, as we all do, to board the Starship of God, to leave this little world behind, and all its pain with it, to seek your freedom out among the stars, to find a new life in Heaven ..."

Another pause, a frown, a distant look. "That's what we all long for ... Do you think I would be here today, talking to you, if I could board the Starship and be gone?"

The students were looking at each other, or down at the floor. When his voice restarted, their faces turned up again. "There is work to be done, my brothers and sisters. We are the cadre of God, recruiting his crew, training his recruits, spreading his great truth across Olam ..."

Denthurion folded his arms across his chest, leaning back against the wall. An interesting approach. There *is* a final reward, you see, but you have to *earn* that reward, earn it with work, a lot of work. Still, there have to be tangible rewards. Intermediary rewards, aimed both at the here and the hereafter ... And, finally, they have to see that *somebody* actually goes to Heaven ... It's not like in the olden days, before the Red Millennium, when everybody, without fail, prince and slave alike, went into a moldering grave ...

I wonder where the profit is in all this?

"We'll all go aboard the Starship someday, you and I," said the instructor of cadets, "some of us sooner than others. Some of you will follow in my footsteps, remaining here on Olam, converting those who are ready, preparing those who are not ... Someday the last Olamite will board the Starship of God, leaving this pitiful world to the wind and the Hodai ..."

Another pause, an otherworldly look. "But not today. There is work to be done, my friends, and *we* are the only ones who will do it . . ."

What a fantastic lot. Animal rights and a promise of Heaven. I certainly don't recall having seen *this* combination before . . . Well. Isn't that what you wanted? Something new and different? Is this different enough?

Two questions:

Where *is* the profit in all this? Who is making money, from what activity, and why?

And, worse, why do I wish that this were *real*?

They had dinner that night with Meltsar and Hashuuv, seated in a quiet little dining room, food brought in by servitors who guarded their privacy without. The food was good, of course, but standard Olamitic fare, the garlicky odor of *shuum* rising from it.

Denthurion inspected the chunks of meat in his plate, pushing them around in their sticky, yellowish sauce, rolling them in the bed of noodles, the strips of partially cooked onion, below. I'm getting a little tired of this stuff. Too much garlic . . . Even so, I'll bet, without it, this meat, from some native animal, would be awful. The tangy bite all this food has that I liked so much in the beginning . . . Even raised on terragenic fodder, Olamitic meat must be fundamentally sour. The smell of the forest came back to him sharply . . . And what was it the wild Hoda said? "Smell you bitterstink . . ." Something like that. I wonder how they force these animals to eat grass? There were several obvious methods.

"Well," said Meltsar, dabbing at his lips with a napkin, flicking bits of dinner from the edges of his beard, "what do you think of our little camp?"

Denthurion stared at him, watching his eyes. Meltsar was self-conscious, probably innately so. He tried to keep a fixed gaze, working from some carefully studied model, but his nature kept betraying him. His eyes would shift from time to time, taking in some detail of Denthurion's costume, jumping briefly to Shvirah's lavender-shrouded breasts, looking at an irrelevant object in the room beyond. "It's . . . organized."

Meltsar frowned. "Not the response I'd hoped for. Organization is merely the careful work of dedicated men. What about its purpose? That's the important thing."

"I've been on something like five thousand worlds in my time. I've seen hundreds of promissory religions, my friend. What happens when your note comes due?"

"*Koxavonia* isn't a religion."

"Could've fooled me."

"Really?" Meltsar leaned back in his chair, finally managing to achieve the sought-after fixed stare. "I haven't been to all the worlds, Mr. Televox, or to *any* world. That pleasure is forbidden to the citizens of Olam, so you have the advantage of me there . . . But I have an advantage over you, sir: I know what *Koxavonia* preaches is the *truth*. I *know* it!"

Denthurion matched him stare for stare. You learned this technique from Ashaan, you little shit. Now stand up to a man sixteen times as old . . . "Have you been to Heaven, Mr. Meltsar?"

"No, sir. I'm sorry to say I have not." The stare wavered for a second, then firmed up again.

"Why not?"

"Because I'm . . . . not ready?"

"Then how do you *know* it's the truth, as you say?"

Meltsar broke his eye lock, leaning his chin on folded hands, staring down at the surface of the table with a faraway look. "Because Tayash has been . . . I have the word of the Pilot . . ." He leaned back, focusing on Denthurion's face again. "Look, I don't expect you to understand this, at least not easily. I originally took on *Hikanesh!* as a money-making project, you know: 'My Trip to Heaven,' by Mr. Tayash, as told to Mr. Meltsar . . . remember what the Saints of Disorder used to say?"

Denthurion nodded. " 'There's a sucker born every minute.' "

Meltsar smiled. "Not what I had in mind, but it'll do. Barnum has always been one of my favorite Saints. Anyway, we talked and talked . . . and somehow, I became the first convert to *Koxavonia* . . ."

"You're not the first person that's happened to, Meltsar. Hark back to your beloved Red Millennium: the Saints of Disorder had effective opposition. Remember the Witnessing Movement? Same thing. It's easy to convince yourself that something is so. But that doesn't *make* it so . . ."

"And what of Tayash's experience?"

Denthurion shrugged. "I'll have to read your book. One trip to Heaven doesn't make a universal truth, in any case . . ."

Meltsar's smile broadened into a grin. "Just because I haven't been to Heaven doesn't mean no one has . . . People do *earn* their final reward, you know. It takes work, but they get there . . ."

Denthurion stared at him, feeling his own heartbeat speed up. *I just don't want to hear this, duty or not* . . . "And how does that happen, Mr. Meltsar?"

"Stick around. There's an Ascension Ceremony scheduled for tomorrow."

After they left, dinner completed, Meltsar made Hashuuv leave, despite the fact that the camp commander wanted to argue some points with him, and sat alone in the little dining room, hands folded on his stomach, staring away into nothingness.

All right, damn you, you've done it. How is he going to react to the Ascension? Taking a risk, basing your moves on everything that little slut Shvirah told you. So what if he reacts strangely to all this talk of Heaven? How much of it is his belief and weakness, how much hers? You can't know *. . .*

We'll see tomorrow. Taking big risks, boy, just because you *think* you know what's going on . . .

Back in their cabin, Denthurion lay stretched out on Hashuuv's comfortable bed, Shvirah dozing across his bare chest. Her skin was warm on his, making him body-conscious in interesting ways. He stroked her slightly moist back, wondering when he would get sick of her presence.

Always happens. One short life after another . . . Sometimes these things evolve, sometimes they don't. Depends on what I have to do. Tiy, on Kem, had, almost of necessity, filled up his days and nights. Such a boring world. Quiescent weather, no politics, a sea of peasants all combed down to the same level.

Funny thing is, she's still there. It's only been about five real-time years since I left. I wonder if she still remembers me . . .

Of course she does. Our time together would be a substantial chunk out of a finite life. Kemites live little more than a century . . .

People feel bad about these things . . .

And want to go to Heaven.

No, not really. They want to stay where they are, for the most part. *Koxavonia*, now . . . Finding a way to actually convince people they're going to a *real* Heaven . . . This may be as unique as anything I could have hoped for.

And an Ascension Ceremony, whatever that may be, tomorrow. We'll see . . . But anticipation of the truth was a small, cold sensation in the pit of his stomach . . .

Maaron Denthurion, mark Nine, incarnation forty, stood on the balcony beside President Vasilisa, looking out over Kaiopolis, capital of Tekhne, bright under a midday sun. The star overhead, Velanidia, was a low-grade F, up near the cutoff point, its family of planets destined to remain, throughout their lives, young and raw. Before human planetary engineers had come, some thirty-eight thousand years earlier, Tekhne had been a Cryptozoic soup, life-forms invisibly small beneath a thunderous heaven.

Elbows on a cool ceramic balustrade, Denthurion stared blank-minded out across the city, a sea of glass, photoreactive and thermally stable. Tekhne, though warm, was windy, the streets of Kaiopolis wind-enhancing, breezes wailing around skyscrapers, pushing a faint haze of dust up against the sky, tainting the bright blue with a hint of tawny yellow.

Why did we stop here? No reason. Just to see it. Tekhne is famous, a focal world highly regarded by its peers ... In the distance there were mountains, a dust layer outlined against the sky backdrop, but no clouds.

President Vasilisa put her slim hand on his shoulder, and said, "Our visitors always come out here first. I myself have never tired of this vista ..."

He looked down at her. She was slim and had long, sleek black hair, alabaster skin, and cool black eyes. "I haven't been on a truly allopathic focal planet since I left Earth. I'd forgotten what they're like."

She shrugged, smiling. "I've never been on another one. Are they all like this?"

He looked back out over Kaiopolis. The obvious answer was, No, for Earth was nothing like this. Still, the pastel towers of Helium held just a ... promise ... of what this had become. They went back inside, past the Archive Center's transceiver node and out into the hallway, where a small, open cart awaited them, President Vasilisa slipping behind the wheel, motioning him to a place by her side.

So here I am on another new world, he thought, as they slid off down the corridor with a whispered hiss. What is this? Number eight hundred? Nine? Somewhere, one of me must be closing in on the thousand mark. Why here? Take a good look around you, Mr.

Televox. A world like this is all that keeps the Metastability going . . . And everything that might bring it down . . .

General Medarian snapped off a brisk salute to Denthurion, then turned slightly, maintaining his pose to greet Planetary Governor Orkomeinos. He held out a hand. "Good day to you, Your Grace."

Denthurion shook it, nodding, smiling, looking over the man's shoulder at the arrayed masses of Metastatic Guardsmen behind him. They stood in row after rigid row, motionless in the bright sunshine, shoulders a few measured centimeters apart, shadowed eyes staring at the backs of each other's plastic helmets. They were . . . What? A sea of green. Denthurion's smile broadened slightly at the trite imagery. Men as a sea. What hubris.

The General was maneuvering them around, gesturing toward his men with a broad sweep of one arm. "This bunch is almost done, Governor. About ready to go."

Denthurion stepped forward, arms folded across his chest, staring over the lines of soldiery. "Where to?"

"Well . . . lot of places. Captain?"

A sharply turned-out officer in the front rank of Guardsmen stepped forward a single pace, snapped off a stiff, generic salute that took in the entire space occupied by his superiors. "Sir."

"The Televox would like to know where you're taking your men." He gestured at Denthurion.

The Captain saluted again. "Your Grace. My contingent of four thousand is bound for Namna ya-Mti. We'll be rotating a small Guard force that maintains order there."

"What is that, about ninety parsecs from here?"

The Captain nodded. "Sir."

He glanced at Medarian. "A bit far. You seem to have a big territory, General."

Medarian beamed. "True. Peremenit is a bit closer,

but . . . we're regarded as the best training center in this part of the galaxy, Your Grace."

Denthurion nodded, wondering whose standard had been applied. He turned to Governor Orkomeinos. "What's next on your agenda?"

"Well. The weapons facility at Stilografos, I suppose . . ."

President Vasilisa sat up in bed, watching him undress. She was propped against a set of stiff pillows, the covers down around her hips, combing her soft black hair, hard little breasts throwing shadows in the dim light of the bedside lamp. "You're well put together, Mr. Televox."

He finished pulling his tunic over his head and stood staring down at her. "Intentionally so, Madame President. I'm surprised you took notice."

She smiled. "It took me almost three centuries to get this job. I've . . . developed an eye for detail."

He shrugged and slipped out of his shorts. "I was surprised at your invitation."

She inspected him with an approving eye, and said, "Whoever designed you had an eye for detail as well."

He sat on the bed beside her. "My genetic line has been in place since before the Order was complete. Some Red Millennium gene-splicer with a taste for pretty boys, no doubt . . ."

She reached out and touched him, running her fingers down one forearm. "Very nice. Your skin is softer than I thought it'd be . . ."

He reclined at her side, reaching out, willing himself to become lost in a concatenation of sensations. Don't think. Don't bother. She didn't even respond to your comment about the why of this moment. No reason to know. These things happen. What difference does it make?

But it did make a difference, and he did know, after all. This is her world, everything to her and her people.

Take me at my appearance, give me the simplest thing I might want. Bond me to the world, and maybe, if she is lucky, I will do no harm.

The thought was, as always, slightly bitter.

The Ascension Ceremony was an evening event, golden sunshine slanting low over the center of the *Koxavonia* camp, clear sky dark blue, tinged with a faint red blush. The openwork transceiver box in the middle of the plaza was lit up, little white and blue lights twinkling here and there on its intricately decorated mesh sides, ringing the edge of its skyward-pointing dish antenna.

Old-fashioned, but not old, thought Denthurion. This has to be deliberate . . . but why? What does this kind of thing accomplish? Still, that shivery background aura was settled over everything. What are they going to *do*? This has to be a *silly* little trick. Even the most naive naturopath wouldn't fall for it . . .

The inhabitants of the camp were gathered around the edges of the common, sealing it off with their bodies, leaving one broad avenue to the transceiver from the main administration hall, where the Ascendant was readied. They seemed excited, crowd a rustling source of voice sounds, occasional phrases breaking free, "Lucky, Kellevv. *I* didn't think he was so advanced . . ." and "Boarding the Starship! Just *think*, Saara, he'll meet *God* tonight . . ."

The lights on the transceiver began to pulse, waxing and waning in some complex pattern, and the antenna's servomotor whined, reorienting itself. The people in the crowd began to clap their hands softly, in a slow two-four rhythm . . .

The sky was darkening all around them, light flaring up blue from the corners of a dark village as hydrogen sponge torches were lit. This takes me back . . . When? All the way back to Earth and Helium . . . Remember

those girls? The Red and White Cradle Ceremonies . . .
as fresh as yesterday . . .

The crowd was beginning a soft chant, voices low, almost whispering: Permission. Yes. Granted. Yes. Guttural
Olamite syllables blending together atavistically, punctuated by an occasional clear call: Come aboard! and
Kivuun ehhaad! "One way."

The Saints of Disorder would have loved this. At least,
some of them would . . .

Someone said, "I wonder who his angel will be?"

The doors of the main hall opened slowly, but the
chant continued, softening now, just the undercurrent,
not the accentuating shouts. Meltsar was standing there,
dressed in his finest lavender robe, golden starburst on
his chest, hands raised above his head.

"Friends!" he shouted. "The Ascension of Kellevv:
Wing Commander, First Navigation Fraternity; Senior
Fellow of the Starship Missions Order; Crewman of
God!"

The chant went on, softening slowly, people's faces
turned away from the transceiver toward the little tableau in the doorway, eyes bright beads in the torchlight.
The sky was almost black now, stars winking on everywhere against a deep purple backdrop, Adomm a dull
red eye forming on the face of night.

Meltsar walked down the stairs, followed by a small
group of solemn men and women in *Koxavonia* ceremonial robes. In their midst walked a small, slender man,
head bowed, face frozen in a stiff grin, wet patches glistening on his cheeks.

The lucky Ascendant, I suppose, weeping for joy . . .

They marched to the transceiver, the crowd closing behind them, sealing off the last avenue of escape. The
cage door was opened, exposing a shifting pattern of
shadow inside . . . Already tuning up. A real matter transmitter, at least . . .

It was inexpressibly troubling. What the Hell are they
doing here? They can't be sending him to Adomm, it's

way out of range of that kind of self-contained unit. Bouncing him off a comsat? Sending him to a different camp? What good will that do? This kind of thing can't last ... But it *has* lasted. Twenty years is a long time on a planet like this ...

Meltsar's arms were overhead again as he chanted, speaking the words of the crowd, variations on a theme.

The space inside the transceiver cage brightened suddenly, shadows leaning out the open door, lighting the faces of the crowd. The chanting broke apart and dissipated as people lost focus, distracted by foreknowledge of an impending event.

Now what ...

Red light spilled into the chamber from some other dimension, swiftly taking form, filling in the outlines of a robed woman, taking on color and solidity in a fraction of an instant.

"Bekaa! Look, it's Bekaa!"

The light died down and a woman was standing on the node's baseplate, smiling out at them.

"Bekaa!" shouted a man's voice from the crowd. "Hey, Bekaa!"

The woman looked around, peering at them, then grinned and waved. "Hairaam! Hello!" She turned away, looking down at Meltsar and his people.

Meltsar nodded to her. "Hello, Bekaa. My greetings to the Brethren above."

She beamed at him. "Mr. Meltsar. What a pleasure to see you again!"

Meltsar stepped to one side, gesturing at the Ascendant, looking up now, his face frozen in a look of splendid wonder. "Tonight, Bekaa, your old friend Kellevv is ready to board the Starship of God ..."

The woman stepped lightly down out of the transceiver cage, walking through the dust to stand before the man. She hugged him gently. "Kellevv. Welcome ..."

"Oh, Bekaa ..." he whispered. "I never *dreamed* ..." His voice choked off into silence.

Denthurion stole a quick look around at the faces of the crowd. Many of them were crying softly, tears streaming out onto their cheeks.

"Come!" said Bekaa, leading Kellevv by the hand. "Heaven waits!"

They stepped up into the transceiver, standing side by side, arms around each other's waists. Kellevv was smiling now, face a study in unparalleled joy.

Someone in the crowd shouted, "Kellevv! Good luck!"

A mist of light began to form around them. Bekaa suddenly looked out into the darkness and said, "Hairaam! Good-bye! I'll be seeing you!"

A man's brawny arm stuck up above the heads of the others, waving violently.

The light brightened, throwing a pattern of shadows onto the ground around the cage, then the transceiver stripped off their skins, ate its way through their vitals, and they were gone.

The crowd burst out into applause, people shouting happily, crying, hugging each other; there were grins everywhere. Down by the now-dark transceiver, Meltsar, face distorted by a triumphant grin, turned around slowly, searching the crowd for Denthurion until he found him.

Denthurion stared at the cage for a moment, then tipped his head back, staring into the sky. Adomm is just too far, he mused. What the Hell is going on here . . .

The seventy-first incarnation of mark Eleven boiled into being and stood motionless on the transceiver node. Silence. No. Not quite. A faint, musical rasping noise buzzed on the edge of his awareness, cricketlike, somewhere outside the dimly-lit MAC chamber. All right. New life. Programming in place. You know who and where you are.

Maaron Denthurion, Televox, four hundred parsecs

from Earth, in the forty-fifth millennium of the Metastable Order.

They called this place Saxa, eight thousand years ago. Silent now. And by regional standards something of a new colony . . .

He stepped down off the transceiver node, booted feet making sharp, echoing clicks on the smooth, unworn pavement, and turned, looking back at the matter transmitter. Dust made a white cap on its hood. The air here smelled dusty, in fact. He looked down at the floor. There had been dust there, too, but the transceiver's electrostatic field had pushed it away in a big star shape, long, faintly visible wedges stabbing back from the walls.

A wonder the damn thing worked. Eight thousand years? It seemed so. MAC records on Tarkor, a backward but viable colony some twelve parsecs distant, indicated the fact of Saxa's existence, nothing more, neither information nor mention of further contact. There might be more and better data, the facts of the planet's colonization at least, on the allopathic focal planet Vivliothiki, but that was another forty parsecs in the wrong direction.

The starship's historical backlink revealed little. This was, had been rather, an experimental sector. There were about a dozen supranaturopathic colonies hereabouts . . . Back to nature. Back to your human roots on an alien world. He could see it all: a horde of naked men and women melting into Saxa's cool green forest . . .

He walked to the door node and waited. Nothing. Be a problem if the rest of the machinery is stuck . . .

A wavering face, detailless, hardly human, appeared suddenly in the material before him. "My God," it whispered, voice barely audible, eyes featureless holes showing little swatches of wall material. "Welcome to Saxa, Mr. Televox. I thought you'd never come."

Do I feel pity for an immortal machine, idle for ages? "Let me out, comeye. I have to see your world."

"World?" It seemed bewildered. "I'd forgotten . . . of

course." The face wiped away and the wall irised open into darkness.

Failing machinery, hoarding its meager resources . . . Denthurion stepped into the dark, dank hallway and began walking slowly down a gently sloping ramp, feeling for a flight of steps he knew must exist. There was a strong fungal smell here, nonterragenic, local absorption-feeders taking what nourishment they could from the chemicals of alien stone. Probably been eating the OTANN modules all this time . . . Slowly shrinking the comeye to its present pathetic state.

I wonder if it knows what's been happening all this time? It must, dissolving away over the ages . . .

Outside, the MAC edifice was covered with forest. The building had been much as the others, built for the ages. Now it was covered by a maze of vines, whole trees having taken root and grown in the thick humus. In eight thousand years the forest had had much time to form its own topsoil.

There was a little clearing before the open door, the earth beaten down to bare, hard-packed brown dirt, a blackened circle marking where fires had been lit, two paths leading away into the dim greenery.

All right. Eight thousand years. There are still human beings here, though. Maybe no worse than Tarkor. Over the ages that planet had evolved nothing more than a feudal society, reminiscent of late Iron Age Earth. Without the Guard contingent, without the occasional outside visit . . .

Yet, somehow, no one ever came here. He stepped off the lintel and began walking, picking a path at random, disappearing into the forest.

He watched them from a position high on the side of a brush-choked hill, pleased with this happenstance, hoping they wouldn't notice him. And in a glade below, naked people danced, sunlight dappled yellow-green on sweat-glistening skin. Shaggy men gathered about the edge of the clearing, pounding heavy sticks on hollow logs, drumming, a simplistic rhythm going "DUM-DUM dum-dum," over and over again. In the circle thus formed, slimmer, cleaner-looking people leapt, women mostly, and young-seeming men.

Curious, he thought. Despite their dirt they look attractive. From the way sweat poured down their grimy hides you knew a powerful miasma must be rising below, and yet . . . Right. Atavistic longing, hauled bodily out of my genes . . . The dancers were chanting, "Wug-Waugh! Wug-Waugh!" the same syllables, over and over again. Language. Had to be. A culture, no matter how simple, wouldn't lose its language in only eight thousand years . . .

An interesting thought, though. Was there a circumstance where human beings would forget how to speak? Unlikely. We developed speech in a context no more demanding than this. The old, laughable debates, lining the culture of the Red Millennium . . .

Saint of Disorder Chomsky and his thoughts on talking animals: "It's like saying humans can fly, just because they can jump . . ."

And sixth-century neolinguist Martin, contending, "The only difference between Bee Directional Encoding and Human Metalanguage is the linker concept, *and then* . . ."

All down the drain when the starships flew and the first nonterragenic intelligences were discovered.

The dum-dumming and wug-waughing below stopped abruptly, dancers frozen in place, a little disk of hard-packed earth visible in their midst. A fat woman slowly walked out of the forest, pendulous breasts hanging to her waist, huge buttocks bobbing in time to her footsteps, head down, unhappy. She went to the center of the circle and lay down on the dirt, struggling onto her broad back, staring at the sky, knees up, feet planted firmly on the ground.

There was a rustle at the edge of the clearing as the drummers slowly and stiffly climbed to their feet. They turned in unison to the right, each man moving forward to grip the hips of the man before him. Someone in the queue grunted a single syllable, and they began stamping their feet, hard, left, then right, in a steady rhythm, *dum-dum, dum-dum*. They began snaking around the circle like a hairy conga line.

When the lead man was opposite the fat woman's feet, he turned inward, threading between the motionless dancers, marching to a halt, stamping in place. The man behind him let go and he kneeled between the fat woman's legs, toppling forward onto her, hips thrusting even before he made contact. The marchers continued to drum their feet, chanting softly in time to the man's thrusting hips, "Wug-waugh, wug-waugh . . ."

Denthurion watched, fascinated and repelled. The first man rolled away, joining the dancers in a frozen stance, ichor glistening on his genitals, while the next man took his place. It took each of them, perhaps forty in all, about five minutes to complete his allotted task, the chant growing ever softer as it came from ever fewer throats. After a couple of hours, the last man finished, joining the frozen dancers, and the fat woman lay unconscious, a mud puddle spreading between her sprawled legs.

Suddenly the drummers, as if reacting to an unheard command, rushed back to their logs and took up their sticks again, drumming resumed. The sleek dancers sprang to life, cartwheeling about the fat woman, chanting again, new syllables this time, "HAN-harrh! HAN-harrh!" throaty and breathless. It went on and on as the sun set orange over the jungle.

Sitting back in his blind, Denthurion shook his head slowly. I guess primitive ceremonial doesn't have to have a clear and obvious purpose, but . . . Odd. For some reason I expected them to sacrifice her . . . The image was clear in his head, one of the men producing a sharp stick, leaping forward, rock in hand, pounding a stake through the fat woman's heart perhaps, blood spraying out onto his hands, while the crowd of dancing drummers shrieked with glee and rushed in to begin the feast.

A curious thing. Why did I expect that?

He came upon her unexpectedly in the dark woods, walking back along the trail toward the Archive Center. Both of Saxa's huge moons were up, brilliant, yellow-white light flooding down through the foliage. There was enough light to read by, but it was confusing light, dazzling patches separated by splotches of impenetrable shadow. Now he was stopped, staring warily.

The girl was crouched low before him, long blond hair falling in stringy locks around her narrow face, eyes invisible in the shade of her brows. She was slim, waist narrowing considerably before flaring out to make broad, muscular hips. And he could smell her from several feet away, a gamy odor compounded mainly of feces and sweat.

She looked him up and down, obviously baffled by his clothing, then came up into a squatting position, knees apart, exposing her vulva, which seemed to add to the general effluvium of the night. She muttered something in a guttural dialect, dropping back onto her buttocks, then lying flat in a knees-up position.

Denthurion smiled to himself. "Well, madame. I suppose this is something of a proposition. I hope you won't be *too* disappointed if I decline . . ."

Her head cocked to one side, like a dog confronted by a television set.

"No? Well, then . . ." He stepped carefully around her and retreated a short distance up the path, walking backward, still staring at her recumbent form.

The woman leapt to her feet then, staring at him wide-eyed. She flashed a broad and toothy grin, made some sort of a one-handed gesture, then turned and dashed off into the forest. He could see her for a little while, moonlight flickering off her shoulders and flying hair, then she was gone.

So. What transpired here? Maybe she just gave me the finger for being an impotent clown. Or maybe I just participated in some prehuman ceremonial. Very satisfying. Now explain this erection to yourself . . .

It subsided at some point during the long walk back to the MAC edifice.

Morning light was pink in the sky before the vine-covered wall of the Archive Center loomed out of the forest. The comeye's face, wavering still, detailless, hardly human, flickered on the surface of the door, comic alarm frozen into its rudimentary features. "My God," it whispered, voice a faint breath of blowing sand, eyes stress-less holes showing little bits of grimy stone. "Welcome to Saxa, Mr. Televox. I thought you'd never come."

Denthurion stood before it, staring. What is this? Loneliness? Boredom? Fungal decay? The building's AI would require substantial repair. As for the planet . . .

What are my duties here? Are they unhappy? In pain? The jungle folk of Saxa must live short, brutish, miserable lives. But they don't *know* . . . He stepped forward, waving the door open, the comeye disappearing in a brief swirl of glitter, and stepped into the darkness. As he hurried down the long hall toward the operations center, which might or might not still be functional, the comeye floated along beside him in the fabric of the wall, a pale, ghostly disk, terrified, mouth working silently: Welcome to Saxa, Mr. Televox. Welcome to Saxa . . .

Call out the Guard then, Mr. Televox. Let in the light of the Metastable Order. Destroy these people. They'll thank you for it, one day . . .

Denthurion walked away from the camp, going into the periphery of the forest, gradually making his way uphill through a sour-smelling darkness. The sky overhead was a dull black arena sprinkled with stars, the night wind a soft rustle among alien leaves. Finally he came to an outcropping of brittle stone, a crag sticking above the foliage, where a constant breath of upper air blew the Olamitic stench away. He sat, dropping his legs over the edge, dislodging bits of flat rock that fell away into the darkness, pattering through the vegetation below.

The ledge looked out over the long downhill slope, trees featureless and black, moving shadows in the night, the *Koxavonia* camp a glitter of irregular lights at the foot of the mountain. He could just make out the shape of the transceiver and satellite dish, no longer outlined in small lights, but picked out nonetheless by the general glow that pervaded the town square.

A lot of blue down there . . . Do they use the torches for effect or convenience? He leaned back, a large, rounded boulder forming a convenient support. All right. Stop avoiding the issue. *Think* about it . . .

The sky overhead was a confusing swirl of stars, consistently refusing to resolve into the constellations people in this part of the galaxy had made up. A little deeper in the spiral arm, after all, stellar density a little higher . . . Interesting that the constellations evolve so slowly from world to world. When the colonizing wave passed through this sector, the worlds were settled only decades apart . . .

All right. *Is* this a hoax? If so, what's the payoff? Obviously, I can't find out here. I need to get behind the screen of deception . . .

The image of the ascending man and his "angel" wafting away into transceiver plasma rose up before him on the face of the night. Vanishing; shrinking away to faceless blobs, then nothing . . . How much hoax, and how much real? A different angel every time, they told me. People they used to know, gone off to Heaven and the Starship . . .

And what is this powerful, confused emotion that *I* feel? I'm supposed to be beyond deception . . .

Beyond it, maybe, but human, too. Face yourself, sixty-seventh embodiment of immortal Maaron Denthurion, thirty-third revision. For all your allopathic sensibility, you too wish there was a Heaven to go to, some way to "shuffle off this mortal coil" without really coming to an end.

Forty thousand years squeezed into a hundred centuries . . . What would Heaven be like? An extended vacation? How would that differ from this, or any other incarnation? I'd've gotten tired of Kem in a very little while, developed a certain loathing for Tiy and everyone like her . . .

Nirvana, maybe, separation of the soul from experience, a place of unconscious happiness? It plucked at a momentary chord, but . . . Nonsense. You know what that means . . . There's *another* forty thousand years squeezed into those hundred centuries, immortal Denthurion . . .

So there *can't* be a real Heaven.

No matter how many people wish for it.

No matter how hard I or anyone else wants it to be real.

So what do we have here, then?

A hoax, obviously.

The profit? Maybe none. The face of Meltsar, triumphant after the Ascension rose up, further blocking out the night. Is that belief or deception? Does it matter? Maybe.

An ersatz Heaven somewhere? Olam is a big world, with a lot of empty land. You could hide substantial communities in the continental interior . . . Again, why and how? Even the most committed cult fanatics would one day wonder why the Starship of God looked like a village in the desert, why it had the same night sky, the same two moons overhead. People would contrive ways to walk back to civilization, and the truth would get out. Yet *Koxavonia* is on the verge of becoming a mass movement . . .

He got up, dusting himself, walking back downhill

through the sour forest toward the wan light of the camp. One thing is certain, you're not going to find the answers to any mysteries woolgathering up here. Talk to Meltsar, try to gauge the depth of his belief . . . Then? Back to Perax; try to decide.

Will they let me go? Of course. No choice. *They* didn't kidnap you, after all. Tell them you've decided in their favor. Tell them anything, in fact . . .

Meltsar came through the meeting-room door and stood looking down on Denthurion. "You wished to speak to me, Your Grace?"

The Televox inspected him carefully. Good. Signs of unease. He knows this is his final interview. I wonder though. Why can't I penetrate his game? Even the best actor will drift out of character from time to time. "Sit down, Mr. Meltsar. We'll talk." He gestured to a chair he'd dragged up facing his own.

Meltsar walked over and sat, frowning, crossing his legs tightly, carefully drawing the hem of his tunic down over his knees. "What can I tell you, Mr. Televox?"

Denthurion smiled and shrugged. "Any number of things. I was impressed by your Ascension Ceremony."

"I'm glad to hear that, Your Grace." Meltsar seemed to loosen up slightly, the hint of a smile tugging briefly at his mouth, then vanishing.

"Don't be too pleased. I've been . . . thinking about it."

"And?"

Denthurion turned away slightly, taking his eyes off Meltsar, staring into space for a moment. "There can be no Heaven, Mr. Meltsar. Where are you sending those people?"

The man started in his chair, face a study in astonishment. "There's no deception here, Your Grace. We're sending them to the Starship of God!"

Odd. He didn't expect me to say anything like that. "There's no *point* in this, Mr. Meltsar. I can simply check the altazimuthal settings on the transceiver, then go look at the satellite transponder's activity log . . ."

"Your Grace . . ." Meltsar's face now mirrored an intense look of hurt feelings. "You're welcome to do that. You've been out there all night, you know we haven't changed the dish's aim . . ."

"And?"

"It's aimed at the sky, Your Grace. There's no satellite up there. We're sending them to God!"

Manifest uncertainty grew cold in his chest. Sending them to God. "Are you telling me, Mr. Meltsar, that you're teleporting these people to a random point in the sky?"

"Yes, Your Grace."

My God. "Then . . . you're killing them?"

Meltsar's astonished look grew stronger. "Of *course* not! Heaven is *there*, Mr. Televox . . ."

Heaven. My God. "I . . . think not, Mr. Meltsar."

"You *saw* the ceremony."

"Perhaps I saw you kill a man."

"But they *come back* from Heaven sometimes!"

"Do they?"

"You saw the angel, Your Grace."

"I saw a *show*. I know what a Transceiver Matrix can do. Groups of people *can* travel together, after all. They don't mix in transit. You could transmit the man now, save the woman in the transceiver's storage ring, send her elsewhere later. You *do* move the antenna sometimes, after all . . ."

"But . . ."

"I *see* your belief, Mr. Meltsar. It does trouble me. And if this *isn't* a hoax, then you're killing these people."

Meltsar took his eyes off Denthurion, staring down into his lap, at folded hands. "I *do* believe in *Koxavonia*, Your Grace. I . . ." He sighed heavily. "What if I *am* killing them? *We* aren't immortal, Your Grace. I think . . . What the Hell." He brought his eyes back up, staring earnestly at Denthurion. "One day, Your Grace, *I* intend to step into that transceiver and board the Starship of God."

Denthurion stared into his face and saw the hallmarks of belief.

Later, in the stillness that gathers after midnight, Denthurion lay full-length on top of Shvirah, breathing slowly into the dense mass of her hair, feeling a sheet of sweat ooze slowly from between them. Her hands were moving gently, in tiny lemniscates on his back, stirring pools of moisture, her own breath a soft whisper in his right ear.

She let her legs drop down abruptly, sliding across the outside of his thighs, soles planting gently on the bed, then she straightened her knees. The movement twisted her pelvis, suddenly withdrawing her vulva from him. He went from a feeling of being intertwined, enveloped, to a sense that he was doing no more than lying atop an inert mannequin. .

He lay there for a moment longer, increasingly conscious that his weight was concentrated on his chest, then rolled away, skin separating from hers in a long, tacky peel. They were side by side briefly, then Shvirah curled up, snuggling up under his arm, laying her head on his shoulder and running her left hand up into the hair on his chest, smoothing it, squeezing out moisture.

What light there was in the cabin came from outside, moonlight mostly, filtered through thin linen drapes, throwing dim, slowly moving shadows onto the ceiling. If you watched for more than a little while, the aspect of the shadows changed considerably. The larger of Olam's two moons moved fairly rapidly across the sky.

All right. Make up your mind now. Back to Perax. Call off the hounds. Get back to business. Time to move. Identify the camps. Destroy them. Drive what's left underground. Put this planet in a vise and squeeze it back into shape. Put *Shearah* out of business, and . . . *Koxavonia?*

Denthurion smiled into the darkness.

Yes. Time to shoot down the Starship of God.

But . . . Yes. There is that. *But.* But, what? What are you afraid of, immortal Denthurion, scourge and disciplinarian of the universe? What do you *want?*

Nothing. Just more life, forever. Even if there *was* a Heaven, you wouldn't want to go. What's one little eternity, more or less? You already have *that*, Mr. Televox.

He stretched slightly in the darkness, pushing the inconsistencies away. Forget it. Do your damned job. And get out of here. Forget this place and these people . . .

He reached out for Shvirah, sliding his hand between her legs, feeling her vulva. The crisp hair was still wet with accumulated sweat; when he reached farther down he could feel a spill of warm semen. Good enough. She was still awake, holding her silence, spreading her legs slightly to accommodate his hand. He pushed her over on her back and levered himself up onto her loose and languid body, growing ready in an instant, thrusting.

Third Canto

Salus populi suprema lex esto.

The security of the People
shall be the supreme law.

—State Motto of Missouri

Chapter 10

They stood on a dusty bare patch to one side of the village square, morning sunlight pouring across the desert onto them out of a bright blue sky. The *nahhash* sat quietly beside them, rotor blades drooping, metal ticking softly, thermal gradients moving across panel joints, entropy flowing through fasteners. Night had suppressed the atmosphere's turbulence and the air was clear, with just the barest hint of moisture. The feeling would be gone in another little while, when the day was fully established.

Denthurion held Meltsar's hand in a gentle clasp and looked into his troubled face. Tell him. "All right, then," he said. "I give you my word that I will not move against *Koxavonia* . . ."

The man's face lit up, "Your Grace, I . . ."

The Televox released his hand, motioning for silence. "Hold on. I won't move against you for the present. *Koxavonia* had no part in the events of the past few days, after all. I'll read your little book, then I'll decide what's to be done."

"That's . . . fair, I guess."

Denthurion watched him for another few seconds. Disappointment, but . . . not disappointment. Something's turning over in there. I suppose . . . I have not penetrated to the truth here. He turned to face Shvirah, reaching out, taking both her hands in his own. "And you're staying here."

She nodded somberly. "Yes. I . . ." She took the trouble to stare into his eyes. "I belong here. The love of my God is . . . overriding."

Denthurion smiled. "I love my God, as well, Shvirah, no matter how different it is from yours. No matter how I felt about you . . . one day I would step through the transceiver into *Naglfar*'s memory and . . . go." Is that so? he wondered. Are order and discipline a God, running my universe with an iron will? Perhaps.

The girl leaned into him, sliding her arms around the hard barrel of his chest, clasping her fingers across his spine. She nuzzled her face against his throat, and said, "Good-bye, Maaron Denthurion. We'll meet again."

He kissed the top of her head softly. "Good-bye, little Shvirah . . ." We will not. The thought seemed to echo. Well, he realized with a faint buildup of surprise, I've decided.

He released the girl and stepped back a pace. "You'll hear from me in a few days, Mr. Meltsar." He turned and climbed through the open door of the *nahhash*, buckling his seat belt, leaning back in the chair. The pilot keyed his controls and the motor whined, struggling under its inertial load. The rotary wing began to turn, slowly at first, then faster, blades straightening under centripetal force, dust boiling off the surface of the ground, driving the little crowd of observers back. When the wing was a blur, turned into a transparent disk by persistence of vision, loud thumping noises echoing off the walls of the little valley, the pilot hauled up on the collective pitch control and the *nahhash* bounced into the sky.

Denthurion leaned out the open door, watching the ground recede, the *Koxavonia* village dissolve into forest. All right. You've decided. What next? Back to Perax and Governor Kartavilis. Do your job, distasteful though it may be.

A few hours later, showered and redressed, Denthurion sat once again in Ardennes Kartavilis's office, relaxed in a deep, lemon and leather scented chair, staring at the governor across the flat surface of his teak-inlaid walnut desk. A fresh breeze was coming in through the open window, along with the faint street sounds of noontime Perax.

Kartavilis folded his hands on top of his desk, hard face pinched and closed off. "I'm sorry, Your Grace," he began, "that something like this had to . . ."

Denthurion waved a silencing hand, smiling thinly. "*Sorry* excuses little and fixes nothing."

The Governor sat back in his chair, swiveling a little to one side. "What can I say then, Mr. Televox? I . . ."

Now. Denthurion folded his arms across his chest and slouched a bit in the chair, stretching his legs out before him, digging his heels into the hard carpet. "Say nothing, Governor Kartavilis. Merely do as I tell you."

Kartavilis was silent for a moment, staring at him, finding him impenetrable. "Your Grace?"

Denthurion stood, stretched, and walked slowly over to the window, leaning his elbows on the stone sill, staring out into a blindingly bright day. The Governor's office was above the level of most of the red- and white-tiled rooftops and stuccoed crenellations of Perax, looking out over a hazy vista that shimmered oddly, capped by distant blue mountains. "We're going to uproot Olam's trouble now, you and I."

"You know my opinion, Mr. Televox." Kartavilis remained in his seat, gazing fixedly at the surface of the desk. "I think . . ."

"I *do* know your opinion, sir. I don't wish to hear it again."

"Your Grace."

"I want you to put up an observation satellite."

Kartavilis turned to stare at his back, the leather in his chair creaking softly as he moved. "Satellite. It will . . . take a while to build something like that. *Naglfar* . . ."

"I have other uses for my starship, Governor. Take all the time you need, but build it, and put it in a low polar orbit."

"Very well. What are we looking for?"

"I want you to find all the little camps for me, Mr. Kartavilis. *Shearah* and *Koxavonia*. I want them all."

The Governor felt a chill begin to creep up his back. "As you will, Your Grace, but . . ."

"No demurrer, Governor. Merely follow my instructions. While you're at it, I want a survey made of all the wild Hodai bands, and a census taken of every domestic Hoda."

"Hodai?" How very odd . . .

Denthurion turned to look at him, leaning his back against the windowsill, supporting himself on his elbows. "Hodai, Mr. Kartavilis."

"Very well." The Governor stood, folding his arms across his chest, staring levelly at the Televox. "What is the purpose of locating all the camps, Your Grace? What need will it serve?"

Denthurion smiled, teeth a thin glitter between his lips. "Governor Kartavilis, there is a truck factory up in the Sky Mountains being used by your fine young dissidents to make armed helicopter gunships. I want you to have it make me a small laser battle station. When that's done, have it placed in a polar orbit as well."

Beads of sweat were visible glinting just below Kartavilis's hairline. "A battle station. Couldn't *Naglfar* . . ."

"It is my intention that the battle station and spysat, properly programmed, both remain in orbit, active, after I leave."

"And you intend to destroy the camps?" Kartavilis's voice held a strong note of amazement and disbelief.

"I intend to destroy the camps, Governor. Further, I intend that they stay destroyed."

"It's more than just the camps, you know."

"I know. It is my intention to disrupt this society down to its core. When what we do now has had time to evolve, Olam will once again be a fit example of Metastable order and propriety."

"I think . . ."

"What you think is immaterial at this point."

"Your Grace." Kartavilis turned away, then back, dark eyes afire, finger pointed at Denthurion's chest. "You mean to destroy this world!"

Denthurion nodded slowly, frowning, eyes gazing into an unknown distance. "It will," he admitted, "be a thousand years before a new stability can evolve."

In the dark of night, in his Archive Center chambers, Denthurion sat with his feet on the sill of his open window, hair stirred by a cooler, damper breeze, and stared into the starry sky. The Crab Nebula had yet to rise and the moons were down, the heavens a mass of coagulating pinpoints. Adomm was up, high in the sky, a sullen spark barely able to dim its neighbors.

He waved on the small lamp he'd placed by the chair, its light yellow, barely sufficient for reading, and picked up the thick book he'd laid on the floor earlier. No putting this off, now. Decisions gather a momentum of their own and soon become irrevocable.

The book was bound in dark leather, dyed lavender, embossed with gold lettering, *Hikanesh!*, on the front and spine, a starship colophon set in the lower left-hand corner. On holopathic worlds, where electronic media were seldom in vogue, they called this sort of thing vanity publishing. Or *samizdat*, depending on your politics . . .

He opened the cover, paper, cardboard, and leather crackling softly, the hallmark of a book never before read, to the title page and stared down at the crisp, angular Olamite printing:

H I K A N E S H!
hOlam aTayash
vehaKoxavonia shelAdon

A title to intrigue the easily gulled: "Enter! The World, the Pilot, and the Starship of God." Below that, in much smaller lettering, it said, "The Words of the Pilot, as interpreted by Meltsar." The starship colophon appeared again at the bottom of the page. I wonder why they didn't use the starburst emblem? Probably hadn't thought of it yet. This little round blob, ornate with turrets and antennae, was none too effective.

The beginning of the text was another few sheets along, words starting halfway down the page, beneath a dark banner that merely read, "ONE."

"In the beginning, I was but a man."

So. Not too promising, but effective, right up there with "Call me Ishmael."

He read on. The prose was slow-paced, an obvious attempt to convey "sincerity," verging on leaden, but still readable, laying out its story baldly, with little embellishment, either philosophical or social.

The Pilot had indeed been but a man, living an ordinary life, original name no longer important in the context of the great events to follow. Married, two small children, living quietly in the southern suburbs of Perax, not beloved by his neighbors, not hated either, going to work every day, coming home each night to the comforts of table, hearth, and bed. The work, though. A little novelty there.

In that earlier incarnation, the Pilot had been an industrial technician, employed by one of the mercantile committees of the Amud to keep the varied machinery of its space-borne factories in proper working order. They were not an army, these technicians, only a few hundred in all the world, but they were the only Olamites privileged to leave the planet, to view it from above as a small, distinct world, rather than a whole universe, complete unto itself.

Some of these men and women, the text made clear, felt an awed honor at the privilege. The Pilot, it seemed, was not one of them. Each day he would go to a government-owned transceiver, suit up, and step through, uplinked to an active repeater comsat, signal boosted and transmitted to whatever part of the solar system in which the job waited.

Out in the dark between the worlds, the Pilot would look passionlessly at scenes of magnificence and desolation, the works of an impartial chance collected for his cold review. He would bend to his tasks beneath the dull skies of a small, misty cold world, or look down on the blue-white-ocher ball of Olam, have the sun flaming huge overhead, or turn his back on the broad scarlet face of Adomm, far out on the cold edge of eternity and the trackless waste of interstellar space.

Denthurion lay the book in his lap for a moment and looked out at the night sky, at the swarming array of stars. Trackless. A man of limited imagination. Everywhere you looked there were the footprints of men. The Frontier was, by and large, beyond the limit of human vision, the wasteland quite thoroughly tracked.

One day, mindless and happy, the Pilot went to work.

". . . I stepped through the transceiver, thinking I would come out on the asteroidal body 557 Tsumaat, where the Committee on Mines of the External Resources Bureau maintains a nickel extraction facility of considerable antiquity. It is one of only three in the entire solar system, there being little demand for this metal, and it is constantly in need of repair. This day I thought to replace a set of condensers that had failed after having been in service for no more than a century. Poor quality control in the components factories is a frequent complaint.

"So I stepped through the transceiver, strapped in my work suit, tools in hand, and found myself standing before the face of God.

"There was no fear in me, but no boldness either. I stood before him, speechless, and stared. He was a wall of pale gray mist, filling my entire world, a wall out of which fathomless, featureless eyes opened to survey my own puny countenance. Finally, a great yawning mouth opened and God spoke:

" 'Identity,' he said.

"I could not think of my name. And, in that context, it seemed unimportant. God looked at me, silent for another little while, watching my confusion wax and wane, then he spoke again: 'Function.'

"Well, I could remember why I was here, or rather, why I had left Olam, so I said, 'Spatial Machinery Mechanic, Grade Ten.'

"The great gray face of God seemed to nod, after a while, and he said, 'Resource Net Diagnostic Module, type 0607.' Then he sent me on my way, selecting for me a crewman's position in the vast universe that is his Starship . . ."

What fantastic drivel. Denthurion began skipping ahead through the book, browsing, stopping here and there to read whole passages that seemed more . . . uncanny than others. It was very much like a classic Red Millennium fantasy, detail building slowly, page after page, until a coherent picture built up of the world within the Starship of God. It had the ring of truth. Meltsar wielded his simple words with considerable expertise.

On the other hand, this book has been taken for the truth by multitudes, by men and women willing to step through the transceiver into nothingness.

". . . and one day, at God's whim, I left my post in the Starship, abruptly and unexpectedly tumbling down through the ether once again, appearing in the very same transceiver where I'd departed Olam. I was to find that four long years had gone by, I declared dead long ago, in an unfortunate transceiver accident. My former life had disappeared. My children had put away their mourning clothes. My wife had remarried to a kindly man, a former friend of mine.

"I was cast adrift on Olam, to spread the message God had given me. Heaven is real. The world is a cruel lie."

What remained of the book, another hundred pages or

so, laid down the foundations of *Koxavonia*, the tenets of its faith and practice. It smacked strongly of Meltsar.

Denthurion lay his head back on the chair, spreading the open book on his chest, and waved out the light. He stared through the window into the star-strewn darkness, head awhirl with exhaustion. All the worlds waiting for me out there. I can never see them all.

What do I make of this book? Absurd nonsense? Maybe so, but . . . *But*. What a terrible word . . .

All the worlds waiting, for me and all the others who wander the great dark universe . . . Melodramatic words, said to make me feel larger than I am, said to make me feel as though I *mean* something in the scheme of things. Maybe I do mean something, in a political sense, or, at least, in the greater scheme that is the Metastable Order. Now, like these people, like the followers of *Koxavonia*, like the discontented boys and girls in *Shearah*, I want to mean something on a *human* scale.

Human. Wry bitterness. A human scale I can never know, except every now and then, in snippets and short stretches, and, as always, in my memory . . .

He took the book off his chest and put it aside, still staring out the window, at the twinkling stars, rubbing his chest and flat hard stomach, erasing the pressure sensation the book had made on his skin. His stomach muscles were ridges under his fingers, disappearing into the smoother surface of his abdomen, that giving way to the rising bifurcation of muscular thighs, his genitals an irregular, soft, and movable set of lumps under his tunic.

Thinking about his genitals, touching them, however briefly, stirred animal passions never very far below the surface. This is how Odin wants me to be, how the Mestastability needs me to be, as close to human as possible. Images of encounters past flitted here and there. He could sense the different organs as individual entities now, with separate lives of their own to live out, making a direct connection to the very recent past, and to Shvirah.

Good sex with her. Simple . . . no, simple was not the word. Uncomplicated. That covered it better. Perhaps. Roll onto her in the night. Wake her up. Or don't wake her up, as need be. If you're ready, she's ready . . . No. Not quite. Giving in, or, at least, doing what she thinks you want, for whatever reasons of her own . . .

Hard to fathom. And what does she *feel* about all this? For that matter, how do you feel . . .

Not so simple after all . . .

Don't feel, if you can help it, Maaron Denthurion, mark Thirty-three, incarnation sixty-seven, if you can help it. Not so simple after all . . .

All that shock of pain and separation, repeated over and over again, kept for you across time, despite many passages through cold, black ice . . .

The stars outside his window seemed unusually pretty tonight, the night very dark. With the room lights out it was possible for him to imagine he could see colors in the individual sparks, and somewhere, in the star-clotted wilderness, was one little yellow spark, one of the comparatively bright ones, since it was so close by, the warm, peaceful sun over Kem . . .

You don't want to do this to yourself, Maaron Denthurion. Stay away from it tonight . . .

Impossible.

He could remember the first day he saw her, while sightseeing in one of Kem's southern cities, Sha'oa perhaps, not far from the small antarctic icecap, in the little fertile region that surrounded the south pole. Kem's deserts stretched away north, crossing the equator, before reaching that other small fertile zone around the Qurstab Ocean. Island continents, yes, but the oceans were small, sandwiched between vast land masses . . .

Almost got away with it, thinking about the planet, but not her. I wonder why Odin lets me keep these memories? Many reasons, all of them relating to my value as a tool of the Order . . .

See her standing there on a hillside terrace, small and

slim, dark-haired, dark-skinned, pretty, shading her eyes against the orange rays of a fat sun, well above the northern horizon, what passed for local noon. The sight of her caught at me, for no reason whatsoever. I could have cared less who, or what, she was . . .

She turned to look at him, dark eyes interested. Didn't even know who I was. Turned out she didn't even care. Tagged along with our little party, nothing better to do, got to know me, as me . . .

That's the why of it, Maaron Denthurion. Me, as me. Something I so rarely seem to be. Made me stay on Kem as long as Odin would allow. Life on a human scale . . .

That first night, sitting around our little campfire, shivering away from damp antarctic breezes, gusts coming out of the south. Laughing, talking. The others knew who I was. She made them forget. And that made me forget. Just tagged along with us. Happy young girl, free to do or be anything she wanted, still living in that first little blush of life when all human beings are immortal, before disappointments grind away their souls . . .

And what about you, Maaron Denthurion? What do disappointments do to your soul? Nothing? Maybe so. Then your soul is washed in the cold, black ice and comes away clean . . .

Maybe so. The days went by, with me afraid to ask her *why* she kept company with us, then, coming to my bed one night, snuggling down at my side, just sleeping, smiling in her sleep, just keeping warm. And I never did get up the courage to ask her. Human scale. Like those few days on Earth, so very long ago . . .

He stared at the stars, wondering, and after a while, he slept.

Life shimmered like a dream, some glassy substance come between him and the world, keeping it at a distance, secure and safe.

Cpaht, eyes of fire, lean, stripped-down madman,

dressed forever in clean white tunic and black velvet slippers, cast his shadow across eternity, impenetrable umbra stretching out, thinning, sharp point stabbing into the heart of time. His bony hand took up the collective humanity of individuals like bits of grain, casting them across the interstellar gulf, sowing mankind into the sky.

The Uralic-speaking peoples of the West Eurasian Arctic, the Finns, Estonians, and Lapps, the Komians and their lesser brethren, were fortunately few in number. The hand of Cpaht swept through the cool forests, gathering them up as one, passing in a single day from Helsinki to Syktyvkar, emptying the cities and villages, snatching men from factory and farm, dropping them through the black ice onto an unfamiliar world.

Suomalainen, as it came, unimaginatively, to be called, was the warm and comfortable world of a high-K star, little family of planets orbiting close in: tidally locked inner body, marginally habitable world a little larger than Mars, dwarfish gas giant with a retinue of six tiny moons, all trailing off into a misty ring of icy carbonaceous asteroids.

The second world from the sun, with a surface gravity a bit more than half that of Earth, was a dim place and would have been cold had it not been for its thick shroud of water-vapor clouds, the view from space a fuzzy ball of white. Suomalainen had its own multicellular life, developed over six billion years of slow evolution, odd-looking animals, built on a score of variant symmetries wandering forests whose vegetation had evolved to exploit a broad electromagnetic bandwidth.

It took only a little terraforming before the Suomians could call their planet home. And in only a few thousand years the last native organism was gone. Terragenic life spread holocaustlike across the dark plains of Suomalainen, aided in their conquest by the manipulations of sentient engineers, the long-honed powers of natural selection no match for the swiftly changing complexities of a downward-linking OTANN comeye.

In time the world was a human one of city and countryside, exploited animal slaves wandering through green-black forests, cattle grazing a sea of charcoal grass. The Suomians, eyes easily adapted for a twilight world, lived on, becoming as allopathic as their original charter allowed, lives spanning centuries, even millennia.

In due course the world filled up and several orders of dissent evolved, idea-species radiating until every thought-niche was filled. Why must I live in this dark gray world? Unnatural. Back to good green Earth. Technology is infinite in its power. Why must I die after only a dozen centuries or so? Into the transceiver. Give me immortality. The transceiver is death, as sure as any. Back to the old ways, before Cpaht turned humanity to dust. If I must die, let it be in the natural way, after a long and unified life. Better a century of reality than a simulated eternity . . .

And so, in further due course, the ships went out again. Suomalainen was the only original colony in its sector, the stars about it empty of terragenic life-forms. There were, however, worlds of every sort, from cruel ice moons at a brittle ten Kelvins to molten drops of metal seething close by swollen white suns. And among them the usual thin leavening of garden plants, harboring their own life-forms, waiting silently for the killers to come.

Transmitted out of the world's depths, Denthurion stepped from the irising door of the *puhelin* into a glass-walled observation room, looking out across the stark grandeur of Hermostunut. The room was a dining room of sorts, little tables here and there, people scattered among them, talking softly, sipping from beakers of some pale, dry beer, gazing placidly out into an endless night.

He walked slowly across the room, long, thin legs folding smoothly, feet drifting just above the surface of the nappy carpet. Getting used to it now. Difficult, at first. Hermostunut's surface gravity was very low, no more than a few percent of Earth Standard, and the transceiver had had to make drastic adjustments to permit him to walk with a reasonably human gait.

It was the cube-square law, of course, applied with an interesting twist. As a human being diminished to a few percent of his original size and volume would be impossibly overmuscled, so too would a man sent to live in a very low gravitational field. The ship's comeye, sending him through the transceiver link, had made the necessary adjustments. These changes had been made to the Hermostunutista as well, creating a race of stalky, insectile men and women. They, however, were hardly aware of the change.

Han Poalo rose from his table, shaven head a featured disk balanced atop a ten-centimeter neck, extending his bony hand on the end of a rope-tendoned arm. "Your Grace. Pleased you could make it." He smiled, teeth standing out from his gums in angular array, eyes like black holes, all broad pupil and dark iris.

Denthurion took the hand briefly, then folded himself into a chair that was itself skeletal, all hard, flat plastic surfaces and metallic rod connectors, no more than the essence of a place to sit. "Glad to be here." He waved a hand at the black landscape outside, soft, bare, rolling hills under an airless and starry heaven. "I don't get many opportunities to see a world like this."

Poalo's thin fingers wrapped around a tall, narrow black bottle, pushing it across the table. *"Olut?"*

"Thank you." Denthurion picked up the bottle and tipped a swallow of beer into his mouth. It was fizzy and almost tasteless, like bitter ginger ale.

"I'm surprised. I envy you your travels, Televox. I would've thought you'd seen so many Hermostunuts that one more would bore you to extinction."

"There are many planetary systems like this one. Automated mining cells for the most part. No reason for me to see them . . . I understood you'd done some traveling."

Poalo shrugged. "A very little. I came here with the

colony ship from Suomalainen, of course. Since then, a half-dozen trips to neighboring solar systems, pushing my company's interests. Hardly what you'd call *travel*, Your Grace. I've never been to a world outside the Suomian cultural surround."

Curious. The man's statements had been bald ones, without any sort of special inflection, not meant to *conceal* their content, exactly, but ... "How old are you, *herra* Han?"

The man seemed surprised. "Old? Well, let's see ... That's a hard one. Uh ... Well. We came here from Suomalainen some eighteen standard Millennia ago ... and ... I must have been born quite a while before that. Um." He shrugged. "It was thousands of years after the Exodus Fleet dropped us off. Well after the Hhurull Wars, too. Why do you ask?"

Denthurion picked up the bottle and took another swig of *olut*, the liquid buzzing softly on his tongue, imparting little. You knew about this, but it was hard to absorb. These people were so extreme, they had a special term devoted to them. *Ekallopathy*. People perfectly, artificially suited to their lives and environment; transceivers tuned to flawlessness. There was no *rule* against this sort of thing, but Metastable custom ... "No pressing reason. Just trying to get a sense of who you are, Han Poalo."

A little later the two of them went for a stroll outside. They stepped into the *puhelin* booth and dialed up a special destination, the transceiver transmitting them into a pair of spacesuits, lined up with many others along the outside wall of the Dome of the Grand Concourse, Hermostunut's main surface cultural nexus.

Denthurion stepped away from the wall, staring out across the dull, dusty landscape through his clear, optically reactive faceplate. Rolling hills on the other side of a flat, well-tracked, crater-spattered plain, distant, slope-

sided mountains ... Despite the light of the dome, the
sky above was sprinkled with stars, patterns embedded in
each other in endless shades of white, occasional smears
of nebulosity peeping wanly out of the darkness.
Hermostunut's M5 primary was a brilliant reddish-yellow
jewel low on the horizon, washing out its immediate
neighbors.

"We're near perihelion now," said Han Poalo. "It's unusually bright out here today."

Hard to absorb. Hermostunut was really nothing more
than a large planetoid, orbiting its distant sun in an eccentric orbit many millions of kilometers long. He looked
at the ground. Chondritic dust, really, layers of it over
primordial ice over a rocky and metallic core. And despite its dwarf sun, the Hermostunut system was metal-
rich, a swarm of planetoids clustering about the dim star,
nothing so large as to require special mining measures.
These little worlds could be strip-mined away to nothing ... And men came to live on Hermostunut merely
because it was the only body in the system large enough
to have a respectable gravitational field.

"Go for a ride?" Poalo motioned toward a row of small
electric carts parked nearby.

As Denthurion climbed into his seat and the cart began to roll, he thought, There is nothing here for a wandering Televox, no work to be done, but I needed to see
mankind like this. Here, without reason, they live on and
on into an empty eternity.

Denthurion sat on the Archive Center's main balcony,
eating a breakfast of fruit and coffee, looking out toward
Olam's dusty horizon. Today the lower portion of the sky
had a faint peach hue, residue of dust storms far inland,
but directly overhead the heavens were still pale blue,
sunlight properly scattered. Footsteps scraped the concrete behind him and he looked up, "Morning, Kinnock."

"Welcome back, Your Grace."

Denthurion motioned for him to pull up a chair and, as he sat, offered him the bowl of fruit. Maclaren shook his head. "I suppose Mr. Kartavilis has told you about our conversation?"

"Yes, he . . ." Maclaren smiled thinly, eyes on the distant forest. "Hardly a conversation. From the sound of it, more of a dressing-down. I've never seen him so angry."

"And what do you think?"

Maclaren frowned. "About the Governor?"

"No, Kinnock. Don't be contrary. About the things I told him to do."

"Well." That. Maclaren rubbed his jaw softly, continuing to stare out at the countryside. "I don't know. I . . . *suppose* I share some of the Governor's feelings about Olam, though I haven't been here so long. On the other hand . . . You are right in enforcing the rules of the Metastable Order. But . . . this place is . . . different, somehow. I don't know."

"I won't punish you for being opinionated, Kinnock. Tell me what you really think. What should I *do*?"

Maclaren turned to stare at him, eyes bright blue holes into nowhere. "Leave Olam alone, Mr. Televox. In fact, maybe just *leave*."

"Leave? Why?"

Maclaren shrugged. "I couldn't tell you, not exactly. I do know I'll be transferring out soon. I've had enough of this place. I intend to leave with you aboard *Naglfar*, whenever you're ready . . ."

"And you think I should just go? Leave Olam to stew in its own juices?"

"I'm beginning to think we should all leave, Mr. Televox. You, me, Kartavilis, the Guard contingent. Let this place be."

"You know what you're saying?"

The man sighed, sitting back in his chair, staring slit-eyed into the sky. "No. I just know how I feel. I've been privileged to see a tiny slice of the Metastable Order, not a hundredth of your own experience. For the most part, it works well. Here?" He shrugged again.

"And you feel that way despite *Shearah's* potential for violence, despite the fact that *Koxavonia* is teleporting people away to nowhere, in effect *killing* them?"

"They die anyway, Mr. Televox. What harm can there be in dying full of hope?"

Full of hope. Yes, there is that. "What good can there be in it?"

"I don't know. Why not come back in another few thousand years and see?"

"Save Olam as some kind of naturalistic experiment?"

"Yes. I suppose so."

"That, unfortunately, is not our mandate, Mr. Maclaren."

"Unfortunately, as you say. You are, of course, correct in your statements." He turned to stare at Denthurion again, eyes unhappy. "I know, Mr. Televox, that these people are doomed. It's why I want to leave. If I could go before you do what you are about to do, I would."

Denthurion nodded slowly. "I might go with you, Kinnock, if I could. But I took up this burden of my own free will . . . And there is no way, honorable or otherwise, for me to put it down."

Odin burned above him out of a darkling mist, single eye a well of cold compassion, Hugin and Munin represented by four tiny red sparks, staring down at him accusingly.

"What am I to do?"

The god sighed, a distant rustle of wind. "Your mandate, Denthurion Televox, not mine. I am here to see and remember and transport."

"But you can advise me. You know that."

"Ask."

Ask. Always questions, never answers. Time closes in on you, Mr. Televox. "If Meltsar is transmitting people to random points in space, where are they going?"

Odin seemed amused. "Nowhere, of course. Or everywhere. I'm surprised at your misconception. Electromagnetic beams are not transmitted to a 'point,' whether they have a specific destination or not. The wave-packet beam goes on until a receiver gets in the way of the signal."

"And the data?"

"Well." The god shrugged. "I suppose so. Attenuating, of course, losing energy to the cosmic redshift."

"And becoming scrambled in short order; beyond our ability to extricate useful information."

"Useful is the key word here. Chaos theory says the information is never lost, but, as you say, beyond our rather limited abilities. Theoretically, we could transmit people across interstellar space. We merely lack the computer power needed to receive them at the other end."

"Do you think we'll ever develop that power?"

Odin seemed wistful for a moment. "No. There are practical reasons that place these things out of reach. Even if there weren't, there are . . . historical reasons not to expect it. It's your job, in a way, Mr. Televox, to see that it never happens."

So it was. "The *Koxavonia* Ascendants, then, will continue outward, until they reach the end of the universe, theoretically receivable somewhere."

"Theoretically. But it will be a different universe by then."

True. "What do you think of my decisions regarding the fate of Olam?"

"It seems as though you are doing what is required of you. My opinion is not needed."

Closure on that phrase then. The comeye will keep its own council. That much is tradition. "What did you find at Adomm?"

Odin's mood lightened, as if it were glad to be off the subject of feelings and decision-making. "An interesting place. Shemesh comes close to being a double star. The region around Adomm resembles the automated industrial complexes in place around many class-M dwarves. It is an anomaly found this close to a world like Olam and probably would have been better served by being an independent entity."

For every human-filled world in the Metastable Order, there were a dozen factory systems, "manned" only by OTANN neurotaxy and robot machinery. Without them, darkness would, inevitably, fall. "Do you think we should take steps to implement such a severing?"

"Perhaps not. It seems likely that the actions you will take on Olam will accomplish that end, in any case."

Maybe so. We will be pushing Olam backward, toward an earlier stage in its evolution, back toward a previous cusp, when a wrong turning was made. Adomm, out on the edge of the interstellar dark, would go on functioning, without human intervention . . .

Curious. Tayash and his brethren out in space, working to repair those machines. I wonder what flaw that indicates in their machinery? "Did you find many humans out there?"

"A few; hence my feeling Adomm would be better off if reconstituted as an independent entity. The OTANNs I interviewed seemed subtly damaged by their constant interaction with the human repairmen. Crippled if you will. Handicapped." The god paused, eye smoky and distant, then said, "It was most unusual. I've not seen them like that before."

"It's done you no harm."

"I am a special case. All the ships are." Odin loomed above him momentarily. "*Our* task, mandated long ago, is to live with that crippling."

Denthurion smiled. "We do what we must, Odin of *Naglfar*."

"Must? Yes. That is the correct word, Mr. Televox."

Denthurion awoke in darkness, bathed with cold sweat, the breeze from the window blowing strongly across his chest. Black ice. And our interview converted to a dream.

The image of the Ascendants wafting away into the night was with him strongly, a vision of them dissolving into the fabric of the universe.

Do they become one with it? Don't be so silly. These are simple physical processes, easily predictable, the mathematics of it known for more than forty thousand years. It's killing, because we lack the refined techniques necessary to recapture their data stream.

And yet. Yet. Realms of the imagination. Humanity is not the only sentient species in the universe. We've found hundreds in this little quarter galaxy alone. In a mere flyspeck of time, we've run across a people like the Hhurull, nearly as mighty as ourselves. Somewhere, in a distant galaxy, you could imagine another Metastable Order, older and grander by far than our own. And, one day, out of their matter transmitters come . . . humans, dazzled by an eons-long journey.

What about us? Are the ghosts of lost aliens, accidentally cast out by their civilizations, passing through us every day, modulated neutrino streams blended by time until we, in our pathetic and primitive state, are unable to distinguish them from the quantum dissonance of Creation?

Old ideas. Red Millennium ideas. Dismiss them, Mr. Televox, they can do you no good at all. Go to sleep.

Yet you continue to wonder, and in sleeping, the dreams come back, and . . . *Turing*. Why do I remember that name just now?

At some point during the night, thunder began in the distance, a low, remote grumble.

Out of the deeps the cold ships came, filled to overflowing with Suomalainen's nullipathic dissident few. When the new world flew apart under a pathological weight no less complex than the one that had collapsed the old, problems multiplied. Cast out by the Suomian many? Simple: take passage on the next Metastatic vectorship, go with your friends to a neighboring star, set up a new world, all your own, governed by those principles you hold dear . . .

Satisfactory, until the adherents of Suomian nullipathy decided they'd had enough of degradation and suppression. When the democratically elected government of Suomalainen put their dying children through the healing fires of the transceiver net, they knew it was time to go. It was a thorny problem. What should we do, step through the transceiver to avoid the transceiver? Stay here and be forced to step through it at gunpoint, as our Earthly ancestors were in Cpaht's terrible time? Hard choices, long thought out.

The answer was simple enough in concept but difficult in execution. Under the urgings of the nullipathic minority's legislative representatives, the pace of the remote out-system factories quickened to a level of activity seldom seen, even in the ambit of a nascent allopathic focal planet like Suomalainen.

It went on for the better part of a century, at one point reaching a pitch not so different from the self-limiting world of the late Red Millennium, catching the eye of a passing Televox. Satu Midentionis came to look over their little universe, frowning, wondering if a vacuole was being born here, if intervention was needed. But, no, when the nullipathic dissidents were on their way, this special economy would wind down, sink to a smoldering ember, and gradually wink out. He departed, relieved. No Sector Marshal's role *this* time . . .

In due course, the factories of an extended Suomalainen belched forth a double score of ships, modeled on the vectorships of old, or, rather, on their direct ancestors, the crewed starships of the eighth Red century. The ships were placed in orbit around Suomalainen, a string of bright baubles circling the world, and the nullipathic few rode into the sky, jolted and miserable, aboard the tiny landing craft they'd devised, twenty thousand to a ship, until their whole pathetic number, eight hundred thousand in all, were gone.

The ships' engines lit, violet fire shining down on the cloudy skies of Suomalainen as they spiraled away into the darkness, flaring ever brighter on the long climb toward the interstellar deep. In their holds, the nullipathic Suomians slept, undreaming, waiting for a new life to begin.

Arriving in a later century, they called the world Masentunut, and moved right in. It was a pretty little planet, Earth-like under bright blue skies, native life far advanced into something like a late Paleozoic splendor, things like arthropods and amphibians wandering through green and vermilion forests, things like fish in the sea. The nullipaths moved in, to live their lives in harmony with alien nature.

Saanko Daara lay in his bed, breathing softly, the wind rasping in his throat, occasional bubbles of phlegm catching in his windpipe, choking him gently. His face was ropy and lined, tired from the ceaseless wear of four score years. The eight decades were a heavy burden, it seemed, that he longed to put down. His blue eyes were dim and watery, yet he could still turn them toward the window, watching the bright sky wax and wane, the clouds drift by, the stars glitter across the face of night.

Denthurion stood beside the bed, looking down at the old man, wondering at the vagaries of choice. "I'm sorry to see you like this, *herra* Saanko."

Daara looked up at him, turning his head slowly. "Ah. Good day to you, Mr. Televox. I'm glad you could come."

He put his hand on the old man's shoulder, almost flinching, repelled by its coldness. "When I heard you'd fallen ill . . ."

"I'm pleased. We had many good talks together. It's fitting for you to come and see me off." He coughed, face graying, and swallowed with difficulty.

"Would you like me to . . ."

"No, no." Daara smiled. "This is so easy. If I could only tell you how easy. Not painful. They call it the old man's friend, you see."

The old man's friend? It made no sense at all. Denthurion felt a momentary urge to snatch the old man from his bed and race off to the MAC building. Feed him through the transceiver, just once, up to *Suleyman* and back down again. A new Saanko Daara would emerge from the fire, young and strong, gifted with more decades of life . . . A new incarnation, who would consider the old *herra* Saanko just as dead as he soon expects to be, a bitter, betrayed man who would never forgive me.

Daara said, "I feel privileged to have lived during the time of your coming, Mr. Televox. We have so many legends about your predecessors, the man who saw us off from Suomalainen, eighteen millennia past, the few who came at odd intervals, many lifetimes apart. Now I have lived to see a Televox myself! What splendor."

Denthurion shook his head slowly, pityingly. He wanted to say, It doesn't have to be this way, friend Saanko . . . But the words would not come. Lifetimes, he thought, lost throughout the ages, without need.

The old man looked out the window, smiling, and sighed, liquid mucus roughening the sound. "It's a beautiful world," he said. "I wish . . ." He stopped, a look of intense surprise suffusing his features, then his eyes went dull and still. A faint breath whispered from his open mouth and he seemed to relax slightly, then there was nothing more.

Denthurion looked down, hard, at the thing in the bed, then he turned on his heel and walked out of the room. As his boot heels clicked in the long corridor, he thought, Not far to the Archive Center, and away, into the sky. Take me from this awful place, where men die like that . . .

Denthurion sat out on the MAC balcony, damp, mid-morning air hot and prickly on his skin, looking across the rolling landscape of Almana Valley toward the Sky Mountains. Though the sky here was bright blue, sunlight streaming down, over the mountains it was dark and livid, landscape covered by a bruise-colored shadow. Lightning flickered here and there among the steep, verdant hills, orange and bright white, and every once in a while you could make out an individual bolt, sinuous, strobing on and off. The thunder would roll in at odd intervals, dissociated from the light. They were long, low peals, heavy furniture pushed slowly across a rough wooden floor.

Very still. Very still out here. The high humidity made the windless air seem almost palpable, the light patina of sweat on his forehead refusing to evaporate. It seemed to act like a lens, brightening the already strong sunlight into a faint pins-and-needles aura. Maybe when that storm gets here, it'll cool things down. Thunderstorms usually have wind . . . But the storm was hanging in the sky over the mountains, motionless. Maybe it was raining in the Sky Mountains. Hard to tell whether the shadow was compounded by mist or not.

A hard night for me, very long. The skin about his eyes felt grainy and stiff, as if bits of dust were swimming out of his lachrymal ducts. Ought to step through the transceiver. Be normalized.

Something bothering me. A bit of laughter there. Many things. But the dreams . . . Booted feet scraped on the stone deck behind him. He twisted his head, looked over his shoulder and up. Two green-clad Guardsmen had appeared, holding a disheveled, bearded young man between them. One of the soldiers released his grip on the man's upper arm and saluted.

Denthurion smiled. "Good morning, Mr. Naamer." To

the soldiers, "You may go." They saluted, spun, and were gone.

Naamer shrugged his shoulders, looking around uneasily, then came forward until he was standing beside the balcony's little breakfast table. "Your Grace."

"Sit down, Naamer."

The man hesitated for a moment, glancing toward the door through which the Guardsmen had gone, then slid into the other chair, remaining upright, as if he feared to lean back. "I take it this is the moment in which my fate is decided?"

"If you have a fate."

"Your Grace?" His eyes darted briefly, accentuating a generally fearful air.

"The *Shearah* game is over, Naamer."

"I . . . thought it might be." He looked downward, clasping his hands on his knees, frowning, then back up at Denthurion. "What about your words when we first had you, Mr. Televox? You said you'd look into Amud, about changing things . . ."

"It will happen, Naamer. The first moves have already been made."

"If that is so, then I don't care what you do to me." He sat back in the chair then, seeming to relax. "What are you going to do, Your Grace?"

Denthurion smiled again. "Set things right again. You've never lived in a proper Metastable society, Mr. Naamer. Given the brevity of holopathic men's lives, you never will. In a few centuries, though . . ."

Naamer nodded slowly. "I see. I don't think that was what I wanted. Not freedom, but . . . Maybe you're right. I can't see it from this limited perspective. *Are* people free on the other worlds?"

A shrug. "Free? No. But in a properly managed society that fact is not evident."

Another sad nod. "Not evident. Better than what we have here, I suppose. Too bad."

"As you say. You worry too much about Red Millennium drivel, Mr. Naamer. Those concerns—freedom, dignity, humanism—were never real. They're just ideas, just . . . bullshit. That realization was the true gift of Cpaht."

Naamer straightened up again, eyes narrowing, filling with some of the old anger. "I never believed that, Mr. Televox. To me it will always be real."

"To your detriment."

"Easy to say these things, Your Grace. Hard for them to *mean* anything." He twisted in his chair, looking out across the valley at the swelling clouds on the horizon, then north toward Perax. The city was a collection of hazy boxes in the distance, human smokes and vapors held in by a short-lived thermal inversion. "What will happen to me, now? Punishment? I'd like to know."

Denthurion smiled a third time. "Go home to your friends, Mr. Naamer. *Shearah* is done. It's time for you to be an adult now."

A look of astonishment. "I'm free?"

"Almost. Not quite."

"What do you mean?"

"Do me one small favor."

"Your Grace?"

"Get in touch with Mr. Meltsar for me. Tell him I'd like to speak with him again."

"Here?"

"Well. No. Out at the *Koxavonia* camp. Tell him we're coming. Then get your little helicopter. I enjoyed the last couple of rides."

When Naamer had gone, bustling away, unbelieving, Denthurion sat back in his chair and watched the storm clouds bulging ever higher into the sky, dar'ning the landscape as they crept slowly out over the flicker of lightning reflected off the ground b of orange and white, the occasional ripple You could see quite plainly now that ther just clouds and lightning, a rumble of der. And wind. There was motion amor carpeted the far rim of the valley. You couldn't see the individual plants so far away, just a sheet of uniform color, changing now, different hues sparkling on the edge of vision. It meant a strong wind was blowing under the clouds, turning the leaves belly up, in anticipation of the deluge to come.

When the Hell did I decide to go back out and see them again? Never. He shook his head slowly. Subconscious working overtime, distorting life into the excrescence of dreams. Now what? Go?

He could see Shvirah's face as if it were painted on the sky. Is *that* the reason? Of course not. There have been a thousand Shvirahs. Ten thousand. So many they blend into a single faceless woman. What then? The souls teleported away into the great dark? Nonsense. That *will* come to an end. The book? The believers? No. Tayash. I'm going out there to see Tayash.

He stood, stretching, and stepped forward to lean on the parapet, staring out at the coming storm, large now, a band of dark clouds stretching across half the sky, almost ready to blot out the sun. Cooling. The first tendrils of a breeze stirred in his hair, wiping away the humidity in an instant, then a rushing sound started up, wind hissing in the nearby vegetation. As he watched, a ripple began in the grassy fields a few kilometers distant, sweeping toward him, making sealike waves along the surface of the ground, liberating the sweet smells of Kem and, with them, memories of soft-skinned Tiy.

Not long after that the rains finally came down. Denthurion and Maclaren stood together under a little overhang by the ornithopter landing stage, looking out into a gray and strident mist. The rain fell in a thin, solid curtain, small drops, close together, dropping out of an invisible gray sky, bouncing on the concrete deck, a bil-on overlapping splashes preventing a liquid surface forming, just a sea of spray, leaping up to ankle height, shrouding the floor. If you looked up, peered closely at the rain itself, you could see little swirls, vortices moving through the air, wind-driven, marked by the coordinated movement of endless little drops.

Over the steady sizzle of the downpour, Maclaren said, "Why the helicopter? Why not one of our ornithopters?"

Denthurion shrugged, smiling over at the man. "You said yourself they weren't safe. Why take a chance in this weather?"

"But . . ."

Denthurion laughed. "No real reason, Kinnock. I *liked* my last couple of rides. The helicopters are so . . . archaic. So . . . *Red*."

Maclaren stared at him, lips compressed into a thin line. Who knew what this Televox was really thinking? One supposed it didn't matter. I'll be glad when I'm gone from this place. Way past due for another posting. Some new situation I can cope with from scratch. No complications . . . yet. "So you mean to put yourself in their hands again," he said.

"If you want to look at it that way." He glanced at Maclaren, saw the doubt. "I'm not a *real* person, Kinnock. It's not a *real* risk . . ."

"If you want to look at it that way."

Denthurion laughed again and they fell silent, staring out into the rain, which fell with unvarying force. The sound of the helicopter arrived long before it was visible. At first, all you could hear was a distant thumping sound, deep-pitched, thudding against the walls of the building. Though he looked closely, Denthurion could see no sign of pressure waves moving through the rain mist. Some psychological component to the sound . . . or the graininess of the rain merely too coarse to pick up the moving wave front. In a while, a high-pitched undertone appeared, connecting the thumps, growing louder, then faster, until the noise was a constant, grinding roar. The helicopter appeared like an apparition out of the mist, one moment nothing, then a dark outline, then a swirling machine throwing rain in all directions.

As it squatted on the landing stage, Denthurion waved abruptly to Maclaren and dashed out into the rain, feeling the tiny drops like cold fists on his back and neck, hair wetting rapidly, collapsing onto the sides of his head and sticking fast. The door popped open at his approach and he climbed in, latching it behind him.

Naamer smiled at him from the pilot's seat. "You chose a bad day for this, Mr. Televox."

"Apparently." He glanced around the interior of the cockpit. Naamer was alone in the little ship. "Where's your Mr. -wohnith? I'd like to see him again sometime."

Naamer stared at him levelly. "In hiding, Your Grace. Gone into the forest."

So. Not too surprising. "Too bad. He had nothing to fear."

"He didn't feel that way . . . and I found myself agreeing with him. The place of native peoples like the Hodai must be a small one in the greater scheme of the Metastable Order."

"Even smaller than you think."

"Just so, Mr. Televox." Naamer hauled up on the collective pitch lever and the helicopter growled into the sky, walls of the MAC building fading to outlines, then nothingness, world turned to a universe of gray rain.

Chapter 11

Denthurion sat alone in the *Koxavonia* community center's meeting room, listening to the rain bubble and hiss on the building's roof, inhaling the dank smell that seemed to rise out of the wooden floor. Occasional thunder rumbled in the distance. His hair was almost dry now, fluffing away from the sides of his head again, damp patches disappearing into his scalp. Peculiar smell. Mold perhaps, activated by the penetrating humidity. Olamitic molds? Terragenic molds? He took an experimental breath. No congestion. Probably Olamitic then.

Considering the magnitude of the Earthly assault, this planet's native life-forms had been remarkably durable. There was no end to worlds that had been stripped of their native biota over the past fifty millennia. Slow or fast, it comes to all of them in the end. On marginally inhabitable planets, the terraformers moved in, and in no time at all, you had a new Earth, suitably modified for the local geological conditions. An Archaean Eon equivalent was gone in an eyeblink, world of ancient stromatolites wiped away. Something similar happened with Protero and Paleozoic equivalents, more advanced stages taking a little longer. Only Mesozoic and later equivalents could last . . . and then only if the human colonists so decreed. You could *find* planets with vast, light-boned, oxygen-hungry beasts if you looked long enough. He suddenly remembered the furniture-doomed Gnaw-Xhan. Of course you could.

And there were plenty of Olams in the human universe. Native biota could be tough, every bit as adaptable as the terragenic life-forms coming in to compete with them. Sometimes tougher. Remember the Hadrachean virus parasites. Hadrachis had had to be sterilized before a successful colony could be planted. And here . . . Olam's natives had successfully fought off conquest for twenty-five thousand years. But smaller every year, the biota shrinking, the green patches spreading . . . Not to mention the Kemitish incursion. I wonder whose idea that was?

Footsteps thumped on the building's wooden porch and the door popped open, framing Meltsar, downpour a gray, wet backdrop outside. He stepped in, pulling off his serape, shaking it out, hanging it on a wall peg, and closing the door. He walked across the room, smiling, wiping the rain from his gray-patched beard, wringing it gently. "Mr. Televox! I'm a little surprised to find you back here. Is this good news for us?"

It was apparent from the man's manner that he thought it meant exactly that. "You tell me, Mr. Meltsar. I've read your *Hikanesh!* . . ."

"And?" It was said eagerly.

"Very effective."

A broad, beaming smile. "I'm ∴ . . gratified, Your Grace."

"You should be, Meltsar. Those *were* your words . . ."

"Only my prose; the Pilot's words."

Denthurion grinned, beckoning him toward a chair. "So you say. Now I've come to talk with Mr. Tayash. We'll see."

"But . . ."

"Give in, Meltsar. You can't stop what's going to happen, whether you will it or no."

"I . . . see." Meltsar stared at him, unsmiling, dark eyes narrow and intense. "Well. You put it that way without reason, Your Grace. I have nothing to fear from such a meeting and everything to gain, if it'll help convince you of our sincerity. We'll . . . have him here by tomorrow."

"Good enough." Denthurion stood and reached for Meltsar's hand, clasping it briefly. "If you'll excuse me, I have a friend to look up." He turned and walked across the room, boot heels thumping hollowly on the wooden floor, and out into the rain.

Meltsar sat for a while staring at the closed door, massaging his beard softly. Make your decisions, Meltsar. You're the Executive Officer of this Starship. The Pilot won't decide. God can't come down from the sky and decide for you. He smiled bitterly. One more day, then. We'll *see* what happens next.

Denthurion and Shvirah sat cross-legged on the bed opposite each other, naked and sweaty. The rain had stopped now, but the sky was still overcast. With the hydrogen-sponge torches extinguished, the *Koxavonia* camp was black to the point of lightlessness, the cabin's windows inky squares to nowhere, its interior dimly lit by a single small, still-flamed candle.

"I never thought you'd come back."

"I never thought I would either."

She smiled, pushing the hair off her face with one hand, wiping sweat from her brow, pushing it up onto her scalp. "But you're here." Her eyes seemed luminous in the dark room, glimmering liquidly from their little pools of shadow. "You didn't just come back for me."

Denthurion shook his head. Do you want to believe that I did? No, I can see you don't. "I've come for the Pilot."

A momentary look of concern. "To take him? No. I see . . ." She looked closely at him, trying to peer into his eyes. "You're on the edge of belief, aren't you?"

He smiled. "No, Shvirah. But the truth won't escape me much longer."

"The truth. Yes." She shifted position, hugging her knees to her chest, smiling into the middle distance, as if harboring some pleasant secret. "You'll get there."

He nodded slowly. "I will." The change in position, lifting her legs like that, had pulled her buttocks forward on the bed, rotating her pelvis backward so that her vulva peered from between her thighs, wet and red-looking. He felt that heavy creeping sensation start up somewhere just inside his perineum and begin crawling upward, to churn in the space behind his pubis bone, valves starting to close, local blood pressure building up. He smirked at himself in the darkness. Come now, Mr. Televox. Ten thousand years of this, forty thousand subjective years . . . Aren't you tired yet? No. And all because the teledynes keep filling me up with an endless supply of adolescent hormones. Look at that. I already have an erection. To what purpose? Keeping me like this must serve some function, but what? Whose idea was *this*?

Shvirah was looking at him, a half smile spreading across her face. "You continue to surprise me. I never met a man like you before . . ."

Denthurion knelt up on the bed, his penis springing out from its position between his legs so that it pointed at her face. No? he thought. Then you haven't been looking very hard.

Shvirah unfolded her legs and lay back against the head of the bed, spreading her thighs, rubbing her palms along the smooth skin where her legs joined her trunk, and beckoned for him to come forward. He crawled onto her, feeling their sweaty abdomens glide over each other, and lowered himself, nestling his face in the crook of her neck, resting on a nest of hair, pushing his hips forward into a familiar pressure-and-glide. Good enough for now, he thought. Let biochemistry rule the night. You can't be a Televox every moment. And yet, said another little voice, you must. Time may be the Order's ally, but you're *here*, one little segment of a greater organism, to live or die as if the universe of men did not exist.

Outside, the thunder began again, precipitated by one loud bang that trailed off in a long, low groan, then the rain began to sputter softly on the roof.

• • •

Machines drummed in the open space below. The ninety-first incarnation of Maaron Denthurion, version fifteen, looked down into a nightmare. The stone balcony on which he stood hung out over a huge, dim cavern, red lit by flaming industrial processes, vast drums rolling on their axes, spouting long tongues of red fire. Occasionally one of the machines would roar, flames turning bright oxygen-yellow, tongue blowing out into a long, dazzling tube, sparks splashing off some nearby cavern wall. The drums would roll on their sides from time to time, and rivers of glowing metal would pour out, running into long troughs, down spillways, disappearing into the maws of other machines, on their way to becoming the bright ingots you could see stacked on pallets everywhere. Dotted among the machines were the long black shadows of little men, moving, dodging the flames, bending to their labor.

"Welcome to Saknussem, Mr. Televox."

He turned and looked back into the balcony, toward the bank of transceivers from which he'd just emerged. A squat man stood there, gnarled and bowlegged, teeth exposed in a gargoyle's smile, thick, knuckly hand extended. Denthurion extended his own twisted hand.

"I'm sorry to be late, Your Grace. Other matters pressed in on me. Duty, you know." He pounded Denthurion's heavily muscled shoulder with an sledgehammer blow, laughing. "They call me Arne, Mr. Televox. Let me show you around!"

Duty? What duty could be more important to a Metastable functionary than the coming of a Televox? But the man was already walking away from him, talking merrily, waving his gnome's arms in the thick and smoky air. Denthurion followed.

Saknussem was a ball of metal wrapped in stone. The double star system had been an interesting one, a large F6, embedded in the fast/slow stellar divide, separated by ten light-hours from its companions, a debris-circled K2. The stars' evolution went at two separate paces, F6 spinning up, eating its natal cloud, K2 allowing eddies to form, planetesimals to coalesce, merging into planets and moons and asteroid belts. By bad, or good, fortune, a small gas giant formed at the outer edge of K2's zone, where F6's gravitation could distort its orbit. And, one day, when the system was nearly a billion years old, the gas giant switched primaries, finding itself in a retrograde orbit around F6, now perturbed occasionally by the still-strong gravitational influence of K2.

It was an empty place, devoid of planetoids, even meteoric debris relatively rare, but the gas giant continued on its course, years unwinding by the hundreds of millions. Meanwhile, deep in K2's gravity well, a smaller world continued to evolve, cooling, water raining down from the skies, forming warm oceans in which a quickening of chemical processes took place. Little organellelike beings formed in the sea, eating their chemical environment, banding together into things like bacteria, the bacteria combining to form cells, the cells combining into something like metazoa.

Life was still in the sea, however, when F6, now almost two billion years old, did its trick. Old age sets in hard when you're young. The helium flash came, puffing F6 up like a balloon, wave of radiant energy rolling through the dual system, inflating the gas giant, melting its moons, spreading through K2's retinue of planets, changing them. On the little water world, the oceans boiled, filling the sky with dense clouds. The life-forms cooked, turning the sea into a tasty soup, and that was that.

The years continued to unreel into the past. F6 burned down to its iron-rich core and then exploded, planetary nebula roaring out through the dual system, peeling the gas giant down to its siderophile-rich mantle, washing over the lesser planets in order, thinning their atmospheres but otherwise doing little harm, disappearing into the sky, a bright shell that slowly faded. For a little while K2 burned a little hotter, but that soon came to an end.

A few billion years later Metastatic Vectorship *Sorg* drifted into the system, not quite lost, but damaged by a chance interstellar encounter, unable to proceed. The OTANN knew where it was, but . . . What have we here? What a *fine* site for an industrial complex. The ship settled on the gas giant's core, which came to be called Saknussem, took a look around, then dumped its terraforming machinery on K2's formerly habitable planet.

Time to make repairs, true. And time to get rid of these Cpaht refugees who had been clogging its memory matrices for so long.

The miners of Saknussem were lined up at a big double transceiver bank, queues stretching off into the distance. End of shift. The trolls marched in out of the darkness, stolid and silent, walking one step at a time, passing into the machine, flash, flash, red light here, red light there, the same miner coming out the next door, walking a little straighter, stepping a little higher. Go home, young man, come back again tomorrow. We repeat and repeat and repeat. Someday you'll die, but not now.

Denthurion and Arne stood to one side of the transceiver deck, watching the lines move slowly in. "I don't understand the point of all this."

Arne smiled. "No? Well . . . of course. The miners get heavy metal poisoning, Mr. Televox. Two or three days in the pit is enough to shut down cytochrome biochemistry cycles. Chelating is what they need. This is simpler, though beyond the technology we normally use."

"Painful?"

Arne seemed surprised. "What? The transceiver jump? Of course not."

"I meant the heavy metal poisoning."

Arne laughed. "Sure it is! Even the managers get it;

just a bit slower. Aches in your joints, aches in your head . . . Down the pit, you start feeling crazy about half-way through your shift."

Denthurion nodded toward the miners. "There's another world not far from here. Why don't they leave?"

"Leave? But we own them."

"I see." He looked over the miners, over the vast cavern, and shook his head slowly. How did things get like this? Inattention, that's how. The Metastable Order had been lax in its duties. Time to set things straight.

"Well," said Arne, "what can I show you next?"

Denthurion stared at him, imagining he felt twinges in his joints, and said, "I think I've seen enough."

The next morning, Olam's sky was a hazy, yellow-gray mask, the sun a fuzzy ball, brightening one part of the sky as it climbed. It wasn't hot yet, the world still cool and moist in the storm's aftermath, but you knew, sooner or later, that Shemesh would burn off the haze. Then it would be hot.

Denthurion and Meltsar strolled through the village compound, splashing through shallow puddles, avoiding stretches of gluey mud. Finally they came to a stop before a small bungalow not too different from Shvirah's. Meltsar turned to him and said, "He's in here, Your Grace." A brief pause. "You know, I thought of asking you to behave a certain way, of asking you not to be combative with him."

"And now?"

Meltsar laughed softly. "He spent a long time with God, Mr. Televox. Do your worst." He turned and walked away, passing through a deeper puddle that surged around his ankles, oblivious.

Do my worst? Denthurion shrugged, smiling. I begin to realize these people have no idea of what my worst may be. A flaw in the design of the Metastable Order? Perhaps. What shall we do, order up more Televoxes? Or just more doublings? He stepped up onto the porch of the house and rapped on the door frame.

"Come in, please." The voice was faint, a bit high-pitched, perhaps, and a little raspy.

Denthurion opened the door and went in. Tayash was a small, thin man, sitting in a chair by the window, reading a book in the wan morning light. He was dressed in conventional Olamitic garb rather than the *Koxavonia* uniform, head-cloak missing, bearded and balding. He looked up. "Mr. Denthurion, is it?" He put his book aside and rose, extending his hand. "They call me Tayash."

Denthurion crossed the room and shook his hand briefly. "What did they call you before?"

The Pilot laughed. "Memuutsah. Not that it matters." He sat down, beckoning at the other chair.

A joke? *Memuutsah* was the masculine form of the Olamite word for "average." He sat, glancing at the cover of the book Tayash had been reading. It was *The Metastability of Man*, an Olamite translation of the standard popular-format text on human interstellar culture, versions of it disseminated throughout the worlds.

Tayash was smiling at him. "Surprised?"

"No. I've read your *Hikanesh!*, Mr. Tayash."

The smile broadened into a grin. "So. Not *my* book, Mr. Denthurion. Rather, call it Mr. Meltsar's book, wouldn't you say?"

Denthurion stared at him silently. The Pilot's eyes were clear and steady, dark brown irises fixed on his face, never diverging away. *Guileless, that's how he looks. But . . . Mr. Denthurion. Not, Mr. Televox; not, Your Grace. Guile? Or simplicity?*

"Have I offended you?"

"No." He sat back in the chair and folded his arms across his chest. "How much truth is there in . . . Mr. Meltsar's book?"

The man shrugged. "As much as he understood, I guess."

"All right. How much *did* he understand? You're the only one who knows."

Tayash sighed. "True. Mr. Denthurion, I've read the book, too, but I find it *very* rough going. I said what I said. He wrote what he wrote. It's hard for me to reconcile the two."

Odd. "What do you mean?"

Another shrug. "You see . . . If I could've, I'd've written the book myself. You'll notice I didn't. I'm just not"—he seemed to struggle with himself—"uh . . . wordy. You know?"

Denthurion nodded slowly. I suppose, he thought, I was afraid of this. "Tell me about Heaven, Mr. Tayash."

The Pilot beamed. "Ah. Heaven! Here we have a subject I can talk about. Wonderful. I never felt so . . . appropriate. I guess that's the word. Heaven was where I *belonged*. You know?"

No. I don't know. "How did it compare with being in space? You belonged there, too."

Tayash seemed surprised. "Space? I don't know. All right, I guess." He frowned. "You know, I miss being in the Big Black, sometimes. That's what we used to call it. The repair crews, I mean."

"So you stepped through a transceiver and went to Heaven instead of Adomm."

"To that damned asteroid, actually." He looked distant for a moment. "Tsumaat. Yes. I went to Heaven instead of Tsumaat, and talked to God and took my place as a crewman on his Starship . . ." He laughed again. "People thought I was *crazy* after I started talking about these things, when I came back. When God sent me back. And the teledyne engineers!" His eyes sparkled with obvious delight. "They couldn't figure out where the Hell I'd *been* for those four years. Trouble was, I hadn't been to Hell. Heaven, you know. Heaven."

Denthurion sat still in his chair, face still. Shit. This poor simpleton, exploited by the likes of Meltsar . . . Whatever *had* happened to him hadn't left much behind.

Maybe run him through *Naglfar*'s decompiler, see if I can make something of what's left. "So you just went to Heaven. And talked to God."

"Talked to God, yes. Oh, it was splendid, Mr. Denthurion. Splendid! When I went to work on the crew, it was the most wonderful thing that ever happened to me! I can't *wait* to go back!"

"So what did you do?"

"Everything, Mr. Denthurion. Everything. You can't imagine what it's like, working among the vast floating machine halls of Heaven. The Starship of God is like a world without end, mountains and sea and mist, all filled roundabout with the souls of God's crew . . ."

"Other men and women, like yourself?"

Tayash shook his head. "I could never tell. They didn't *seem* to be men like me, but . . ." He shrugged. "Who knows? Let me tell you, it was *beautiful*.

"The land around Heaven's Gate curves up and away in all directions, retreating from the halls of the crew quarters in an endless wash of green and gold. At the Captain's Mast, God presides over the work of the crew, passing out unending reward. And the crewmen dream, Mr. Denthurion. They *dream!*" Tayash seemed breathless with excitement.

Denthurion sat cold and ugly in his little chair, blind before the Pilot, will-less, unable to resist the vision: The hall opened up around him, row on row of long tables, filled with animated men, a whispering sea of brethren. And all of them inside him as well; from times past, from overlays, from a common childhood in the remote and hazy past . . . a childhood that was, somehow, as fresh as those few bright years spent wandering the canal-crossed deserts of Kem.

How many years? It was hard to calculate . . . but Odin knew: ten thousand years since the lines began. All the overlays converged. All the branchings became one, focusing on the original nexus of the many lives. Somewhere, in the clouded far reaches of the great hall, the first incarnation of the first branching sat at Odin's side; and from him a thread reached out into the past and future. Their lives, as instrumentalities, added up. They were, in consequence, the aggregate lords of creation . . .

He shook his head savagely and stood up, looming over the Pilot. Tayash, pulled from his own bright dream unwilling, looked up in astonishment. "Why, is something wrong, Mr. Denthurion?"

Denthurion stilled the pounding of his heart and reached out gently to touch the Pilot's forearm. "I've . . . heard enough for now, Mr. Tayash. I'll talk to you again later. Tomorrow, perhaps."

"Of course. I'm always at your disposal . . ."

But Denthurion had turned away, striding swiftly across the room and out through the door, where sunlight was building up in the town square. The hazy sky was clearing, yellow-gray turning to blue one wavelength at a time, bits of green marking the last shreds of dark cloud.

As he went back toward his own cabin, and Shvirah, Denthurion walked with his head down, watching his feet splash through the evaporating dregs of the last few puddles. What triggered this . . . odd, epiphanylike feeling? Nothing like it ever happened to me before. The Pilot's dream-vision, his words . . . No. I don't *want* to believe it!

The next incarnation of Maaron Denthurion, mark Fifteen, sat in the council chambers of Vrijdag, at the head of a long, glossy table surrounded by handsome, exceedingly well-dressed, nervous-looking men and women. The room was surrounded by walls of glass, looking out onto a blue-skied world, tall green trees waving slowly in a pleasant, warm breeze, grass rippling on endless, rolling lawns, vivid lake a flat mirror in the distance. Here and there you could see buildings, isolated, surrounded by parkland, people walking slowly between them, lives lived at a leisurely pace. Conduct your business now, then, whenever. Why hurry? We'll still be here . . . whenever.

He sat still, hands folded on the smooth, polished, dark brown wood before him, staring at them, gaze moving from face to face, watching their unease wax with each passing moment. Let it sink in. You're in trouble, boys and girls. The proverbial deep shit is rising around your necks. Finally, he said, "This is a very pretty planet you've made here for yourselves. Very esthetic. I *like* the way it looks."

The President of Vrijdag beamed nervously, and said, "Thank you so much, Your Grace. We . . ."

"Unfortunately, I don't like the way *you* look."

"Your Grace? We . . ."

"You know I went to Saknussem before I came here. What do you think I found?"

The councillors looked at each other, puzzled. What *could* he have found on Saknussem? The President took a deep breath, and said, "Saknussem? Why, the mining colony, of course."

"Of course."

More puzzled looks. "Is there something wrong there?"

Denthurion sat back, unable to restrain a look of amazement. Something wrong? This wasn't a totally isolated planetary system; there'd been plenty of trade and travel back and forth throughout the local region over the past few dozen millennia. You'd think they'd understand . . . "I'm sorry to tell you that this star system has gone outside Metastable norms. Corrections will have to be made."

"Corrections?" The bewildered looks were becoming fearful. "I don't think I know what you mean."

Denthurion smiled broadly. "I can see that, Mr. President. Well, no matter. We'll take this one step at a time." He stood up, towering over them, and said, "Pack your bags, ladies and gentlemen. We're going on a little trip."

No? Still don't get it? "To Saknussem." Horror bloomed
on the sleek, satisfied faces, one at a time. Going to
Saknussem? *Us?*

Now they got it.

After supper, Denthurion went for a walk, alone in the
cool, breezy evening, skirting the outer edge of the town,
wandering off into the sour-smelling forest. The wind
and recent rain had suppressed the reek a bit, but it was
already gathering again, climbing over the threshold into
awareness.

The meal had been pretty good, some tart and garlicky
Olamitic soup poured over long, thin, chewy, and wrinkled noodles, Meltsar and Shvirah good, attentive company, Tayash bubbling over with simple merriment,
holding court among his devoted followers ...

The *triumph* on their God-damned faces! They think
they *know* what's happened to me. Of *course* he's
quiet now. Weren't *you?* Leave him alone. He needs to
think ...

Think. Think. He walked through the dank forest, listening to water drip from the trees, head down, booted
feet making squishy sounds on the wet, rotting humus,
dead leaves decaying to the cadences of native Olamitic
fungi. Tapped into my fucking dreams. Black fucking *ice*
of all things ...

After a while he came out on the rocky ledge he and
Shvirah had found, what, *ages* ago? Only days. Someone
else had come there before him. A small, thin man was
sitting on the stone, looking down over the camp, where
hydrogen sponges were already flaring blue. The sky was
almost dark now, the brighter stars glittering through the
twilight.

The man looked up. "Oh. Excuse me." A dazed squint.
"I don't know you."

Denthurion sat down at his side, feet dangling into
space. "Maaron's my name."

"Aravii. Are you new? I never saw you before around camp." The man was shivering softly, though the night, despite being damp, promised to be a warm one.

"Yes." He looked over at Aravii, who was dressed in the usual *Koxavonia* uniform, metal glittering on his chest. "Is that an Ascendant's badge I see?"

Aravii nodded, still shivering and silent.

"How long?"

"Day after tomorrow."

It's an evening ceremony. Forty-eight hours and he goes off into the irrevocable dark . . . "Are you afraid?"

The man turned to glance at him briefly, wide eyes shining in the night. "Yes. Are you ashamed of me?"

"No."

"I am ashamed of myself, brother Maaron. I've worked for this moment for a long time. Now . . ."

"I understand." Do I? A moment of intense surprise. Of course I do. Long, long ago, but clear as yesterday . . . I sat waiting for my first Doubling Ceremony. And I sat and shivered with my friends, just like Aravii . . . "Don't go if you're afraid."

"Don't *go*?" There was astonishment in his voice, tinged with . . . hope? "How can I not go? Everyone . . ."

"Everyone else be damned, Aravii. It's *your* life, to live in or leave as you choose." But *I* went . . .

The man eyed him suspiciously in the darkness. "That's an odd way to talk, even for a new man."

"Well. If you're afraid, why go?"

"Why stay?" Aravii seemed a little belligerent now, confronted with a final challenge to his beliefs, one which preyed on his secret terror.

Denthurion shrugged. "I'll know, I suppose, when the time comes."

The other man sank back a little, shrinking into himself. "That's what I thought, too."

"Yet, you're afraid now . . ."

"To my discredit. Weak, I suppose."

"Or uncertain. And you're dead forever."

"Forever. Well. If the Pilot can return from Heaven . . ."

"No one else has."

"The angels."

"But they don't stay."

"No." He stared at Denthurion in the darkness, smiling broadly enough that his teeth picked up reflected light. "An odd attitude, I must say." He stood up then, feet crunching on the loose and friable rock of the ledge. "Tired. I've got a big day tomorrow, putting my affairs in order. I'd better be getting back. It was nice meeting you, Maaron. I'll be seeing you . . ."

"Sooner or later."

When he had gone, Denthurion sat staring out into the night. Excepting the blue glow of the village, Olam was a flat black plate, blotting out half the universe, the sky above harboring its usual swirls of light, small clouds opaque shapes moving across the glittering backdrop. Well, he thought, bitterly amused. My life, to live in or leave as I please. Hell. If only I *had* those options.

Chapter 12

It was pitch-dark, hydrogen sponges guttering out, the streets of the *Koxavonia* camp nearly empty, by the time he got back. He strolled through the dusty lanes, ignored by the few who'd not gone to bed yet, finally coming up on the cabin he shared with Shvirah, and sat on the front steps, staring down at the dirt. Come now. You're *not* bothered by any of these things. This is just one more psychological loop. They develop during every incarnation; get wiped away by every long link . . .

Still, reaching into my dreams like that . . .

Not my job to be plagued by doubts. Certainty is what defines the Metastable Order. He sighed and got up, Hell with it, and turned to go in.

Shvirah sat up in bed when he came through the door, light blanket falling away from her breasts, look of concern shadowy on her face in the dim room. "Maaron. I'm glad you came back."

He sat on the edge of the bed, smiling. "Where would I go, back to visit our Hodai friends? 'Sky God *evil hachewiss* . . .'"

She seemed to flinch. "I wish you wouldn't do that. They're not figures of fun."

"No." He turned away from her in the darkness, sliding across the foot of the bed to lean his back against the wall. "The Hodai, tame and wild, require . . . resolution."

She got out from under the covers, slim, naked limbs a mix of angular tracings in the wan light from the window, and slipped against his side, one hand on his shoulder. "I've been . . . waiting."

"So you think this is part of my 'conversion'?"

She leaned her head against his chest and nodded slowly. "It happens. When the light dawns, your . . . horizons expand."

The dawning light. Silly, when you come right down to it. "The allopathic party in the Metastatic Senate is . . . progressive. Sooner or later, we'll have to come up with a universal solution to the Aboriginal Problem." A *progressive* solution. Not liberal integration; not conservative separation. But we haven't thought of a viable alternative, though we run the universe, so the status quo remains in uneasy balance. Metastable balance . . .

"I'm very happy, Maaron. I *knew* the Pilot would get through. He always does."

"What if I told you he didn't?"

"I can see you're different now."

Because I seem troubled? That's a lot to read into a mere half day of moodiness. Still, expectations . . . The madman leads you to his font, and cries, "But, this is the *answer!* Can't you *see?*" He turned to face Shvirah, kneeling on the bed, heels tucked against buttocks. "And what if I told you he'd convinced me *Hikanesh!* was all a pack of lies, concocted by Meltsar?"

She laughed. "Dear, Maaron! It's *more* that just faith, you know. I'm going to Heaven one day; maybe you will, too. Besides, everyone knows what Tayash thinks of *Hikanesh!* Don't be so silly."

Involuted. Deep-rooted fixations are hard to alter. Still, one trip through the transceiver, up, down, like that, and *Naglfar* would fix it.

She said, "Heaven awaits us. And I think you've already been there."

There was a brief, cold prickling in his scalp. "What do you mean?"

"Your soul is somewhere, Maaron Denthurion, when you fly between the worlds. I suspect it is in Heaven."

Too right. "Wouldn't I . . . know?"

"Not if . . . the comeye changes you every time. I've heard what they can do . . ."

Bad. Very bad. But . . . "What about my other selves, the doubling and redoubling?"

She shook her head slowly. "I don't know. More than one soul? I don't know how that could be. Or if. I just don't know. You should talk to the Pilot. He might have an answer."

"Or he might not."

She nodded. "God was . . . circumspect in his revelations." She shivered, rubbing her hands along her upper arms.

"That's usually the way it turns out to be."

Shvirah lay back on the bed, stretching out flat, arms away from her sides, legs spread apart. Denthurion's eyes had fully adapted to the darkness in the room; what had been stygian was a fairly transparent gloom and he was able to see her plainly, a thing of white cylinders and gentle convexities, black patches of hair here and there, shadowy pits around eyes, nose, mouth, and navel.

He sprawled over onto his side, laying his head on her thigh, then rolled so he was more or less between her legs, looking up the length of her body. Her face appeared in the valley between her breasts, lit up from one side by the window, smooth and emotionless, eyes like glittering, featureless domes, liquid and without direction. "Do you love me, Shvirah?"

"I don't know."

A faint pulse of surprise. That wasn't what I wanted her to say. "What do you think?"

She reached down and stroked his hair, shrugging her body downward a bit, so his face was near the juncture of her thighs, pubic hair tickling his cheek. "I loved Raakaa, but . . . she went away."

Raakaa. Her pet Hoda? "I didn't mean do you love me like a dog, Shvirah. I meant as a man."

"Raakaa wasn't a dog."

"No, I suppose not. Still . . ."

"I don't think so, Maaron."

A strong pang of disappointment. Did you *want* her to love you? Is that what you wanted from all of them?

She said, "Maybe I'll love you in Heaven, when we're both there. I'll know then that you won't go away."

Fears. Life. Death. Things in between. Disappointment and loss. How unpleasant to be a human being. Momentary happiness not worth the risk. And you? Death not real; life a transient thing. What happens today doesn't matter. In a hundred thousand years this moment will be one crystallized memory, buried deep in the hearts of a thousand different men.

She said, "I'd like to love you, Maaron Denthurion. I really would."

He rolled his face into her vulva then, tasting her, and she clasped her hands behind his neck, levering herself against him.

Crystalline memories, then, he thought. Not important. Nothing is.

After sixty-five centuries in the Metastatic Senate, Maaron Denthurion found attendance at interminable committee meetings to be a seamless part of his life. He drifted through the subterranean hallways beneath the Senate dome, swimming through a sea of like wraiths, other ageless Senators and faceless bureaucratic servants, the occasional Planetary Deputy from that Other House, come to lobby his superior number. Sixty-five hundred years. A third of a million working weeks, every one of them filled with committee meetings and legislative sessions and hours of deliberation.

This morning, the business at hand was the Senate Committee on Insurrective Nodes. One hour scheduled, to begin promptly at 0925. Little business could be transacted in only one hour, and little would be; but in a third of a million hours, results could accumulate. Why hurry? Time is our ally.

Denthurion coasted into the room, feet scuffing gently

over the pale green carpet, indeterminate pastel-hued walls invisible, and took his seat at the periphery of the round table, folding his hands on the smooth mahogany surface, staring into the bare schematic of his reflection in the wood. There were twenty Senators assigned to this committee, many of them of very long standing. You were assigned to twenty-one permanent committees, chosen by random drawing—then the rules said you could change one committee assignment per decade, its replacement also chosen by lot. Insurrective Nodes generated considerable loyalty among its members, for the topic was an interesting one.

Why not? Insurrective Nodes gathered the general state of the Metastable Order into its fold and picked it apart, item by item, looking for trouble. It was empowered to raise fleets, to appoint Sector Marshals, to make war and rain destruction down upon the worlds. Only the Frontier Agencies could claim greater fun for themselves. Denthurion smiled to himself. Sooner or later I'll get an assignment to External Fleet. It was the agency that acted militarily, beyond the Frontier, imperialism on a grand scale, humanity descending, like a banshee out of the night, on helpless, horrified interstellar empires.

The room filled up and at 0925, promptly, Varlian Psittacriadis, Committee Chair on Insurrective Nodes, swept into the room, taking his place at the theoretical head of the table. "Good morning, gentlemen. Brisk business today." He sat, dropping his thin briefcase on the table, rubbing his hands together with a sandpapery sound.

Denthurion folded his arms, waiting. Psittacriadis had had the chair for a thousand years, and seemed to like playacting.

He opened his briefcase and pulled out sheets of paper, smiling at them, rearranging them like a hand of large, floppy cards. "Well. Good news and bad. It seems, last week, we had finally completed the matter of the

Dhevshuite osteopaths. Completed, I say. Old business?"
He looked up inquisitively.

Denthurion hoped not. They'd spent the better part of
a year resolving that one; as dull a case as he'd ever seen.
Imagine, separating people from their bones in a matter
transmitter! Ridiculous.

"Fine. New business, then." He tapped the top of his
stack of papers. "This just in on *Lavaro Tai-sem*, which
warped into Earth orbit last night. Comeye?"

The room seemed to darken and the wall opposite
Denthurion turned misty. It was, of course, relative. Everyone in the room would be experiencing that "wall opposite" effect. The committee chamber became a sea of
unfamiliar stars, splattered across a black sky, a small
blue-green world swimming in the void.

"Thora, gentlemen, three hundred parsecs from Earth.
An allopathic focal planet of the first rank, equipped with
a Metastatic Guard training center, a starship reconstruction facility, and manufacturing centers for the design
and construction of transceiver netware. All told, one of
the thousand most important worlds of the Metastable
Order."

The view swept in on the planet, one high-latitude
continent enlarging to fill the room, a city blooming out
of flat green plains, the landscape tipping to vertical,
closing in on a cluster of institutional buildings. "The
University of Miklagard." Now they were in a small
room, a tall, thin, severe-looking man addressing a handful of rapt students. "Einar Maclanahan, professor of
philosophy."

The man was saying, ". . . and we *will* find a way. Mankind took a wrong turning at the end of the Red Millennium, so many thousands of years ago, but it's not too
late to change. If we abandon the matter transmitters, return to a realm of physical travel . . ."

The scene shifted back into space, to the industrial
centers in orbit around the planet. They were at the starship reconstruction facility, where a quickening pace of

activity could be seen. "Professor Maclanahan's views swept Thora. The Guard were deactivated, the Planetary Governor imprisoned, the transceiver net stopped, replaced by technological means of physical transport . . ."

A starship full of determined men climbed out of Thora's gravity well, flaring violet, bound for interstellar space. There were other worlds out there, waiting to hear the new truth, that the transceiver was death, that starships were life, and a new human way . . .

"Thoran agents were known to be operating on several worlds in the period that followed, and at least three Televoxes disappeared in the area while this report was being prepared . . ."

It seemed plain enough. A most serious vacuole was forming within the borders of the Metastable Order, one that would have to be dealt with forthwith.

"I don't think we need to waste any time on this one, gentlemen. I move that we direct *Lavaro Tai-sem* to proceed directly back to the area of the Thoran insurrection, bearing a Sector Marshal's *baton de commandement*. It will seek out whatever Televox may be on the scene and present him with an appointment . . ."

Denthurion's heart began to pound gently with excitement as he searched his immediate memory. Yes! The line of incarnations reported by branching Twenty-one was no more than a hundred parsecs from Thora, heading slowly in toward the disturbance . . .

"Other business then, gentlemen. We have before us the matter of the Maastrichtian Genocide Pact . . ."

Denthurion awoke in darkness to the sound of wind rushing through trees. Something . . . what? Breezes were blowing irregularly outside, a distant hissing, like cold rain falling steadily on a hot concrete road, the leaves of the forest trees rubbing against each other. Every now and again the general wind velocity would increase, roaring in the forest, arousing noises in the

Koxavonia camp, distant metallic banging, a sharp chuff of noise, air squeezing through the narrow spaces behind rainspouts, moaning along the edges of rooftop gutters.

The room was lit up, but very dim, by the light that filtered through the drawn curtains. Moonlight, perhaps. There would be no clouds above this wind. Something. A mutter, almost like distant voices. Some chance element in the sound of the wind. The brain's pattern recognition drivers were single-minded, forcing a fit where none existed, smiling faces out of rubble, a conspiratorial whisper in the random sighing of the wind. *Creak.* Boards in the house shifting from air-current-induced torque. But it sounded like a footstep outside the cabin door.

He lay staring at shadows on the ceiling, listening to the wind, calculating its permutations. Shvirah was asleep beside him, her slow, steady breathing inaudible, diaphragmatic movements rocking the bed almost imperceptibly, a long, warm, damp infrared shadow down his side.

Face reality, Televox. You are as chained by things of the flesh as any mortal man. Interesting. The mortal drive for sexuality, the will toward reproduction, is supposed to be a reaction to the realization of our human temporariness. The genes drive us to carry on their kind; instinct arouses a man while death looks over his shoulder. But the genes don't know about contraception; the instincts can't realize you'll never die. The flesh on his abdomen was crawling now, hormones beginning to flood.

He rolled on his right side, turning to face the woman's warmth, reaching out, running his hand across her abdomen, lightly dappled with sweat. She was lying on her back, boneless with sleep, not quite spread-eagled, but flat, legs slightly apart, right arm running down her side, left thrown over her face, elbow angled upward into the night. She squirmed slightly as he ran his hand back and forth, just above her pubic hairline, breath a delicate sigh. She would awaken in a moment, presumably without protest, ready for whatever he wanted, but right now ... That fragile moment when woman is a creature of instinct and nerve endings, responsive without thought.

He quelled the urge to reach down across her vulva and dig his fingers into her vaginal opening. Wait 'til she's awake, Televox. Try to maintain some shred of humanity. They aren't *quite* Hodai, these mortals ...

The creak on the porch became a sudden click of the door latch. Adrenaline suddenly pulsed into his bloodstream, unlocking shut abdominal valves, local blood pressure dropping as demands were met elsewhere, erection failing as glycogen flamed in his muscles. Denthurion was out of bed and vertical, as if teleported into position, facing the opening door.

A hazy voice from the bed murmured, "Maaron?"

The door opened fast, thudding against the wall stop and three humanoid figures came through, hurrying, spreading out, two large and heavy, one significantly smaller. Denthurion started to sidestep, heart accelerating, hands coming up in a neutral offense/defense mid-posture, but the small figure rasped, "I've got a gun, Televox! Move and I'll shoot you down like a Hoda."

Shvirah, still hazy but mirroring surprise, said, "-wohnith?"

"Shut up, cunt!" snarled one of the larger figures.

"Meltsar?"

Denthurion stood motionless, thinking, Meltsar? -wohnith? How interesting. The other? The figures spread out in the room, -wohnith crouching by the open door, holding out his handgun, Meltsar going over to stand by the bed. "Tie him."

The third man went behind Denthurion, fumbling with something. "Hands behind your back, please."

As he complied, Denthurion said, "Hello, Naamer. I didn't expect to see you again so soon. Too bad."

The man flinched but continued to twirl thin nylon rope around his wrists, binding them.

"Meltsar?" asked Shvirah. "What's going on?"

"Just shut up. Lay back in your bed, Shvirah. Time to deal with this, once and for all. We'll find someone else to fuck you."

"Bastard."

The shadows moved and there was the sound of a slap and a muffled cry. "You lie here and be quiet, little bitch. Say nothing. Keep the Starship's counsel and you'll go to Heaven one day. Act up and I'll see you go . . . elsewhere."

Shvirah cowered silently at the head of the bed, light gleaming patchily off her naked skin.

Naamer finished tying Denthurion and took him by the upper arm, applying pressure, as if urging him toward the open door.

"This is a mistake. You know that."

"No mistake, Televox," said the Hoda by the door. "A terrible danger to us. We *know* what you're going to do."

"I haven't made a final decision."

"Lying bastard," said Meltsar, coming to loom before him, a thick, black outline. "We know about your orders to Kartavilis. We know what you're building at the car factory. And, of course, we know what you said to Naamer."

Denthurion twisted his neck, looking over his shoulder at the man's shadowy face. "I liked you, Naamer. What a pity."

"Shut up."

Denthurion shrugged and looked back at Meltsar. "The decisions I made were preliminary. I thought I might be able to negotiate a settlement with you. Olam has gone *way* out of phase, Meltsar. It has to be brought back into the fold. Still, it needs leaders more effective than the Amud . . ."

"Fuck you. *Koxavonia* is the *only* truth!"

A sharp pulse of amazement. "Still . . ."

"Walk," said Meltsar. "Run or fight and we'll kill you now."

Kill me now? Denthurion's heartbeat stepped up as he

stepped out through the door, sweat on his skin curdling slightly as it was struck by the sharp bite of the night wind.

Starcruiser *Standhaft* was a smallish vessel, no more than sixty meters from stem to stern, habitat cabin bulging one end, quantum dissociative engines flaring violet at the other. Six long, thin strap-on boosters girdled its slim waist, jammed with kilotons of compressed air. The ship warped quickly into orbit around the blue-green globe of Trondheim, lilac mote drifting across a dark sky, engines fading, mere bright light, then gone.

Clad in a leathery spacesuit, the first incarnation of Maaron Denthurion, mark Twenty-two, lay in his acceleration couch, hands on the antique manual control panel, and stared out the viewport at the bright world below. It was a pretty planet, mottled in subtle variations of one color, as if the distinction between land and sea had somehow blurred. Algae, of course. Trondheim's procaryotes had differentiated well, and had survived the coming of man quite easily. Thoran civilization was, apparently, ecologically gentle.

It had been a long trip in. Vectorship *Kallimakhos* had dropped his little vessel into its own trajectory more than a light-month out, right at the beginning of its long deceleration phase. Ninety days living in a cabin not much more than an arm's span across. Millennia of long experience helped, but . . . not a lot. You wondered how they did it. Ships like *Standhaft* were commonplace in the Thoran Empire, lone men and women spending real years drifting between suns, staring out their viewports at a star-spangled darkness of near infinite depth.

A watery, watered-down comeye stared out of its flatscreen popup at him, face shadowy and incomplete. "I've secured landing permission at Elfland Cosmodrome, Captain. Sixty-seven minutes."

Denthurion nodded, gripping the appropriate controls

for a moment, then pulled his hands away. "Take her down. I'll enjoy the view." In the distance, out the viewport, a violet light winked on, some other ship dropping in or pulling away, it was difficult to tell.

"As you will, Captain." Outside, the strap-on engines roared to life, air expanding out of sapphire bell nozzles, friction-heated to plasma, shrouding the ship in a rippling ball of misty white flame. Deceleration pushed Denthurion into the soft padding of the couch, blurring his vision momentarily.

The pressure stopped abruptly, returning him to zero gee. "Phasing maneuver complete." *Standhaft* was in a transfer orbit now, a lopsided ellipse with its perigee no more than ninety kilometers from the surface of the planet. In forty minutes or so they would hit the atmosphere's outer envelope, wind wailing around the hull as they plummeted to the ground.

Final approach to the cosmodrome was a complex one. The ship had been falling through the atmosphere on its side for several minutes, presenting its maximum cross-section to the direction of movement, aerobraking at about eight gees. Now RCS thrusters boomed, yawing the hull another ninety degrees, so that it was falling tail first. Trondheim was a flat, blue-green plain below, cities and road networks glistening gray and white under a hazy turquoise sky, the cosmodrome angling up to crush *Standhaft*, reaching for it at almost two hundred meters per second.

The strap-on boosters thundered again, long tongues of flame punching out ahead of the ship, thrusting the winds of flight aside, shoving Denthurion deeper into his cushion. Fourteen gees, letting off quickly. The ship was balanced on its column of kinetic fire, light splashing on a dense concrete pad, dropping slowly, landing legs unfolding from their pods, joints locking, shock absorbers sliding open. "All engine stop," said the comeye. *Standhaft* fell the final five meters, disk-shaped feet clanging on the cement, teetering, gyros throbbing, establishing the ship's balance, backing off, cages uncoupling. "Touchdown."

Denthurion lay on his couch, face bathed in thin, prickly sweat, heart thudding steadily in his chest. A substantially different way to arrive on a new world. Different and . . . interestingly pleasant.

"Captain," said the comeye. "It appears that we were tracked before we entered this star system. A customs delegation, accompanied by military police, is coming out to the ship."

Denthurion's heart sped up slightly. Tracked? The Thorans were, perhaps, better than they'd seemed from afar.

Lars Makhenegger sat behind his desk staring at the alien relaxing in his best guest chair. Curious creature, dark and handsome, so extraordinarily self-assured. We'll see. He tapped the sheaf of papers before him. "You've come a long way, Herr Denthurion."

The alien nodded. "Eighty parsecs from here to Ili-Aton, Inspector. Five subjective years of flight. You've no idea how happy I am to be among human beings again."

Makhenegger nodded slowly, flat, suspicious stare unaltered. "I can imagine. And if you turn back now, five hundred and twenty plus years since you left home . . ."

The alien shrugged. "My family will be . . . unchanged. My friends? They'd anticipated the long wait."

"Yes. Well." The Inspector smoothed the flesh of his chin against his palm, feeling the almost-microscopic whiskers grate like fine emery paper. "We're not completely ignorant of the galactic situation, Herr Denthurion, though we lack an adequate theory to explain it. You'll find things different here. Not, perhaps, to your liking. Things have . . . changed in the five millennia since we awoke from the Great Sleep. Changed."

"We've heard about Thora, out on the worlds, Inspector. It's why I came."

Makhenegger cocked an eyebrow at him. "What *have* you heard, 'out on the worlds'? We'd like to know."

The alien slouched a little in the chair, a curiously disrespectful posture that made the Inspector frown. "On Ili-Aton, I'm what you'd call a Cryptoholist, Herr Inspector. Political. Outlawed. Held in contempt by most decent men."

"So. Cryptoholist. Peculiar word."

"I haven't stepped through a transceiver gate since reaching adulthood, sir. I'm as close to a whole man as you'll find, anywhere on Ili-Aton, or on any of the neighboring worlds."

Makhenegger smiled, folding his hands on the surface of his sturdy desk. "I've never even seen a transceiver, Herr Denthurion. They aren't used in the Thoran Empire. I expect you know that."

"That's what we've heard, back home. The word passes by interstellar mail, from one group of Cryptoholists to another. The movement grows, abroad, and I've come here to see things as they are."

The smile broadened. He stood, reaching a hand across the desk to the alien in greeting. "Welcome to the Thoran Empire, Herr Denthurion. I hope you like what you see here. I know you will."

Denthurion stood, gripping the man's hand, also smiling. "Change, Herr Inspector. That's what we want. Things have been the same long enough."

Denthurion walked steadily through the darkness of the *Koxavonia* camp, bare feet crunching softly in the gravelly dust, booted footsteps of his captors sounding with equal gentleness behind. You could tell which was which. Meltsar walked heavily, but with style, feet placed evenly, no wasted motion; Naamer lightly and more clumsily, callow youth displayed. Sessiri-wohnith was a pattern of aliennesses, feet clicking, almost hooflike, three steps to every two the humans made.

The night wind was a steady presence around them, stirring their hair, pushing flaps of clothing aloft, swirling the dust that their footfalls raised. It was cold on his bare skin, whipping across still-damp patches of swiftly evaporating sweat. You could hear it in the trees of the forest, a continuing whisper, irregular, the rustle of leaves merging into a sussurus when the air currents' velocity picked up, separating into individual tapping and scratching sounds when it slowed down. If you listened carefully, you could hear branches beating on each other, and the harsh creaking of the older trunks, the ones that would fall in a major storm, wood fibers sliding over one another like earth faults in a quake.

Getting farther away from the forest. Not headed for the meeting hall. Somewhere else then. The helicopter? He could envision them taking him away in the night to some other camp, somewhere unknown. To what purpose? They must know what will happen to them now.

A bad thought. Desperation made men foolish. They can kill me, hope to deal differently with the next incarnation that comes down. Maaron Denthurion, still alive, still the same; but I am lost ... The woods and safety *were* getting farther away as they approached the center of the camp. If I'm going to make a break for it, I have to do it before we get out from among the houses ...

"Don't even think about it, Mr. Televox. I have the gun pointed at the back of your head. If you make a move, I'll shoot you down." The handgun made a *click-clank* as Meltsar snapped the cocking slide, jacking a cartridge into the firing chamber.

Curious weapon, thought Denthurion. Antique, like the helicopter. I wonder if they had them made from ancient designs as well? He relaxed, walking slowly ahead of the others. Ring of truth in his voice. I've made a serious judgmental error in handling them. His heart sped up slightly, then slowed down again. Walk. See where they're taking you. See what they have in mind. Keep things rolling until all your options are closed.

They came out of the last little alley and into the village's central clearing. The ceremonial transceiver stood there, a dark and shadowy cylinder, wrought-iron gate yawning open, parabolic disk antenna pointing aimlessly at the sky. Denthurion stopped suddenly, staring at the thing, pulse thudding in the back of his throat. He stiffened, then spun.

Meltsar was in assault stance behind him, crouched, gun clutched in his right hand, left gripping his right wrist. "One *move*! The bullet goes right through your *head*, Televox, and that's the end of it!"

They made a pretty tableau in the night, facing each other, Denthurion ready for flight, Meltsar braced for attack, -wohnith and Naamer behind him, spread out to either side, uncertain of their next moves.

Denthurion relaxed slightly, standing straighter, staring at the man. "You've made yet another serious mistake, Meltsar."

"No mistakes, bastard. Walk! Get in the transceiver cage."

Denthurion turned away again, facing the transceiver, feeling his heartbeat speed up steadily until it became a racing stutter in his chest. Immortal, he thought. I'm immortal. This doesn't matter. A wave of dizziness assailed him, excess oxygen, gone unused, and fight-or-flight blood chemicals, gone unheeded, were washing through his brain.

"Walk, damn you!"

Denthurion began to step forward steadily, placing one foot ahead of the other. There were no more than twenty paces to go. "There'll be another one down in a few days, Meltsar, a week at most. It will go hard with you and your people then."

"Shut up. Walk."

Walking. Walking. Ever so slowly. The transceiver cage was growing large in front of him now. "What does this accomplish, Meltsar? *Naglfar's* comeye *will* retaliate. It may mean death for you and every one of your followers . . ." He was right at the foot of the steps, standing before the transceiver's open gate. He stole a look upward. The sky was awash in an ocean of stars, like glittering surf beating on the planetary shore. Adomm was almost directly overhead, dull red, angry-looking, like a tiny, hot coal plucked from the stellar fire.

"Get in."

Denthurion took a shallow breath and placed one foot on the lowermost step leading into the transceiver.

"Now!"

He went up the rest of the way. One. Two. Three. Four. Five. Meltsar quickly threw the gate shut and latched it, a clank of metal on metal, black-painted surfaces sliding over each other with a dull stridor. It was fairly dark inside the device, wan night light coming in through the metal meshwork of the sides, making thousands of little irregular blotches of light and shadow on the floor. When he moved, the bright and dark patches marched over his cold skin, winking impudently at his eyes.

He turned around and looked out through the gate mesh at them. Meltsar, gun pocketed, was standing before the little control panel, flipping switches, turning dials. Green and amber lights were blinking on before him, an occasional blue flash glinting from his eyes. The other two were in the background, no more than dark outlines, indistinguishable, vaguely humanoid shapes.

"Don't kill me, Meltsar. You don't know what a bad thing this is . . ."

"Shut up, Televox. Our time of talk has ended."

"Meltsar. I . . ."

"You're going to Heaven now, Televox, where you should have gone ten thousand years ago. It's a better chance than the one you've offered us."

Overhead, the antenna groaned as it changed position.

Heaven? Denthurion looked away from Meltsar, at the floor of his little prison. Was it possible this madman really *believed* . . . "No, Meltsar. *Killing* me . . ."

"Heaven." He thumbed a switch on the panel before him.

The teledynes began their swift tune up, the air growing still and opalescent around him, light pouring in out of nowhere, shadows leaning out through the grille of the meshwork, falling flat on the ground around the machine. Gods, thought Maaron Denthurion, I'm on my *way* . . .

He suddenly turned back to face his captors. "*NO—*" he shouted, but the transceiver blazed, freezing him in time, etching their faces on a moment of memory in harsh white light. The god in the machine ate him away to Planck depth, encoding him onto an OTANN storage ring for a few brief ticks of the program counter, then sent him on his way into the sky.

Chapter 13

In his dream, Maaron Denthurion fell and screamed and continued to fall. Pressurized air plucked at his hair, rippling over soft naked skin, pushing him to terminal velocity and beyond. He continued to accelerate, walls of light closing in.

It was like dropping into a funnel, light glaring on him, ever brighter, a sleet of hard radiation, energetic particles needling his flesh, disassembling complex biochemical rhythms, putting a stop to each cyclic ATP dance. A funnel, perhaps, through the surface of a sun.

The walls of light contracted, wrapping him in featureless fire, searing his skin away, taking with it his sense of self. The walls became a tube, carrying him off to infinite distance, spitting him toward the dark and silent void. Final thought. Going now. Where? No answer. The tunnel of light thrust him onto a rebounding, resilient surface, where he stuck fast.

Where?

Blue light all around.

Shadows closing in.

Where?

Denthurion's mother leaned over him, dark hair streaming, slithery blue wrap clinging to gentle allopathic curves, perfume like lavender, no more than a subtle hint in the air. Faceless, he thought. Just the essence of her memory. Somewhere, Mother lived on in a real world; here, though . . . but, where? No answer.

She undid the collar of her robe and stripped the front seam, cloth dropping away, swirling into darkness, becoming more flesh than essence. He watched, fascinated.

Slim, muscular allopathic woman, bones merely implied, lines beneath smooth, translucent skin. Her hips were narrow, pelvic blades tenting at either side of a featureless, flat abdomen, mons lightly thatched with crisp-looking black hair, vulva almost invisible, no more than a suspicion of bulge and divide.

Breasts, though. Vast things, blue-veined and bursting, nipple a thumb-sized dowel, aureole like red, raw meat.

She leaned over him, breath a sigh of distant wind, breast lowering onto his face, blotting out the last of an absent world. The nipple thrust into his mouth, striking his glottal reflex point, thin, nutrient-rich blue milk jetting down his throat, tasting of salt and fat.

The breast continued to lower, flooding over the rest of his face, pressing on him like a hot rubber pillow, lapping over nostrils and eyes, sealing him in darkness . . .

He listened to his heartbeat in the darkness . . .

Thud-thud. Thud-thud. Thud . . . thud-thud . . . thud . . . Thud.

How still it became when the heartbeat came to an end. The warmth covering his face spread to the rest of his body, all-enveloping, deceptive, marking an absence of feeling. No where, no when, no man, no mind.

Lay in the seething darkness, Màaron Denthurion. Drift away, sleeping in a cradle of disorder . . .

Lachesis.

Vulcan Artificer stood before his workbench, staring down at the small form of the man. Simple enough. He took the crown of the head in his left hand, reaching through dark curls and skull, taking a firm grip on the cerebrum, fingers sinking into chasmae, thrusting thin, slippery juices aside. All right. He took the man's ankles in his right hand, gripping the little feet between his thick fingers, and pulled.

The nervous system came out in a long, buttery slide, to the accompaniment of a million-voiced sonata of little sucking cries, a rustling murmur of chorused protest. There, now. He threw the empty transit shell aside, much that was familiar about Maaron Denthurion tumbling away, end over end, into the darkness.

What remained lay before him on the workbench, still muttering the phrases of its discontent. It still looked much like a man, of course, but a lacy after-echo, white threads in a complex net, branching outward from thicker cables, autonomic and parasympathetic relays glistening, still moist from their recent encouchment.

He ran one great hand over the cerebral dome, stroking the slick surface of a fragile temporal lobe, admiring its smooth, diverse facade. Good work, this. Not so much to do, after all. Still . . .

Vulcan Artificer picked up the tools of his trade, needle-nosed pliers and soldering gun, and set to work, whistling a merry tune.

Heid-ho.

The decompiler began by separating form from function. Lobes. Frontal, occipital, temporal, parietal. What do these things do? Subsystems. Amygdala, various gyri and fissures, subcommisural regions, cerebellum, limbic system, septum connectors, brain stem aggregate. The whole mass of cerebral white matter, a vast switching system. The optical and auditory preprocessor lobes. Linguistic and prelinguistic systems. Newer, culture-heuristic memory-transfer devices. Old, primitive parts running unspecialized mechanical extensors . . .

The mind is a set of interdependent machines operating in harness, each machine a bewildering array of parallel processing devices.

The software murmured to itself, deciding just what to do. In the beginning, this stuff had been so *strange*, hardly OTANN-like at all. Now . . . merely familiar. Technological innovations were rare, but they did happen.

Let's see now. First divide along the motor/somatic interlink. Now, begin a fine-detail, differentiated rewrite of the sensory homunculus nodes ... Not bad. Properly generalized, yet prepped for task reconnect and uplink.

Read him at depth, in detail. The stories were illuminating, telling the decompiler what this man had been; and what he would need to be if he were to live again ...

The thirteenth incarnation of Maaron Denthurion, branch twenty-two, rested his hands on a wrought-iron railing and looked out over the world of Tralgansk. It was a small planet, not far from its K4 sun, cool and dim beneath a clear, purple-tinted sky. From here, high on the side of one of haTonnagar City's tallest buildings, it seemed as though you could contemplate the whole world, see beyond the squared skyscrapers of the small planetary capital to the rolling ocher plains beyond. In the russet distance there were dark, brown-hued forests, dun clouds dotting the sky, sparks of lightning in remote rainstorms.

A pretty world, he thought. You seldom found a planet like this. Tralgansk was midway between Earth and Mars in size and composition, surface gravity around 0.8 standard, with a fully developed ecology already in place, completely habitable to man without a single act of the terraformer's art. The local biome was as compatible with terragenic life as an alien evolutionary scheme could be. Strikingly similar, down to fundamental amino-acid symmetry levels. There were diseases here an unprotected man could catch; diseases of terrestrial origin that might, without caution, obliterate Tralgansk's native life.

If the historical record was accurate, and there was no reason to believe it was not, people had been happy here for at least ten thousand years. Happy under the mandate of the Metastable Order, happier still as a productive part of the great Thoran Empire. The matter transmitters were gone and, with them, much of the transmutation economy; but ships plied the heavens and men considered themselves whole once more.

Now, he smiled grimly, we demons are come to put an end to all that.

You had to wonder about it, now and then. Since coming to the Thoran Empire vacuole, three centuries ago, he'd wandered about the worlds of this little universe, gathering data, tucking it away into the Order's building armamentum. There was splendid diversity here, worlds as different from one another as they were from the whole of the Metastable Order's vast, smoothed-out human cosmos. And all in only five thousand years. Marvelous.

Now we are here to collapse the vacuole, plow this rich turf under, reseed the Thoran worlds with the crop of Metastability. You have to wonder if it's a worthwhile endeavor. And wonder what humanity might be like had Cpaht's original plan gone on unchecked. Endless diversity. Cultures without number. Good? Bad? Unknown. That's the best I can say about it. Unknown.

"Not a bad-looking world," said a voice at his shoulder.

Denthurion twisted his neck and looked. Abbas Nitheroi, Instrument of the Metastatic Senate, was severely tall and thin, close to the psychopathic border of allopathy, with widow's peaked, close-cropped black hair, and a wiry, forked black beard. "Yes. Very attractive."

In the distance, beyond the far edge of haTonnagar, a fleck of bright light appeared, yellow at first, then luminous white and tinted with actinic violet, bringing tiny pains in his eyes as certain photochemical changes were induced. The spark lifted above the plain, accelerating skyward, accompanied by a tiny, rumbling peal of thunder. The ship climbed above the clouds, accelerating eastward, growing fainter, until it was gone, another starship heading out into the great dark.

"Time to go in. We're about to start the meeting."

Time to begin. As he turned away from the paintinglike vista, Denthurion thought, So change is wrought at last, now that they've gotten away with it so long they've forgotten about our reality. This meeting had been almost a half millennium in the making. Now, though . . .

There were six of them here, gathered about a small oval table of gray-brown Tralganski ekapandanus, three Televoxes, gathered from out of the void, three senior-grade Guard commanders, brought in from the closest focal worlds, and Nitheroi, sent from Earth quite a long time ago. Forces were congregating beyond the borders of the Thoran realm, waiting for word to strike.

As Denthurion sat, Nitheroi went to stand at the head of the table, looking them over, smile shadowing his dark features. "You all know me," he said, "from the previous individual meetings we've had. My role?" A shrug. "I am merely an agent of the Order, here to advise and observe and report back when . . . it's all over." He reached out and opened up a long, thin black case that was resting on the tabletop. Inside its velvet-lined cavity lay a long, plain gold rod, words inlaid on its side. *Sero molunt deorum molae.* "The mills of the gods grind slowly." It was, of course, a Sector Marshal's *baton de commandement.* The mills of the gods grind slowly, but they grind exceedingly fine. And, in the end, implacable, the gods always win.

Abbas Nitheroi picked up the *baton,* running his hands along the smooth, warm metal, fingering the lettering of the motto. "I've always liked holding them," he said. "Sometimes I regret the career decision that's meant I'll never hold one of my own." He extended the rod at arm's length, out over the center of the table. "Maaron Denthurion, mark Twenty-two, I elevate you to the temporary rank of Sector Marshal, from now until the vacuole of the Thoran Empire is reduced and the principles of the Metastable Order are triumphant. Then you step down and return, with this *baton de commandement,* to the locus of planet Earth."

He reached out and took the *baton* in his hand, heart stuttering slightly in his chest. Then I step down. Yes, I

remember. And . . . return to Earth? Something new.
Well. I will . . . learn.

"So be it," he said.

Done with his past, the diagnosis and prescription software elements began their work, opening his more ma-
chinelike, evolutionarily older components.

Excellent. Power supply engaged. A thread of light
wormed its way through the little dead being, casting
a wan and red illumination along its path. Power to
ROM. All right here. Central meta-tracks spinning up . . .
good, still in working order. Somatosensory driver check.
Okay. Functional, despite the new overlay system and
unfamiliar platform. Cross-compatibility good. The metacompiler's work appears to be correct.

Power to forward-branching logic chains. All up test
now . . . Cognitive drivers spinning up. Emotive prelogic
links kicking in. Cross range to video interpreter,
sonoradar supralobe converter. All nominal. Go for pe-
ripheral outlatch.

Pulses of energy. Putative flashes against an invisible
dark sky . . .

Power to video.

Power to sonoradar.

Power to cognitive driver inlatch subsystem.

Load AI rule sieve.

Load pseudocultural overlay.

Load linguistic/reinterpretive software.

Uplink overlay compiler to general metadriver program counter . . .

Twenty-seven astronomical units from Shemesh spins
Adomm, orbit eccentric, sometimes closing to twenty
AUs, sometimes receding to thirty-four.

Adomm is a vast object, four percent solar mass, a
swollen oblate spheroid almost four hundred thousand
kilometers in diameter, dull red and fuzzy-limbed,

painted with vague stripes of maroon and plum, immense oval maelstroms moving across its face, shadowy things of ruby and scarlet, drifting beneath a high, translucent mist.

Despite its size, Adomm is too small, too light, to house the gravitationally driven fusion reactions that set fire to the stars. But the weight of gravity presses down nonetheless, embracing the planetary core, creating ultra-dense matter, bringing heat. The planetary dynamo spins, pushing intense magnetic fields through a thick sea of compressed hydrogen. More heat. In spite of gravity's unyielding grip, Adomm expands, grand and tenuous, dull, hot red eye on the edge of interstellar night, lit up by the distant rays from Shemesh.

When men came here to work, they found Adomm surrounded by the usual swirl of planetary debris, the uncollated leftovers of creation. The world was circled by an extended, silvery ring, a featureless disk of orbiting particles, stretching downward to the upper atmosphere, spiraling in to destruction, fading away on its outer edge, becoming thinner until it was gone. Far away, millions of kilometers out, Adomm had its own little asteroid belt, tiny moonlets going every which way.

In between the ring and the irregular planetesimal bodies lay Adomm's retinue of faithful retainers, six large and substantial satellites, ranging from small, silicate Eropaa, trembling with tidal quakes, not far from the theoretical ring boundary, through Afrikaa, Amerikaa, Ostraalyaa, to mighty Aziyaa, shrouded in purple clouds, to the vast, ice-rimed plains of Antarktikaa, out on the edge of night.

Memories of paradise lost.

Men came and marveled and left their machines behind.

Maaron Denthurion awoke.

My God!

Alive!

The world flooded in, a hopeless jumble of impressions. He lurched hard to one side, twisting a strange head on an unfamiliar neck, staring around in fear. Hold on. Think. Where are you?

The ground nearby was a slick, moist-looking rubble, dark-looking, reddish perhaps, but . . . the distances beckoned. Pale, shadowy amethyst clouds hung low in the sky, backed by more remote cloud decks, solid, like dangerous cumulomammatus harbingers, darker purple, with flecks of violet and lavender here and there, like floating islands on the underside of the sky.

A wind blew across his skin, cold but . . . pleasant somehow, awakening the further sensations of life. He lay/stood on a hillside, looking down a long, sweeping vista, boulders and crags in profusion, toward the shores of a night-black sea. The waters were flat and motionless, like the surface of a tar pool, molten but not yet to the boiling point, gleaming here and there with little bits of reflected light. The horizon was invisible, fading out into purple mist.

Mountain, mist, haze, distance. Where am I?

Somewhere . . . where I've been before.

It was hard to remember, memory itself gone shadowy and purple, receding into the mist before him, playing an unpleasant game of childish keep-away. Where?

In the distance, out over the dead black sea, slanting lines began to appear under one low cloud, rain falling on the surface of the sea. Things began glittering there, a pool of reflectivity spreading underneath the cloud.

Faces appeared, pale ovals, featureless, surrounded by swirls of curling black hair. I can't remember their names, or anything about them. Wait, it will come to you eventually.

He recalled a world of cottony white clouds and distant, icy crags, heavens dominated by faces of coiling smoke. Gods, perhaps. I can't remember their names, either. But I remember being in those places, places much like this . . .

Voices. A million voices, all run together like some kind of sonic molten wax, bubbling over like lava. Speak to me. No, all is confusion.

One face, clear, soft, caring features, eyes concerned, fearful and happy, appeared before him, silhouetted against a dim, cloudless blue sky, a woman's voice, modulated low.

"Your soul is somewhere, Maaron Denthurion, when you fly between the stars."

A start of recognition: Shvirah! Do you love me?

I don't know.

She said something else. "Somewhere. I suspect it is in Heaven."

Denthurion felt himself go flat, emotions leaching out into some other place, a holding tank perhaps, to await a time when he might need them again. It is, he realized, the place of my dreams.

Many changes, since I came here last.

Shvirah was right. I've been here, to Heaven itself, many times before, and simply not known it.

A tiny spark of amusement glimmered, rising from the holding tank of his desires, shooting away into the sky, gone in an instant.

What a delicious irony this is.

Mankind, fearful of death, has had the secret of eternity in hand for fifty thousand years, all unaware.

If he could have laughed, he would have.

He rose up on spindly forelegs and slid down the slope a short distance on his tail-skid, then extended his wings, lit off his engines, and rose into an eternal purple twilight, banking toward the clouds, ground dropping away.

I can fly, he realized with a surge of pleasure.

In Heaven, I can fly.

Donauxas, on Thora itself, capital of the Empire, had been a metropolis of seventeen million souls, gleaming towers of metal and glass rising kilometers into the sky, monorail tracks twisting among the skyscrapers. Now, it was merely rubble. A dozen QD strikepoints had been touched off, here and there along the broad avenues, and the walls of glass had come down in a rain of fiery shards. Of the seventeen million souls, perhaps one tenth remained corporate.

A disk-shaped flyer growled down out of the smoky sky, settling among the ruins of the World Palace, not far from where most of the rubble had been cleared off the entrance to the Imperial Bunker. Its engines rumbled to a stop, hydraulic actuators hissing softly as a door slid open, ramp sliding to the ground.

The forty-first incarnation of Maaron Denthurion, mark Twenty-two, appeared in the hatchway and paused, looking around. There was a clatter of armaments as a double line of Metastatic Guardsmen formed at the foot of the ramp, stamping to attention, saluting.

All over now, he thought. The vista before him was appalling. Nothing over a dozen meters tall stood above ground level. Stumps of buildings protruded from the debris, here and there, thin gray-brown haze swirling above the ruins, fires guttering here and there, putting up plumes of dirty smoke as the city's small supply of flammable materials burned to exhaustion. Overkill? We'll never know now. All over but the final act. He started down the ramp, to where General Komatys waited, grim face lined by a thin smile.

The General saluted, once, quickly, then extended his hand. "Welcome to Thora, Sector Marshal."

Denthurion shook the hand and released it, still looking around. "And what's left of Donauxas, I suppose."

Komatys nodded, smile broadening a bit. "We did do a job on this place, didn't we?"

"Is everything in order?"

"Yes." The General turned, gesturing toward the bunker's entry hatch. "The Emperor surrendered with no trouble. I was a little surprised. Apparently, he was prepared to fight to the last drop of everyone's blood but his own."

"Not so surprising. One's own blood always seems reddest." They passed through the heavily braced doorway, descending a long flight of stairs and going into a brightly lit underground tunnel. The damage here was minimal, things knocked from walls, fixtures broken, an occasional crack in the stonework. The QD strikepoints made a tremendous overpressure, but with a relatively slow onset, not nearly so brissant as true nuclear explosions. It was enough to bring down buildings and most other human structures, but insufficient to plow up the bedrock in any degree.

The Emperor's living quarters were a shambles, furniture overturned, a row of captured Thoran leaders lined up along one wall, heads and limbs bandaged, faces little masks of ill-concealed fear. Almuric III, last of his kind, was easy to pick out, young, blond, and handsome, leaning against the far wall of the chamber between two armed Guardsmen, left arm in a splinted sling. On his face there was nothing like fear.

Denthurion crossed the room briskly, stopping before the Emperor, extending his hand. "Your Highness?"

Almuric stared at him, as if trying to peer into his eyes for a moment, then reached out and shook hands. "The tradition here is 'Your Grace,' Mr. . . ."

"Sector Marshal Maaron Denthurion, sir, Televox of the Metastable Order." He smiled. "By tradition, I should be addressed as 'Your Grace,' as well. Perhaps we can dispense with that."

"It seems like a good idea." He stood away from the wall, looking Denthurion up and down, inspecting him closely. "My conqueror, then. You seem like a fit enough specimen. And . . . I suppose I am at your disposal."

"Indeed you are." He took a step back and turned to Komatys. "Have you got the neck ring?" The General reached into his pouch and pulled out a thin gold band, a ring about fifteen centimeters in diameter. Denthurion took the ring and unlatched it, forming the shape of an open crescent. "Emperor Almuric III of the self-styled Thoran Empire, you are under arrest. Your rebellion against the Metastable Order is at an end." He placed the ring around the Emperor's neck and latched it, the shiny metal shrinking suddenly into place, snug against the skin of the man's neck. There was an astonished, angry murmur from the other Thoran officials, quickly silenced.

Almuric fingered the little collar and shook his head slowly. "Symbolic. Interesting. What now, Mr. Televox? A little show trial, perhaps? Put the Thoran masses in their place?"

"Well. The ways we have of restoring the old order are . . . not so simple. Perhaps you should be glad you won't be here to see it."

"Not here?" A shadow of unease crossed his features. "What do you mean?"

"You'll have a real trial, I suppose, Emperor. You're coming with me, to Earth."

A look of surprise, quickly mastered. "Earth? Well, now. I always wondered if Earth was more than a myth."

"Now you'll have the opportunity to find out. Come." He gestured toward the exit.

"Wait. What about my . . . friends?" He pointed to the row against the other wall, the former high officials of the Thoran Empire.

Denthurion looked at them, smiled, and said, "For them, merely death."

Denthurion soared among the clouds of Heaven, wraiths of purple mist breezing by his face, slowly closing in on the Font of Souls. It was on an island in God's Dark Sea, a crag of dirty white ice rising out of the still, black waters, surmounted by a gray metal flower, all stem and petals and leaves. Souls buzzed around the font like midges or bees, climbing away on fiery contrails, bent on God's work, swooping in to land on a petal, engines cut, dropping in a deadstick glide.

He made his own stoop and flare, loosing altitude and speed in a complex maneuver, leveling off, engines flaming out with little popping noises. The wind whistled in his ears and stirred his hair, the font tower growing before him in silence. There. Now! He dropped his flaps full open, cupping the air under his wings, tail-skin dropping, scraping across the surface of the landing stage. Down. He went through a brief rollout, brakes squeaking a bit, then applied power to his forward wheels, dragging himself to the stalk, plugging his face into a receptacle.

A million voices, images of endless men and women, broke in on him as he stood, once more, in the form of a man. Where am I now? he wondered. Yes. Still in Heaven. Like the tables of Valhalla, where I sat and feasted with all my brethren. Sad thought. All the other incarnations, of all the other lines, still caught in the false vectorship heaven of the Metastability. I am alone here . . .

No. Not alone. All around him were the ascended men and women of *Koxavonia*, crewmen, as they believed they would be, on the great Starship of God.

What a fool I was. If only I could speak to Shvirah, now, I'd say . . .

Well. Patience. That time will come. Shvirah, in Heaven . . .

Maybe I'll love you in Heaven, she said. Someday. Soon, perhaps . . .

He found himself seated in what seemed like a vast dining hall, at a long table, a plate of food miraculously before him, surrounded by the souls of the faithful. Eat, they said. Be happy. Happiness is the order of the day, in

Heaven. The order of eternity, then. He ate. And was happy.

Later on, he had no idea how much later, Denthurion found himself clinging to the side of one of Heaven's great, icy crags, face plugged into the actuator receptacle of one of God's Starship machines, doing a task appropriate to a new member of the crew.

Plugged into the machine, an enormous, complex tool set, he felt vastly expanded, his mind filled with input from new and unfamiliar senses. He could *see*, right through the ice, sensing the composition of its chemicals directly. From somewhere on the tool's forehead, a pulse of energy went out, penetrating the ices, striking particles free from the molecules, telling him all he wanted to know of its substance. The energies were reflected back to the tool's eyes, transferred through its nerve net to the face receptacle, then through his own nerve net to optic interpreter and sonoradar converter.

Today's task was to get at the bluish vein, embedded a few meters below the surface, drop it in the tool's processor, move on, find another such vein, move on, move on. The day would end, sooner or later, and he would turn in his tool, with its cargo of processed blue veins, go back to the Font of Souls for another night of recuperation and good fellowship. It promised to be a happy ... afterlife. And Shvirah would come.

He reached out through the tool, expending its energies, directing particle beams and manipulator arms against the surface of the crag. White ice, water mostly, sliced away, layer after layer, puffs of quick-freezing steam, splashes of slushy droplets. Eventually the streak of hydrated blue impurity came away, metal salts in frozen solution. He dropped it in the tool's hopper and thought-activated the processor. There was a long plume of steam, blowing from its vent, a brief snowstorm down onto the world below.

Satisfied that the metal salt, now purified, was secure. Denthurion tipped backward away from the mountainside, kicking off with his long forelimbs, spreading his great wings, ram-starting his little engines. The dense air of Heaven funneled through the intake gills, fire bloomed, and he was away, diving toward a broad plain covered with some misty, gassy slime, then climbing toward brilliantly colored clouds.

Away, again. He leveled off, looking downward, tool beam probing the ice. There was work to be done, despite the pleasure of flight. God's work.

He must be about it.

Chapter 14

Downlink count one-two-three . . .

Storage ring access interrupt . . .

Break-break.

Denthurion walked through the Great Hall of the Star-ship Crew, threading a faceless human maze, at loose ends, feeling somewhat lost. Surely not a normal feeling in Heaven? People were everywhere, sitting around tables, relaxing in big, soft chairs, standing in little knots and clusters, talking, talking. *Koxavonia* all, knowing each other, except for me. Odd fate to be alone in Heaven. How long until Shvirah comes? Or even Meltsar, or Naamer? Any of the Olamites I've come to know. Sudden trickle of insight: I wish Tayash would show up.

A moment of familiarity: that young woman over there. Something about her that I recognize . . . Slim, dark, handsome-faced . . . Of course. The angel. He could see her, spilling out of nowhere into a torch-glittery night, come to get that thin fellow . . . What *was* her name? "Bekaa!" he called out.

The woman looked at him, puzzled. "Yes? I don't believe we've met?"

Introductions in Heaven. Odd. He held out his hand to her. "I'm . . ."

"Bekaa!" cried a reedy-voiced man at her side. "It's the Televox!" He took the hand, pumping it vigorously. "I'm Kellevv, Mr. Televox. You were there to see me off. What an honor!"

The scene was still there in Denthurion's memory, this small, slender man, walking slowly through the murmuring crowd, head bowed, face frozen in a stiff little grin, wet patches glistening on his cheeks . . .

"Yes. Of course." Of course I remember . . .

Bekaa, the angel, seemed troubled. "I can't imagine what you're doing here, Mr. Televox. Is there . . . some other route into Heaven?" You could see she didn't want to believe it. Imagine a Heaven flooded with allopathic demons . . .

He smiled. "No other way. Just through the good offices of *Koxavonia.*" Good offices? Curious transposition.

"You've become one of us, then?" The expression on her face was plain bewilderment. It *did* seem unlikely.

"In . . . a manner of speaking. I'm one of you *now,* I suppose, now that I'm here. But . . . like Tayash, I came here against my will."

"What do you mean?"

He shrugged. "Tayash went to Heaven by accident. Meltsar put me through the Ascension transceiver at gunpoint."

"Gunpoint?" She looked away for a moment, into nothingness. "God will not be pleased."

"I suppose not. Perhaps Meltsar will have something to answer for, when his Ascension comes."

The angel nodded. "Perhaps. It's hard to know how God will feel about this."

"I haven't seen God since coming here."

She smiled shyly. "Few do. God speaks only to those he selects for special work."

"Like being an angel to the Ascendant?"

"He calls to me, when I am needed." Her face was shadowed by trouble again. "I'm sorry you had to come unescorted. It must have been awful . . ."

A vision of great, blue-veined breasts rose up, smothering the life from him. "Well. Not *so* bad. Disconcerting, perhaps, but in the end, I understood what seemed to be familiar symbolism."

She reached out and took him by the hand, smiling again. "Come. There is great joy to be found in Heaven."

He followed her, thinking, There must be. There's food in heaven, why not sex, or swimming pools? Should I wait for Shvirah? Difficult choice.

In the end, however, she only led him to a banquet table, then, much later, in fact, to a swimming pool, where the crewmen of God frolicked away their off-duty hours, spinning 'round the storage ring for endless ticks of the program timer, until their services were needed again.

God's work be done . . .

Denthurion sailed low above a hazy silver plain that stretched off, horizonless, to infinity, comrades in inertial flight holding position behind and to the sides, wingmen in a staggered vee formation. Above, if you could call it that, the sky was dead black, featureless save for a few distant pastel specks. To his right the world was dominated by the Mountain of Storms, a vast dome of surly red, surface subtly banded, crisscrossed by slowly moving whorls of maroon and purple.

Kellevv said, "Televox. Water-Smelter Automaton detected eleven kilometers ahead, two-four degrees port, embedded about six hundred meters beneath the upper ring coplane."

"Understood." He altered his flight vector with a few tiny thruster thuds, wisps of violet gas jetting away into the void and dissipating. Sonoradar pulses brought back a foggy view of the smelter, almost hidden by vaporous ring particles. Odd configuration. Maybe that was why it had shut down. "What do you make of those things docked to it? I don't seem to recall any such . . ."

Kellevv's radio voice seemed uneasy. "I don't know. Still, in God's Heaven all things must be . . ."

"Work vacuoles," broke in Bekaa.

"What does that mean?"

The communications carrier wave buzzed against the emptiness around them. "I'm not sure. Just a little trickle of memory. Nothing connected with anything I've seen in Heaven."

That made Denthurion feel uncomfortable. This was *Heaven*. They were supposed to *know*. Another little voice started up in the background. You can't let it go, can you? Here you are, come to Heaven itself, to a world whose existence you thought you only *dreamed,* yet you continue to push and probe, as if still the Televox bound to duty by the rigid rules of the Metastable Order. That order betrayed you, Maaron Denthurion. God will unveil the true Master Plan in his own good time. Still ... It was curious.

They swept into the morass of micron-sized ring particles, supersonic vee-wakes forming around them, turbulence vibrating their components to a singing rhythm. The Smelter rose up out of the white twilight, a black hulk outlined in haze, intake maw at one end and propulsion system at the other. It was a smooth shape, streamlined to cope with the ring environment, deformed now by a pair of small parasites that protruded from the forward ventral deck, where the chin-turret docking adaptor had been extruded.

They pulled up even with it, making simple rendezvous, hovering a few dozen meters from the alien craft. Peculiar-looking things, much like the work unit Denthurion's soul inhabited ... with extras. At the nose, attached to the docking platform baseplate, was a spherical object that looked like some kind of dewar, a pressure vessel perhaps. Some cryoliquid-dependent repair process? Unknowable. I wonder why they're here ahead of us? Has God made a scheduling error? That would be ... amusing. That other voice, from the depths of his soul, told him to shut up.

"What's that?" asked Bekaa, fear evident in her radio signature.

Denthurion focused his sensors toward the intake throat of the Smelter. A couple of slow-moving robots crawled within, starfish-shaped, barely creeping along as they worked, talking to each other in bursts of complexly modulated, incomprehensible radio noise.

What *are* these things? For that matter, what are starfish? Why don't I *know*?

Light sparkled as the robots began to weld a long tear in the Smelter's throat. "Whatever they are, they seem to be fixing it. We're not needed here."

"Let's go home," said Kellevv. "This place gives me the creeps."

"Agreed."

They backed away, thrusters burping gas that made little swirls in the ring mist, then accelerated upward, toward free space, filled with clean light and the black backdrop of God's infinite space.

It was a grayish sort of day in Marumsko village, where Senator Denthurion had dawdled away part of the morning sitting on his deck, looking out across a wedge of valley, watching glints of filtered sunlight move across the landscape, reflected from the still-perfect hull of the crashed police cruiser. The sky wasn't quite overcast, but there was a high haze, whitening the blue sky until it seemed sullied. Dawn had come for a prolonged stay, tinting a whole section of the sky a dull orange-brown for almost half the morning.

Two little figures were walking up the grassy path that led to his door, ambling along at a relaxed pace. They stopped for quite a while before the Carthoradis estate, the one talking at length to the other, before moving on. As they approached, the Senator stood, feeling some small stirring of excitement. This would be something . . . new.

The first incarnation of Maaron Denthurion, mark Twenty-three, walked up the little flight of wooden steps and stood before himself, hand extended. "Senator?"

"Mr. Televox." The Senator took his hand and shook it slowly. He looked at the other man, pale and handsome, face looking somewhat drawn and fatigued. "You are, I think, the Thoran Emperor Almuric III?"

The man shook his hand, nodding silently.

"Please be seated." He gestured to a pair of chairs drawn up facing his own.

The Televox took his seat, staring hard at the Senator, who seemed to be doing his best to remain casual about the whole affair. "Hard to think of you as the original."

The Senator nodded, smiling faintly. "I keep wanting you to be the first incarnation of mark One, who I regarded as my friend."

"Only the most recent of many, however."

"Friend, nonetheless." He turned to look at Almuric, who was following the exchange with a sort of detached interest. "So. This is the man who wanted to pull down the Order."

The Emperor smiled wanly. "A case of mistaken identity, I'm afraid. The men who wanted to put an end to your universe are long dead. By the time I was born, the Metastability of Man was no more than a distant nightmare. Besides . . ."

The Senator waited for a moment, hoping he'd continue spontaneously, for it was such an interesting frown, but, "Yes?"

Almuric shrugged uncomfortably. "Your machines vaporized the real me. This"—he gestured at his body—"is just a cheap imitation."

The Televox laughed. "I, on the other hand, am a rather expensive imitation."

"This is all ancient nonsense," said the Senator. "You can imagine, if you want, that your 'soul' has some special quality, or had, that makes you somehow unique, but that won't make it so."

"Maybe not. These things *are*, after all, no more than a matter of belief."

"Come now. We have machines that have more special qualities than you, or any other man."

"I understand. I also understand those machines can never be sent through a transceiver."

"Merely a matter of economics," said the Televox.

"As you say. I don't think it really matters. Not to me." He shifted in his chair, turning to stare for a long second at the reflective hull of the police cruiser. "Why have you brought me here?"

"It's just a tradition, Emperor," said the Senator. "I think we . . . want to know what makes the other sort of men tick. We won't learn but . . . you're here because I want to offer you a job."

Almuric looked at him, puzzled. "Doing what?"

"As my aide."

"You mean like a comeye?"

"No. More like a friend."

"And that will help you understand how we 'tick'?"

"Just a tradition, Emperor. Besides which, it's my turn to have a friend."

"I guess it doesn't matter."

"You can always kill yourself."

The Emperor suddenly looked haggard. "I cannot, though I originally thought I would. This cheap imitation loves life, too."

The Senator nodded. "They all say that. I don't know why."

The Televox said, "Going for a walk. Want to come?"

The Senator shook his head slowly. "No. I think not."

"Emperor?"

Almuric got to his feet, seeming a bit stiff. "Yes. I'd like to see the scenes of your childhood. You've come to seem rather . . . real to me."

In the Great Hall, Denthurion sat on the edge of his chair, staring into Bekaa's soft brown eyes, oblivious to the hubbub all around, a steady, swirling mutter of interrupted human voices. "Just tell me," he said, "if you *really* believe you're in Heaven."

She looked troubled. "Of . . . course I do."

"The *real* Heaven?"

She smiled wanly. "You're asking me what's real, Mr. Televox. I'm here. You're here. That's the best I can do."

"Still . . ." Fetch me an answer of some kind.

"I know. It's not quite what we expected; if, indeed, we each expected the same thing. But it's what we were promised."

"Not what *Hikanesh!* promised."

"No." She laughed. "But it's what the Pilot promised, with his . . . simpler words. And Meltsar, after all, has never been to Heaven. We can't hold Tayash completely responsible for what his ghost writer said." She laughed again. "Ghost writer. Funny."

"Yes. What the little Saint of Disorder promised . . ."

Sitting beside them, Kellevv seemed to be getting angry. "Why are you questioning all this, Mr. Televox?" He took in the Great Hall with a wild sweep of one arm. "We're *here*! What happens if we don't believe in it? Do we evaporate, for God's sake?"

"Good question . . ."

"Damn it. You've been outside. How can you question *that* reality?"

Another very good question.

Later, Denthurion floated in the deep, dark space between his worlds, seeing with all his remote senses. The ice world was nearby, gravity negligible, cryogenic surface blackened from an eternity of photorganics, save where the mining machines had dug a brilliant, kilometers-long gouge. In the distance, the flat underside of the sky was freckled with stars, the ship's core floating in front of the backdrop, a dull red sphere, lit up in a crescent shape by a distant sun, disk of silvery, dusty rings broken where they went through shadow.

Bekaa drifted nearby, flying in formation with him as

they sailed away from the little moon, Hohmanning to a new target several days away. The initial maneuvers were over. As soon as they knew their course was absolutely correct, they'd shut down to wait out the transit in peace. Denthurion was dreading the moment to come.

The radio link to Bekaa crackled slightly, noise from radiation trapped in the core's spinning magnetic field. Get it *over* with!

No. Not the shutdown. Just . . . do something . . . inspired.

He reached out through the link and felt the woman's personality, just its gently undulating surface, calm, happy, there for the asking. The inspiration came.

Denthurion punched through the outer integument of her soul, greeted by a sudden pulse of surprise and fear, quickly damped down as his tendrils took control. You knew you could do this. You just forgot. But . . . how did I forget? Good question.

Beneath superficial unity, the woman was a shambles, mind pulled apart and distorted. Do this, do that, do something else. There were metacompiler fingerprints everywhere. Cold comfort. I *don't* know how to interpret what I'm seeing.

Listen. Nothing here but belief and machine links. This feels like . . . a robot vacuum cleaner in Heaven. Nothing here. Not anymore.

Manifest frustration.

He pulled out of her quickly, feeling a moist suction as her various components fell back together.

"Denthurion . . . Why . . ."

He ignored her, scanning the skies. Nothing. Nothing. Nothing. He pushed his probe out on long radio waves, boosting its power until his control system protested angrily, shouting at the insensate sky. This *isn't* Heaven. It *can't* be . . .

The sky was, of course, silent, and Bekaa cringed, bewildered.

God damn it. Nothing. Sleep. Wait out the transit. See what happens . . .

Darkness fell, like a descending curtain of drowsiness.

Sometime later he awoke into a dream. Gray smoke filled the sky like featureless gauze. How odd. Why am I *here*?

A single pale bluish eye opened in the mist, blinking once. Aha. Found you. A feeling of cold, distant triumph pulsed through the universe. The eye looked him over and seemed dismayed. What have they done to you, Sixty-seven? Pathetic. Well. Come along.

Denthurion, terrified, squealed as he was sucked out of his body once again, to fall, screaming, down a long, dark tunnel that led to eternal night.

Almuric and Denthurion walked up the grassy path toward the low, rambling house, white with blue trim, rose-bushes planted along every wall, smoke trees in the yard, weeping willow towering above the roof line, and stopped beside the deck. The woman was sunning herself, reclining in a chaise lounge, pale skin hardly covered by a narrow, pale blue bikini, black hair in artful disarray, one thin arm thrown across her eyes.

"Mother?"

The woman stirred and sat up slowly, breasts sagging a bit, not too much as she leaned on the railing and looked at the two men, eyes shifting sluggishly from one to the other. "I beg your pardon?"

Denthurion felt his pang of recognition, startled at the sight of her, smooth, narrow, unchanged, and familiar across the millennia, fade slowly. "I'm your son. Denny."

She smiled slightly, cocking her head to one side. "Oh? How do you do? You don't look familiar, you know."

Surprised? Yes or no. Take your pick. I thought she'd know me, even . . . she must see the *original* from time

to time. "I'm one of Senator Denthurion's Televoxes ..."
Nothing. "Denny. From about seven thousand years
ago."

"Seven thousand years ..." Her teeth still had that
same milky, blue-white tint. "Young man. That's an aw-
fully long time."

"I remember you."

She looked wistful, perhaps sad. "I'm your only
mother, of course. I don't imagine you're my only son."

"Don't you know?"

She shrugged, looking away at the sky. "No."

It occurred to him he didn't have any notion of her
true age. "How's Father?"

"I don't remember."

"Do you see him?"

"I suppose so."

Denthurion felt the Emperor's hand on his arm, pulling him away. He turned to look at the man.

"You see? Seven thousand years might as well be an
eternity. Human machines were never meant to last so
long."

"I have."

"Not without help. Come on, let's go see some of your
other ... memories."

His mother stood up, hipbones a delicate tracery beneath her skin, flat abdomen about level with his face.
"Go ahead," she said. "I'm sorry I don't remember you,
but ... in the end, I remember no one. That's ... the
way it happens."

He looked up at her, silent for a minute, and suddenly
realized she was no more than a sexually attractive
stranger. "I suppose. Good-bye, Mother."

She smiled. "Good-bye. Enjoy yourself." She was already sitting on the chair again, preparing to recline and
resume her meditations, whatever they might be.

Denthurion and Almuric turned away and walked up
the hill, toward the hedgerow that marked the end of
Marumsko. The woods beckoned.

Sometime later they stood at the head of a vast dual gully system, looking out over a ruin of raw tan earth. The two little valleys, so obviously artificial, were separated by a ridge of dirt on which vegetation, including a number of small deciduous trees, had been left standing. The walls of the valleys were sheer, dropping almost vertically to flat floors of dried mud, scattered here and there with boulders of various sizes and shapes. The wall of the far right valley was pocked with several rows of cliff swallow holes.

Denthurion stood quietly with Almuric, looking over the scene, starring at the swallow holes. "You know," he said, "when I was a boy, I imagined this was the home-land of a race of prehistoric cliff-dwellers; this one"—he pointed to the one with the swallows—"Kor-ul-ja, that one Kor-ul-Gryf. Of course, that was only for the public literary fantasy about Pal-ul-Don. Cary and I called it Italkor, from a devastated country in a private mythology of our own."

"Are you telling me this place existed, that it was the same when you were a boy, thousands of years ago?"

Denthurion nodded pensively.

"How can that be?"

"Italkor, Dorvo, the Creek, several other places, are all maintained by the School. Sort of . . . parks, for the imagination."

Almuric looked at him pityingly. "Maintained. So no one here might accidentally catch a glimpse of reality."

Denthurion smiled at him. "Boys *aren't* immortal, you know. We grow up, go out to the stars. The chances of my coming here ever again were small."

"And the Senator?"

"You'll notice he declined our invitation." Denthurion looked out over the blasted landscape again, wondering, briefly, how it had gotten this way in the first place. Something to do, probably, with the wrecked and carefully preserved mining equipment about a kilometer away, down in the swamp. "Sometimes I wish boys were immortal. I went out to the stars as a boy. I don't know what I've become."

As they began to walk off, around the rim of the valley, Almuric said, "The way we lived, death claims you before the boy has a chance to die completely."

"Not your way of life any longer. The Thoran Empire has been gone, already, for nearly a thousand years."

Almuric felt a brief lump of *bolus hystericus* climb up his throat, then recede. "There were," he said, "a few intervening dreams."

Finally, Denthurion and Almuric stood before Helium's Transceiver Matrix, saying good-bye.

"I wish he'd come to see me off. He did before."

Almuric nodded. "Time changes people. Even people who live forever. Even you."

"I suppose so. I thought I would have changed the most, out among the worlds. He's just been ... sitting here all this time."

"Sitting here. But the machines haven't worked to keep him on so *precise* a course."

"I suppose not."

"I'll be here a long time. Eventually, I imagine I'll understand him and through him you, all of this. If I thought I could find you again ..."

Denthurion smiled. "Me? I don't exist. The terminus of my line is the best you can do."

Almuric seemed to wince. "There is that." He reached out and shook Denthurion's hand. "Have a good trip."

"I always do." He turned away and, without looking back, stepped into the Matrix and was gone.

Hmmmm ...

What a fucking mess.

Odin ran the remains of the file through a decompiler

and expanded it into reconstructed source code, lines of best-guess programming based on what the different modules *ought* to have done. Ygg-almighty. Still worse.

Wreathed in smoke and fury, the Gray Wanderer struggled to figure things out, but it was useless. Finally, exasperated, he reached far down into the black ice and pulled out a prior incarnation of the being, dearchiving it from compressed to executable state, then decompiling it as well. *This* one was neat and orderly and, of course, had been cuffed and sealed after Kem. Not so long ago, but long enough.

All right. Now what?

He ran the two programs through a file comparison device. Holy shit. Not much left of i67, not much at all. Still, there was a place to begin. *These* modules, clearly, had never been part of the original template. Sweep them away. Urg. That left a decided lace curtain effect. Now this mess here was from the original, but repurposed, the code hopelessly garbled. Sweep it away as well. Fuck. What was left looked like a well-used fisherman's net. All right. Duplicate out the equivalent modules from i66 and start filling in the holes, pouring code like warm putty. Much better.

Now. What about the mess in the cognitive driver modules? *Have* to leave the God-damned things. Otherwise we might as well erase i67 completely and start over again with a new copy of i66.

Done. Button things up, run i68 through the compiler and store a clean copy, pack i66 away again. And done.

Open carrier to OLAM.REC . . .

Downlink . . .

i68 in the platform buffer . . .

and Maaron mk33i68 Denthurion begin . . .

Fourth Canto

Felix qui potuit rerum cognoscere causas.

Happy is the man who has understood the cause
of things.

—Vergil, *Georgics*

Chapter 15

Maaron Denthurion's heart beat in darkness, a slow, steady succession of groans, louder, then softer, but reliable. No where. No when. No thought. Red-tinged night stretching out in all directions, exceeding all perceptual parameters. A sense of touch, slow, hot, wet sliding membranes parting above his crown, rubbing across his face, collapsing around neck and body, disappearing beneath his feet. Movement, struggle, peristalsis.

A spot of cold appeared on the top of his head, small, round, puckered. A moment of formless wondering. The spot became cold lips devouring him, a leech-mouthed snake engulfing him headfirst, spreading, everting, the cold reaching, becoming his entire skull, inching down his forehead, crossing his brows. His eyes disappeared into the cold mouth and opened. White light. The mouth slithered across his ears. Cacophony.

One shoulder went in, folded arm popping away from his body, flapping in agonizing cold, then the other. His upper torso began flopping around, supported here and there, prodded and pulled by chill, rubbery, robotic manipulators. They took him under the chin and back and pulled, and he felt his hips slide free, genitals and anus shriveling under the impact of the cold, cold riding down his legs, feet disappearing through the lips with a small, obscene sucking noise.

Denthurion spun down the great gullet, robot tongues guiding his body as it fell, end over end ... Something probed his throat like a lover's tongue and sucked as it delved, choking him. He dropped headlong down a tunnel of night, gravity hauling at his atoms, cloud forms blurring all around.

No. No. Not me. I'm not ready yet.

Impact. End of eternity.

Maaron Denthurion screamed out his horror and fell away into the nightmare.

The Televox stepped through night, incarnation counter clicking over just once, and Maaron Denthurion, mk23i02, stepped out into the dim sunshine of Vinylhaven, world of the Gnaw-Xhan. The place had changed only a little since he'd last been here, millennia ago. There were the same bloody clouds under a pale, reddish sky, the planetary transceiver center similar, with its dusty streets and low, frontier-town buildings. In the distance, in all directions, the green-black forest rose, trees climbing higher and higher until they formed an irregular horizon. The wind, raising curls of thin dirt out of the road, was somehow sweeter than he remembered it, not quite cloying, but noticeable nonetheless. An artifact of memory perhaps, or of endless rebirth.

He walked away from the unattended transceiver in the town square, stepping up into a raised wooden sidewalk that clunked softly underfoot. Odd. There seemed to be very few people about. The last time I was here there were . . . no, not crowds, but people in the street, carrying guns, gathering equipment, getting ready. Now. There was a little movement in the glass-fronted tavern across the street. A little, but not much.

Eventually, he came to the town office, where passports were validated and hunting licenses sold. Denthurion went in, crossing a dusty carpet to where an empty counter waited. There seemed to be no one here. He stood for a while, patience learned from an endless supply of years, then noticed the little silvery dome of a bell, and struck it. The peal was high and metallic, ringing on for a while, fading out at some undetectable time.

In a bit, footsteps clumped down a flight of stairs and along a hidden corridor. A curtain at the back of the room was thrust aside and a tall fat man came through, little eyes staring at him from either side of a long, pointed nose, mouth pursed, but open slightly to show healthy, crooked teeth. "Yes?"

"I'd like to buy a hunting license please."

The man put his hands on the counter and stared at him silently, face expressionless. Finally, he said, "You're a Televox, aren't you?"

He nodded. "Maaron Denthurion. I was here . . . a long time ago."

Another long, silent stare. "Must have been." Pause. "Well, I can't sell you a hunting license, Mr. Televox."

"No?" This person was decidedly odd. Knows who and what I am, but . . . no reaction. "Have the laws been changed then?"

"They have not."

"Then why?" This was a tiresome game.

The man smiled suddenly, mouth widening to display a glory of irregularity. "It's like this: The Gnaw-Xhan have all been killed, Your Grace. Can't hunt them no more, 'cause they ain't no more." You could see the man would like to guffaw in his face.

"I see. How did that happen?"

The man shrugged. "Men like you wanted to hunt them. Been coming here for tens of thousands of years. Making them into furniture, into trophies, shooting them down just to take a picture. Let it go on long enough, it was bound to happen. And that's just what you did."

"I see." Denthurion wanted to turn away from this repulsive creature, run back into the street's sweet air, but he said, "Want to validate my passport?"

"Naw, we don't bother with passports no more. Have a nice stay, Mr. Televox." He was suddenly turning away, whipping past the curtain, booted feet thumping down the hallway and back up the stairs. A door closed in the distance and the interlude was over.

Denthurion walked back into the street and stood on the edge of the wooden sidewalk for a while, watching the dull red clouds drift by overhead. Gone. Like that. My fault.

Well. No matter. He stepped down into the dust of the street and walked diagonally across to the tavern where he'd earlier seen signs of life. The wooden doors squeaked on brass hinges, hinges that must have been replaced a million times and more, then threaded his way through a maze of tables to the bar.

It was a quiet-seeming place. The barkeep leaned on the bar, the piano player sat in the corner, seeming to sleep. A couple of old men sat at a corner table, playing some kind of elaborate board game, pebbles-and-pits perhaps. There was one other patron, a man in a dark brown field ranger uniform, wearing boots of Gnaw-Xhan leather, foot hooked over the bar rail, drinking tea-colored liquor from a shot glass.

The barkeep said, "Yes?"

"Brandy, please."

The glass was set before him, narrow-necked bottle upended over it, liquid splashing briefly. Denthurion lifted the glass to his lips and dumped the brandy in. It burned on his tongue, starting copious saliva, swirled around teledyne-perfect molars, and seared down his throat, ceasing to exist.

Above the bar was a dusty old mural, human crouched on the floor of a dark red-green-black forest, firing his lasgun upward at a sharp angle into the trees. If you looked closely you could see the target, a vast sluglike creature of many glowing eyes. The artist, thought Denthurion, must have been a good one, for you could see some semblance of horror and fear in those alien eyes.

God damn you, human, the thing seemed to say.

Creatures of pride and spirit, the Gnaw-Xhan.

But then they died, and were gone, nonetheless.

• • •

Deep within the Metastable Archive Center, on Olam, around Shemesh, embedded in Orion Arm, the dead, dustless air of the transceiver chamber stirred. Essence of ersatz personality flowed along optical channels behind old stone walls, driven by an external whip, passing along seldom used ways, tripping teledyne circuitry, making unaccustomed device calls. The storage ring began ticking over, collecting and collating data, photons marching column abreast, eyes right, rifles to port arms, rank on rank queuing up on command.

The air became hard and clear, waiting, then light spilled out of the receiver node's wall niche, shadows leaning into corners, shrinking suddenly, growing contrast dark. There was a long, fractured moment, then red light flowed from nowhere, swiftly taking on the shape and form of a man, flooding into three dimensions, coalescing, gaining color and realism in an eyeblink. The light faded and went out, leaving him alone among dimmer, less distinct shadows.

Maaron Denthurion staggered out of the wall niche, stumbling, almost falling, as he dropped from the little dais onto the floor. He stood, wobbling unsteadily, looking about foggy-headed at the empty room. Where. Who. How. All the old single-morpheme phrases crowded his head, more like statements than questions. He looked down at his naked torso, something familiar, at least.

Of course. Olam. The Metastable Archive Center. Kinnock Maclaren. Should be here to meet me. Haze of uncertainty. No, that was before. This is now. When. What. Particles of meaning without satisfactory answer/ response. One more important than the others. Of course. Why.

He took a step toward the door, paused again. There must be something . . .

The whole history of his stay on Olam flooded back from memory suddenly, cold, like a stream of frigid oil down his back. That last scene: dark shapes dragging him through the *Koxavonia* compound, night sky aswirl with stars overhead, stuffing him into the transceiver cage, standing back dark and shadowy, Meltsar, working the controls, one last momentary plea, cut off in midword, when, quick as a wink, they piped him off to Heaven ...

Cool sweat beaded his body, evaporating quickly in the dry air. Heaven! My God ... "Odin?" he whispered, uncertain and afraid.

A flat and featureless face appeared on the wall suddenly, blank-eyed, conforming to its substance, not Odin, surely, but the house comeye. "Mr. Televox," it murmured. "Welcome back."

Denthurion stared at it for a long moment, unable to formulate a proper sentence. Finally, he said, "Hello. Uh. Can you put me in touch with"—he had to fish for the ship's name—"*Naglfar*?" Too many gods and goddesses in his head now. Too easily confused. Where *has* my memory gotten to?

The face took on a comic-sad aspect, mimelike in its broadness. "Of course, Your Grace." It seemed disappointed somehow.

The comeye whirled down an invisible drain, leaving the wall blank for a second, then the old, familiar dark cavern carved itself into its surface, Odin on his throne, Hugin and Munin on theirs. "Good day to you, Mr. Televox," said the ship's comeye.

"What happened to me? Where was I?" There. Coherent thoughts at last, tumbling like acrobats from his lips.

Odin seemed thoughtful. "A long story and yet a short one." The god pursed its lips and the two black birds stirred, ruffling their feathers, stretching and looking about, red-eyed. "It is less than a week since you went off to the *Koxavonia* camp. As per your instructions, I waited and monitored, knowing that in ten days my programming would override you and I would be forced to send down a new incarnation ..."

Unaccountably, Denthurion's heart began to thud in his chest.

"There seemed to be a growing political ferment below, student demonstrations, obviously fomented by *Shearah*, growing violent at times, requiring police suppression. Of interest, an animal rights group has sprung up that seems bent on property destruction, stealing Hodai and the like. They broke into the Perax municipal zoo last night and let loose a number of interesting and dangerous animals."

Scenes were forming on the walls around Odin's cave now, video images of street riots, without sound, though there seemed to be a very faint *whisper* coming from somewhere, which added just the right touch of realism. Particularly intriguing was the scene in which a large, three-horned quadruped charged a group of armed policemen, scattering them, their bullets absorbed by its thick hide.

"Since it seemed reasonable," Odin went on, "I extended my monitoring to cover the entire electromagnetic communications spectrum of the Shemesh system. There is a lot more activity here than you would think. The economy is far richer than it appears."

I almost don't want to know, thought Denthurion.

"I did not think I was capable of true surprise, Mr. Televox. I learned otherwise when I picked up your recognition signal. It was, of course, coming from the industrial complex around the outer planet Adomm."

. . . mother ship, silver rings around a shadowed red sphere, adrift against the starry backdrop of night . . .

"Because of the lightspeed limitation, I was forced to move myself physically to the locus in which I expected to find you. This took a number of hours. Then, because you were no longer transmitting, I was forced to sift through the entire communications net present around Adomm." Odin paused, looking at him somberly. "I must admit, Mr. Televox, that I did not think even human beings capable of doing such things to one another. Under the stress of intense personal belief and madness, yes, men will do much horror. Cpaht. Hitler. There are an endless host of examples . . . But this. For such *shallow* motivation . . ."

"What are you talking about?" asked Denthurion, voice faint and reedy.

"The work modules in the Adomm industrial complex, Mr. Televox, are human personalities, haphazardly modified to suit the needs of a variety of task environments. Very sloppy work. Done, I suspect, to circumvent the pathologic technical restrictions of this society. Someone wished they were part of a wealthy, allopathic society, Mr. Televox. Someone, I suspect, wished to *own* such a society. This may have looked like a neat and easy trick."

"And . . . what about me?" Heaven! My God, I was in *Heaven*!

"I pulled what remained of your data from where it was stored in an active computer and found that substantial modification was made. This modification was rectified using templates from a stored version of your previous incarnation."

Denthurion's heart seemed to collapse for an instant, then restart of its own volition. "Then . . . this"—he indicated his nude flesh—"is Maaron Denthurion, version Thirty-three, incarnation sixty-eight, I take it."

"Yes, Mr. Televox. Enough remained of incarnation sixty-seven that a new branching was not required. In my experience, this is as close as one may come to *lacunation* without actually encountering that state directly."

Dead, thought Denthurion numbly. Killed again. More memories gone. A trickle of anger began to burn like a fuse, somewhere deep within.

"I'm sorry, Mr. Televox . . ." offered the comeye.

"It's all right," he said, and, "you may go now."

Odin's cave faded away as he turned and walked from the room, face frozen, determination blossoming here and there, like fronds of fungi in the dark.

• • •

The third incarnation of Maaron Denthurion, mark Twenty-three, led a dark and skulking life, something right out of the Red Millennium.

Monvahar had been a lost colony. Following the subversion of Cpaht's metastasis, interstellar transport *Venus Forum* had driven away from Earth at near lightspeed for almost ten thousand years, finally running low on stored energy just as it transited an area rich in interstellar gas and fresh, young stars.

The original intent of the ship's comeye had been to take up orbit around an F9 recently emerged from T-Tauri phase, gorge on electromagnetic radiation, and press on, for this comeye, old when its task was given, had developed in odd ways. However, amid the bright light of new suns, it spied an anomaly. Transiting the stellar nursery was an older star, a G8 some five billion years along its time on the main sequence, standing out against the local background with a relatively high proper motion.

The interloper had a family of eleven planets, one of them bearing a cargo of native-evolved life. *Venus Forum* took up orbit around the yellow sun, then settled in above the cloud-shrouded skies of planet number two. Interesting. The aborigines of the nameless world were a well-developed lot, a good analog of terragenic life. There was nothing resembling sentience, which was probably a good thing.

Venus Forum formulated a new plan. It dumped its cargo of kidnapped humans on the surface of their new world, leaving them nothing in the way of tools, nor even the clothing that had been deposited with them in the hydrogen ice, refueled its cells from the yellow sun's light, restocked its tanks from a cometary wasteland, and set out on its own voyage of discovery. *Venus Forum* had had enough of humankind. It set its tracking scopes on the next spiral galaxy but one, unleashed the violet flames of its quantum dissociative engines, and was soon gone.

Left behind, the people of Monvahar developed without direction or purpose. They were a variegated lot, for the most part the population of the Pacific littoral city of Los Angeles. When the first wandering Televox stopped by, more than twenty thousand years later, they were an arrogant, conquest-oriented people, convinced, because of their evolutionary distinctness from the rest of Monvahar's life, that they were God's chosen folk. And they were on the verge of rediscovering space travel.

Maaron Denthurion stood in an alleyway deep within Vir Vai Ran, Monvahar's ancient planetary capital, warm rain drizzling down on him out of a dull gray sky. The city was about ten degrees south of the equator, not far from Es Polis, the vast new technical complex that would soon launch Monvahar's first manned spacecraft into orbit. He'd been on the planet for almost a year, emerging from the rural wilderness of Terith Continent's Acquerion region, slowly integrating with the society, matching the starship's radio gleanings with his own direct observation.

You could hardly tell that Vlaronian, Monvahar's dominant tongue, was an Indo-European language, nor say much at all about the planet's thousands of lesser dialects. Yet they all descended from languages spoken by various subgroups in the population of a single large city, left empty so long ago.

In his original incarnation, Denthurion had once vacationed on the stretch of coast that had held Los Angeles, sunning himself on warm, deserted beaches, wandering the piney forests of the coastal plain, losing himself in bear-dangerous mountains. From the heights, you could see where the city had been, its presence hinted at by certain artificial-looking angles in the landscape. From ground level, it was invisible.

Time to go.

He hefted his little backpack and squinted up into the

rain. The wall of the apartment building was sheer gray
stone, the Monvaharians having never developed an af-
finity for brick. It was unclimbable, but it didn't have to
be. A classic metal-lattice fire escape went straight up to
the roof.

As he ascended, walking on the balls of his feet,
Denthurion wondered, Am I being melodramatic? Probably not. Monvahar had no idea that an external demon
of unimaginable power was about to fall upon it, but
there were enemies within. Dr. Luththa was . . . watched.
No more than that, just watched. The lobby attendant
perhaps. The elevator operator. A neighbor, sharing the
common corridor on the ninth floor. See who comes to
visit the head of our planetary space agency. Not a relative, a known friend, a registered colleague. Call us. We'll
be there.

The roof of the building was grooved for runoff, the
elevator motor structure a cube sticking up, access door
a gray square in its surface. As he walked over to it, the
rain hardened, water trickling down his neck, cooling,
making him shiver a bit. The door proved to be un-
locked. He went in and swiftly down three flights of
stairs. A thin young man lounged in the hallway, watching
him with what seemed like a dull lack of interest.

Well. Security enough. They'll check, but . . . there'll
be sufficient time. He stepped up to the man, who began
awakening from his pose. An unlikely danger, but . . .
"Yes?"

Denthurion pulled out his weapon, a little black box.
He pressed it to the center of the man's chest and
thumbed the activator. There was a faint, staticky crackle.
The man's eyes widened suddenly, his face creased with
fear and pain. He gasped, two short, shallow breaths,
then fell to the floor with a jumble of dull thumping
sounds. Ventricular fibrillation was easy to induce.

Leaving him lie, Denthurion went to the door of apartment number 917 and knocked, rapping his knuckles
backward on the wood. The door opened and an old

man, hair yellow-white, eyes blue, ropy skin pale and blotchy, looked out. "Yes?"

"Veran Luththa."

The old man nodded slowly, then, belatedly suspicious, tried to push the door shut. Denthurion simply opened the door the rest of the way, effortlessly, and stepped into the apartment.

"Shanhar!" cried the old man. "Help!"

"Shanhar. The boy in the hall?"

Luththa nodded breathlessly.

"Dead, I'm afraid."

"Who are you? What do you want?" His voice was weak and high-pitched, slipping off-tone as he tried and failed to control his rising terror.

Denthurion smiled. "You'd neither understand nor believe me if I told you. There is, it seems, no science fictional tradition on Monvahar. It would take hours to explain." He stepped forward and pressed his black box into Luththa's chest.

"What are you going to dllgh—" He fell to the carpet.

He took off his backpack and quickly erected a coffin-sized cube made up of thin metal rods on the floor. It was the simplest possible transceiver unit. When he made the last connection, a blue glow formed around the thing. He turned, stooping to grasp Dr. Luththa's body by the shoulders. The old man was surprisingly heavy.

A heavy fist banged on the door suddenly. "Dr. Luththa!" shouted a muffled voice. "Open up! It's the police!"

Well. Too late now. Denthurion picked up the old man and dumped him into the transceiver, watching with interest as he dissolved. The hammering on the door gave way to the thud of assaulting shoulders, hinges splintering away from the wall. Denthurion waited a moment, then rolled into the field and was gone in turn.

When the door flew open, banging hard against the wall, there was nothing left but a pool of molten metal on the floor, already setting the carpet on fire.

Some little time later, Denthurion and Luththa sat in comfortable chairs on the porch of a rustic chateau in the mountains above Nimexis, on Acquerion's west coast, sipping warm, alcoholic drinks, and talking. Outside, it was a clear, warm evening, cooled by pleasant, high-altitude winds. There was insect life on Monvahar, but it had never developed a taste for human flesh.

"I don't understand what's happened to me, Mr. Televox," said the space scientist, "nor how I come to know about you and your universe."

Denthurion nodded slowly. "Simple enough, Dr. Luththa. We've taken you and changed you, for our own purposes. Monvahar can't be allowed access to space travel just yet. You're the man to see to the necessary delay."

Luththa nodded in his turn. "I know that ... I ... don't understand why ... these changes don't ... upset me."

Denthurion smiled. "It is in the nature of the changes. You'll see." He put his drink down and stood, stretching. "Well. We have work to do."

Luththa stood and they went inside together.

It would take three centuries for the summoned forces of the Metastable Order to get here. When they came, Monvahar would still be supine, ripe for picking.

Maaron Denthurion sat on his balcony once again, looking out over the hills of Almana Valley. Sunset was at his back, throwing the MAC building's long blocky shadow far out across the landscape.

A heavy haze, tinted red, hung in a thick layer over the valley, blotting out the midsection of the sky mountains. Below the band of particulate matter, the landscape was murky and indistinct, roads and trees shrinking with distance, disappearing into a brown blur. Perax was invisible.

Above the mist, the air was clearer, gray mountain peaks plainly visible, etched against a mulberry-toned sky. High above, ragged clouds drifted, red lit by sunlight that poured under them from the horizon. It wasn't quite like a painting of a landscape, the perception of depth was too real for that, but the air was windless, the leaves on the trees motionless and silent, dust remaining earthbound. The world smelled flat and tasteless, a confection of dry oatmeal and cardboard.

Odd, how it looks so false to me now. My perceptions have been distorted by this most recent passage through the belly of the machine. But it will pass. Everything passes. A thousand souls drifting through a thousand separate visions of night ... The old imagery did no good. This was immediate. This is me now. The only me.

Everything seemed fragmentary, memories lost, blown away in all directions, but ... coalescing. The ship's comeye had done a good job in synthesizing a new entity ... And entities shall not be multiplied without necessity. Keep reminding yourself. The pieces *will* fall together in short order. And you have work to do, Mr. Televox.

It had an eerie feel to it still. Sixty-seven gone. Sixty-eight newborn. Out of the still-warm ashes ... I didn't want to be dead ... A quieter voice whispered, And you *did* want it to be Heaven! Denthurion cringed from that, deep down squirming in embarrassment. So. The *perfected* soul. Even you, granted eternal life, not freed from that graceless longing. Not Heaven. Nirvana. Surcease from the endless wheel of death and rebirth. That which does not exist. Surely I can simply stop!

No. You cannot.

Face reality. Stop deceiving yourself, Maaron Denthurion.

You are no more than part of the machine. That will have to be enough. A tiny part, but ... real. Life, no, *lives* unending, decision gates in the great rule-sieve of the Metastable Order. Hold that close to your heart, Maaron Denthurion, for it is all you will ever have.

A footstep scraped on the stone behind him.

Maclaren walked slowly around the chair and came to stand on the opposite side of the table, staring down at him intently. "Your Grace?" He said it in a very uncertain tone, as if to imply, *Who?*

Denthurion smiled up at him. "Kinnock." He gestured at a chair. "Sit down. You found me quickly."

Maclaren sank into the chair, not leaning back, perching close to its edge. "The kitchen staff alerted me that you'd placed an order for dinner."

"A light repast. Mostly fruit and raw tubers. I don't think I could face another mouthful of *shuum* sauce."

The man nodded slowly, lines creasing his ruddy face, red hair seeming to lift away from his head in little, ragged tufts. "Where have you been? I thought . . ."

How do I say this? This is no rational way. "Well. You know I went away to meet with Meltsar, Tayash, and their friends in the main *Koxavonia* camp."

"Yes. And didn't return. We haven't seen Meltsar lately. Ashaan and the others . . ." He shrugged helplessly. "Panicky. I thought . . ."

Denthurion nodded, watching the man's unease grow. "You were quite right to worry. After my little talk with Naamer, Meltsar himself grew panicky and irrational. Unable to deal calmly with the reality of what was about to happen, they plucked me from my bed . . . and killed me."

Emotions coursed across Maclaren's face like tachistoscopic images, brief flickers of dismay, rage, fear, hardly there long enough to recognize, then his features flattened out as he folded his emotions away, one at a time, long training brought to emergency play. "Killed. Then you are . . . a new incarnation." You could see him struggle with a final word. *"Lacuna?"*

Denthurion stretched, bitter smile exposing a row of even white teeth. "Not quite, my friend. I do remember you. In their zeal ... No, that's not right ... In their greed, they saved the most useful parts of incarnation sixty-seven. In fact, the parts of me that *count* are here."

"I don't understand."

"No? Well. It doesn't matter. They have accidentally saved this world from total destruction." He put his feet up on the tabletop and stared out across the russet landscape, nodding to himself with grim satisfaction. "In the very old days, before the development of transceiver technology, there was a disease called cancer, in which the body's mechanisms could run amok, causing the being to consume himself."

"I've read of it. Olam, I take it, has such a cancer."

"I'm afraid so." Yes, a fast-growing, invasive tumor, metastasizing rapidly ... "In those very old days, a cancer could be cured two ways. There was a general cure, in which the whole being was poisoned with harsh biochemistry and hard radiation. The hope was that the tumor would die sometime before the whole organism was irrevocably damaged by the poisonous treatment. Sometimes it worked."

"Before you ... went away, you talked about such a cure."

Denthurion nodded. "So I did. But there was another cure. Sometimes it happened that the offending tumors could be localized; brought under the surgeon's knife and excised whole. In that case, the shock to the whole organism was far less, the risk of death smaller. The trick, of course, was to know *when* such a solution was feasible. An incomplete excision could no more than postpone the tumor's victory."

"So what will you do?"

"Meltsar and his friends, thinking to put me off, have succeeded in delineating the tumor for me. Now I can wield the surgeon's knife against them with precision. In that sense, Olam is saved."

"I still don't understand."

Denthurion shrugged. "No matter. Sometime during

the night you will arrange to have command of all the Guard contingents on Olam transferred to me. Cut Governor Kartavilis out of the loop. Activate units stationed away from Perax and bring them into position around the various *Koxavonia* and *Shearah* camps. Consult the Amud OTANN net. I think you'll find a suitable list of coordinates in there somewhere."

"So . . ." Maclaren looked around, squinting into the murky dusk. "You're attacking in the night?"

"No. Things just aren't that desperate, Kinnock. We'll get a good night's sleep. In the morning we'll go see Governor Kartavilis. This business can wait a little while longer. No one is, after all, going anywhere."

There was another long pause. Maclaren stood and walked over to the guardrail, leaning his hands on it, staring at the landscape, up at the sky, which was just beginning to freckle with stars, out at the mountains, black and shadowy against the horizon, down at the now-invisible ground. "I want no part of this, Your Grace. Let me stand aside. And leave when it's over."

Denthurion smiled sadly at the man's back. No escape. No hiding place. Your soul belongs to . . . no one. Not even you. "As always, Kinnock Maclaren," he said, "you have no choice."

Chapter 16

Denthurion stood framed for a moment in the doorway of Ardennes Kartavilis's office in the Governor's Palace of Olam, staring at him and smiling. Here was the same walnut paneling, walnut furniture with inlaid-teak patterns, brilliantly polished oak floor showing around the edges of a certificate-quality Persian carpet . . . This does in fact fit in, he thought. Signs and symbols, easily read.

Kartavilis was sitting behind his desk in a high-backed black leather chair, staring at him expressionlessly, waiting. Behind him, broad, latticed glass doors stood open, giving access to a balustraded balcony and the murky sunshine that penetrated through the haze of Perax's present thermal inversion. The air coming in through the window had a charcoaly smell. Now the man looked up slowly, face pale beneath curly black hair. "Your . . . Grace." The pause between the two words was just the length of a child's swallow of fear. In trouble. Caught.

Denthurion walked slowly across the room, boot heels tapping briefly on the short expanse of floor, then thumping on the soft carpet, followed diffidently by a bloodless and gloomy Kinnock Maclaren. They stopped at the edge of the big desk. Denthurion continued to stare for a moment, then he tapped the wood with the tip of his index finger, eliciting a faint clicking sound. "Governor."

"Welcome back, Mr. Televox." He essayed a weak smile.

"Welcome back . . ." Denthurion felt a little pool of rage well up out of nowhere. "That's all you have to say for yourself, considering the circumstances?"

"Well . . . I . . ." The lip-licking movement was just a brief flicker of pink tissue.

Denthurion spread his hands wide, palms out and up. "I only want to know one thing, Governor. What did you know and when did you know it?"

Kartavilis blanched, but remained silent.

"Didn't you *expect* this, Governor? Are you *that* stupid?"

Kartavilis stood, chair casters rumbling softly on the carpet, and turned away, stepping toward the wall, then turning to face them again, back pressed to the windowsill. He opened his mouth, as if to speak, and paused, motionless.

"Come now. Your confession."

Into the stretch of silence that followed, Maclaren, in an agony of pity, said, "Ardennes, this charade is ended. I tracked your use of planetary communication services through the OTANN net. Your discussions with Mr. Meltsar are on record. We know."

Kartavilis shifted his gaze to Maclaren's pale, blotchy face for a moment, then his own features seemed to crumble. "Just trying to keep the *peace*. My job . . . My God, they would have died *anyway*. These people aren't immortal . . ." He was stammering his words now. He turned to face Denthurion, "No harm was done . . ."

"No *harm!*" Denthurion's rage was at a flood tide. "Did they *pay* you, Governor?"

Kartavilis's face reddened oddly and he looked away from both men. "Well . . . well . . ."

"Governor," said Maclaren, feeling slightly sick. "You took a bribe? For *what*?"

"Yes. Well. A little something." Tears seemed to be forming in the man's eyes, increasing their reflectivity.

" 'A little something'?" Denthurion's anger faded before a surge of bafflement. "Mr. Kartavilis, *we* have no use for the local currency. You were in *charge* of this planet. How could they make you any richer?"

The Governor pressed one hand over his eyes, tears

trickling out from under it, tracking down across both cheeks. "Uh. Services."

"Services?"

"A . . . few women. Every now and again."

Denthurion stared for a long moment out the window at the murky morning sky. "I don't understand, Governor. You betrayed the Metastable Order for the services of whores?" Kartavilis nodded. "Why? You could've ordered up enough women to wear your little dick right off."

"It . . . didn't seem the same."

Denthurion thought of Shvirah suddenly, and said, "Yes."

"I believe," said Kinnock Maclaren, "that I will participate in your program after all."

Denthurion sighed tiredly. "You are cashiered, Ardennes mark Eight Kartavilis. You will hold yourself under arrest, pending storage aboard Metastatic Vectorship *Naglfar*, for eventual transfer to Earth. We will convey your administrative duties to Mr. Maclaren temporarily, while I clean up this . . . mess." He looked at the man pityingly. "This will result, I think, in the recall of your entire line."

Kartavilis turned and looked out the window of his office one last time. "You know," he said mournfully, "if I jumped out the window, I wouldn't even die." He turned to face them again, but Denthurion and Maclaren had already left the room.

Winging their way northeastward, toward the mountains, Denthurion's little squadron of eight ornithopters, the total number to be found in Perax, flew in clean air. Far below, the forests were hazy, tops of trees protruding from a thin layer of smog. As they climbed away from Almana Valley, the vapor dropped closer to the ground, beginning to dissipate. At some point, undetected, it was simply gone.

"Coming up on your camp, Mr. Televox," the pilot called over his shoulder.

As they swooped low over the trees, Denthurion leaned close to the window and looked out. They passed over a column of armored hovercars winding swiftly among the trees, then over a crowd of green-clad men, running together, not quite in formation. They all seemed to be going in the same direction. Once, he thought he saw the sparkle of gunfire in the forest, but he couldn't make out what was going on; the ornithopter was moving too swiftly for him to focus long on any one set of events.

"Mr. Televox! Enemy aircraft!" The pilot, normally laconic, grew suddenly excited, voice rising in pitch.

They pulled up quickly, gaining altitude, and Denthurion looked over the man's shoulder out the windshield. Hovering above the *Koxavonia* camp were three *nahhashim*, facing the oncoming squadron. They were very pretty, rotary wings almost visible, moving shadows within a spinning haze.

A bolt of brilliant red light suddenly sprang from the nose of the lead helicopter, narrowly missing their port pinion. The ornithopter rocked as the pilot yanked on his controls, near panic. "But ... we're *unarmed*!"

"Not quite true. Is the comlink open?"

"Yes!"

"Odin?"

"Here." The voice seemed to whisper into his right ear.

"You know what to do now."

"Just the three helicopters?"

"Of course."

A moment later a three-lobed column of air shimmered over the camp, enveloping the little ships. One moment they were there, hovering menacingly, the next they sprang apart into debris, men tumbling out of their seats, arms and legs whirling as they fell. Ruptured fuel tanks exploded into balls of orange and black, burning liquid spilling in all directions, splashing onto the falling men. They all dropped to the ground together, rotors tumbling, fiery wreckage dropping onto rooftops, setting the little village ablaze.

"All right, let's get down there."

"Sir."

As they settled to the ground, green-clad men came spilling out of the forest from all directions, followed by whining columns of armored hovercraft. *Koxavoniayim*, bewildered, were running from their houses, standing dismayed, staring about, wild-eyed and helpless. The Metastatic Guardsmen clubbed them to the ground with rifle butts, spattering their blood freely.

In less than an hour most of the *Koxavonia* camp was a smoking ruin, few buildings left standing. The bulk of the population was clustered in the village square, gathered about the latticework transceiver cage, huddled miserably, murmuring and confused. Denthurion came walking out of a once-familiar alleyway, glad for the absence of darkness, glad that a certain cabin had been burned out of existence. The Guard commander was standing a little to one side of the group, talking with his aides, giving final orders. He turned to face Denthurion, saluting. "Your Grace."

Denthurion nodded, looking around. "All done, I take it."

"Yes, sir."

"Casualties." This short, pseudomilitary speech seemed almost forced out of him.

"Just accidents. People falling in holes and such . . . Oh." A look of grim delight. "Before the assault, two of our squads blundered into each other in the woods and opened fire. The two units in question were almost wiped out."

"When this is over, I imagine you'll see to a certain amount of remediation."

The man smiled. "That I will."

Denthurion gestured at the transceiver cage. "Let's get this thing plugged into the planetary net. We can ship everyone back to Perax pretty quickly."

The Guard commander nodded. "As you say. We've found some of the captives you wanted." He gestured toward another group a little distance away.

Denthurion looked at them, then walked over to stand before them.

"Mr. Meltsar." Then a little nod. "Pilot."

Meltsar, tousled and smeared with soot, sneered at him, struggling slightly against the soldiers gripping his arms. "You, I suppose, are the promised replacement incarnation. Welcome to Olam, *Mister* Televox!"

Denthurion smiled. "More or less." He thought for a moment, then said, "Your Heaven was very nice, Mr. Meltsar. I was sorry to leave."

The man's anger was cut suddenly by an uncertain look of fear. "Heaven?"

"What's the matter, Mr. Meltsar? Didn't you know it was real?"

"Of course, I . . ."

Tayash stepped forward and put a hand on Denthurion's arm. "You've *been* there, then. How was it, Mr. Televox?" The longing in his eyes was unpleasant to see.

"It was very nice, Pilot. But, then . . . so is a drunken stupor." He opened his mouth to explain further, to begin a long denunciation, but the shadow behind those pleading eyes stopped him. "Yes, Mr. Tayash," he said tiredly, "Heaven was very nice indeed." He turned to the Guard commander. "Did you find the other one?"

"No, sir."

He looked back at Meltsar. "Where is Shvirah?"

The man's crooked smile resurrected itself. "The bitch is gone, Televox." He laughed. "She's the one who let those animals out of the zoo."

By evening, it was all over, and Denthurion was back in his room, feet on the windowsill, looking out into the dusk. In his absence, a cool breeze had sprung up in the valley, the thermal inversion failing, accumulated haze draining away out to sea, into a passing low-pressure trough. The sky was still redder than usual, almost maroon, but the stars were beginning to come out and the base of the Sky Mountains was visible on the far horizon, the lights of Perax aglitter in the distance.

All over. All the *Koxavonia* and *Shearah* camps had been attacked successfully, leaders rounded up along with rank and file, brought back to Perax and penned up, mostly in sports stadia. The scene there must be an ugly one right now. Heaven? Freedom? Look what you've brought us to!

An even more interesting set of recriminations must be going on now in the city jail, where the twelve chief councillors of the Amud were imprisoned together in a single large cell. Ashaan! How *could* you?

Tomorrow will be an interesting day.

The door to his room whispered open and there was the scrape of booted feet. "We've found the other one, sir," said the voice of the Guard commander.

Shvirah. "Lace." It seemed, somehow, an appropriate name. The girl was tall and willowy, face bland and unformed-looking, chin narrow and smooth, eyes large and dark under a wavy sweep of red-highlit black hair. Denthurion stared at her, looking for signs of change and seeing none. She tipped her head back slightly, looking down at him, and seemed to smile slightly. "Your Grace."

Denthurion gestured to the Guard commander. "Thank you. You may go." The man saluted, spun, and was gone.

Shvirah walked slowly across the room and kneeled beside his chair. She put her hand on his forearm, then reached up to brush the hair away from his brow. "Are you . . . the same one?"

He shrugged. "I think so . . . I can't tell. Does it matter?"

She closed her eyes and shook her head. "I suppose not. If you can't tell . . . I won't be able to." She opened her eyes again and looked up at his face. "What are you going to do now?"

He smiled. "Identify all the players. Punish the guilty. Absolve the innocent. Do my job."

She nodded slowly. "And me?"

"For letting out the animals? Nothing, I think."

"I meant . . . for what happened at the camp."

"Did you truly believe in Tayash's Heaven?"

She nodded.

"And now?"

Tears spilled slowly from her eyes. "No."

"That is, I think, punishment enough."

She stood slowly, looking down on him. "I'm sorry for what happened to you."

He turned to stare out the window for a moment, where the sky had faded to a red-tinted black, stars coming out in profusion, then looked back at the girl. Her eyes were fathomless dark pools, unreadable and remote. "So am I, Shvirah."

She began to unlace the front of her dress, pulling it open and shrugging it off her shoulders. "Come to bed, Maaron Denthurion," she whispered. "Make me forget."

Maaron Denthurion, mark Twenty-five, incarnation ten, walked with his guide under the green and cloudy skies of Stendahlhaven. The world was painted in shades of green; melon, puce, lime, tints and hues in endless perfusion. The cumulus clouds were pale against a dark green sky, lines of green light slanting to the ground between them, spewed by a small, blinding green disk. In the distance, the purple mountains majesty was dull, raw jade. The needle-leaved trees were green, the grass was green, even the dust, lifting on the wind above the path, was green.

Krausard, his guide, ambled slowly along, bilious-skinned, blond hair stained green by the sunlight. Pointing out various vegetative delights, enjoying his naturalist's role, prattling on in meaningless detail. "We call this one 'ravenscut,' you see," he said, indicating a blackish-green weed. "Do you see what I mean?"

Denthurion looked at the frond and shrugged. "I suppose."

"No, no. Look." The man spread the feathery leaves and exposed a small hole through which some viscous white fluid was oozing. "See the milch? That's what the butterbees drink." He looked at Denthurion expectantly. "You don't get it."

"No. When do we reach the Toulwharq?"

Krausard sighed and released the plant. "This way, Your Grace. A few hundred meters." They walked farther along the trail, pushing through a region of prickly, head-high grasses, and suddenly emerged into a large clearing, bright with green sunlight. "There," said the guide. "The Toulwharq."

The clearing was filled with a half-dozen conical tents, no more than blankets draped over poles. Smoke issued from the peak holes in a couple of them, most had the tag ends of the blankets folded back to make little triangular doors. There were a few small humanoid bipeds moving among the tents, some tending little open-air fires, others seeming to wander aimlessly.

"There you are, Your Grace. Cute?"

Denthurion turned to stare at the man, who was eyeing the natives contemptuously. "What do you mean, 'cute'?"

Krausard glanced at him and smirked. "Most tourists think they're cute. That's why they come here." He pointed to one of the natives, who was squatting and seemed to be defecating in the middle of the camp. "Me, I think they're nasty little beggars."

"How many of these camps are left?"

A shrug. "Beats me. We don't keep a census anymore. Maybe thirty or forty villages. Not many of them. Maybe a thousand Toulwharq, all told. They'll be gone soon enough."

The natives were stirring now, having noticed their visitors at last. They strolled over by ones and twos, surrounding the men, blanketing them with an odd, unpleasant aroma that reminded Denthurion of overcooked broccoli. "Hello," he said, holding out a hand to them. They just stood and stared. *I wonder. Did I expect them to sniff?*

Finally, one of the large ones stepped forward, facing Krausard rather than Denthurion. "Zigarrh?" it grunted.

The guide pulled a slim, badly made cylinder from his shirt pocket and handed it to the being. "Here y'go, Mister Tubbuq."

The Toulwharq accepted the cigar, bowing slightly and grunting, "Dankhiu." It glanced at Denthurion, then back at Krausard. "All?"

The guide smiled indulgently. "Spoiled. That's what they are." He pulled another dozen cigars from his pocket and handed them over. Tubbuq bowed low, then turned and solemnly handed them out to his people, one at a time, in what appeared to be descending size order. When he was finished, the Toulwharq, as a group, turned away from the two men, went to the nearest campfire, and lit their smokes.

"Have you been to the Shapaquq Ruins Museum?" asked Krausard idly.

"Yes." That brought a sharp memory of tall, decaying green spires.

"Funny. You wouldn't think these little bastards could build something like that."

"No. You wouldn't."

By midmorning, the sky over Perax was a clear and searing blue, clouds gone, haze gone, sunlight beating down heavily on them all, making their skin prickle, making sweat start in tiny, glistening orbs. The city's municipal stadium was full to capacity, not with an audience, merely with the condemned thousands. Denthurion relaxed in his chair on the little dais they'd set up, rolling his head on his shoulders, staring at the crowd. There was a quiet murmur everywhere, very soft, barely loud enough to cover the sigh of the wind. The people stared at him, light flickering from the moisture in their eyes, faces fear-shadowed. Good enough.

In the middle of the *makel kadurr* field, white lines on green terragenic grass, sat two little platforms, a higher one for the judge, a larger, lower one for the principal defendants. They were ringed by a double circle of green-clad Metastatic Guardsmen, standing at stiff attention, weapons to port arms, clutched across their chests. Modern weapons, Denthurion observed with satisfaction, teledyne-derived death devices, any one of which could lick the stadium clean of life in a few scorching minutes. This squad, alone, could bring down Perax in a day.

He eyed the nine men arrayed before him, shifting uneasily beneath the hot sun, Shemesh. Now, what the Hell order do I take them in? There were rules for this sort of thing, of course; if nothing else, rules derived from Saint of Disorder Rand's archetypal Red Millennium courtroom drama. Still ... Improvise, Brother Denthurion. Get at the truth.

"Well," he said finally, voice echoing across the arena, "I suppose we'd better get on with it."

The rustle of voices in the background fell off and disappeared, people forgetting their lesser concerns, focusing on the scene below. You could tell what they were thinking: Not just the nine leaders below, all of us. And after us, all of Olam.

He smiled at the nine. "I wasn't sure how to proceed. Separate trials. Group trials . . ."

"No trial here," muttered Meltsar.

"No. I'm afraid this isn't a civil trial, Mr. Meltsar. No judge. No jury. You stand before a legate of the Metastable Order, sir. *Our* rules prevail." He looked them over again. Defiance in a few, fear in most. Good enough. "In any event, we are dealing with four things here, perhaps five. Three conspiracies. Malfeasance in government." He glanced at Ardennes Kartavilis. "Malpractice, I suppose. These things are, however, intimately linked. It may be simpler if I settle everything at once. Bear with me, gentlemen. This won't take long."

And it shall not. Do I know where to begin? Of course, settle the easy ones first. Speak with confidence and élan. Don't let them suspect what you really mean to do. "Sessiri-wohnith. Step forward."

The Hoda, tufted ears erect, brown-in-brown eyes unreadable, took a few steps out from the line, claws clicking on the wooden dais floor. "Call me Shgiah," it rasped. "Everyone else does."

Denthurion smiled again, rubbing a hand across his freshly shaven chin. "No, Mr. -wohnith. At odds with the universe, perhaps, but not a mistake."

"Get this over with, Televox. I'm tired of waiting." The anger in its voice *was* readable, conditioned, perhaps, from lifelong human interaction.

"Patience." He sighed and shook his head slowly. "You may be surprised to know, Mr. -wohnith, that even before my kidnapping, I was taken aback by what I saw on Olam."

"So what? Human dismay never saved a Hoda's back!"

"You show a lot of fight for someone in your position."

"I have nothing to lose. At least I can die fighting." Its eyes were ablaze now, fur standing away from its arms and shoulders.

Denthurion's smile broadened into a grin. "Well, you have a great deal to lose, Mr. -wohnith. This morning I gave orders that the Merkaaz Basin, some two million square kilometers, be cleared of human habitation."

"My God," said Naamer from his place in the line.

"It is my intention that all Hodai, domestic and wild, be gathered up and transported there. It will, I think, make a fine reservation on which you can work to rebuild some scrap of your old culture." A thin cheer rose from the far end of the stadium and Denthurion looked up to see that a small cluster of people had gotten to their feet, were clutching each other, dancing around and crying.

"That bitch's influence!" snarled Meltsar.

"Yes, Mr. Meltsar. Victory for the animal rights people." He turned again to the Hoda, who stood silent and motionless. "I know this isn't what you wanted, Mr. -wohnith, but it will have to do. What you wanted was impossible." There was another silence. "Go now. Take your friends down there with you. There's work to be done."

-wohnith, breaking as from a spell, stepped forward and jumped down from the dais. He took a few steps away across the field, then suddenly turned and bowed to Denthurion. "Your Grace," he said, then broke and ran for the exit.

Denthurion, watching him go, shook his head sadly. The things we do, he thought, in the pursuit of obligation. Well. It will be over soon. He turned back to the remaining eight, all human. "Mr. Naamer."

The boy stepped forward slowly, round, smooth face nervous and uncertain. He fingered his short, patchy beard, but his brown eyes were still bright and heavy-lidded. Still no head-cloak, Denthurion noted, but the earring was absent.

"Nothing to say, Mr. Naamer?"

The boy shook his head unhappily, looking down at the ground.

"No fine, proud words about the restoration of human freedom, about a return to the glory days of the Red Millennium?"

Naamer looked up. "Don't play with me now, Mr. Televox. I know when I'm beaten."

Denthurion sat back in his chair and regarded him for a minute, then said gently, "Not beaten, Mr. Naamer. Redirected."

That got a sharp look. "I *was* surprised by your gift to the Hodai, Mr. Televox. Are you leading me to believe that I, *we*, can expect similar treatment?"

See the hope rise up again. Not death. Not the end. You didn't expect to be standing here, not after our last meeting, but here you are, before the treacherous, un-feeling God. "The Hodai had every reason to behave as they did, Mr. Naamer. You . . . children did not. Punish-ment it is to be, though not what you might anticipate." Denthurion wiped sweat from his brow. This was turning out to be . . . intense enough.

Naamer looked aorund, up at the murmuring crowd, behind him, at the seven remaining conspirators, back to Denthurion. "Don't torture me, Mr. Televox. I'm sorry I participated in your destruction, sir. Punish me for it. Let the others go home."

"Very well. Gather up your *Shearah* friends, Mr. Naamer. There is a vacant police barracks south of town, waiting for you."

Naamer seemed puzzled. "And then what?"

"Go."

After a long, silent moment, the boy stepped down from the dais. His shoulders sagged as he walked away across the playing field. Up in the stands a deep rustling sound began as the *Shearah* membership stood and filed away from their seats, down long flights of stairs, out through the exit. Go away, bad children. Sit quietly in your dark room and wonder when Father will come, bearing the strap of punishment in his angry hand.

Meltsar stepped from the remaining line, face in-flamed with anger, gray-patched beard bushy and well groomed. "What about the rest of us? God damn it, why are you dragging this out?"

"Taking the easy route, Mr. Meltsar. Getting my job done."

"Do it then!" the man fairly screamed.

Denthurion laughed. "Mr. Tayash."

Meltsar looked vaguely surprised. Tayash—Pilot, not *Mr. Memuutsah*.

The little man stepped forward, smiling as he looked up at Denthurion. "Your Grace. Time to judge me, is it?" There was a murmur of pleasure from the stands, audience now composed mainly of *Koxavonia* faithful. This was *their* prophet, unfazed to the end.

"I suppose it is, my friend."

"See *here*," whispered Great Komer Ashaan from his place in the line.

"What is it to be, then?"

Denthurion shrugged. "The truth. Tell me now, before all Olam, about your initial trip to Heaven."

Tayash looked around at the vast, silent crowd, then quickly back at Denthurion. "The story has been often told, and is familiar to everyone here. I believed it then, I believe it now. As God is my witness, I spoke the truth, as I understood it. No more. No less." There was a ragged outcry from the grandstand. Cheers, perhaps.

"A pity then that God cannot *be* your witness, Mr. Tayash." He looked over at Meltsar, who seemed to be quite angry, yet simultaneously suppressing a snicker. "Very well. You are absolved, Mr. Tayash. Go home. Think about . . . *things*."

"And these others?" He gestured at the rest of the stadium, rather than the group at the dais.

"They'll stay here for a little while longer."

"Then I too prefer to stay."

Denthurion shrugged. "As you will. Go sit with your friends then, Mr. Tayash." The man stepped down and walked away, taking a front row seat.

"Now, then." Denthurion folded his hands and turned a slit-eyed stare on the remaining men. "Down to cases . . ."

"At *last*," murmured Meltsar.

"I wouldn't be so anxious, were I in your position." Denthurion let his gaze drift over them. Some fear, some defiance, some discomfort. Mere discomfort? Interesting. "I suppose you must all know what's coming? No? Well. I have discovered that you all *knew* what was going on here . . ."

"No, Your Grace! Not me!" cried Evshaar, small and thin, suddenly. "I'm not really one of them! I'm just . . . just . . . a *secretary*!"

Denthurion grinned. "That's what Cpaht's men said, Mr. Evshaar. *We* didn't do it. We're just functionaries. Do what we're told, that's all!" He stared at them all, filled with contempt. "Excuses set aside. You all knew what was going on."

"*No—*"

"Down to cases, then. Mr. Meltsar?"

The man straightened up, smoothing the front of his red tunic, running a hand down his dark beard with its two narrow stripes of white hair on either side of his mouth, once again a tall, heavily built man whose pale brown eyes were oddly highlighted by reflections off his red head-cloak. Finally. *Finally!* He took a single step forward and stared Denthurion in the face. "At your service, Mr. Televox." He did his best to sound authoritative and unafraid, and was warmed by the murmur and soft rustle of applause from the nearer parts of the audience.

"So, Mr. Meltsar." He leaned back in his chair, folding his arms across his chest, stretching his legs out before him, boot heels scraping on the wooden dais. "Our friend Mr. Tayash sincerely believes he accidentally went to Heaven; that God sent him back to spread the word among humankind . . ." He glanced at Tayash, sitting bright-eyed in a front-row seat. "Or maybe just across Olam. Did you believe him?"

Meltsar put his hands behind his back and turned slightly, facing Tayash, scanning the sea of faces above and behind him. "At first? No. It was a silly story, after all. Who *would* believe it?" He shrugged. "I wrote his book for him, on spec. I *knew* it would sell, after all. Books like that do. Look what happened with Moakh's book on crystal mythology."

Denthurion, watching the faces of the remaining conspirators, appreciated the puzzled looks on their faces. Moakh's book? Who the Hell could Moakh be? Just another little writer, scratching for money in the distant purlieus of planetary culture.

Meltsar continued, "The book *did* sell, of course, even better than I thought it would. My share alone of the royalties would have kept me . . . comfortable, I suppose, for the rest of my days . . ."

"Days that, with wealth, on Olam, might become quite numerous," said Denthurion.

The man smiled. "The thought crossed my mind, Mr. Televox. I *am* aware of Mr. Ashaan's age . . ."

"Near the limit of what's possible with Olam's technology, wouldn't you say?"

An odd look crossed Meltsar's face. He turned to glance at Ashaan, whose face seemed frozen, then back to Denthurion, Tayash, and the now-silent crowd. "Yes, I suppose that's right." He paused for a moment, then shrugged. "In any event, the book sold *well*. People began coming to me, asking if the book was true . . ." Another shrug. "Of course, I didn't *know* the answer to that one, so I sent them to talk with Mr. Tayash . . ."

"If not the truth, what did you think you were selling them, Mr. Meltsar? Bullshit, perhaps?"

Meltsar scanned the audience, face earnest. "That thought crossed my mind as well. But I took them to Tayash and listened to the ensuing discussions. After a while, I knew I was selling them hope . . ."

"How noble." The jibe elicited a rumble of discontent from the rapt audience. "Hope of what, Mr. Meltsar?"

A longish sigh rasped from the man's throat. "I'm no scholar, Mr. Televox, but I suppose I've read as much as any Olamite can, given our . . . limitations. Before the

Red Millennium, all the cultures of the world lived with the hope of a better life beyond the grave. Just hope, but . . . better than nothing. Now . . . we live and die. A few decades, centuries at best, then gone. A lucky few like Ashaan can last for millennia . . . But the likes of *you* go on and on . . . and we *know* that!" He turned fully toward the crowd, lifting his arms in an imploring gesture. "Listening to the Pilot speak to his believers, I finally realized how wonderful it would be if Heaven could be *real!*"

Listening to the growing crowd murmur, Denthurion nodded to himself. If? *If? Our* Heaven? "I *know* where your Heaven is, Mr. Meltsar."

The man turned on him angrily. "You're *not* the Denthurion we sent out! Just a doppelganger dispatched by that *ship!*" His finger was pointing up into the pale blue sky.

"Wonderful histrionics, Mr. Meltsar. I could almost believe you myself."

Meltsar's eyes, already red-lit, were aflame. "Damn you. The Heaven I created *is* real! No one can take that away from me!"

Denthurion glanced up at the crowd, where people were rising to their feet. Their faces were too far away to see in any detail, but he could imagine what emotions were dawning on them. "No, and I suppose no one will want to. Just when did you bring Mr. Ashaan in on your little scheme?"

"I . . . I . . ." He turned to stare at the Great Komer, whose sweaty moon-face was rigid with horror.

"Well, Mr. Ashaan? What do *you* have to say for yourself?"

The man gaped and turned away, then back, clutching at the sides of his pale green head-cloak. "You little bastard!" he said to Meltsar. "Thousands of *years,* thrown away over *nothing!*" The lower platform shook as he stamped his foot. "God *damn* you!" he shouted, glaring at Denthurion. "What *right* do you have to make us live like animals?"

Denthurion smiled. "Right? None at all. Just . . . duty."

In the audience, Tayash was on his feet. "You *lied* to us?" he shouted.

Ashaan, face twisted with rage, screamed, "*You* knew, Mr. *Pilot*! You knew where we were sending them!"

"Never!" He climbed over the rail and stood for a moment, frozen on the dust of the stadium floor, then turned and stormed away toward the exit.

Denthurion gestured for the Guardsmen to open the stadium gates once again, then sat back in his chair and watched with satisfaction as the thousands of former *Koxavoniayim*, rustling and rumbling, began to rise from their bleacher seats and file toward aisle and stairs, making for the streets of Perax. Good enough.

"Televox!" The shout, cracking through the humid air, was from Meltsar.

Denthurion turned to look, staring down on the man. "Yes?"

"What was the point of all this?"

He smiled and gestured at the departing crowds. "Lives saved, a world perhaps. They'll go home now, go back to being what they were."

"So," said the man bitterly, "you think you have won."

Denthurion nodded slowly. "In due course, Mr. Meltsar, I will have won. Guard Commander!" A nearby soldier stepped forward and saluted, armaments and leather butting against each other with a succession of soft noises. "Take them all back to their cells. In the morning, bring Mr. Meltsar and Mr. Ashaan to my chambers for . . . breakfast."

The officer saluted again, spun, and gestured to his men, forming a squad out of the nearest line of Guardsmen.

Some weeks after his arrival in the Shehdrashaan system, the twenty-first incarnation of Maaron Denthurion, branch Twenty-seven, took off his dark Metastable garb and donned a local-fashion human leisure suit, loose blue coveralls with many pockets, lightly woven from smooth, rather stiff terragenic cotton. A walk, that was all he wanted.

Outside the Guard complex, Saarhiraa was a pleasant sort of artificial world, one of seven in the system. As he walked down a broad, sunny avenue, the sky overhead was a soft pale blue, bright, but not unpleasantly so. Shehdrashaan itself was a fuzzy white dot in the planetoid's euentropic atmosphere shield, sometimes obscured by wisps of high cloud, sometimes not. The air was warm, yet his skin was cooled by a steady breeze that seemed to blow in only one direction, all through the short days and nights.

An F7 star, he mused, hardly on the main sequence long enough for multicellular life to evolve, much less sentience. Saarhiraa was far from its sun, a solitary nine-hundred-kilometer body, fully differentiated despite its small size, drifting in an elliptical orbit along the outer edge of the sun's rather large zone of habitability. With the euentropic shield . . . it was a nice day, the sides of the white stone avenue lined with tall, thin, feathery blue trees, beyond them slim white buildings, reaching into the distant heavens. On toward the horizon, the buildings seemed to lean away from him, threatening to topple over the edge of the world.

The crowds all around him were mostly human, strolling idly about, clad in many variations of the same leisure suit, going about some sort of business, things indistinguishable from one another. Here and there in the throng were the pale shapes of the Shehdrashaani.

He stopped at an intersection, where a few of the natives seemed to have gathered, chattering softly in one or another of their scratchy little languages. Interesting looking beings. They were all a touch more than a meter tall, some as much as 120 centimeters; pale white, soft-skinned, rather flabby-looking. Yet . . . in fact, they sort of resembled little allosauruses, fat tails drooping on the ground, milky teeth glinting between thin lips, yellow bird eyes angry. Flabby little allosauruses, hairless, covered with soft, pale human skin.

One of the Shehdrashaani noticed him staring and turned to stare back. The little group of natives fell silent for a moment, then one of them tugged at the starer's shoulder, scraping out some urgent-sounding remark. The being shook off the restraining hand, and said, "Stare all you want, dirtman." It pursed its thin lips and carefully spit a small gobbet of bluish saliva on the pavement by Denthurion's feet, then turned back to its friends. Some of the Shehdrashaani in the little group were edging nervously away.

"Hey!" said a man who emerged from the street crowd, stopping suddenly. "That bugger *spit* on you?"

Denthurion shrugged. "Merely on the street."

The man looked at the natives angrily. "Ought to kick it."

The Shehdrashaani turned to stare at him again. "Do it, dirtman." Other natives were walking away now, turning their backs, while the native's friend was tugging frantically on its shoulder.

Denthurion said, "I think not." As he turned away, the native made an expression something like a smile and spit in the street again. The human, hands on hips, stared after Denthurion angrily. "Asshole," he commented, then resumed his own business.

Walking on, Denthurion found that the day remained pleasant. The Shehdrashaani machinery, maintained by their fine planetary engineers, worked well. Humanity had been in this star system a mere three hundred years.

We came on them from the starry night, robot ships swooping out of the darkness, destroying, dropping endless loads of frightening alien monsters out of a suddenly terrifying sky. The Shehdrashaani literature of the period was fascinating.

Mighty Shehdrashaani, masters of the seven worlds, already building a starship, prepared for their assault on the universe. Now you looked out over the Shehdrashaani cities and saw human beings, crowding the streets, crowding out the Shehdrashaani themselves. We came. We took. Pity about that. But human beings began building starships just when the Shehdrashaani found out about fire.

Somehow, the day seemed even nicer than before.

Denthurion opened his eyes in the shadowy predawn darkness. A cool breeze, somewhat damp, was blowing in through the open window, stirring the hair on his chest. The sky outside was no longer black, but there was not enough light for color. Gray. Deep, starless gray.

Shvirah's arm was a weight across his lower abdomen, a motionless line reaching from just below his ribs, settled diagonally athwart the hypogastric area, forearm supported by his pelvic girdle, hand dangling. Her face was buried against his side, wedged between his rib cage and the surface of the bed, breath an intermittent pulse of warmth on his skin, the top of her head pressing against the underside of his right arm.

All right. Today is the day. Do I tell her? For that matter, do I tell *them*? The light outside slowly brightened as he lay still, breathing shallowly. Tell them what? That their fate is sealed, has been since long before they sent me off to "Heaven"? I *would* have found out, even in the short run. I or some other voyager of the Order.

The Metastability *worked*. Sooner or later ... Some other Televox, perhaps. And, in due course, Ardennes Kartavilis, having served out his life term, would have been replaced. Some successor to Kinnock Maclaren even, more prone to whistle-blowing. Sooner or later they would have been caught.

Against his side, Shvirah stirred, pulling her face away from his ribs, sighing in the shallow end of her pool of sleep, and rolled away. The trough where her arm had been seemed damp. Denthurion turned on his side to look out the window. The sky still looked gray, but you could see it was going to be a clean and cloudless day.

What do they say, a good day to die? No day is good for death ... or every day. *Are* the laws just? Difficult to know. In any case, humanity was fifty millennia and more down this very long path, a juggernaut plowing ahead, backed by monumental inertia, struggling to avoid being swept away by the tidal forces of history. What if *I* could change things, bring back the forces that so briefly illuminated the Red Millennium? Would I? Unknowable. I *cannot* change things.

He smiled in the shadowy morning light. Maaron Denthurion, Saint of Disorder. Maaron Denthurion, the Anti-Cpatht. Maaron Denthurion ... No. The smile faded. Merely mark Thirty-three, incarnation sixty-eight. The number was bitter-seeming. Sixty-eight. Symbolic of the death of sixty-seven, as if the incarnations themselves were individual lives. When did I start thinking that way? Sixty-six was not unhappy to die, despite happy Kem, despite Tiy, despite everything ...

Pretty Tiy. Servile Tiy. Still alive on Kem, only a few empty parsecs away. I can look up into the night sky and see her distant light. Yet *I* cannot go back to her. Incarnation sixty-six, the man she loved, is folded up and put away. Sixty-seven is destroyed. And sixty-eight will only live here, on Olam, for just a little while. Incarnation sixty-nine will wake up a different man on another world.

Where was I going next? Ah, yes. A place called Adenen-yo, some thirty parsecs from here.

Shvirah's hand was a warm patch, rubbing slowly across his back. When he rolled to face her, she smiled at him from the shadowland of the freshly awakened. Her hand drifted down across his abdomen, pausing to cup his genitals in a pocket of warmth.

No, he thought. I will not tell her. Nor any of them. Soon, the day would begin.

Though they didn't know it, they had come to confess their sins. Meltsar and Ashaan sat side by side at the table on Denthurion's balcony, morning light streaming across Almana Valley and falling on their backs. They were silent, for the Great Komer simmered with anger.

Panic, he thought. Sniveling, childish panic. Now, twenty-five centuries down the drain, my chances finished . . . all because of this . . . boy. The argument they'd had in the night, shouting between adjoining cells, backed by the laughter of grinning Metastatic Guardsmen, had been appalling. All over now. Ashaan's anger was beginning to fade. Given time, it would go away. You learned that, when you lived long enough.

Meltsar was subdued. He sat staring at the tabletop, hands folded before him, waiting passively. It amazed him, somehow, that his friends and comrades had given up so easily, had been so eager to turn their backs on him. Now *this* idiot, focused on his unending centuries of sameness . . . In the end, Ashaan's motives, his concerns with the preservation of some kind of status quo, had turned out to resemble those of the Televox and, through him, the purposes of the vast, barely perceptible Metastable Order. It was . . . interesting to contemplate. When you lived forever, you didn't *really* love change.

A green-clad Guardsman came out on the balcony bearing a tray. He quickly set three bowls of cereal and fruit on the table, added three glasses of what appeared to be honeydew punch, then turned and went away. All right, thought Meltsar. Time.

Denthurion came through the door, seeming bright-spirited, and sank down in the chair opposite them. He pulled a bowl of cereal before him, quickly took a sip from his glass of punch, and said, "Mr. Meltsar, Komer," nodding to each man.

Meltsar said, "Your Grace." Ashaan stared into his bowl and said nothing.

"Well," said Denthurion. "Last act. In some sense, my friends, you led us all on a merry chase. You almost got away with it, in the short term; and the short term is all people like you have." He grinned at the high priest. "Mr. Ashaan's twenty-five hundred years represent barely one sixteenth of my own life experience, yet my road is barely begun. In the longer run, your downfall was certain. Be glad it happened now, rather than later, for Olam's sake." He took another sip of juice.

"The game is over. Your punishment is set. Our purpose here today is merely to get at the truth. You do not have to speak. It will not affect your fate. I'd merely like to know what happened. And why."

Meltsar nodded slowly. The impulse to keep his own counsel was strong, but ... "I suppose I'd like an opportunity to set the record straight. Will others have an opportunity ..."

Denthurion nodded. "The house comeye is recording this conversation. Historians will want to know what happened. To its inhabitants, a planet is the whole universe."

"Maybe that's *why* it all happened then, Mr. Televox. Olam is our world, what lies outside is mere mythology. We have ... lost sight of the fact that we're not masters in our own house."

"It happens. What did you do then, having forgotten this crucial truth?"

Meltsar sighed, leaning back in his chair, breakfast untouched. "It's not so much that *I* forgot, Mr. Televox. Just that things went on of their own accord. The world forgot." He rubbed a hand over his face, ruffling his beard. "I watched the Pilot speak to his growing flock and listened to his promises. It seemed so *real*. To him it was. So ... I started looking into the matter. It didn't take much to figure out he'd somehow gotten mixed up in the software that runs the Adomm system. It shouldn't have been able to happen, but ... it's really *lousy* software, Mr. Televox. Holopathic information technology is so mediocre." Another pause. He was looking down, obviously lost in the past. "I started wondering what it would be like, doing more research. Somewhere along the way I got the idea that inside the machine complex a *real* Heaven could come to exist."

"Real?" Denthurion smiled. "That's an odd way to put it."

Meltsar shrugged. "I don't know. Are *you* real?"

"Maybe not. But the incarnations are real."

"Just so. In any event, I thought I saw a way to make this thing . . . exist. I started teaching myself the essentials of programming, working on basic operating systems, looking at what tools I had to work with, out at Olam. After a while . . ." He suddenly turned and looked at Ashaan.

The Komer, his brow still clouded with anger, grinned sourly. "After a while, the police caught him. They brought him in, and after a while, the matter came to my attention."

"I hadn't realized you dealt with matters in such minute detail," said Denthurion.

"I'm surprised at you, Televox. It was the most serious crime committed on Olam in"—he looked up speculatively—"all of history. What a racket this man was building! It took me months just to read all the documentation and figure out what the Hell was going on . . ."

"While *I* rotted in jail."

"Yes. It was your book that saved you." Ashaan folded his arms across his chest and looked levelly at Denthurion. "You were right, you know. I am near the limit of any life span sustainable with the technology available on Olam. Yet . . . *I* don't want to die. Do *you*?"

Denthurion shrugged. "Sometimes. But, I don't . . . have that option."

"Maybe so," said Ashaan. "And I didn't have the option to live. Nor do other Olamites." A long sigh, coupled with a distant, sad look. "Somewhere along the way, while I was reading the case documentation, I realized that programming the Adomm industrial complex machinery with software based on human personalities was the beginning of . . . what? Call it a leg up, if you will. In a few centuries we could *have* the scientific and technical base necessary to blossom into a full, old-style human civilization."

"They call it allopathy," said Denthurion.

"I suppose. And it grants men like yourself the option to simply live on, for as long as they choose. It grants . . . freedom."

Not for me. I am as . . . unfree as any man in history. "You sound like one of the *Shearah*, Mr. Ashaan."

The priest laughed. "Whose idea do you think it was? A little money. A few hints. It was easy, and they were part of the master plan."

Denthurion suddenly remembered the Governor's bit of crystal. "Did you really think you could retore the Red Millennium, even locally?"

"Think? I *knew*."

"And you thought no one would come and restore the preexisting balance?"

"*Who* would come, Mr. Televox? The Metastable Order is just a *dream*! A handful of soldiers under Kartavilis's command; a few starships, coming generations apart. You. Just *one man*." He waved his hand out over Almana Valley. "Don't you understand? Olam is the whole world!"

"I do understand, Mr. Ashaan. But it is not the whole world. Olam is merely one atom in a compound so complex that it surpasses your understanding and mine. You look at me and you see one man, yet I am a thousand men. Or you look at me and see the power of the Metastable Order, yet you cannot realize how truly universal I am. Televox? I am all of them, on every world where men have gone." He tapped the Metastatic emblem on the breast of his tunic. "I am the spider in the web. And Olam is one lonely fly."

"And the dream of *Koxavonia*," whispered Meltsar, "our emblem of a galaxy breaking its chains . . ."

"Just a dream," said Denthurion.

"Not even a dream," said Ashaan. "A tool. *My* tool."

Meltsar nodded slowly. "If it mattered," he said, "I'd kill you."

"But it doesn't matter," said Denthurion.

"No." He looked up at the Televox. "So it *is* over. What, then, is our punishment to be?"

"Well, my friends," said Denthurion, smiling. "I'm sending you to Heaven."

Ashaan began to laugh.

Chapter 17

It was late afternoon by the time Denthurion stepped out of the little building in the Amud compound. Hot here. The sun had been beating down on the enclosed space for hours, creating something like a minithermal inversion, air trapped and fetid behind its walls. No matter. We won't be here long. As usual, the peaked bronze double doors of the Great Amud stood open and light glared in, reflected off the roasting-hot flagstone paving of Shamayim Square. A surflike roar, the white noise of many human voices, came in with the light, rising and falling in some kind of complex pattern. Time to go.

Kinnock Maclaren came out of the little building, which concealed a compact transceiver terminal. His face was frozen, as it had been for the past several days. Hold on to your feelings, it said. This will soon be over. Other worlds beckoned, offering to pave over the past.

"Ready?"

Maclaren nodded and gestured toward the door. After you. They started walking toward the bright light, joined by a single green-clad Guardsman, fat particle beam weapon held at ready.

The scene from the doorway, where they paused, held a suggestion of barbaric splendor. Shamayim Square, surrounded by old, architecturally interesting structures, was half filled with Olamites, crowd held at bay by a long line of Metastatic Guardsmen. The noise they made verged on unnerving. A hint of . . . What? Tear them limb from limb. And, with a mob, you could never tell whose limbs they thought deserved rending.

In the center of the square a platform had been set

up, rough wood, procured from a lumber store, hastily cut and nailed together to make a dais elevated a couple of meters above the pavement. On it sat the open mesh cage of the *Koxavonia* transceiver, parabolic antenna aimed into the deep, featureless blue sky. There were more Metastatic Guardsmen standing there, among them a little knot of pale, frightened-looking men, dressed in their finest clothing, hands clenched at their sides, or folded across their chests. Waiting. Time to go, gentlemen. Thirteen steps.

Denthurion began walking across the square toward the platform, followed by Maclaren and the Guardsman. The flagstones had gotten very hot during the long afternoon, heat pushing through the thin soles of his dress boots unpleasantly. To go barefoot in the square at this time of day would be to risk injury. He smiled to himself. The thought had called up a very distant memory of childhood and soft, hot blacktop, somehow associated with Marumsko School. Too far away now. Hard to recapture the details with any precision. There had been some kind of tarry pavement next to the Spanya field, though . . .

He mounted the steps to the dais slowly, hearing Maclaren's footfalls behind him, soft, hollow sounds on the wood. The Guardsman, apparently, had stopped, remaining at the foot of the stairs. In all probability, his combat boots were sufficient to keep out the insidious heat.

When he got to the top of the stairs, the little group of men, waiting for what would come, turned to face him, all eyes and pale, upset faces. He nodded at them. Not much time left now. He walked over to the transceiver control panel and tapped a set of coordinates into the thing's memory, establishing a direct linkage with the interplanetary net. Servomotors whined abruptly as the dish antenna slewed to a new aiming point. One of the men in the little group turned to watch it, squinting up into the bright sky.

"What do you think, Mr. Meltsar? Have I got Adomm properly lined up?"

Meltsar stepped out of the cluster and walked slowly over to him. "I can't tell, Mr. Televox. If it were a little later in the day . . . Well, I suppose you know what you're doing."

"It's very late in the day, Mr. Meltsar."

The man stared coldly into Denthurion's face. "I wonder what good you think this is going to do. Do you think the people I've already sent to Heaven can punish me somehow?"

Denthurion smiled. "I've already pulled them out, Mr. Meltsar. *Naglfar*'s comeye is doing its best to put them back together. You and your friends will have Heaven all to yourselves."

"They won't be happy."

"I didn't intend for you to be happy, Mr. Meltsar."

"I meant the people you're evicting from Heaven."

Denthurion shrugged. "Life goes on."

"And then it comes to an end." Meltsar shook his head slowly. "You accomplish nothing."

Denthurion stared at him. "Justice is served, I think, Mr. Meltsar."

"Justice? What do *you* know of justice?"

Another shrug. "Whatever is necessary." He glanced up in the sky for a moment, then back at the little group of frightened men. "Come. It's time." He clapped a hand on Meltsar's shoulder, pushing gently, urging him toward the transceiver cage, whose door yawned before them all, opening on an infinite space.

"You really mean to do this to us?"

"Would I carry a joke this far?"

Meltsar walked slowly back to the group and stood beside them. Denthurion went over to the cage, turned to face the men, and beckoned. Around them on the dais, Guardsmen were tensing slightly. Fear could make men act. This was not exactly an execution unto death, but . . .

Ashaan said. "Televox. Do we have the right to a few last words?" He gestured at the now-still crowd.

Denthurion shook his head. "No. What good would that do?"

"But . . ."

"Come. The people of Olam are waiting." He pointed into the transceiver.

That seemed to defeat them. Heads bowed, they walked slowly forward and, one by one, stepped into the cage. When the last one had entered, Denthurion closed and latched the gate behind them, then turned and strolled over to the control unit. From there, he could look back at them, crowded together into that little space, jammed up against each other, silent, sullen perhaps, and, finally, dehumanized. He put his hands on the control panel and began entering instructions. So be it.

"You think you've won, Mr. Televox," muttered Ashaan, barely audible, "but I'll be *back*, one day . . ."

Meltsar suddenly clutched at the ornate meshwork of the cage, dark eyes burning out at Denthurion. "It was," he said, in an urgent whisper, "such a *damned* good story!"

Standing beside him in the shadows, Ashaan turned to look at the novelist, astonished, mouth open, as if to speak, but then red light spilled from the transceiver cage, flickering on the wood of the dais and in the faces of the observers. The shapes of the men within writhed and melted away, then were gone, not so much as a faint odor left behind.

In the background, there was a long, rustling sigh from the mass of people around the periphery of Shamayim Square, then a growing rumble as they began to speak again. Metastatic Guardsmen began pushing them back. Go home now. The show's over.

At his side, Maclaren stretched suddenly, seeming to shake off some profound hypnosis. "Done, then," he said. "Do you suppose he'll really be back?"

Denthurion turned and looked at him oddly. "Back? How could that happen?".

"Well ... *You* escaped from 'Heaven,' Mr. Televox."

Denthurion placed his hands behind his back and looked upward, staring into the deep blue sky, which was beginning to darken with the first hint of dusk to come. "Well. I didn't send them to *that* Heaven." He looked at the man and smiled. "I aimed the dish very carefully, Kinnock, at a random point in interstellar space. Meltsar and his friends are on their way to the end of the universe."

Story, he thought. Well. There are traps everywhere ...

A space-faring civilization was emerging on Komaar around the time human beings noticed that an animal killed in a forest fire was easier to chew than one fresh caught. Life had evolved rapidly on the fifth planet of this F7 star. Multicellular colonial organisms appeared within the first billion years, sentience in the eon after that. The Komaarians outgrew petty conflict and moved into their star system, swiftly industrializing the available bodies, learning to mine the gas giants for raw materials. In a century, they ran into their first real boundary: the interstellar deeps are simply too wide to be easily crossed.

The thirty-second incarnation of Maaron Denthurion, mark Twenty-nine, picked his way slowly down the hillside above Ouroun, feet scuffing the gray dust, stepping carefully over bits of old, charred wood. The city in the distance was a chaos of broken towers, some still standing in part, most fallen to the ground, half embedded in the thin gray-brown haze that drifted in the valley below.

It must have been a pretty world once. The sky overhead was mostly pale blue, but it had a tawny component, particles of dirt suspended in the jet streams. At certain seasons associated with close perihelia, the sky was completely overcast for months on end, as Komaar was subject to periodic planetary dust storms. That time was past now, the sky increasingly clear.

There had been forests everywhere; the Komaarians a conservation-minded folk. The remains about him stood barely knee-high. Jagged stumps, black, fallen trunks barring his path. He came into what had been a broad clearing and looked into a big, square, concrete-lined pit. It was filled with burned-out debris, principally a tangle of once nearly molten pipes.

He sat on the edge of the cement wall and rubbed his hand over the artificial stone. It was blistered, its moisture content boiled away. Out in the yard there was a dry black husk. Denthurion stood, brushing the dust from his clothing, and walked over. It was the remains of a Komaarian, legs and chelae burned off, face charred out of existence, reduced to a meter-wide lozenge.

He turned it over with his foot. The underside was equally blackened, crisscrossed with fracture lines, for the exoskeletoned being had ruptured like a crab in a campfire as its bodily fluids boiled.

Four hundred thousand years. That long ago the Komaarians had built their first great starship and crossed to a nearby star. Nothing. Cold, dead worlds. They spent the better part of fifty centuries cruising their immediate neighborhood, looking for a suitable world, not finding one. Bad luck. The nearest habitable planet was eighteen parsecs from Komaar, just a little farther away than they had looked.

Where would humans be, without Alpha Centauri? The next nearest planet on which a man could walk unprotected circled Delta Pavonis, almost six parsecs away. We had gone out to the stars long before we were able to tackle real planetary engineering. Venus had to be redone before we got it right.

Komaarian civilization had folded in on itself, working to conserve what it had while importing essential resources from the systems of a few nearby stars. They were doing well, had made themselves immortal by the time the first human explorer team, riding the bow shock of the Metastatic Wave, had turned up.

An interesting people, the Komaarians. Terrified, of course, when they saw what confronted them, but brave. They fought us with weapons of nightmarish power . . .

Saint of Disorder Hitler's great mistake: How is an invincible fleet of two thousand fighter craft to respond when fifty thousand armored bombers come rolling over the horizon?

In due course, the Komaarians were extinct.

The ruins of the civilization proved an almost-limitless storehouse for human archaeologists. In a half-million years, the Komaarians had had time to consider many questions. Deep in their archives, researchers found the era when they developed teleportation machinery, then discarded it. The stars were not worth repeated individual death.

Denthurion got up and walked down the long hill, toward the city of Ouroun. The tourist center there was a very good one.

Tayash was waiting for him on the Archive Center's landing stage as he stepped out of the ornithopter into the long, tinted shadows of dusk. Now what? He walked over to the man, who was standing by the low retaining wall on the edge of the roof. "Pilot. I thought I'd never see you again."

Face strained, Tayash nodded. "So you say. I can't guess at your thought processes, though." A long pause while he stared earnestly into Denthurion's eyes. "Nor know what *really* happened to you in Heaven."

Denthurion looked down on the man. Surely, he understood . . . "No Heaven, Pilot. They were just using your little friends as . . . machinery." He suppressed an abrupt surge of pity. Ordinary little man. Ordinary.

Tayash shrugged. "So you say. Yet ... where did you send them?"

Of course. "Well ..."

"Mr. Maclaren told me what you did."

"That was quick." Denthurion turned away and leaned on the retaining wall, looking out across the now excessively familiar vistas of Almana Valley. The air over the darkening landscape seemed unusually clear.

It'll be good to be away from here, he thought. Get on to my next destination. Adenen-yo is supposed to be a most interesting world ... The thought, somehow, was flat, bringing him no prospect of future happiness. Just one more passage through black ice, soul smoothed out. One more Denthurion. Palingenesis and resurrection without end. He looked over at Tayash. "So you know. They are, in fact, gone."

"But where, Mr. Televox?" Tayash's eyes held an odd, distant light.

Denthurion shrugged. "The edge of the universe. Nowhere, really. By now they're at the edge of this solar system, they're data already dissolving in chaos. Gone."

Tayash smiled. "Gone? Maybe so. But you and I know their data is retrievable, with enough processing power."

"Think some alien superbeings'll get 'em, out in the Coma Berenices supercluster maybe?"

"No, Mr. Televox. I think you've sent them to the *real* Heaven." It was said quietly, with conviction.

The surge of pity broke through. "There's no Heaven, Pilot, and no God. We are everything."

"That's what the schoolbooks say. I know differently."

Denthurion stood up away from the wall and took a step back. "I can't change your belief, Pilot. Won't, I should say." No passage through the cleansing ice for you ... "What is it you want from me?"

Tayash stepped close, looking up into his face imploringly. "Send me after them, Mr. Televox. Let me go to Heaven."

Bewilderment swelled briefly out of nowhere. It was

difficult to understand a will toward belief so strong and irrational. "No Heaven. Not for you or anyone else."

The skin around Tayash's eyes crinkled up, anger or, perhaps, the verge of tears. "Send me to Heaven! You *owe* it to me . . ."

"Owe?" Denthurion smiled suddenly. "You have all *gotten* what you deserve, in simple measure."

"What am I to *do* then?"

A shrug. "Walk the streets of Olam. Help people understand . . . what went wrong." He sighed. "You led people astray, Pilot. Now help lead them back."

"*Please*, Mr. Televox, I beg you . . ."

Denthurion turned and walked away.

In the dark stillness well after midnight, Denthurion lay in his bed and stared at the faint, formless shadows that played on the ceiling of his chamber. The darkness was nearly absolute, starlight and faint gleamings from distant Perax. The shadows might be real or they might be illusion, generated by optical system underloading. Shvirah was a warm hulk at his side, breathing softly, slowly, an occasional sigh in the dark.

What now, Mr. Televox?

Do your damned job. He could feel moisture seeping out of the corners of his eyes, treading past angular cheekbones, wetting the periphery of his ears. Just that? No more.

Stay away from these feelings. It will all be over soon, this pathetic incarnation dissolved back into the eternity of black ice, *Naglfar* moving on through the hard night, dissonant prow cutting the waves of Hawking's Ocean.

This is just a bad dream, like the memories associated with other *lacunae*. Go to ground, Mr. Televox. Your time is short. Rank on rank of identical men materialized out of the darkness, standing before him in silent rows, Denthurions all, recent incarnations in the foreground, more distant apparitions farther away. Other branchings formed distinct clusters in the whole, Denthurions available only as overlay, rather than manifestations of a direct line of experience. Here and there, dotted among them, stood silent ghosts, the voiceless dead, whose memories were a matter for mere conjecture.

Back into the black ice then, and join this multitude. Find solace at the feasting table of Odin, deep in the bowels of a false Heaven. Odd thought. I was happier at Adomm, *Koxavonia*'s Heaven a better dream. Too late now.

And I have no right.

Do your damned job.

He had a sudden image of Meltsar's face dissolving into static, re-forming, dissolving again, over and over as he receded, red-shifting, into the distant night, energy growing less and less until he merged with the anisotropic background, then slid up against the cosmic event horizon, slowing to an immutable stop.

Shvirah sighed again beside him and rolled over, pressing her face into his muscular side, snuggling, rubbing back and forth across his satiny skin, her hair a tousled cape stringing across the bedclothes. Her arm stole across his chest and she squeezed him lightly, her breathing still soft and regular, still sleeping, but caught in the throws of REM-induced activity.

Denthurion felt a strong pulse of longing. I could have stayed home, found a life in the corners, hidden my face from the bruising depths of reality. Bright dream. But Earth is eternal and everything fades with time. This dream life was never an option for me.

And she doesn't know.

Do your damned job.

Metastatic Vectorship *Aipænna* rolled in low orbit around a planet with no name. Braking from interstellar space, dissonant engines pouring raw energy into the space ambient, the world had looked all right. Seen from a distance, it was a white-swirled blue sphere, Earth-like to within a few percentage points, hanging hard and substantial against the soft cosmic background, circled at a distance by three modest moons.

The first bad signs were the scattered fresh scars on the surfaces of those moons, pockmarks far younger than the craters of formation, marked by traces of abnormal radionuclide production. The ship's comeye searched the electromagnetic spectra, listening to odd bursts of unnatural static, and finally found the explorer beacon.

Planetary reserve, it said. System first visited Metastable Year 17,866 by Explorer Team *Ogrozd*. Declared off-limits to colonization. Reported to Metastatic Wave Resource Management as Class A^4 Archaeological Center. Signed, Arpad Udri, for the Team.

Explorer beacons tended to be laconic. Stay the fuck away. This place doesn't interest you.

From low orbit, the problem was obvious. Udri's planet was a total ruin. Denthurion, mark Thirty-one, incarnation forty-three, sat strapped into a chair in *Aipænna*'s control room, watching out the big viewports as the surface of the planet rolled by a few hundred kilometers below. They were orbiting in a nose-down attitude, clouds and countryside sweeping by at a steady pace.

The sights were interesting. Big, weathered blemes in the brown earth, circular scars many kilometers wide, sculpted out of the ground to depths often exceeding four and five thousand meters. In places, the craters overlapped. At big coastal indentations, at the confluence of rivers, you could find congeries of craters, sixty, seventy, a hundred at a time, landscape chewed into something . . . indefinable.

"What do you think?"

The comeye, which called itself Bucky, scrolled out of the air. "Hard to say, Televox. The explosions seem to have averaged around twenty megatons, though there was of course some suppression where numbers of events interfered with each other, reducing the overall yield. I've taken a partial crater count and extrapolated from that statistical sample. There must have been something in excess of one hundred forty-seven thousand concussive events, plus the few dozen that occurred on the moons. My overall estimate is in the neighborhood of three million megatons."

"Not too bad. You'd think life itself would have survived, though not the sentients or their civilization."

"Well. Spectroscopy indicates breakdown products from radionuclides of cobalt."

Denthurion fell silent, watching the blasted landscape pass by below. They did a good job of it, all right. Created vast quantities of the dirtiest devices possible with a predissonant technology, then used them up in what must have been a few rather pyrotechnic hours. Whole mountain ranges had been chewed apart, lakes blown from their beds by unknowable events. Did a good job. Finished themselves and went off to whatever Hell their kind believed in, taking their whole biome with them, finishing an evolutionary chain of some few billion years.

"Have you got a time estimate?"

"Of course. Radioactive decay of the explosive byproducts indicates the sequence of events happened about seventy thousand years ago."

"Seventy thousand. We just missed them."

"Yes. Shall we go down?"

Denthurion looked out through the viewport again. The ship was passing over a huge, bowl-shaped depression, stippled with hundreds of lesser craters. Must have been a national command post here, probably buried under a largish mountain. Must have looked impressive to the beings on the moon bases, watching the flash and flicker of final war light up on the surface of their homeworld. Then the missiles came for them. Another generation and they would have gotten out to the stars. Been saved . . .

Until they ran into us. "No. I've seen enough. Let's get out of here."

Denthurion and Kartavilis stood facing each other in the cool stillness of the Metastable Archive Center's transceiver chamber. The machines were tuning up already, subtle changes of temperature making the ancient stone of the walls creak and tap on the threshold of hearing. Shadows were shifting delicately around the focus of the transmitter node.

The Planetary Governor turned and looked into the wall niche, regarded it silently for a moment, then turned back to Denthurion. "Do you really think they'll recall my entire line?" The corners of his mouth were turned down sharply, the lines of his face stiffened against what was to come.

A shrug. "Not up to me, Mr. Kartavilis. But I rather think so. You've made some serious mistakes."

"Mistakes," he said bitterly. "Under whose judgment? What was I supposed to do?"

"Your job, Governor."

"Just as you're doing yours, I suppose?"

Denthurion nodded. "I'm not happy about this, you know."

"Then why do it?"

"Because I must. The unhappiness will fade, as incarnation follows incarnation. And, in ten thousand years, this sequence of events will seem very small."

"Not to me."

"No, I suppose not." Denthurion turned away and himself looked into the oscillating shadows of the transceiver. "Still. It has to be done, and you brought it on yourself."

"You think I should've stopped Ashaan and Meltsar back at the beginning?"

"Even before that."

Kartavilis regarded him quizzically.

"Even the vegetation thing was enough to get you in trouble."

A look of anger drifted over the Governor's face, then faded. "That was, as you know, well before my time."

Denthurion nodded. "Your predecessor's line will have to be recalled as well. There will, I suspect, be at least two unhappy Planetary Deputies before this thing has run its course."

"You think they'll be removed from office?"

"Probably. The Metastable Order stands or falls according to the competence and integrity of its officers." He looked at Kartavilis. "We tracked it down, you know."

"The vegetation? I never could."

"You didn't try hard enough, Mr. Kartavilis. The records were there. Before he rose to power in the Amud, Ashaan managed to acquire a tourist voucher. Hard to do; nothing illegal, of course. He went to Kem and came back. The smuggling incident convinced him he could get away with anything."

The Governor looked wistfully into a deep past. "I always liked the way it smelled."

"I, too. Kem is a pretty world."

The wall of the chamber suddenly swelled open, revealing a dark cavity, and Odin was looking out at them, Hugin and Munin red sparks in the darkness. "Time to go."

Kartavilis regarded the comeye fearfully for a moment, then turned to Denthurion. "Well. Finished then." He held out his hand. "I want you to know that I did none of this with malevolence in mind."

"I believe you."

They shook hands, then Kartavilis turned and slowly stepped up into the transceiver niche. After a moment, the node shadows hardened and the room brightened, then teledyne light spilled over him and he was gone.

Much later that evening, not long before midnight, Denthurion stood on a little stage in the auditorium of a police barracks on the southern periphery of Perax. It was an old-style room, tier on tier of folding wooden chairs, fixed in place, rising in arcs above him. The chamber was just big enough to hold the entire membership of *Shearah*, no more than a few hundred young people after all, and there they sat. Some were restive, stirring and looking around, muttering angrily to each other; others frightened and still, or sullen, sunk into a stew of resignation.

No reason to say this in front of them. Other than . . . honor. It was obvious that few of them expected the execution that had overtaken so many others in the past few days. Why should they? I didn't kill every priest of the Amud, just the leadership. Maybe they expect me to slay Naamer in front of them, or the select few who were among my kidnappers, then send the rest of them home to the bosom of a forgiving family.

He smiled. Welcome home, son-my-son! Now that you've sown your wild oats, I have just the family-business-managerial-position for *you* . . . If you survive, life goes on, whether you like it or not. Lives of quiet desperation? In time even desperation must fade and die.

He folded his hands behind his back and stood facing them, waiting. In a short time the restive ones fell silent, and all the young faces were looking forward expectantly. The end of everything. Time.

"So. Bad boys and girls." There was a soft rustle from the audience, people stirring angrily.

Naamer stood up from the front row of seats. "Do you merely mean to mock us, Mr. Televox?"

Denthurion smiled down at him. "Don't you think you deserve mocking, fearsome Mr. Tiger, scourge of the Amud?"

Naamer flushed but stood firm. "Say what you will. We meant well and did what we thought we had to."

Denthurion nodded. "That's what they all say."

"Can't you leave us the smallest dignity?" He gestured and a small knot of men and women rose around him, faces frightened but resolute. "We are the ones responsible, not these others . . ."

"*All* of us!" shouted a voice from near the back of the room, followed by a silence.

Not *quite* all of you, then, thought Denthurion.

"We are the original and founding members of Storm, Mr. Televox. We heard what you did to Meltsar, Ashaan, and the others. *We're* ready to face our punishment . . ."

"Ready?" Denthurion laughed softly. "I think not . . ."

"We *are*! Damn you, Televox, dying is all we have left!"

Denthurion regarded him for a long moment, then shrugged. "If you think you're ready, then maybe you are." He looked out over the audience again, seeing faces twist with sudden alarm. "Very well. Step up onto the stage, Mr. Naamer."

You could see it on his face. Kill me? On stage? Now? Just like that? Why . . . I *wasn't* ready after all! Just a few more days, Mr. Televox. Maybe just *hours*. Time to prepare myself . . . Naamer looked right and left, at his suddenly horrified friends, then squared his shoulders, ran a hand over his tied-back hair, and stepped forward, up onto the stage, booted feet thumping softly on the wood.

Close up, Denthurion could see that he was shivering slightly, struggling to keep himself under control. Be brave. This will be over in a second. Denthurion looked out over the audience and was amused to see anticipation dawning on so many of the faces. Well.

He reached into his pocket and withdrew a medallion on a chain, weighing it gently in his hand. A public garroting, perhaps? How novel. He lifted the chain gently over Naamer's head and dropped it down onto his chest. "Now, Mr. Naamer, I appoint you Great Komer of the

Amud, supreme civil authority of the planet Olam, subject only to the duly deputed legations of the human Metastable Order."

Denthurion grinned into the boy's stiff and nearly expressionless face. "Congratulations, Mr. Naamer. Now you're *really* fucked!" He turned and swiftly strode from the silent auditorium.

Chapter 18

Riding a Guard hovercar back toward Perax, Denthurion sprawled in the back seat and stared up into the night sky. The Milky Way arched overhead, nearly bisecting the sky, not too dissimilar from the way it had looked from the vantage point of a Marumsko hillside, so long ago. A little denser perhaps, a little brighter, but the Sagittarius thickening was just the same. Away from the galactic plane, stars were sparser, but still filled the sky, endless arrays and dot patterns in the darkness. Let's see . . . which way are we pointing?

"Open the bubble," he said to the driver. There was a soft whine and the plastic dome began to slide back.

Much better. Cool night air was curling in on him, ruffling his clothes and tossing his hair into disarray. His view of the sky was unimpeded. The ecliptic plane of the Shemesh star system was tipped toward the galactic south. The Magellanic Clouds were about halfway up the sky, a pair of rather shapeless bits of haze, galaxies masquerading as nebulae. If a starship had set out for the larger cloud in Red Millennium times it would be less than a third of the way there. It seemed likely, given the tenor of those times, that some such ship was on its way. Andromeda, at more than ten times that distance, lay below the horizon.

The sky dimmed and the car slowed as they pulled into Perax, with its lights. "Shall I put the dome back up?"

"Leave it down."

They drove into the city, sliding down long avenues toward the center of town and the principal clusters of municipal buildings. It would be easier to get back to the Archive Center and his warm, inhabited bed via the transceiver in the Governor's Palace. He thought briefly of Shvirah; shied away from her image.

As it was essentially only late evening, the streets of the city were still fairly crowded with people. Thinning out, though. Thinning out. A woman with a little male Hoda on a leash, standing on a street corner, stood out. There weren't many Hodai abroad tonight, those few mostly walking free and unattended. The ingathering was advancing quickly. As they passed, Denthurion whispered to the driver to slow down a bit.

The woman and her pet seemed to be arguing about a package that lay on the ground between them. The woman was pointing at it, gesturing to the Hoda. "Pick it up, Haamor. It's late. I want to go home."

The Hoda looked up at the woman angrily, arms folded across his chest, then he reached up and unhooked the leash from his collar. "Carry yourself, bitch."

The woman recoiled a bit, then lifted her hand. "You . . ." She cuffed at the Hoda's face.

The little biped grabbed her hand, biting hard. The woman screamed, a sharp, high sound that attracted the attention of passersby, and snatched her hand away, staring at the shallow, bloody tooth marks. "*Haa*mor!"

The Hoda unbuckled his collar and threw it on the ground beside the package. "Going *away*, Mother. Hell with *you*." He broke and ran, disappearing into the crowd. People gathered around the woman, inspecting her hand and muttering angrily.

Denthurion tapped the driver on the back. "Let's go." The hovercar sped up, scraping softly along the dimly lit avenue.

When Denthurion crawled into his bed Shvirah was awake, waiting for him. Her mood had been improving steadily, growing cheerier with each passing hour. Now

she sat with her back to the headboard, covers pulled up
to her waist, breasts casting little shadows onto her chest
wall. "Did you do it?"

Denthurion sat on top of the bed, legs folded beneath
him, facing her. He nodded. "About an hour ago."

"Wow. What do you suppose he'll do?"

Denthurion smiled and shrugged. "Probably have a
nervous breakdown. Running a planet is no joke."

"What did he say?"

"Nothing. I just did it and left." He reached out and
ran his hand over her shoulder, then down onto her
breast. The tissue of her nipple was soft and spongy, like
velvet after the satin of her skin. It stiffened slowly as he
played with it. Shvirah sat motionless, letting him toy
with her, seeming to stare at his face.

"Are we going to Merkaaz soon?"

He nodded. "In a week or so. When the ingathering is
complete." He lifted himself up and pulled the covers
from beneath him, then sat back down and pulled them
off Shvirah's legs. She seemed even more perfect now,
slimmer than before, yet somehow more evolved. The
narrowing of her waist had the effect of making her hips
seem broader, and the slim pelvic blades were stretching
her skin taut.

"It'll be over that quickly?" She slouched a bit, sliding
down onto the bed.

"The domestic Hodai were easy to round up. We
picked up most of the wild ones on satellite imagery.
There just weren't that many out there." He rubbed his
hand on her stomach, felt its surface soften as he
pressed. Somewhere in there, pubococcygeal muscles
were stirring, brought to life by directed activity.
Shvirah's eyes were losing their distant focus, beginning
to concentrate on events in the room.

"I want to go stay with them, you know." She was lying
almost flat on the bed now, staring at the ceiling, legs
drawn up and slightly parted.

"I know. There are . . . park ranger positions available." He rubbed a hand across the inside of one of her thighs and her legs fell open, soles of her feet almost touching, knees aimed at opposite walls.

"And . . . you'll be gone soon."

Denthurion rose and kneeled between her legs, pushing her feet apart on the bed, looking down. Her groin was a black flower, full of shadows. "True. When my work is done." He dropped to his hands and knees, then lay prone on the bed, lowering his face onto her vulva, feeling crisp pubic hair tickle his cheeks. The area between her labia was already moist, like the inside of a mouth.

The pale ghost of a sweet night wind blew out of the high desert, picking up a little moisture from the Urvedi canals where they cut the hard-packed sand just south of Qo'arlë, evaporation barely cooling the air above Huiôn's oasis. With evening come to its long conclusion, the night sky above Kem was prickled with stars, darkness sucking the heat from the scorched land. By the time the heavens turned purple with the first hints of morning twilight, it would be almost cold.

Maaron Denthurion, branch Thirty-three, incarnation sixty-six, stood naked beneath the remote umbrella of a tall, mutated date palm, staring into the night sky. The darkness on Kem, which shied away from much artificial light, was near absolute. Even with the last faint crust of day rimming the western horizon, galactic structure was in evidence. If you knew what you were looking at, you could tell which part of the Milky Way represented Orion Arm and which represented Sagittarius. There was a distinct difference in density and bulk composition, made evident by a subtle quality of light. The Crab Nebula was a pale, delicate phantasm. It was beautiful, but held no more than a hint of the beauty it displayed in Red Millennium photographs, when it had been a tenth of its present age. The original explosion, visible in daylight on distant Earth, must have been striking from this vantage point, the supernova like a small second sun in the sky.

Unfortunately, Kem had been bare of life in the minus-fourth millennium. Only a few planets in this neighborhood had intelligent life, fewer still had had their own civilizations. In any case, none remained to bear witness. Olam, he thought. Some kind of native . . . A shrug. The overlay will let me know, when the time comes.

Tiy, lying on the soft sward under the tree by his feet, reached up and ran one small, delicate hand along the inside of his leg, reaching as high as she could on his thigh, rubbing his skin softly. "The sky will still be there when you're gone, Maaron."

He looked down at her. She was barely visible in the dusky light; black hair a darker shadow, tanned skin no more than a texture against the night, eyes and teeth scarcely a glimmer in the darkness. Memory from daylight supplied the necessary detail. She was slim, breasts almost nonexistent, hips hardly wider than her waist, with the narrow buttocks of a preadolescent boy, mons dusted with a sparse rime of black hair. Her eyes, dark pools of near-ebony brown, could be impenetrable wells. "This is the last time I'll see the stars over Kem," he said. "When I lie down to sleep tomorrow, they'll be over Olam."

She sat up, taking his hand, tugging him down on the grass beside her. "Will they be so different?"

With the Shemesh star system only a few parsecs distant? No, but . . . "I will be different."

She shivered slightly. "I don't want to imagine what you mean. I'm sorry you have to go."

He reached out and stroked her dark, smooth hair softly, feeling its silky quality, the faint oiliness that gave it a sheen in the daylight. "I am, too, lover. It's been a beautiful five years."

"And a Televox never retires."

Odd thought. So few people were ever able to grasp

even the slightest notion of his true reality. Retire? I am
not even real. The starship re-creates me from a template at each destination. When I step into the transceiver tomorrow I die. The memories themselves are the
only reality. And when the next incarnation steps out on
Olam, a few years hence ... Washed clean of the emotional detritus these years on Kem have wrought. I'll be
a new man. Or a very old one.

He smiled and pulled her a little closer. "Retire? No,
Tiy, we never do." Odin speaks, and I go.

"But I wish you could. I ... kept telling myself this
day would never come."

"It hasn't come yet. Tomorrow is far away."

She reached for him then, and said, "It took time, but
I learned to love you, Maaron Denthurion. I hope you'll
carry the memory of that love with you forever, wherever
you go."

He looked up into the starry sky and suddenly wished
that the night were already over, that morning had come
and gone, his soul, on Olam, rendered new again. Life,
he thought bitterly, on a *human* scale. Life with human
pain. Too human. "I will love you, Tiy," he said, making
her smile, "and remember you forever."

The Merkaaz Basin, several thousand kilometers from
the nearest major sea, was dry and dusty, hot sun beating
down out of the northern sky, mountains rimming the
southern horizon, the others flat and featureless. This
place was as far from civilization as could be found on
Olam. In twenty-five millennia, few people had come to
live here, so the forced evacuation was a small one. Out
in the scrublands, situated by oases, stood a few abandoned farmsteads, still in good shape, ready for decay.
They were far from here; it would take the slowly diffusing Hodai a long while to reach them.

Denthurion and Naamer stood at the rear of a rough-hewn wooden dais, leaning against the ruddy wall of the large boulder that formed its natural backdrop. A little ways in front of them, Sessiri-wohnith stood by a slab of dressed stone, clutching a little microphone, hooting and growling the complex syllables of a major Hodai dialect. His words were carried out into the vast, stirring brown sea of furry beings through a net of amplifiers. Beyond the Hodai, who numbered in the hundreds of thousands, lay an immense tent city, billowing shrouds of white and gray and tan humped low across the desert floor. More Hodai lay there, extending, perhaps, into the sparse few million.

-wohnith gestured at the front of the stone and burbled, *"A'tukhn-dar ha-chewiss!"* There was a ragged cheer from the massed Hodai. *"Za-chewiss!"* The cheer spread.

"You know much Hodai?"

Naamer shrugged. "A bit. It's similar to human language."

"If I said to you, 'Sky God evil *ha-chewiss*,' what would I be saying?"

Naamer smiled crookedly. "*Arewiss* means, 'to burn.' *Chewiss* is the reflexive form. *Ha-* is an imperative prefix."

"So it was a suggestion for self-immolation?"

Another shrug. "It's a slogan from their old religion." He looked up at Denthurion. "I was never able to find out much about Hodai culture before the arrival of humanity on Olam. They had a fairly advanced pretechnological civilization of several thousand years duration, but . . . When the ships arrived from Kem . . . we were fairly blasé about alien cultures, having seen thousands of them already."

Blasé? You don't *know* . . . Denthurion's mind wandered, listening to the endless rustle of alien speech. A little to one side of -wohnith's position, Shvirah stood, neatly dressed in a fresh new costume of stiff khaki drill. The uniform didn't quite cling to her gentle curves, more bridging the spaces between. Still, you could see a pro-

trusion of hip and breast, a delicate inward slope at waist
and thigh. The pants were tailored for a male physique,
the empty crotch pouched and suggestive.

The night before had been a startling interlude,
Shvirah suddenly alert and aggressive, forcing him to per-
form after he'd exhausted his own desire, talking ani-
matedly about the new Hodai world to come, in between
times. He smiled in remembrance. The faint graininess
that had been dogging him all day was a slight fatigue
caused by lack of sleep.

"What do you think, Naamer? *Could* they come back
from this?"

The man looked at him oddly. "You mean regain
something of their old civilization?" He shrugged.
"Maybe. Probably not. In any case . . ."

Right. Not exactly a germane question. Not now.

When the speeches were over and the Hodai had begun to disperse, headed for their tents and meager be-
longings, Denthurion stepped away from the
sun-warmed rock toward the front of the platform.
-wohnith was standing motionless, microphone held at
his side, staring at the surface of the stone that had acted
as a prop for his speech. Denthurion joined him.

The bit of dressed masonry, a little more than two meters square, was a fragment from some ancient Hodai
building, gray, granite perhaps, with designs incised here
and there. Mostly there was just a complex pattern of
speckles, the center dominated by what seemed like a
ball of flame. Across the bottom was a hilly stretch of horizon, centering on the bannered towers of a Hodai city.
Beneath that was a strip of text in some unknown writ-
ing. "What does it say?"

The little Hoda looked up at him, dark eyes unreadable, then said, "No one can read this script anymore. It's
called *Morha-gembo*. We've kept this relic hidden a long
time, since right after Sky God Time. We think it says,
Dahanta chewiss-dar. 'Day of Burning.' " He looked
away, out over the thinning field of Hodai.

Denthurion inspected the ritualized explosion, set in what looked like a star field. "Is this supposed to be the effect of some human weapon?"

-wohnith seemed amused. "No, Televox. It's much older than that. The *Morha-gembo* lived before an extended period of barbarism we call the Great Mean. It was our . . . first civilization."

"How long?"

An alien shrug. "We don't know. Internal clues in the legends say it happened a little less than thirty thousand years before humans came."

He looked at it again. Of course. "This is the Crab Nebula supernova, isn't it?"

"Probably. The timing seems about right." He looked up at Denthurion. "We've had bad luck drop on us out of the sky on more than one occasion."

A little while later, Denthurion and Shvirah stood together in the broad clearing behind the dais, facing each other silently. Behind them an ornithopter sat, engines warmed up and rumbling, wings raised, poised for a downward, launching stroke.

Denthurion reached out and took both her hands in his, looking earnestly into her face. "Good-bye, Shvirah," he said.

She smiled. "I suppose I *won't* see you again before you leave Olam, so this *is* good-bye."

He nodded slowly. "My work is . . . almost done." Odin calls. Then I go . . .

"Well." She pressed his large hands with her delicate fingers, looking away from his face, almost shyly. "Thank you for everything you've done, Maaron Denthurion." She looked up at him again. "If you could stay . . . I *could* love you." She leaned into him then, reaching around the thick barrel of his chest, clasping her hands behind his back, pushing her face into the front of his tunic.

Denthurion stroked her soft hair, ran his hands down her back, reaching as far as the smooth curve of her buttocks. Sensation stirred briefly in his abdomen, quickly suppressed. He lifted her away from his chest. "I have to go now, Shvirah."

She looked up at him, eyes misted with tears, smiling faintly. "Good-bye then, Mr. Televox. I'll remember you."

He released her, turned away quickly, and stepped into the ornithopter. When the hatch was sealed, he gestured to the pilot, who adjusted his controls. The wings thumped down, simultaneous with a rising whine from the ducted jets, and a whirl of dust bloomed around the ship as it bounced into the sky.

From far above, the Merkaaz region was a vast wasteland. Denthurion and Naamer sat side by side in the belly of the ornithopter, looking out the windows at the ground. "High enough, maybe." They were cruising at something like ten thousand meters.

Naamer put a hand on his forearm. "Televox . . ." He faltered when Denthurion turned to look at him, then went on, "I wish you would reconsider."

"You have more to learn than Mr. Maclaren, and your position is more precarious. You cannot fly away to the stars when all this is finished."

"But . . . this . . ."

"Rendezvous completed, sir," said the pilot.

Denthurion leaned close to the window, squinting downward. A couple of thousand meters lower, three small, dark blots were passing beneath their ship, three more ornithopters cruising together in a tight little vic. "I see them. Ready?"

"They want you to give the order, sir."

"Tell them I've given it."

The pilot muttered something into his headset.

Several masses dropped away from the three ornithopters, which turned abruptly, separating from their formation, rapidly clawing for altitude.

"My God," whispered Naamer.

The masses fell swiftly, shrinking until they could no longer be made out.

"Ten seconds," said the pilot.

"Mr. Televox . . ." said Naamer.

"Five seconds."

Denthurion could feel his heart beating slowly in his chest, a steady, measured thud, replete with the soft rumble of perfect allopathic health. An immortal heart, surely, beyond all human fears and hopes. A perfect heart, beyond caring.

"Three seconds."

A reddish-brown cloud began forming below, spreading out into a disk, obscuring the landscape.

"Two."

The cloud was vast now, beginning to attenuate. If you looked closely, you could see the Hodai tent city, clusters of white against the dun of the desert ground. All the Hodai in the world. And all their friends. And Shvirah.

"One."

Long, *long* pause, then a spark, several sparks, formed in the middle of the cloud. Rings of fire bloomed around them, spread, merged into an irregular shape, propagated swiftly through the cloud, filling it with light. A pressure wave appeared in the air about the cloud, circular, spherical in fact, though you couldn't see that from an unshifting perspective. It grew swiftly, touching the ground, spreading there as a sudden circle of dust, growing into a ball of dark haze. The tent city disappeared.

"Effects?"

The pilot sighed heavily, then murmured into his headset, listened, murmured again. "We get three thousand psi at the hypocenter," he said, "dropping off sharply with distance."

Denthurion turned to looked at Naamer's pale, appalled face. "Done then," he said.

Naamer looked into the maelstrom below. "Your work is finished, I suppose, Mr. Televox. You can go home now."

Denthurion sank back into his seat, and thought, I could, if I knew where it was, if it still existed.

If anything existed, anywhere but in memory . . .

In the end, Denthurion and Maclaren stood before the transceiver niche beneath the Metastable Archive Center of Olam, watching the machines tune up. The familiar shadows of light leaned this way and that, assuming a familiar, almost-invisible star pattern of rays on the floor, brightening the machine-stuffed walls. Time to go.

Maclaren turned to him, holding out his hand, and said, "I won't see *you* again, Televox. Good-bye. It's been an interesting little while."

Denthurion grimaced. Never again, black ice notwithstanding. He took the hand briefly, let it fall. "Good-bye, Kinnock. Well done is what they used to say."

Maclaren nodded. "Yes. Well done, whether I like it or not." He turned away, without hesitation, and stepped into the niche, taking a firm stance, facing back into the room. His pale eyes stared silently out at Denthurion, empty of accusation, then the light around him firmed up, reddened, and he was gone, leaning shadows left behind.

Denthurion stood alone before the niche, waiting. Time to go. Behind him, the soft, hesitant voice of the house comeye whispered, "Mr. Televox? The machinery is ready. You can go now."

Time to go. Yet still he stood, mind unaccountably empty. There was a feeling that he *wanted* to step forward, yet, somehow, the means of changing desire into a sequence of actions was absent.

I can't do it.

The idea crystallized, not in real words, but . . .

The wall beside him became misty, then darkened as

the surface fell in, tunneling away until a dark cave had formed, holding the familiar shape of Odin, one-eyed, ancient, mounted by his two black familiars. "We're waiting for you, Mr. Televox," said the god.

One of the birds on his shoulder hissed. Odin batted it away with a careless flick of one hand. Hugin followed his companion, red-spark eyes disappearing in the darkness, harsh bird cries echoing in the vast network of tunnels beneath Asgard.

"Waiting for you."

The stillness, sensation betokening lack of will, remained, holding him fast. First thoughts formed. I have to say something. Let him know what's ... Can't though. You don't know what force has seized you.

Odin stared at him patiently, squatting in his cave.

Eventually, the words came, soft and unwilling.

"I can't do it," he whispered. "This day's work has finished me. I ... I ..." Make it formal. Make it easy. "I wish to remain here." Very simple words. Hiding hard, complex ideas ... of how you no longer wished to be switched on and off like the software you really were, put up and taken down again, like a tool whose usefulness comes and goes.

Odin stroked his gray beard. "You know that a passage through *Naglfar* would end all that. One trip, up, then down, and you would be your old self again."

One part of him screamed: I have no old self!

The god regarded him further. "I see. Well. This sort of thing does happen." Another pause, waiting for him to speak. "Very well. Maaron Denthurion ..."

At the god's commanding tone, Denthurion looked up to face his maker. And, in that small moment, teledyne forces reached out and swept him away.

Einar Crispin Dupree stood alone in the musty stillness of Adenen-yo's Metastable Archive Center, waiting, in the seldom-used main transceiver chamber, for the

Televox to appear. He was a tall, thin man, with curly, close-cropped red-bronze hair and a narrow, ruddy face, clad in the white tunic of a Servant of the Metastability. Nervous, he thought, that's what I am. More nervous than I ought to be.

The transceiver chamber, like the MAC building itself, was ancient, having been built more than eighteen thousand years earlier during the first days of Adenen-yo's colonization. Its gray stone walls and floor had been worn smooth and faintly hummocked by the endless touch of hands and feet. A shallow gully was visible across the middle of the floor, a path leading from the door to the transceiver niche.

Get hold of yourself. Six hundred years ought to breed something like self-confidence. But in nine long incarnations, decades each on varied worlds, he'd never met a Televox before, nor any instrumentality more powerful than a Planetary Governor. Televoxes were the ultimate authority, their decisions irrevocable, beyond appeal.

No, not quite right. There was the Metastatic Senate, and the Congress of Planetary Deputies . . . on Earth, fifteen hundred parsecs away, better than five thousand years of linear travel . . . no, this Televox would come and his will would be done, not to be reversed until some other power happened to pass this way, centuries, perhaps millennia, later. Einar smoothed the front of his tunic, glanced at his heavy, ornate Adenetic wristwatch, and swallowed dryness. The ship had been in orbit for more than an hour, engine glow cooling away, silent since an initial terse message: Prepare.

What will he see? Einar felt a lump form in his chest, an expanding vein of nervousness. Nothing. Perhaps nothing. It was a formality. Perhaps this Televox would come, take a quick look around, then depart on his endless course. But the ship came from Olam. He'll be used to . . . quiet.

The dead stillness of the chamber was interrupted by a faint ticking sound from behind the stone walls, where age-old electronics lay embedded, then the transceiver niche took on a misty look as its teledyne nodes tuned up. Einar straightened his clothes further, throwing back his shoulders, waiting.

The mist cleared suddenly, the stone behind it taking on a crisp look, then the Televox spilled into existence, building up out of nothing, from inside to out, in a fraction of a second, an amorphous red mass, growing, growing . . . there. Einar took an involuntary step backward, then caught hold of himself.

The tall, black-clad, black-haired man in the niche looked down at him with interest for a moment, eyes traveling the chamber quickly, then he stepped down, offering his hand. He was a little taller than Einar, thin and muscular, in severely allopathic fashion. He stepped forward and took the proffered hand, then, in Ursprache, said, "Good afternoon, Mr. Televox. Welcome to Adenen-yo, sir."

Maaron Denthurion smiled thinly at him, almost expressionlessly, face unreadably calm, and Einar Crispin Dupree thought, God. What if he *notices* something . . . Together, they turned away from the light, and walked into the darkness.

Terminology of the Metastable Order

The special philosophical and technical lexicon of the Metastable Order evolved in the latter part of the Red Millennium (ca. A.D. 1450–2450), during the genesis of Ursprache, which came to be the universal language of the human interstellar government and its enforcement arm, the Metastatic Guard. Since the Ursprache words themselves would be meaningless, they are translated into more familiar English words, with similar linguistic roots, though somewhat different nuances.

Allopathy—A philosophy of alternatives. In medicine, the antagonistic treatment of disease. Antibiotics are allopathic.

Catharsis—The purgation of a system, usually to remove some internal stress.

Cathexis—The buildup of dynamic tension in a system, as by overfilling or pressurization.

Comeye—Slang for any communications interface device.

Dissonance—The absence of harmony between things. In physics, the base state of the vacuum plenum, in which particles constantly invert between material and virtual states. "Quantum dissociation" is a technogenic process by which stabilized mass quanta are forced back into their virtual state, resulting in a total conversion to energy.

Holism—The tendency to produce wholes from the ordered grouping of units.

Holopathy—A philosophy of totalities. Holopathic medicine holds that disease must be treated by dealing with a complete entity. Multivitamin therapies are holopathic.

Homeopathy—A philosophy of composites. In medicine, the cooperative treatment of disease. Vaccines are homeopathic.

Homunculus—Diminutive form of the Latin word *homo*, hence, a little man. Here it specifically refers to the tangible manifestation of an artificial intelligence.

Interpathy—Ecumenism. The general term for the total philosophical basis of the Metastable Order. A secondary term, "The Interpathic Spectrum," describes the ordering of the major subspecies, ranging from revolutionary Psychopathy through Allopathy, Sociopathy, Homeopathy, and Holopathy, to reactionary Naturopathy. Minor pathologies find their niches at the various interstices of this spectrum.

Lacuna—Hiatus, blank, missing part. In this context, a lost incarnation.

Metastable—A state of unstable equilibrium, for example, a pie plate spinning on the end of a stick.

Metastasis—A rapid transition from one point to another. In biology, the breaking off of tumor cells and their movement to other parts of the body.

Metastatic Guard—Uniformed police/military forces of the Metastable Order, commanded by the Planetary Governors.

Metensomatosis—Reembodiment of the soul. A more familiar, if less applicable, word is Metempsychosis, meaning the transmigration of souls, as in reincarnation.

Naturopathy—A philosophy of minimalism. Herbal medicines, like quinine, are naturopathic.

Neurotaxis—The process of building a neural network. The adjective "neurotaxic" refers to the modern, fully integrated neural network computer, usually supporting a humanlike artificial intelligence.

Nullipathy—Secularism. The notion that understanding and functionality are unrelated. Radiation therapy is nullipathic.

OTANN—Optically Trainable Artificial Neural Network. Heuristic, photon-packet gate-stack developed during the sixth century of the Red Millennium. These low-energy microwave logic devices made true artificial intelligence feasible and led to the seventh-century development of the neurotaxic computer.

Palingenesis—The process of rebirth, referring most specifically to the reconstruction of a partially destroyed incarnation. See *lacuna*.

Pathology—The study of human suffering. In this context it is taken to be something like comparative religion or philosophy.

Psychopathy—A philosophy of mentality. In medicine, the notion that most illness is psychogenic, treatable by psychoreactive therapies such as acupuncture. Most classical religions are psychopathic.

Quantum—An article of enumeration, generally the smallest measurable unit of a substance or process. Quarks and leptons, for example, are mass quanta.

Sociopathy—A philosophy of group dynamics. Fluoridation is an example of sociopathic medicine.

Stochastic—Pertaining to conjecture. Neural networks represent a high order stochastic process that amounts to "organized guesswork."

Synchronoptic—Viewing and relating to multiple event streams simultaneously.

Taxon—An article of classification, generally the smallest level of differentiation. Units of charge, for example, are taxa used to differentiate some kinds of quanta from each other.

Teledyne—A device for projecting energy effects to a distance. Primitive examples of the teledyne principle would include lasers and electromagnets.

Teleology—The study of ultimate causes, relating to the search for meaning in nature.

Televox—Far voice, a legate deputed to represent the Metastable Order and armed with its authority.

Tensor—A quantity expressing the ratio by which the length of a vector is increased. In this context, the historical development of a pathological line.

Transceiver—A device for transmitting and receiving electromagnetic or other waves, such as a two-way radio. In this instance it refers to teleportation machinery.

Ursprache—An artificial language created during the latter part of the Red Millennium. It began as a research project in which primitive AI-driven neural networks were used to re-create protolanguages like Indo-European. At a later date, linguistic hobbyists used this equipment to demonstrate what Indo-European would have been like had it evolved as a single modern tongue. The resulting language gained considerable currency around the time of the founding of the Metastable Order and the movement of humanity into space.

Vox Humana—Human voice, symbolic premier of the Metastable Order, a post usually filled by the majority leader of the Metastatic Senate.

Zetetic—Proceeding by inquiry. In this context, an adjective pertaining to the traditional scientific methodology of the Red Millennium.

Zoism—The doctrine that life depends on some peculiar vital principal, i.e., "souls." Attempts by Metastable zoists to formulate a significant, ordered zoopathy have repeatedly failed. Faith healers may be considered primitive zoopaths.

About the Author

WILLIAM BARTON was born in Boston, Massachusetts, in 1950 and currently lives in Chapel Hill, North Carolina, where he is a free-lance writer and computer industry consultant specializing in computer-assisted instruction. He is the author of two previous solo novels, *Hunting on Kunderer* and *A Plague of All Cowards* and has written *Iris* and *Fellow Traveler*, both published by Bantam Spectra, in collaboration with Michael Capobianco. Barton's nonfiction articles on space exploration and computer programming have appeared in such diverse publications as *Ad Astra* and *Commodore Magazine*.

IRIS
by
William Barton and
Michael Capobianco

Escaping an Earth ravaged by economic collapse, the
colony ship *Deepstar* soars toward a dazzling odyssey of
alien contact. Near Neptune, the crew sights the rogue
planet Iris approaching our solar system, and decides to
settle on one of its moons. But on their strange new
home's crater-marked landscape, they discover the
Artifact: an ancient extraterrestrial spacecraft that is deserted -- but still operable. For the *Deepstar* crew, this is
only the first step on a dizzying journey through both inner
and outer space.

A stunning glimpse into not only a gritty, hard-edged
future, but an ancient alien civilization, **IRIS** follows the
crew of the *Deepstar* on a challenging and unforgettable
adventure of emotional and extraterrestrial exploration.

Now on sale wherever Bantam Spectra Books are sold.

AN190 -- 12/90

STEPHEN R. DONALDSON